SCOURGE THE HERETIC

WHEN INQUISITOR GRYNNER investigates a derelict Imperial trading vessel adrift in the Halo Stars, he and his operatives discover everyone aboard is dead, apparently killed by powerful psykers. As the vessel hails from the Calixis sector, he contacts his colleague Inquisitor Carolus, who runs a network of agents in that area. But there is no such thing as a straightforward Inquisition investigation, and pretty soon Inquisitor Carolus and his team find themselves up to their necks in trouble. The smuggling operation proves much more dangerous than it seems – can they root out its dark secrets before being destroyed themselves?

Dark Heresy

SCOURGE THE HERETIC

Sandy Mitchell

For Rebecca, who hit her first deadline,
just as I overran mine.

A BLACK LIBRARY PUBLICATION

First published in Great Britain in 2008 by
BL Publishing,
Games Workshop Ltd.,
Willow Road, Nottingham,
NG7 2WS, UK.

10 9 8 7 6 5 4 3 2 1

Cover illustration by Clint Langley.
Calixis Sector map by Andy Law.

A CIP record for this book is available from the British Library.

ISBN 13: 978 1 84416 512 4
ISBN 10: 1 84416 512 4

Distributed in the US by Simon & Schuster
1230 Avenue of the Americas, New York, NY 10020, US.

See the Black Library on the Internet at
www.blacklibrary.com

Find out more about Games Workshop
and the world of Warhammer 40,000 at
www.games-workshop.com

IT IS THE 41st millennium. For more than a hundred centuries the Emperor has sat immobile on the Golden Throne of Earth. He is the master of mankind by the will of the gods, and master of a million worlds by the might of his inexhaustible armies. He is a rotting carcass writhing invisibly with power from the Dark Age of Technology. He is the Carrion Lord of the Imperium for whom a thousand souls are sacrificed every day, so that he may never truly die.

YET EVEN IN his deathless state, the Emperor continues his eternal vigilance. Mighty battlefleets cross the daemon-infested miasma of the warp, the only route between distant stars, their way lit by the Astronomican, the psychic manifestation of the Emperor's will. Vast armies give battle in His name on uncounted worlds. Greatest amongst his soldiers are the Adeptus Astartes, the Space Marines, bioengineered super-warriors. Their comrades in arms are legion: the Imperial Guard and countless planetary defence forces, the ever-vigilant Inquisition and the tech-priests of the Adeptus Mechanicus to name only a few. But for all their multitudes, they are barely enough to hold off the ever-present threat from aliens, heretics, mutants – and worse.

TO BE A man in such times is to be one amongst untold billions. It is to live in the cruellest and most bloody regime imaginable. These are the tales of those times. Forget the power of technology and science, for so much has been forgotten, never to be relearned. Forget the promise of progress and understanding, for in the grim dark future there is only war. There is no peace amongst the stars, only an eternity of carnage and slaughter, and the laughter of thirsting gods.

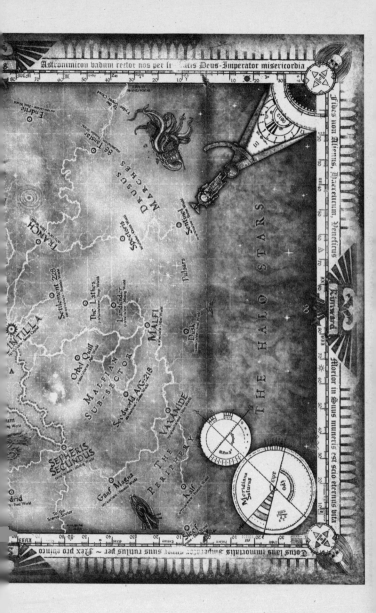

THE HALO STARS

DRUSUS MARCHES

Endric ...

...s Instar...

TRANCH

Spectoris ...

Settlement 228

The Lathes

Landunder ...

MALFI

Pulsars

Dusk

...NTILLA

Obol Quill

MALFIAN
SUB-SECTOR

Sechtor AFG-218

THE
VAXANIDE

SEPHERIS
SECUNDUS

THE
PERIPHERY

Gunf Magna

Naff

...drid

Reef

Meridiana
Saturn

PROLOGUE

Astra Incognita: the Halo Stars
049.933.M41

PIETER QUILLEM FELT sick, a sensation he was depressingly used to, despite years spent in the service of the Inquisition: a calling which, in the very nature of things, tended to strengthen the stomach by repeated exposure to abominations that would have left a more sensitive soul reeling. In his time as an acolyte, and latterly as an interrogator, he had discovered reserves of mental and spiritual fortitude that still occasionally astonished him, but no amount of physical courage or faith in the Emperor could quell the rising nausea that assailed him every time he found himself in open space. He took a deep breath of recycled air, stinking of old sweat and flatulence, and triggered the attitude jets of the tiny shuttle, steadying the slow tumble that had begun to trouble his inner ear.

As the stars around him steadied he felt the swelling tide of sickness recede, and sighed faintly with relief, misting the viewport ahead of him for a moment before the environmental unit's machine-spirit recognised and compensated for the minute increase in humidity. As the thin layer of armourcrys cleared again, the full extent of the galaxy was revealed to him, a refulgent spiral glowing with rich, warm light in a thousand subtle hues. From here, on its very fringes, he could see the Emperor's holy demesne almost in its entirety, stark, clear and beautiful, burning like a beacon in the endless night of infinity. For a moment Pieter wondered if this was how He on Earth perceived it all, before dismissing the fleeting thought as both fruitless and bordering on the impious.

'Are you quite well, Pieter?' The voice in his vox was dry, precise, and carefully modulated, and even without seeing the face of his mentor the young interrogator was perfectly able to picture it. Inquisitor Grynner would have tilted his head almost imperceptibly to one side as he spoke, his deceptively mild blue eyes blinking behind his spectacles, as though the answer might be both unexpected and informative.

'I'm fine, inquisitor.' He spoke a little too quickly, before adding, 'Thank you for asking.' Grynner knew about his susceptibility to void sickness, of course, as he seemed to know about everything, and his sympathy was undoubtedly genuine. Nevertheless, as usual, he'd delegated the task of on-site investigation to one of his entourage without a second thought, preferring to remain in his quarters aboard the starship from which the shuttle had come, calmly assessing whatever information his operative uncovered. Jorge Grynner's formidable intellect was a weapon as potent, in its own way, as the storm bolter built into the power suit he wore on the rare occasions he deemed his personal intervention to be necessary, flensing truth from lies, ferreting out secrets so deeply hidden that no one else even suspected they were there, and he preferred to let it do so without distraction whenever possible. In a way, Pieter supposed, he ought to be flattered that Grynner called on him so often. It was a mark of the inquisitor's confidence in his abilities, an accolade not lightly given.

His mind recalled to business, Pieter turned his back on the wonders of the Emperor's realm, not without a certain sense of relief. Awesome as the sight of the entire galaxy undoubtedly was, it was disquieting to contemplate too. The billions of stars behind him didn't just seethe with humanity, they were infested with uncountable xenos breeds as well, every one a threat, all of them gnawing away at the heart of the Imperium. The Ordo Xenos, which Pieter and his mentor served, defended it as best they could, but the task was an immense one, and the responsibility almost overwhelming.

Looking out into the infinite brought little comfort. Out here, the stars were few and sparsely scattered, but the darkness was still speckled with pinpoints of light, most of them galaxies like the one blazing at his back. All of them no doubt swarmed with life too, and there was no way of telling which, if any, harboured an as yet unrecognised threat to the Imperium. Even more disquieting, in its own way, was the dark void between them. It could conceal almost anything, as the tyranid hive fleet which had slammed so unexpectedly into the eastern arm a couple of centuries ago had so graphically proven.

There. One of the pinpricks of light was drifting almost imperceptibly against the fixed backdrop of the others, and Pieter triggered the manoeuvring jets again. Gradually, the mote grew, taking on form and definition, and Pieter concentrated on the battered bulk freighter thus revealed, picking out as much detail as he could to distract him from the roiling of his stomach. As he drew closer, it rotated gently beneath him, auspex arrays and engine pods drifting past like hills and valleys of pitted metal.

'No sign of external damage,' he voxed, although Grynner already knew that. A fresh excrescence rotated into view above the metal horizon, and he made for it with another burst of manoeuvring thrust, recognising the assault shuttle the inquisitor had dispatched an hour or so ago. As he corrected his course slightly, a new detail caught his eye, a thick metal hatch some metres in breadth, the second '*a*' of the vessel's name, the *Eddia Stabilis*, arcing across it. 'Their gun ports are still sealed.'

'Indeed.' Grynner's acknowledgement gave nothing of his thoughts away, but Pieter suspected he was far from surprised. The distress call they'd picked up from the freighter had been garbled and panic-stricken, but had made no mention of another vessel in the vicinity. He felt his pulse quicken a little. 'Can you see any of our colleagues yet?'

'Yes.' With a flare of relief, Pieter noticed an armoured figure standing next to the open portal of a small cargo bay, a bolter held ready for use across its chest, despite the fact that the *Eddia Stabilis* seemed completely devoid of life. It watched impassively as he guided the shuttle into the makeshift hangar, before plodding across the intervening expanse of hull plating to join him. He couldn't tell which of the kill team it was, the left pauldron of the Space Marine's power armour, which by tradition had been left in the original colours of its owner's home Chapter, hidden by the angle of his approach. Not that it would help much anyway, he suspected. The Astartes veterans which the Deathwatch had assigned to the inquisitor's security detail kept to themselves most of the time, disdaining the company of the rest of his retinue, and he wasn't even sure of some of their names.

'Interrogator.' The Marine greeted him formally, the deep, resonant voice, typical of his kind, buzzing in Pieter's vox receiver. 'The others are inside.'

Brief and to the point, the apprentice inquisitor thought. Whether or not the modified supermen of the Astartes ever indulged in so human a vice as small talk among themselves, he had no idea, but their dealings with Grynner and his staff had never been anything other than brisk and efficient.

'Good,' he responded, as the Marine entered the cargo bay, the closing outer door finally cutting off the disorientating view of the universe behind him.

Pieter took a deep breath, beginning to feel better already, and waited for the sable-armoured giant to begin repressurising the hold. At first sight it seemed little different from dozens of other shipboard chambers he'd passed through over the years, although the walls were discoloured with age, and the air pumps showed signs of hard wear, the votive wax seals of the enginseers flaking a little. Clearly the tech-adepts responsible for their maintenance were less punctilious in their duties than their counterparts aboard the *Emperor's Justice*. Or, more likely, too overworked, trying to keep the antiquated vessel functioning at all.

As soon as the pressure had risen sufficiently, Pieter cracked the seal on the shuttle's hatch, and sniffed the air cautiously as he stepped down onto the deck plating, fighting the impulse to tilt his head back in a futile attempt to read some expression in the Space Marine's blank visaged helmet. He was tall himself, a hair under two metres, but even so his eyes were only level with the aquila emblazoned across the sable ceramite chest plates, and the grimly functional bolter, which the power armoured giant hefted as easily as a normal man might a stubber or lasgun. As his guide turned to lead the way, his left shoulder came into view, and Pieter glanced at the heraldry revealed there, vaguely relieved at being able to put a name to him at last. Orjen the Space Wolf, the only one of his Chapter to be serving with the inquisitor's Deathwatch team.

'The air's fresh,' Pieter reported, for the listening inquisitor's benefit. The boarding party's instrumentation had recorded the fact, of course, but the mindless mechanisms lacked intuition, the subtle ability to draw conclusions not immediately apparent from mere data, which was why Grynner had sent him across in the first place. He coughed a little. 'As fresh as it ever gets on a tub like this, anyway.' Dry and musty, from being recycled and replenished innumerable times over the centuries, the atmosphere was overlaid with all the familiar shipboard odours: the faint musk of human bodies, which seemed to have permeated the very decks: old food and cooking fat; burned incense from the endless round of repairs and maintenance required to keep the ancient vessel functioning; and the ever-present hint of latrines. As the inner door clanked slowly open, and he followed his black-armoured guide into the corridor beyond, he became aware of another odour as well, sharp, metallic and all too familiar: fresh blood.

'Holy Throne!' The exclamation escaped him unbid-
den, and Orjen glanced back briefly in his direction
before resuming his watchful posture, bolter at the
ready. The deck plating was sticky with the mortal
remains of what, judging by the quantity of metal
interspersed with them, had been a group of the vessel's enginseers. It was hard to be sure, though.
Something had torn them apart, twisting the pieces
inside out, and patterning the walls and floor with
whatever remained. Despite the presence of his hulking protector, Pieter found his hand straying to the
bolt pistol holstered at his belt, and fought down the
impulse to draw it. Whoever – or more likely whatever
– had done this was long gone.

'Watch your step,' Orjen advised unnecessarily.
Telling himself that the sudden surge of gorge in his
throat was nothing more that another spasm of void
sickness, Pieter trotted after his black-armoured guide
as fast as he decently could, trying to pick significant
details out of the mess that might provide a clue as to
the nature of the fate that had befallen the unfortunate
tech-priests. No signs of claw or talon marks, or anything that might have been the residue of a weapon...

'You reported signs of battle damage,' he said, quickening his pace a little to keep up with the Marine's
unhurried stride, whose every step covered two of his
own. The matt black helmet swayed a little, in what
might have been a nod.

'Down here.' The Space Wolf turned down a cross
corridor, shadowed between the luminators set into its
ceiling, at the end of which Pieter caught a glimpse of
a flight of stairs. Trying to recall the layout of the vessel, assuming it had started out fairly typical of its class
and that half a millennium of shipmasters with their

own ideas of what constituted an efficient use of space hadn't changed it too much, they probably led up to the command decks. If there were any answers at all to be found, that's where they'd be, he hoped. Orjen gestured down a side passage, and Pieter gagged again, the rank stench of charred flesh searing the back of his nostrils. 'The ship's security contingent.'

'How can you tell?' There hadn't been much left of the bodies, that much was obvious.

'Because they put up a fight. You can still see the impact damage of las-bolts and stubber rounds on the walls. Didn't do them much good, though.'

'So I see.' The corridor had been scoured by what looked like a heavy flamer. Something didn't seem right, though, and after a moment of worrying about what it might be, the answer suddenly came to him. Flamers would have left the unmistakable odour of burned promethium behind, quite clearly detectable even over the stench of its victims' remains, and Pieter couldn't smell a trace of it. The hairs on the back of his neck began to prickle. Only one answer seemed to make sense, and he silently prayed to the Emperor that he was wrong. 'What were they trying to defend down there?'

'The shuttle bay,' Orjen told him, adding what was already obvious, presumably in case the interrogator was as dense as most Astartes seemed to think unmodified humans generally were. 'The shuttle's gone, of course.'

'Of course,' Pieter echoed, trying to make sense of the situation. 'And the wraithbone?'

'Gone too,' the sable giant confirmed. 'We're still sweeping the vessel, but if there was any left aboard, the Librarian would have felt its presence.'

'No doubt.' Pieter followed him up the staircase, the hulking Marine seeming to fill the entire companion-way. They'd been shadowing the *Eddia Stabilis* in the belief that it was smuggling some blasphemous eldar artefacts, although where to, and at whose behest, they had still to discover. Perhaps that was why the crew had been killed, to preserve the secret, although how their hidden antagonists could have known an Inquisi-torial vessel was in pursuit he had no idea. In any event, if even the tiniest fragment of so unhallowed a substance was still aboard, a psyker as powerful as Brother Paulus would certainly have detected it at once.

There was no time to speculate any further, however, as Orjen moved aside at last, and Pieter realised they'd reached the bridge. Another black-armoured giant stood slowly to greet them, easily recognisable by the servo-arm grafted to the back of his torso plate, even before the interrogator noticed the icon of the Iron Hands on his left shoulder: Ullen the Techmarine.

'Have you been able to retrieve anything from the cogitators?' Pieter asked without preamble. In his lim-ited experience of interacting with the members of the kill team, Ullen had even less time for the social niceties than most of his battle-brothers.

'I have not,' the towering Techmarine rumbled. 'The primary logic banks have been desecrated. Any data this system contained has been totally obliterated.'

As he stood aside, Pieter saw that he meant that quite literally. The brass frames and cogwheels of the calculating engine had been ripped apart, like the bod-ies of the luckless tech-priests below, and only fused and blackened stumps remained of the polished wooden control lecterns. There was no chance at all of finding out the freighter's intended destination from this collection of scrap.

Belatedly, he realised that the stench of blood and burning was strong again, and he began to discern fragments of the bridge crew among the wreckage. Swallowing hastily, he activated his vox.

'Inquisitor,' he began, 'we seem to have run into a bit of a hitch.'

'DISAPPOINTING, I GRANT you,' Jorge Grynner said, absently polishing the lenses of his spectacles on the end of his neck cloth. He returned them to his nose, and blinked at Pieter with an expression of vague perplexity, his grey, formal robes making him look more like a senior member of the Administratum than the personal embodiment of the Emperor's will. Pieter, however, had known him for far too long to be fooled by his unassuming manner, and seen far too many heretics make the fatal mistake of taking this façade of bureaucratic prissiness at face value. Those pale blue eyes missed nothing, and the mind behind them was as sharp as a monomolecular blade. 'That freighter was the best lead we've had for some time.'

'We could try extrapolating its course,' Pieter said, sitting forward on the lip of an overly upholstered armchair, and trying to look attentive. The inquisitor's personal quarters aboard the *Emperor's Justice* were as unostentatious as their owner, the floor thickly carpeted, and the bookshelves lining the walls of dark, polished wood. For the most part, the small suite of rooms was fastidiously tidy, only the desk behind which its owner sat cluttered with data-slates and neat stacks of paper. 'There can't be that many systems this far out they might have been making for.'

'Assuming their destination was actually in a stellar system,' Grynner pointed out mildly. 'Nevertheless, I have asked our Navigator to look into the possibility.' He sighed. 'I must say, though, I'm far from hopeful.'

'So what's our next move?' Pieter asked. 'The wraithbone's vanished, and we haven't a clue where it was going. We can't even be sure a Faxlignae cell was really behind the smugglers.'

'An operation of this size, involving interdicted xenos artefacts?' Grynner asked, his air of surprise more a rhetorical trick than an accurate reflection of his state of mind, Pieter thought. The inquisitor smoothed thinning grey hair in no need of straightening, and confirmed his pupil's assumption with a wintery smile. 'The list of organisations capable of coordinating such a thing is rather short, Pieter. I think we can safely infer their hand in this.'

'Didn't you once tell me we should never assume anything we can't prove?' Pieter asked, without thinking. Grynner's smile took on a tinge of genuine warmth.

'Quite right, my boy. Nevertheless, it's the only working hypothesis we've got.'

'All right,' Pieter conceded. 'We got a positive lead on a Faxlignae operation, which ought to have led us right to them. What went wrong?'

'Something quite unforeseen,' Grynner said, looking thoughtful. 'The Deathwatch Librarian reports having felt traces of some violent psychic event when he first boarded the vessel, which certainly seems likely given the state of the bodies you found. Perhaps that was related to the presence of the wraithbone, if it was ever aboard at all. Or perhaps the substance was removed by whoever took the shuttle, and we should be looking for a powerful psyker or two.'

'What would psykers be doing aboard a Faxlignae vessel?' Pieter asked. 'We know they've been scavenging xenos tech across half the segmentum for more than a century, Emperor knows why, but they've never shown any interest in psykers before.'

'That is a conundrum,' the inquisitor conceded. He nodded thoughtfully. 'And one we're not really qualified to unravel. Not without some assistance, anyway.'

'What sort of assistance did you have in mind?' Pieter asked. By way of reply, Grynner rummaged for a moment among the collection of data-slates on his desk, before activating one. The face of a man that Pieter had never seen before appeared on it.

'Carolus Finurbi of the Ordo Hereticus. A good man, as witch hunters go.' Grynner nodded thoughtfully, lost for a moment in some private memory. 'We've shared information before, and he may be in a position to help us in other ways too.' The mild, blue eyes turned abruptly on his apprentice. 'Remind me, Pieter, where did we pick up that unfortunate vessel's trail?'

'The Scintilla system,' Pieter said. 'Scintil VIII void station, to be precise. In the Calixis sector.'

'By all means, let's be precise,' Grynner said dryly. 'Carolus maintains a network of agents throughout the Calixis sector. If anything pertinent to our investigation involves rogue psykers at large there, it's quite likely he'll have some useful information for us.'

'I'll contact him at once,' Pieter said, rising from his seat.

'Good.' Grynner breathed absently on his spectacle lenses, and polished them again. 'You may need to be patient, however. He tends to be somewhat elusive.'

ONE

Forest of Sorrows, Sepheris Secundus
Calixus Sector. 087.933.M41

'JOIN THE GUARD and see the galaxy,' Drake said bitterly, pulling his cold weather camo cape around him a little tighter. Thin flurries of snow danced through the trees surrounding him, the dark clouds scudding above the branches, which waved in the wind like questing tentacles, promising a real blizzard before morning. He shivered, the formless sense of foreboding that had been muffling his soul from the moment the platoon had been deployed here intensified by the biting cold and the constantly moving shadows.

His companion shrugged. 'You can. It's up there.' He pointed to a thin strip of clear sky, beyond the trees and the ominous bulk of the snow clouds, in which a few stars twinkled in a desultory manner for a moment or two before the roiling darkness overhead obliterated them. Drake scowled at the faint pinpricks of light, as though they were somehow responsible for his frustration and slowly numbing feet.

'Thanks, Vos. You're a real ray of sunshine, you know that?'

Vos Kyrlock shrugged, and hefted his precious chain axe, checking once again that the mechanism was still free and unfrozen. He carried his standard issue lasgun slung over his shoulder, as dutifully as any other Guardsman, but the close combat weapon was his pride and joy. It hadn't taken his instructors long to realise that he'd never attain anything more than basic competence with a ranged weapon of any kind, but his natural aptitude for brawling was quite exceptional. Drake, on the other hand, was quite the opposite, his instinctive affinity for las weapons already honed by years of service in Queen Lachryma's household troops, the Royal Scourges, the nearest thing to a properly functioning Planetary Defence Force to be found on Sepheris Secundus.

The two men were completely different in most other respects too. Drake was thin, blond and wiry, his perpetual air of simmering resentment manifesting in a kind of nervous energy, which made him seem on edge even when he was relaxing, and Kyrlock was tall and barrel-chested, hair the colour of dying embers, whose sardonic manner kept most of the people he came into contact with firmly at arms length. To their mutual surprise, they'd become friends almost as soon as they'd met. Satisfied with the condition of his favourite weapon, Kyrlock shrugged. 'We'll be out there soon enough.'

'That's what the recruiter told me,' Drake said bitterly, 'six rutting months ago.' He ducked under a low branch, and almost tripped on a tree root concealed by the snow. Kyrlock followed, sure-footed in the dark woodlands, his bulk gliding between the shadowed trunks without disturbing so much as a twig. Drake swore colourfully as the branch he'd ducked under brushed against his helmet and deposited its load of snow down the back of his body armour.

'At least you had a choice,' Kyrlock reminded him. 'Most of us just got told to volunteer.' It was rare indeed for the mining world of Sepheris Secundus to be tithed for an Imperial Guard regiment. The labour of its countless serfs was vitally important to the economy of the entire sector, and their poor standard of health made them, for the most part, useless as soldiers. However, the increasing number of skirmishes and raids around the Eye of Terror in the last few years had imposed its own demands.

Something big was coming, that much was clear, and the sectors closest to the bleeding wound in the fabric of reality had begun to prepare for the worst.

Drake laughed bitterly. 'Stupidest decision I ever made,' he said. 'I should have stayed in the Scourges, like my father and grandfather did.'

'Without any hope of promotion or advancement?' Kyrlock asked, having heard the story innumerable times before.

Drake's face darkened under the wan starlight. 'That's right. Just because my mother was a chambermaid: mutant rutting snobs. At least in the Guard you get promoted on merit.'

'Well, that's us guaranteed an aquila apiece,' Kyrlock said, referring to a company commander's badge of rank.

'Assuming they ignore your criminal record,' Drake retorted, tugging the barrel of his lasgun free of a bush that had far too many thorns. 'What was it you did again?'

'Smuggling firewood into the Commons,' Kyrlock said cheerfully. 'Easy for a forester. I was going in and out of the Gorgonid all the time with timber for pit props and the like. No problem sticking a few sacks of twigs and offcuts on the truck. You'd be surprised what people will pay for good kindling.' A nostalgic smile appeared on his face for a moment. 'Or. There were a couple of habwives who…'

'Had husbands who told the overseer,' Drake interrupted testily, catching his shins on a trailing tree root. Kyrlock nodded, unabashed.

'Rather petty minded of them, I thought. Anyhow, the Baron needed able-bodied men to meet his Guard quota, and didn't want to lose his most productive workers. So here I am, instead of hanging for tithe evasion.'

'Lucky us,' Drake said. Kyrlock's liege lord hadn't been the only one who'd seized the opportunity the Guard tithe presented for ridding himself of the most troublesome malcontents among the workers he owned, and the undisciplined rabble he'd found himself surrounded by had been a stark and unwelcome contrast to the Scourges.

'Could be worse,' Kyrlock agreed. 'Quite like home, really.' An anxious expression flitted across his face for a moment. 'Do you think they have trees on other planets too?'

'I hope not,' Drake said, neither knowing nor caring. Kyrlock looked as though he was about to take issue with that point of view, but before he could reply, the short-range vox receivers in both men's helmets hissed.

'Drake, Kyrlock, where the rut are you?'

'Just completing our sweep, sergeant,' Drake replied crisply, ignoring his companion's derisory hand gestures. Neither had a particularly high opinion of Sergeant Claren, who owed his rank to his former civilian occupation as an overseer in the mines rather than any grasp of military matters, and who, both suspected, must have done something to irritate an officer in order to have been seconded to this bleak and desolate outpost. That had certainly been the case with them, and, so far as they could tell, most of the misfits and troublemakers in the fledgling Secundan 3rd had been assigned to the same platoon, and sent down here almost as soon as the regiment had been officially founded. Drake, with more experience than most of how the military mind worked, tried not to ruminate too much on the various ramifications of the word *expendable*, although it was hard to see what sort of enemy they might be expected to face in this desolate wilderness.

'Good,' Claren said, from the warmth and comfort of his command Chimera. 'Wyler's got frostbite. You can take over his sentry post.'

'We'll be right there,' Drake confirmed, cutting the link abruptly before Kyrlock could comment verbally. 'You son of a mutant,' he added, sure the sergeant couldn't hear him.

'Well, it could be worse,' Kyrlock said philosophically.

'Could it?' Drake turned, and led the way back towards the outpost. Stark and forbidding, it loomed against the night like a small fortified hill, studded with lights, which somehow failed to reveal anything other than an oppressive sense of greater darkness beyond them. The great metal gates hadn't been opened since the Imperial Guard platoon had arrived and set up their camp, insulated survival bubbles for sleeping and a larger one for messing in, although he'd seen a few shuttles arrive and depart beyond the ramparts. All had been devoid of insignia.

Now and again, men would appear on the walls, their uniforms similar to his, although their armour was grey and their fatigues dark red. That had been a real shock. On Sepheris Secundus, red was the colour of the royal family, and for anyone not of the blood-line, or in their direct service, to wear it was almost an act of treason. Many of his comrades, particularly former Scourges, had been incensed by that, but Drake had found it strangely exciting, a reminder that a wider galaxy existed beyond this world, with exotic customs of its own. He had no idea who the strange soldiers were. They'd ignored all attempts to hail them, and after a few days the guardsmen had given up trying to attract their attention.

'Sure it could,' Kylock said, producing a bottle of something from beneath his camo cloak. 'Claren won't be out checking up on us on a night like this, will he?'

'I doubt it,' Drake agreed, his spirits lifting for the first time since coming on duty. He glanced up at the blank grey walls of the fortress. 'It's not as if anyone's going to break in there while our backs are turned, is it?'

The Citadel of the Forsaken, Sepheris Secundus
087.993.M41

BY THE TIME Drake had made his fate-tempting remark, and he and Kyrlock had begun trudging back through the snow towards their newly assigned sentry post, it was already far too late to prevent an intruder from gaining access in any case. The intruder had been there for some time, although none of the people who saw it, worked alongside it, or exchanged pleasantries in the corridors or over a bowl of reconstituted protein in the commissary with it knew it for what it was, seeing only the face and form of an old friend or colleague. Now, at the appointed time, it made its move.

'Having trouble?' a junior tech-priest asked, slowing his pace a little, eager as always to discuss the minutiae of the Omnissiah's bounty with a fellow initiate. The intruder shook its head, withdrawing it from the inspection panel it had opened.

'Nothing serious, Brother Polk. A faint arrhythmia in the primary heat exchangers, I fancy.' The intruder stood politely aside, making the sign of the cogwheel. 'Do you hear it too?'

'I'm not sure,' Polk admitted, stepping forward to look inside the hatch, the joints of his augmetic legs hissing slightly as they came to rest again. 'But then your hearing is greatly superior to my own, as is your understanding of the Omnissiah's infinite generosity.'

'You're too modest, my friend,' the intruder urged. 'Do you not feel the faintest of tremors in the casing?'

Polk reached out with a mechadendrite, caressing the revealed piping with its tip. A faint expression of doubt flickered across the portions of his face as yet unreplaced by metal. 'Perhaps,' he said at last. 'Do you require assistance in rectifying the anomaly?'

'I believe not,' the intruder assured him. 'The matter seems trivial enough, but it should be corrected if we are to be true to the Omnissiah, whose perfection is reflected in all things.'

'Of course.' Polk made the sign of the cogwheel again. 'Then I shall leave you to your devotions.'

'And I to yours,' the intruder replied, 'which are no doubt more pressing.'

'Perhaps they are,' Polk admitted. 'An imperfection exists in the auspex arrays.'

The intruder nodded as though unaware of the fact, in spite of having taken some time to ensure just such a state of affairs. 'Then it should be rectified forthwith.' It was mildly irritating that the subtle sabotage had been detected quite so quickly, but it had covered its tracks well, and had no doubt that Polk would be unable to complete his repairs until it was far too late. It waited until the young tech-priest had passed out of sight, and resumed working on the systems behind the panel.

Icenholm, Sepheris Secundus
087.993.M41

'THANK YOU ALL for returning so promptly,' Inquisitor Carolus Finurbi said, looking from one expectant face to another. The air was cool here, high in a discreet quarter of the planetary capital favoured by the minor noble houses, but not unpleasantly so. The reflected light that bathed the suspended city struck through the stained glass wall of the villa, which his team had rented as a base of operations shortly after their arrival on Sepheris Secundus. Little puddles of colour blemished the floor and furnishings where the light had acquired the hues of the decoration it had passed through, mottling the hanging tapestries and the floor cushions on which he and his operatives sat. The use of the material for almost everything was a local custom that he hadn't expected. Even the bedrooms and balnearea were walled with the stuff, privacy ensured only by the density of the pigment infused with the glass. 'I gather your enquiries have had little success.'

That much was obvious from their body language. He knew this particular team of his Angelae, the informal name his network of operatives had adopted, better than most, having recruited all of them personally, and felt uncomfortable about reading their minds unless he had to. Today, there would be no need for that, though. Their disappointment hung heavy in the air, like the scent from the perfumed candles in the intricately wrought glass holders which the house servants had placed next to the open doors leading to the balcony. The gentle breeze from outside spread the perfumed smoke throughout the room. As he'd expected, Horst, the generally acknowledged leader of the group, spoke for them all.

'I'm afraid you're right, inquisitor.' The former arbitrator shrugged as he spoke, his dark hair taking on a momentary tinge of yellow as the movement of his head took it through the penumbra of the halo of some minor local saint embedded in the glittering wall. 'You can't move on this Emperor forsaken rock without hearing rumours of some Chaos cult or other, but every time you try to chase them down they just evaporate. Either they're incredibly well organised and connected, or…'

'They simply don't exist,' a melodious voice chimed in. As it spoke, Carolus could feel its echoes, warm and intimate, caressing the surface of his mind, and smiled at the psyker across the room. Elyra Yivor returned the smile, her violet eyes meeting his gaze for a moment. Her unspoken thoughts echoed in his head. *There's something else, isn't there?*

All in good time, he returned, holding eye contact for an instant longer. The blonde woman's smile stretched a little, and Carolus found some pleasant and intimate memories rising to the surface of his mind. The years had been kind to her, he thought, even without juvenat treatments.

Flatterer, Elyra sent, savouring the memories too. *I was never that beautiful, or athletic.*

You were to me. A faint haze of regret drifted over his thoughts. *But you were right. It would never have worked out between us. Our duty to the Ordo Hereticus always came first.*

The Emperor gave us these gifts, Elyra reminded him, just as she had in person, so painfully, all those years ago. *What for, if not to use them doing His holy work?*

Right as always, my love. Carolus broke the link between them, unwilling to be distracted any longer by the echoes of past regrets. As ever, the exchange had been all but instant. The echoes of Elyra's last verbal comment were still hanging in the air as his attention returned to the here and now. The derisive snort that broke in next scattered them, like the shards of broken light scintillating from every surface of the vitreous room.

'They're there, all right, believe me.' The speaker was a young woman, the green eyes beneath her purple-dyed fringe hard and unforgiving. 'I've been right down to the lower levels, several times. It's crawling with muties.' The other people in the room looked at her expectantly. Keira Sythree had been the last to arrive, and was still dressed in the skintight synsuit of an Officio Assassinorum operative, its chameleonic surface seeming to ripple in a vain attempt to match the ever-changing colours being reflected on it from the refulgent glass surrounding her. The only constant hue, apart from her pale face and purple hair, was the crimson bandana holding her fringe out of her eyes.

Horst coughed diplomatically, the sound echoed a great deal more raucously a moment later by the tech-priest in the corner. As all eyes turned to him, Brother Vex shrugged apologetically. 'Sorry. Still need to do a bit of work on the new respirator.'

'As I was about to say,' Horst went on, the merest trace of irritation entering his voice, 'Keira's just returned from another recon sweep in the Gorgonid.' He gestured beyond the open doors, and the glass-tiled patio beyond. From where he sat, Carolus could clearly see the vast pit gouged into the mountains beneath the glass city, which hung suspended above it on innumerable cables slung between the highest peaks. Watching the sunlight scintillate from a thousand palaces and a million surfaces, he was reminded of an arachnid's web dusted with frost on a crisp winter morning.

Looking down was a vertiginous experience. Over a kilometre below, the vast opencast workings of the largest mine on the planet seemed to seethe and shimmer in the faint traces of sunlight that managed to force their way through the near constant cloud cover, thin wisps of dust and vapour rising here and there, apparently at random. For a moment, Carolus was at a loss, trying to understand how something so dark and shadowed could be obscured by heat haze. Elyra supplied the answer: *it's the people.*

Only then did the truly gargantuan scale of the workings impinge on his conscious mind, and he drew in his breath. The rippling motion he could see was the movement of countless serfs, too far away to discern as individual human beings, all hacking away at the mineral wealth of Sepheris Secundus with the most primitive of hand tools. The bottom of the pit was in complete darkness, too deep for the westering sun to penetrate, if it ever did, and the faint glow of innumerable flares, torches and luminators competed with the natural light, blurring his vision even more. How Keira had managed to penetrate that seething anthill of humanity undetected, and return again, he had no idea, but the girl's talents were truly exceptional. Not for the first time, he thanked the Emperor for the insight that had allowed him to discern them, and the tutors of the Collegium Assassinorum for honing them so skilfully.

'So I see,' he said dryly. He gestured towards the crimson bandana. 'I take it you haven't been wearing that in public.'

'No.' Keira reached up to touch it reflexively. Red was the holy colour of the Redemption, the violent sect in which she'd been raised, and she always wore at least a trace of it. She glanced briefly at Horst before going on. 'Mordechai explained the local dress code very carefully.'

That must have been an interesting discussion, Carolus thought, and pushed aside the temptation to lift the memories from their minds. Instead, he nodded judiciously. 'Thank you for your forbearance,' he said. 'I realise how important your faith is to you.'

'No problem,' Keira assured him, glancing again at Horst with what, in anyone else, Carolus would have taken for a fleeting expression of mischief. 'I got some red underwear.' Horst looked uncomfortable for a moment, no doubt unable to avoid picturing the effect it would have on the body that the girl's synsuit already revealed in considerable detail. 'Sort of a compromise.'

'I see.' Carolus hid his surprise. When he'd last seen Keira she wouldn't have dreamed of making light of her Redemptionist principles, and would probably have killed anyone who did. Clearly, exposure to the wider galaxy was having unexpected effects on the girl. So long as that didn't compromise her efficiency or her lethality, he could live with it. 'What did you find at the bottom of the hole?' Once again his eye was drawn to the human anthill so far below, and he suppressed a shudder.

'The mutants seem organised,' Keira reported, her mind recalled to business. 'There are far more of them than anyone up here suspects, and they have the usual shrines to the Changer. I've pinpointed most of them for cleansing. No signs of widespread Chaos worship beyond that, though, and no sign of what you're looking for, either.'

'I see. Thank you.' Carolus reached out to pick up a delicate crystal tea bowl from the low table in front of him, and sipped, ordering his thoughts. The blend was unfamiliar, but not unpleasant, a faint trace of spices behind the bitterness. Similar glass tables, their surfaces composed of interlocking panes of vibrant colour, forming abstract patterns that echoed one another without ever quite repeating, stood in front of the others, who sat or sprawled on their cushions according to their personal inclinations.

Horst was cross-legged and straight backed, his brocade jacket hanging open to reveal his holstered bolt pistol as he reached forward to pick up one of the delicate sugared cakes from the plate the servants had placed in front of him along with his tea. Keira sat, like

Carolus, on her folded calves, her weight forward, poised to move in an instant if any threat presented itself, the hilt of her sword within easy reach of her hand. She sipped her tea carefully, her eyes rising from the steam from time to time to regard Horst and the inquisitor in turn without expression. Hybris Vex simply sprawled, the plain robes of his calling and few visible augments looking utterly incongruous in this vulgarly polychromatic room, and Elyra... Elyra was simply as poised and elegant as the woman in his memories always was, her pale blue kirtle setting off her eyes to perfection. Her upright posture emphasised her faint stoop, a little more pronounced than it had been, as though the burden of her talent weighed physically upon her a little more with each passing year, but that didn't diminish her at all. If anything, it seemed to call subtle attention to the inner strength he'd always admired in her. Meeting his eyes again, the blonde woman smiled.

'Sorry, Carolus. It looks like you've come all the way from Malfi just to hear that we've hit a dead end.' She tilted her head, acknowledging her colleagues. 'We've been turning the planet upside down ever since we got here, and we haven't found a trace of the kind of operation you told us to look out for.'

'I'm afraid that's true, inquisitor.' As always, Horst looked uncomfortable with Elyra's use of their employer's given name, and emphasised his title a little as he spoke. 'There are undoubtedly heretical groups on Sepheris Secundus, which I'm sure we can root out given time, but nothing on the scale your message indicated.'

'Quite so,' Vex interjected, coughing again as he spoke. He balled his fist, and thumped something under his robe, which gave off a metallic echo. 'Ah, that's got it. I've been through the last five years worth of Arbites datafiles, and there's been no mention of any psyker activity beyond the usual stuff. Latents and rogues have been rounded up for the black ships, and that's about it.'

'You secured the cooperation of the Arbites?' Carolus asked, with a hint of surprise. Unlike most worlds of the Imperium, the Adeptus Arbites maintained a considerable presence here, maintaining law and order directly from the fortress garrison that the Secundans referred to as the Isolarium, rather than delegating the task to local enforcers as they usually did. The feudal nature of Secundan society made any conventional police force impossible to run, and the nearest equivalent, the Royal Scourges, were too martial in outlook and too hidebound by tradition to make effective investigators.

Under most circumstances the handful of Arbitrators left to oversee the dispensation of the Emperor's justice on an Imperial world would make useful allies for a team of Inquisitorial operatives, but on Sepheris Secundus, where their main concern was to ensure an uninterrupted flow of raw materials to the hive worlds of the Calixis sector, and riot control was a higher priority than intelligence gathering, confiding in them seemed like an unnecessary security risk.

As if divining the inquisitor's doubts, Vex shook his head. 'Not as such. I just poked about a bit in their datanet.' He shrugged. 'They seem a bit busy anyway, keeping the serfs in line, so it would have been churlish to bother them unnecessarily.'

'How very considerate,' Carolus said, hiding his amusement. The tech-priest would have been able to gain unlimited access to the files he wanted simply by showing his Inquisitorial credentials, but he wouldn't have found that nearly as much fun as outwitting the arbitrators' encryption and security protocols, and his message dispatching the team had indeed emphasised the need for discretion. If his suspicions were correct, a very large and well-organised conspiracy was at work, and there was no telling how far its influence might have spread. 'I'm sure you've all done more than I could possibly have asked of you, as usual.'

'That makes it even more galling to have let you down,' Horst said, 'especially as you've just come halfway across the sector to get here.' Like all his agents, the former arbitrator knew that keeping in touch with so wide a network of operatives as the Angelae Carolus was difficult and time-consuming, and the inquisitor would normally intervene in person only if things were getting desperate. Most of the time, they received their orders and dispatched their reports by astropath, like everyone else in the far-flung organisation.

Carolus smiled reassuringly. 'I wouldn't say that, exactly,' he said, and felt a tingle of Elyra's amusement brushing against his mind.

Here it comes. Whatever he hasn't been telling us…

How right you are, he responded, and began to speak.

Forest of Sorrows, Sepheris Secundus
087.993.M41

'THAT'S GOOD STUFF.' Drake took another pull at the bottle, and returned it to Kyrlock. The large man shook it, listened dolefully to the gurgling that indicated it was almost empty, and drank in turn. 'Keeps the cold

out all right.' An unaccustomed sense of warmth and
well-being suffused him, despite the bone chilling
wind howling across the lip of the foxhole just above
his head, driving its load of snow almost horizontally
towards the barely visible fortress in the distance.
'Where did you get it?'

'Vorlens,' Kyrlock told him, naming one of the
Chimera drivers. 'He's been distilling it round the back
of the maintenance shed.'

'Good old Vorlens,' Drake said, forgetting for a
moment how much he disliked the man, and trying
not to wonder what Vorlens had been distilling it
from. He narrowed his eyes, raising his head for a
moment, and ducked back under cover, his eyes full of
snow. 'Looks like it's setting in for a long blow.'

'Looks like it,' Kyrlock agreed, draining the last of the
bottle, and sending it spinning into the dark. He'd
spent most of his life in a forest like this one, and
could read the weather easily. 'It's going to be a real
mess by the morning.'

Drake nodded sagely in agreement, although neither
of them could possibly have predicted just how cata-
strophically accurate that forecast would turn out to
be.

The Citadel of the Forsaken, Sepheris Secundus
087.993.M41

THE INTRUDER RETURNED to its quarters inside the
fortress, unnoticed and unremarked, and sat at a perfectly ordinary message terminal. Working quickly, for
its task behind the panel had taken a little longer than
expected, it picked up a set of tools and prised the back
off.

If Brother Polk could have seen what ensued, he would have been aghast at the desecration. The intruder worked rapidly and methodically, without even a hint of the proper prayers and rituals, modifying the circuitry and adding a few components that even the most senior acolytes of the Omnissiah would have been hard-pressed to recognise. At length, satisfied with its work, the intruder activated the messager, transmitting a single, highly focussed vox pulse, and began to return its internal workings to their original condition.

High Orbit, Sepheris Secundus
087.993.M41

IF MUCH OF the sky could ever be seen from the surface, and any of the ill-educated serfs were ever inclined to raise their gaze from the unremitting toil of the workface, they could have been forgiven for believing that the stars moved, or at least that a considerable number of them did. At any given time there were thousands of ore barges in orbit around the ravaged planet, their heavy lifters glutting their cargo bays with the mineral wealth wrenched from the cloud-wreathed surface below, swarming like metal flies around a choice piece of carrion.

Externally, nothing marked one particular ship as anything out of the ordinary. It moved smoothly among its fellows, taking up its station with leisurely bursts of its manoeuvring thrusters, and broadcasting all the required authorisation codes.

After a while, a shuttle departed, and fell towards the planet below, its hull plates glowing a deep, rich red as it began its long plunge through the atmosphere, following the coordinates contained in the vox pulse its carrier vessel had received a short time before. Had anyone been able to observe it, they would have been surprised by both its shape and function, but no one did. Exotic technologies shielded it against most forms of detection, and the more specialised auspexes at its intended destination had been blinded by subtle sabotage. As the landing craft penetrated deeper within the atmosphere of Sepheris Secundus, and the air began to thicken, imparting lift to its aerodynamic hull, its occupants readied their weapons.

TWO

Icenholm, Sepheris Secundus
087.993.M41

'IN THE LAST twenty years,' Carolus began, after another sip of tea, 'the number of rogue psykers of Epsilon grade and above apprehended on Sepheris Secundus has fallen by almost three per cent. I sent you here to look for signs of an organised Chaos cult, because that seemed to be the most likely explanation.' He smiled ruefully. 'However, your lack of success in finding one of sufficient size and influence to offer that many wyrds a refuge leads me to suspect that we're dealing with an even more insidious conspiracy.'

'What kind of conspiracy?' Horst asked at once, his investigator's instincts piqued. By way of an answer, the inquisitor placed a data-slate on the table in front of him, and activated its built-in hololith. A face appeared in the air above it, rotating slowly, fading in and out of focus in the manner typical of such devices.

'Tobias Vetch,' Carolus said, 'delta-grade wyrd, killed on Vaxanide by another team of my Angelae two years ago.'

'Good for them,' Keira said, 'but so what? That's parsecs from here.'

'Quite.' Carolus nodded. 'But I encountered Vetch myself, eight years ago, on Iocanthus. He managed to slip away while we were rounding up his confederates.'

'So he caught a ship,' Keira said. 'People do, even heretics.' Her voice tightened with loathing on the last word.

'Wyrds don't,' Elyra said. 'Not easily, anyway. Starports are full of sanctioned psykers of one sort or another, and it only takes one to get close enough to feel what they are.'

'Maybe he just got lucky,' Horst said.

'Possibly.' Carolus nodded thoughtfully, as if considering the suggestion. 'But if so, he got lucky twice. I have strong reason to suspect that he was also on Fenksworld for a while, along with her.' Vetch's face was replaced by that of a hard-faced woman, apparently in her early thirties. Elyra's eyes narrowed.

'Ariadne Thane? I thought we killed her on Luggnum, along with the rest of her coven.'

'So did I,' Carolus said, 'but this pict was taken in 989, six years after that.' He called up an image of Thane leaning on the balcony of a hab block typical of an industrial hive. 'Fenksworld again. By the time I learned of her presence there, and sent an Angelae cell to deal with her, she'd disappeared, along with Vetch. The search was commendably thorough. I have no doubt at all that they'd already left the planet before it commenced.'

'Then someone must have helped them,' Vex said simply. 'It's the only logical conclusion.'

'That doesn't alter the fact that we've been here for months without finding a trace of any group organised or powerful enough to mount an operation like that,' Horst reminded everyone. He shifted his head slightly, squinting as the glass saint's halo brushed yellow across his eyes, to address the inquisitor directly. 'What makes you think they're active here, on Sepheris Secundus?'

'Two things,' Carolus said slowly. 'One being the state of servitude practically the entire population live under. Most accept their lot, it's true, but a few refuse to do so, creating the never-ending problem for the local Arbites that Hybris has already alluded to.'

'Which helps us how?' Elyra asked.

'A rebellious serf's prospects here are limited, to say the least,' Carolus explained. 'Which leaves them only one recourse.'

'Getting off-world,' Vex said flatly. 'Quite a trick if they can do it.'

'A trick that a small but growing number of them seem to be pulling off,' the inquisitor assured him. 'Given the number of ships that depart from here each day it's impossible to tell which may be involved, but it's become abundantly clear in the last few years that at least a handful of shipmasters on a regular run aren't averse to taking the odd unauthorised passenger with them when they leave. No doubt for as much remuneration as the market will bear.'

'I see where you're going with this,' Horst said, nodding in agreement. 'If there's a way off-planet for runaway serfs, then the missing psykers might be using it too.'

'That brings me to the second thing,' Carolus explained, plucking one of the tiny sugared cakes from the plate in front of him. 'If I'm right about the scale of the conspiracy, and the resources available to it, then this planet is a prize they can't possibly resist.'

Lower atmosphere, Sepheris Secundus
087.993.M41

THE DROP-SHIP banked sharply, threading the gorge between two mountain peaks wreathed in snow, the wind of its passage thrashing the trees in its wake as the smooth metal hull soared easily through the turbulent air. Thick, driving snow obscured the viewports, and vicious crosswinds buffeted the fuselage, but the pilot remained calm and unconcerned, feeling the aircraft responding to the slightest touch of the controls like something alive.

A hololith, the image within it so sharp and steady it might almost have been a solid sculpture of glowing light, relayed an image of the surrounding terrain, every feature meticulously rendered with such fidelity that he had no need to look at the blurred, obscured reality beyond his cockpit. Status displays, translated into readily understood Gothic, scrolled across thin, flat pict screens of xenos manufacture and unparalleled clarity.

'We're on our final approach,' he voxed to the compartment behind him, seeing the red icon of the target edging into the fringe of the display.

'Acknowledged,' the strike leader said. Howling like a daemon, clawing the snow from the trees as its belly skimmed their uppermost branches, the drop-ship swooped like a shrike on its unsuspecting prey.

* * *

Icenholm, Sepheris Secundus
087.993.M41

'You HAVE GOT to be joking,' Horst said without think-ing, and then flushed, embarrassed. The inquisitor wouldn't joke about something like that, especially not in the middle of a briefing. He clearly wasn't the only one to feel that way, though. Vex was ashen, his normally dark brown face a pasty grey colour that con-trasted oddly with the metallic sheen of his augments, and Elyra looked shocked and horrified. Perhaps she was arguing with their patron telepathically, or per-haps she was simply stunned beyond words.

Keira's expression was unreadable, of course, but even if her feelings had been visible, it probably wouldn't have helped much. The psychotic bitch was in a world of her own most of the time anyway. Reminded again of her presence, he tried to ignore the disquieting fashion in which the rippling colours play-ing across the girl's synsuit emphasised the curves of her body.

'Why would there be a secret holding pen for the Black Ships on Sepheris Secundus?' Elyra asked, incredulity raising her voice half an octave. 'I thought the Arbites took care of that at the Isolarium.'

'Something on the scale you suggest does seem hard to believe,' Horst agreed, seizing on the distraction gratefully.

'Does it?' the inquisitor asked dryly. 'There are con-tainment facilities for psykers on most Imperial worlds. Given the unusually high population of this one, and the unusually high incidence of mutation among it, I would have thought it obvious that the one here would be somewhat larger than usual.'

'It does seem reasonable,' Vex said, his voice steadying with an effort that only Horst's years of experience, winnowing truth from lies, allowed him to detect. 'In the years since the last Black Ship called here, over a thousand psykers have been apprehended. The Adeptus Arbites facilities at the Isolarium would have been overwhelmed long ago, if they were forced to contain them all.'

'All right, I concede that,' Horst said, 'but I don't see how you expect this holding pen to provide a lead to the conspiracy.'

'Isn't it obvious?' Keira asked, smiling at him in a faintly superior manner, to which the afterimages of his involuntary erotic reverie lent disturbing overtones. 'A thousand psykers, lined up and ready for grilling. If there is a group taking them off-world, then there's a good chance they made contact with at least a few of them before they got picked up.'

'Good point,' Horst conceded, receiving another disconcerting grin in return. Before he could start worrying about it, though, the inquisitor broke in.

'That is why we're going there now. Just a short sub-orbital hop.' He reached up to shake the thin glass bells above his head, signalling for a servant. 'You've got ten minutes to collect any gear you might need.'

Forest of Sorrows, Sepheris Secundus 087.993.M41

'LISTEN,' DRAKE SAID, raising his head and straining to hear over the battering roar of the blizzard. As it had intensified, they'd scraped out a snow hole in the bottom of their makeshift fortification, which, together with the residue of the alcoholic glow, had kept them surprisingly warm despite the freezing temperature. 'Do you hear that?'

'It's just the wind,' Kyrlock said dismissively. 'Holy Throne, you city boys, anyone'd think you'd never been outdoors before.'

'You're probably right,' Drake said, unwilling to leave their refuge unless he had to. But then, given the amount he'd drunk relatively recently, it was beginning to feel as though he didn't have much of a choice. He wobbled reluctantly to his feet, feeling the blizzard lash against his face as he drew level with the wind again. 'Couldn't hurt to check, though.'

'Please yourself,' Kyrlock said, showing no sign of being willing to follow, not that Drake had expected him to. Clearly divining the real purpose of his friend's excursion into the howling storm, the former forester grinned, the edges of the facial tattoos of his home barony appearing from beneath the chinstrap of his helmet as the skin stretched. 'Make sure you keep your back to the wind, or it'll come off in your hand.'

'Wouldn't be the first time for you,' Drake retorted reflexively, and clambered out into the teeth of the flensing gale, before Kyrlock could think of a suitably obscene riposte.

He hadn't taken a couple of paces before the unutterable foolishness of leaving their refuge became all too clear, but the residue of alcoholic warmth within him, and the thought of Kyrlock's derision if he returned ignominiously with an unemptied bladder, combined to keep his legs moving until he reached the comparative shelter of a tree a handful of metres away. In its lee, the wind and the never-ending barrage of sleet moderated to the merely almost unbearable, and mindful of his friend's facetious advice, he quickly created a cloud of rank-smelling steam, which was whipped away almost at once. Trying to explain frostbite in that particular extremity to the medicae orderly was a conversation he'd rather not have.

As he turned away from the rough bark of his refuge, the wind seemed to moderate, almost imperceptibly, and the sound he thought he'd heard before shrilled momentarily into audibility. The high, teeth jarring shriek of a powerful engine, and the rumble of its passage through the atmosphere, rose for a moment through the rolling thunder of the wind, through the blizzard-lashed forest. Shielding his eyes as best he could, Drake looked upwards, straining for a glimpse of anything out of the ordinary through the wildly gyrating branches and the whirling kaleidoscope of snowflakes.

'Vos!' Kyrlock couldn't hear him above the howl of the wind, of course, but that's what the helmet voxes were for.

'Warned you.' His companion's voice was still bantering. 'But if you want me to come and help you look for it, you can stick that...'

'Shut up and listen!' Drake demanded. As he strained his ears over the bellowing storm, he thought he could detect the sound again, a rising note in the discordant symphony surrounding them.

'What for?' Kyrlock asked, responding to the unmistakable note of urgency in his friend's voice, all trace of levity gone.

'For that!' Drake responded, raising his voice as the sound rushed out of the darkness, building so quickly that within seconds it was something he felt rather than heard, resonating deep within his body. Something huge and dark howled overhead, the blast of its passage combining with the bellowing wind to create a vortex that slammed him off his feet. Deafened, half-blinded by whirling snow and a stinging barrage of thin green needles wrenched from the branches above him, he floundered, disorientated, in the middle of a drift. After a moment, he slithered to his feet, eyes stinging, and spat out fragments of bark.

'What the hell was it?' Kyrlock asked, his voice forcing its way past the ringing in Drake's ears. A more alarming possibility seemed to strike him, and he hesitated. 'Danuld? Can you hear me?'

'Just about.' Drake looked around, all sense of direction gone, and fought down a rising surge of panic. After a moment, a thicker swirl of snow in his peripheral vision resolved itself into the comforting solidity of Kyrlock, his outline blurred by his grey and white camo cape, and he sighed inwardly with relief.

'What do we do now?' Kyrlock asked, as Drake unslung his lasgun, checking the power pack with cold numbed fingers. A full charge: good.

'Report it,' Drake said. 'What the rut do you think?' He activated his vox again. 'Sergeant, this is Drake. Are there any shuttles due in?' He waited, bracing himself for some sarcastic rejoinder, but the only sound in his ears was the faint hiss of static. 'Oh great, comms are down. This is just getting better and better.'

'Why's that?' Kyrlock asked, deferring to his friend's greater military experience as instinctively as he would have done to a social superior.

At a loss, and unwilling to admit it, Drake shrugged. 'Too much wind,' he suggested. 'All this stuff blowing about must be blocking the signal.' He glanced around again, trying to get his bearings. 'Which way do you think it went?'

'That way,' Kyrlock said decisively, pointing into the murk in what looked to Drake like a completely random direction. Nevertheless, he knew his way around in a forest, so his judgement ought to be sound.

'Come on, then,' Drake said resignedly, beginning to lead the way into the trees in the direction Kyrlock had indicated. 'Let's go and check it out. Whoever they were, they were way off course. If they've crashed they're going to need help, and Emperor preserve the poor sods, we're probably the best they're going to get.'

The Citadel of the Forsaken, Sepheris Secundus
087.993.M41

INSIDE THE FORTRESS, the drop-ship's arrival had gone unnoticed, just as the intruder had planned. Brother Polk was still deeply immersed in the bowels of the auspex array, chanting the litanies of fault diagnosis as he traced bundles of wiring from one junction box to another. The problem was most perplexing, every individual subsystem appearing to run perfectly, although the primary one they made up between them continued to fail every time he tested it. Polk found that irritating, the impediment to the smooth perfection of the machine as irksome as a hangnail would have been if he still possessed his original fingers.

'Have you made any progress yet?' a clipped voice asked him, and, suppressing the annoyance at the interruption, which, as a mere human weakness, an acolyte of the Machine-God was supposed to be above, Polk wormed his way out from under the primary power coils to answer.

'I have successfully eliminated a number of possible causes,' he replied, straightening, and thanking the

Omnissiah that he'd had his vocal cords replaced by a toneless voxcoder that would purge his response of any lingering traces of resentment at the interruption.

His interlocutor stared at him for a moment in a fashion his subordinates found satisfactorily intimidating, but the white-robed tech-priest remained irritatingly impassive. Feeling vaguely disconcerted, a sensation he found neither familiar nor welcome, Captain Severus Malakai of the Inquisitorial storm troopers cleared his throat. 'Any idea how much longer this is going to take?' he asked.

'The Omnissiah's work is complex,' Polk told him unhelpfully, 'and no one can count the steps on the path to enlightenment.'

'I'll take that as a no,' Malakai said, turning to go.

'Is there any added urgency?' the tech-priest asked, and Malakai glanced back over his shoulder.

'We've got an inquisitor inbound, ETA about thirty minutes, assuming the mad bastard doesn't plough into a mountain, trying to fly in a mess like this. It would be helpful if you could restore coverage before he arrives, in case we need to guide him in.'

'I will pray to the Omnissiah to speed my hand,' Polk assured him, returning to work.

'Good. That's a weight off my mind, then,' Malakai said sarcastically, as the tech-priest disappeared under the tangle of cables behind the wall panel.

DEEP INSIDE ANOTHER panel, near the genetorium, a timer ticked downwards, and, secure in its living quarters, the intruder glanced at a chronograph on the wall.

Guiding the body it wore to its feet, it prepared for action, although it didn't really expect to have to intervene in person. Its preparations had been meticulous, and everything would undoubtedly run as smoothly as it anticipated.

Only moments to go. Were it as human as it appeared, it would undoubtedly have smiled.

Lower Atmosphere, Sepheris Secundus
087.993.M41

'GET READY TO deploy,' the pilot instructed, watching an identical countdown on one of the screens surrounding his control station. The smooth, rounded surfaces of the flight deck still seemed strange, despite the comforting familiarity of the blocky Imperial technology grafted into several of the systems, and the flesh and metal hybrids of the servitors manning all but one of the other consoles. The exception was the gunnery station, where a hard-eyed woman in body armour sat; one of the other specialists their patrons had engaged for this mission. The pilot had no idea who she was, and preferred it that way. No names had been exchanged at the briefing, and although some of the men and women riding in the astonishingly large cargo bay behind him had clearly known one another, they'd kept their own counsel.

The money was good, and that was all that mattered. The path that had brought him here had been a long and winding one, mostly downhill, but this was it, the big score, the one that would set him up for life. Hell, if he'd known in advance what he'd be flying, he'd have done it for free. Emperor alone knew who, or more likely what, had built this ship, let alone how his employers had managed to get their hands on it, but he'd never had so sweet a ride in his life.

'Standing by,' the strike leader voxed in response, and went silent.

The pilot turned to face the gunner for a moment. 'Time to warm up your toys, sweetheart.'

'Everything's ready,' the woman assured him calmly, her eyes never leaving a panel of what looked like targeting displays. 'And if you ever call me sweetheart again, I'll have a new pair of earrings and you'll be singing soprano.'

Frigid bitch, the pilot thought. Well, who cared. After tonight, he'd be able to afford all the women he wanted. Spotting a suitable clearing, he fed power to the gravitic compensators, and the great curved hull settled gently into the snow.

Forest of Sorrows, Sepheris Secundus
087 993 M41

'DRAKE, KYRLOCK, RESPOND.' Sergeant Claren leaned over the vox-unit in the platoon command Chimera, gripping the microphone as if it were one of the throats of his delinquent troopers. 'Emperor help me, if the pair of you are drunk again I'll have you flogged to within a micron of your miserable lives, is that clear?' He waited for a moment, although he wasn't sure quite what for; an indignant denial, perhaps, or more of Drake's mocking pretence of respect for his authority. All he could hear, however, was the hiss of static.

'It's no good, sir,' the vox operator ventured after a moment, clearly apprehensive about drawing down the wrath of the angry sergeant by speaking up. 'All the comms are down. I've recalibrated, and recited the litany like the manual says, but I'm still not getting anything.'

Claren nodded thoughtfully, taking the measure of the situation. This was beyond his power to rectify, and if anyone could be said to be at fault here, it clearly wasn't him. Good enough. It never occurred to him to send for a tech-adept to sort the problem out. Born and raised in a society where every decision was made by someone further up the hierarchy, the notion of acting on his own initiative was as foreign to his nature as disobedience or heresy. The way forward was clear. He would report the matter to the lieutenant when he woke in the morning. In the meantime…

Relieved, he settled back into his seat and picked up his mug of recaf. 'Looks like we're in for a quiet night, then,' he said.

'EMPEROR ON EARTH!' Drake said, crouching as low as he could behind a tree on the edge of a large clearing in the forest. The drop-ship was massive, its smooth, metal hull utterly out of place surrounded by growing things, its rounded surfaces striking the Guardsman as both utterly alien and infinitely threatening. 'They're xenos!' None of the ore shuttles he'd seen on their constant scavenging runs to the Gorgonid had looked anything like this.

'I don't think so,' Kyrlock contradicted, handing him an amplivisor. Drake took it, focusing on the small knot of figures, dwarfed by the gargantuan scale of the vessel they'd come in, disembarking from the access ramp at the rear. Close to, they were unmistakably human, at least the ones whose features weren't obscured by visored helmets. A few of them cursed as they first felt the force of the biting wind, familiar Gothic swear words hurtling towards the hidden Guardsmen along with the stinging snowflakes. 'Mercenaries, you reckon?'

'Must be,' Drake agreed. 'Two squads at least.' It was hard to be sure of their numbers, the swirling snow blending the strange troopers with their shadows and blurring their outlines, but he was sure he could see over a dozen of them, maybe twenty or more. If only they weren't huddled so closely together, it might be easier to do a headcount.

Whoever they were, they knew their business, deploying with a speed and efficiency his own sham-bolic platoon couldn't have hoped to match, even in calm weather. Grateful for the camo cape that con-cealed him, he huddled lower, and flicked his lasgun's safety catch off. Kyrlock did the same, and Drake held out a hand to forestall him.

'Don't shoot unless they spot us,' he counselled, keep-ing his voice low despite the screaming engines of the strange, rounded spacecraft and the howl of the wind between the trees. For all he knew, the invaders might have some kind of sound detector among their motley collection of wargear. They certainly seemed to have pretty much everything else. All wore flak or carapace armour of some kind, but every set seemed to have been individualised to some extent, or made up of scavenged components that didn't quite match. Their weapons were an odd collection too. Many carried lasguns like his own, or stubbers of some kind, but he could see a couple of flamers as well, and several of the troopers carried guns he couldn't recognise at all, despite a lifetime spent in or around the military. 'If they do, fire to suppress, and pull back into the woods.'

Kyrlock nodded, flicking the fire selector of his las weapon to full auto. He wouldn't have much chance of hitting a target anyway, but he could spray and pray like the best of them, and if they managed to slip away among the trees he was sure his familiarity with this type of terrain would enable him to evade any pursuit easily enough. Danuld too, if he managed to keep up. 'Shouldn't we report this?' he asked.

'I've been trying to,' Drake said. The hissing in his vox was louder than ever, the chances of getting a signal through absolutely negligible, and he was certain by now that the jamming was deliberate. 'Looks like we're on our own.'

'If we head back that way,' Kyrlock suggested, waving an arm in the vague direction of the fortress, 'we might be able to get through to Claren in time to warn them.' The mercenary band was dispersing, melting into the trees in the direction he'd indicated, and he'd feel a lot happier staying behind them if he could. Danuld seemed scared of them, and he'd been a professional soldier before joining the Guard. If they stayed put, or sought refuge deeper in the forest, there was no telling what else they might run into. To his relief, Drake was nodding in agreement.

'Let's do it,' he said. If he added anything else, Kyrlock never heard him. The spacecraft's engines rose in pitch, a shuddering whine that resonated through his bones. Then the gigantic vessel lifted in a cloud of steam as powerful fusion jets vaporised the snow surrounding it. The huge metal shape rose slowly above the trees.

'Come on, then!' Drake said, and began to run, following the diminishing howl of its engines and the wind scattered footmarks of its enigmatic passengers.

The Citadel of the Forsaken, Sepheris Secundus
087.993.M41

THE INTRUDER NOTED the hour as the hidden timer reached zero, unsure of whether it had actually felt the faintest of tremors through the floor, or had been the victim of an atypical spasm of imagination. The explosion in the ducting behind the genetorium was small enough, as such things go, but its effects were catastrophic.

Upper atmosphere, Sepheris Secundus
088.993.M41

THE SHUTTLE INQUISITOR Finurbi had requisitioned had just crested the peak of its suborbital parabola, when he tensed in his seat, his face draining of colour.

'Carolus?' Elyra asked, concerned. She knew him well, better than any of the others, and could see the effort maintaining his composure was costing him. A pyrokene herself, she was unable to initiate direct mind to mind contact, but could recognise the signs of a sudden psychic shock impinging on the consciousness of a powerful telepath. 'What's wrong?'

The moment she spoke she regretted the words. Her companions all shifted in their seats, uneasy, glancing sidelong at the inquisitor. In order to lead them effectively, he had to seem infallible, invulnerable, and she cursed herself for throwing even the slightest doubt on his fitness to command, not to mention drawing attention to the closer bond they shared, which she suspected Horst at least found threatening.

I'm fine, Carolus mind touched, the words overlaid by reassurance and gratitude for her concern. *Thank you for asking.* Verbally, he addressed them all. 'There's a strong psychic disturbance at our destination. I have no idea, I'm afraid, what's causing it.'

Elyra watched her companions digest this information in their various ways. Horst looked worried, but

then he always did on a suborbital hop, suffering the
agonies of void sickness as they passed through the
brief zone of zero gravity. Vex nodded, as though
examining this new and unwelcome fact from every
direction, before coughing raucously and thumping
his chest plate again. Keira simply sat impassively,
waiting to find a heretic to kill, only the faint, subcon-
scious twitch of the hand hovering above the hilt of
her sword betraying her impatience to begin bloodlet-
ting as quickly as possible.

'Inquisitor.' Their pilot's voice broke in, diffident and
apologetic, like any Secundan addressing someone of
higher social status. 'We're in receipt of a message from
our destination. They advise caution in our approach.'

'Quite,' Carolus said, his composure apparently fully
restored, although Elyra could see how thin the façade
really was. 'I gather the weather conditions are quite
severe.'

'Yes, my lord,' the pilot said, apparently happier with
a more familiar and less terrifying honorific, 'but that's
not the reason. They say that they're under attack.'

THREE

The Citadel of the Forsaken, Sepheris Secundus
088.993.M41

'WHAT THE HELL–' Malakai began, before the rest of the sentence was drowned by the sudden blaring of alarms. The luminators in the main control chapel had merely flickered for a moment, nothing more, but that and a faint tremor through the rockcrete floor had been enough to warn him that something was awry. The tech-priests manning the lecterns around the chapel, over which twin statues of the Emperor and the Machine-God loomed, both finely wrought in polished glass, just had time to look at one another in consternation, exchanging twittering messages in their arcane secret tongue, before the lights failed altogether. A moment later they flickered back on, blood red, turning the peaceful sanctuary into the semblance of an abattoir.

'Primary generators are off-line,' a female acolyte of the Omnissiah reported, her droning vox-coder draining her words of the panic her posture was screaming into the room. 'Secondaries compensating… Secondaries off-line too.' As she spoke, the sanguineous emergency lighting failed, plunging the echoing room into stygian darkness.

To Malakai's relief the blaring alarms fell silent too, and he was able to hear himself think at last. 'You two, with me,' he ordered, plucking a hand luminator from his equipment pouches, and drawing his bolt pistol with the other hand. The pair of storm troopers on guard by the door of this most holy of sanctuaries fell in at his shoulder as he ran from the room, their hell-guns already cradled, ready for use. Behind them, as they left, a few of the tech-priests kindled luminators built into their augmetics, turning the chapel into a nest of whirling fireflies as they began to pray for guidance, or debate the reason for this sudden and catastrophic displeasure of the Omnissiah.

'Malakai to all stations,' the guard commander voxed as they ran down darkened corridors, scared and startled faces flickering briefly through the cone of light he cast ahead. 'Condition Extremis: repeat, Extremis.'

Despite years of facing the worst horrors the warp and the galaxy could throw at him, he felt a cold trickle of sweat running down his spine at the words he'd never thought he'd use. The command channel was hissing with static, but a few voices were still able to respond, thank the Emperor. By now, the psi dampers would be down, and the thousands of psykers penned up in the containment blocks would suddenly have become aware that their unholy powers were returning. With any luck the shock would incapacitate most of them, if only for a moment or two, but any such respite would be short-lived at best. After that, all hell

was going to break loose, and there was nothing anyone could do about it.

Forest of Sorrows, Sepheris Secundus
088.993.M41

'Sergeant.' The vox operator coughed apologetically.
'A message, sir. From the fortress.'

Claren stared at him in astonishment. 'Are you sure?'
he asked. The vast, looming structure beyond the camp
hadn't even so much as acknowledged their presence
before now. 'What do they want?'

'Whoever's in charge,' the vox man said doubtfully. 'I
told them Lieutenant Kreel's asleep, and they'll have to
call back in the morning, but they won't go away.'

'I'll deal with it,' Claren said. Browbeating some
importunate upstart was a skill he'd learned well in his
former life as an overseer in the mines. Rising to his
feet, he took hold of the microphone. 'This is Sergeant
Claren,' he began, 'duty watch commander–'

'Shut up and listen,' the voice on the other end
said, crisp with the expectation of instant obedience,
and Claren's determination to be obdurate wilted as
abruptly as if he'd come face to face with an irritable
baron. 'Get your rabble on full alert now. Surround
the bastion, and kill anyone who tries to leave.
Understood?' The voice was fading as it spoke, sub-
merging in the rising sea of static that had already
swallowed the voices of the outer sentry posts.
Before Claren could muster a reply it had disappeared altogether.

'What are we going to do, sir?' the vox man asked, an
expression of bovine incomprehension on his face.
'The lieutenant said he wasn't to be disturbed.'

'We've had an order,' Claren said, working out the ramifications and beginning to think like a soldier for the first and last time in his life. Whoever had given it clearly outranked his own immediate superior. 'Sound the general alarm.' Technically, that wouldn't violate the lieutenant's instructions either, as the noise would wake him without Claren's direct intervention. Feeling remarkably pleased with himself, the sergeant reached for his lasgun.

He'd almost closed his fingers around it when the Chimera erupted in a white-hot fireball, blasted apart by a plasma bolt of almost inconceivable power.

'THRONE PRESERVE US!' Kyrlock ejaculated, as he and Drake reached the treeline just in time to see the fiery demise of their detested superior. The strange, smooth hull of the alien drop-ship swept over the Guardsmen's encampment like a living, vengeful embodiment of the shrieking elements, stabbing downwards and outwards with beams of incandescent energy that gouged smoking scars through the permafrost beneath the snow, blasting apart hab units and vehicles alike. Dorsal turrets strobed too, pouring a relentless stream of fire into the walls of the fortress, which began to crumble and burn under the inexorable onslaught. Emplaced weapons atop the towering edifice began to reply, but without any noticeable effect. Drake placed a restraining hand on his arm as he took another pace forward.

'Rut this,' the blond trooper said bluntly, dragging his friend back into the cover of the woods. 'If we go out there, we're dead.'

It was hard to disagree. Those of their comrades who had lived through the initial strike were running around in the open, terrified beyond all rational thought, intent for the most part on nothing more than simple survival. Only a few even attempted to return fire, their las-bolts vanishing into the whirling white-out as if they'd never existed.

The aerial leviathan turned lazily, and cut another swathe of devastation through what remained of the camp, casually picking off a lone Chimera that seemed to be attempting to flee, the lascannon in its turret continuing to spit futile defiance right up until the moment a hypervelocity projectile shattered its thick armour like porcelain beneath a careless boot.

Most of the vessel's staggering firepower continued to be directed against the fortress, however, carving a huge gash through walls, which, until that moment, both Guardsmen would have sworn on the aquila were completely impregnable. Before their astonished and horrified eyes, a section of rockcrete over a dozen metres across splintered and fell, crashing to the ground with an impact that shuddered through their boots even at this distance.

'Look there,' Drake said, pointing. The foot soldiers they'd been trailing were running forward to enter the breach, scrambling over the scattered rubble, gunning down any surviving Guardsmen foolish enough to attempt to engage them with the same casual disdain with which, as a Royal Scourge, he'd poured lasgun fire into the ranks of rebellious serfs armed only with mining tools.

Belatedly remembering the amplivisor he carried, he raised it again, focusing the device on the invading mercenaries. Their vanguard was inside the stronghold by now, meeting serious resistance at last from the red uniformed soldiers garrisoned there. The advance was stalling, and he wondered for a moment how they could possibly hope to take the whole fortress with only a couple of dozen men.

'Something's not right,' Kyrlock said, as the swooping vessel overhead swatted a battery of lascannon, which had been blazing away at it from the ramparts with very little noticeable effect beyond some superficial dents and scorch marks.

He was right, Drake thought, an ozone prickle of apprehension running across his skin. A strange sensation of pressure was building all around them, as though the air was somehow becoming thicker, and the whirling snowflakes seemed to slow, hanging suspended in the coagulating wind.

The Citadel of the Forsaken, Sepheris Secundus 088.993.M41

'REPORT,' MALAKAI BARKED, reaching the thick metal doors leading down to the underground containment area at last. A full squad of storm troopers was formed up in front of the cyclopean entrance, their faces grim, and he assessed the assets available to him without conscious thought, bleakly aware that a hundred times their number might not be enough to avert the imminent apocalypse.

A heavy weapons crew was crouching behind the gunnery shield of their tripod mounted autocannon, but most of the men were armed only with their standard issue hellguns, which they kept trained expectantly on the ominous portal. Thin tendrils of purple lightning played across the dully reflective surface, crackling faintly, imparting an itchy, greasy feel to the air. Malakai noticed that someone had had the sense to set up a portable arc light pointing directly at it. If the warp spawn inside somehow managed to get it open, with any luck they'd be dazzled just long enough for the waiting troopers to open fire.

Not if, Malakai thought: when. There were over a thousand of the walking obscenities down there, and only a dozen troopers at his shoulder. Calmly, he commended his soul to the Emperor, and waited for the inevitable.

'Sir.' Jessun, the sergeant leading the squad, saluted, no doubt having come to the same conclusion. 'The doors are still holding, but there's a lot of energy building up behind them. We estimate they'll be out in a matter of minutes.'

'The gas?' Malakai asked, already certain of the answer. In the event of a complete power failure, a dead man switch was supposed to release a lethal nerve toxin into the containment area, specifically to prevent this nightmare from happening. Jessun looked puzzled.

'Should have been released when the dampers failed,' he said. 'Maybe one of the psykers was able to nullify it somehow.'

'Maybe.' Malakai was suddenly aware that the persistent hissing in his helmet vox had disappeared. 'Command post, report.'

'We've countered the jamming signal,' the droning voice of a tech-priest informed him, 'and sent word of our plight. The inquisitor is responding with all speed.'

'Good.' Malakai felt his spirits lifting for the first time since the incident began. Inquisitors were the unfailing right hand of the Emperor. For a moment, he began to think that perhaps things might be brought back under control, after all.

Then, with shocking suddenness, the doors collapsed, and he was swept away by a tidal wave of lethal insanity.

Forest of Sorrows, Sepheris Secundus
088.993.M41

'EMPEROR PRESERVE AND guide our steps. From all things foul and warp spawned, shield us,' Drake mumbled under his breath, repeating as much of the half-remembered catechism of protection as he could call to mind. Things had gone far beyond the merely wrong. The snowflakes were moving slowly through the clotted air, dancing and swirling apparently at random, no longer driven by the gale, which had been sweeping them along, forming patterns his mind refused to recognise, but which hurt the back of his eyes. The air felt hot and humid, and hard to breathe.

Nevertheless, he kept the amplivisor raised, trying to follow the progress of the firefight in the devastated fortress. The mercenaries seemed to be falling back, the superior numbers of the red uniformed soldiers beginning to tell despite their tenacity. Then, without warning, everything changed. Abruptly, the defenders broke, turning to face some new threat from within the redoubt, and the mercenaries swept on, triumphant.

'What's going on?' Kyrlock asked at his shoulder, and Drake lowered the lenses at last, a casual gesture, which was to save his life.

'I haven't a clue,' he admitted, just as something erupted into existence between them with a *crack* of displaced air and a nimbus of violet lightning. A young woman stood between them, barefoot in the snow, clad only in a thin grey robe. A tattoo almost identical to Kyrlock's marked her cheek, indicating that she had once been the bonded serf of the same baron the former forester had cheated of his tithes, and she gazed at the two Guardsmen through emerald eyes, from which the last vestiges of sanity had long since fled.

'You're a bad man,' she told Drake conversationally, the violet aura continuing to play around her, 'but everyone can Change.' She reached out a hand towards his face. 'Change with me.' She blinked, her eyelids closing from the sides instead of downwards, and a thin, forked tongue emerged from between her lips.

Stricken with horror, Drake stumbled backwards, certain that her touch would bring infinitely worse than death, and tried to bring his lasgun up with panic stiffened fingers. For a moment, he thought he was going to be too slow, and flinched, anticipating the burning touch of the sparkling witchfire, but before either of them could complete their intended movement, Kyrlock had struck out with his chain axe. The mechanism sparked as the metal made contact with the mutant woman's crackling aura, but the teeth whined on, beginning to bite into flesh. With an abruptly curtailed shriek, she vanished as suddenly as she'd arrived, another miniature thunderclap marking her passing.

'Thanks, Vos.' Drake shuddered, his body tingling with the after-effects of blind panic, and threw up in the snow.

Lower Atmosphere, Sepheris Secundus 088.993.M41

'How much longer?' Keira asked impatiently, caressing the hilt of her sword again. Her cache of throwing knives, one on each forearm and one in the small of her back, were familiar, comfortable weights, solid and reassuring. She checked the mechanism of her cross-bow pistol for the dozenth time, and returned it to the clip on her hip. She knew that the weapons seemed primitive to her companions, but growing up on the belly of Ambulon you got by with whatever the Emperor provided, and she'd proven her competence with them in countless Redemptionist crusades before the inquisitor had recognised her worthiness and recruited her to smite the enemies of Him on Earth on a far wider stage.

While other members of her family had coveted the incendiary weapons most members of the sect favoured as the surest way of purifying the Emperor's realm and the most visible sign of His holy wrath, she'd come to appreciate the silent lethality of blade and bow, ranging ahead of the rest of the congregation to strike down the sentries of the unrighteous before they could give warning of the retribution about to descend on their compatriots. Her tutors in the Collegium Assassinorum had refined her natural gifts, to the point where nothing in life seemed so satisfying as a silent stalk and a silent kill, returning another sinful soul to the Emperor for final judgement.

Horst chuckled indulgently. 'Are we there yet?' he whined, in the tone of a petulant child, and exchanged a wry smile with Vex.

Keira flushed, feeling the strange sensation of pressure beneath her sternum that seemed to swell up whenever Horst showed signs of noticing her. It was disconcerting, uncomfortable, and curiously pleasant, although she couldn't put a name to it, and lately she'd developed the habit of trying to attract his attention deliberately in order to experience it a little more often. This was hardly the time for distractions, though, so she turned back to her weapons, losing herself in the litanies of the assassin, and began to focus her mind on the task at hand.

'Another ten minutes or so,' the inquisitor said, his voice calm and reassuring, 'maybe a little less.'

'I'd estimate between eight and thirteen,' Vex put in helpfully, 'depending on the precise weather conditions at our destination. The last reports we had were less than encouraging.' As if to emphasise the point, the shuttle shuddered, battered by a sudden crosswind, and then steadied itself.

The inquisitor nodded. 'Thank you, Hybris,' he said dryly. 'Precise as always.'

'Precision is one of the Omnissiah's greatest gifts,' the tech-priest said cheerfully, and began to check the mechanism of his autopistol. 'But under the circumstances, I think I'd rather rely on this one.'

Nodding in agreement, Keira began the meditation of the blade, attuning herself to the precise weight and feel of the pieces of razor sharp steel scabbarded around her body. Their keen edges thirsted for the blood of the unholy, and her hand twitched again, subconsciously sharing their eagerness to shed it.

The Citadel of the Forsaken, Sepheris Secundus
088.993.M41

IF THERE WAS any warning of what was about to happen, other than the violently flickering balefire sparking and arcing across the face of the portal in front of them, Malakai did not perceive it. With a rending shriek of tortured metal, adamantine slabs thicker than the length of his forearm burst and tore like tissue paper, and a tsunami of unleashed psychic force swept them away down the corridor. None of the storm troopers even got the chance to fire, picked up and whirled away on the tidal wave of warp energy like scraps of flotsam. Some died instantly, touched by the full force of that malignant flood, their bodies torn apart or incinerated by power beyond any mortal comprehension, while others slammed into unyielding rockcrete walls or metal stanchions hard enough to shatter bone and liquefy flesh.

Malakai was luckier than most, crashing to the floor before reaching a more solid obstruction. He felt his ribs break beneath the protective outer layer of his body armour, and skidded into the angle of two walls, bouncing from one to the other, killing most of his momentum as he did so. Looking up, he was just in time to see the twisted remains of one of the thick metal slabs plummeting towards him, and flinched involuntarily, expecting his life to be over in a moment.

The Emperor, however, was merciful. The upper edge of the shattered door ploughed into the wall less than a metre above his prostrate form and wedged there, creating a small, triangular space beneath it. Blinking his eyes clear of the pattering rockcrete dust, and trying to ignore the lance of pain in his chest every time he moved or coughed, Malakai scrabbled in the rubble surrounding him for his bolt pistol.

To his complete lack of surprise, the weapon had gone. Comms were down again too, the vox in his helmet ominously silent. After a moment, his questing fingers found a deep, spongy gash in its hard outer layer, the legacy of an impact that would certainly have shattered his skull without the protection it had provided. Breathing hard, he began to explore his tiny refuge for a way out.

In front of him, a tangled mass of debris and detritus barred the way, tumbled across the narrow triangular opening. As his eyes adjusted to the claustrophobic darkness, he began to discern thin shafts of faint grey light seeping in through a number of narrow chinks in the rubble. He was at a loss to explain it for a moment, but the reason finally occurred to him. The thought was so shocking that he drew in his breath involuntarily, provoking a sharp dagger thrust of pain from his damaged ribcage. The walls had been breached, and the faint pre-dawn light leeching through the clouds outside was penetrating inside the massive structure. How such a thing was possible he had no idea, and with his helmet vox smashed he had no way of finding out.

Taking advantage of the feeble illumination, he wormed his way backwards, finding the other end of the space blocked by the crosswall he'd ricocheted around so painfully. A faint glimmer of light managed to slither round the rim of the metal slab, but the gap was barely enough to get his fingers through, even if he could have turned around in the narrow area bounded by wall, floor, and canted metal ceiling. So, forward it was. He'd just have to shift the rubble, preferably without bringing the whole lot down on his head.

As he took careful hold of a chunk smaller than most, about the size of his fist, and began to try working it free, he became aware of sounds outside, the crackling of small arms and the hoarse cries of men in combat. The familiar miniature thunder crack of hellguns was overlaid with the sharper snap of conventional las weapons, and he wondered for a moment if they were being wielded by the mysterious invaders, or if a few of the conscript rabble outside were still making a fight of it. The former, he strongly suspected.

There were other sounds too, unfamiliar ones, but before he could analyse them further they were drowned out by an ululating roar of triumph from deep within the oubliette below the citadel. The sheer volume of it, and the insane malevolence of it, chilled his blood. Working as fast as he dared, he worked the chunk of rubble free, creating a large enough gap to see through.

Once he could, he regretted it instantly. The tumult in the distance was growing, like the battering of surf against the shoreline of hell, reinforced by the scuffling of countless feet. The feeble grey light seeping in from outside was being replaced by a brighter flickering, a polychromatic aura that made him feel sick to his soul. He saw them at last by the light of the shimmering balefire: a shambling, scurrying horde, grey robes flapping, eyes wide with wonderment or complete insanity, laughing, shrieking, weeping, or grimly silent, flooding towards the outside world.

'This way! Hurry!' an authoritative voice called, amplified to bone shaking resonance, and Malakai just caught a glimpse of a figure in body armour gesturing from the end of the corridor. Its face concealing helmet was crested in the eldar fashion, but the flak encasing its torso looked as though it had once been Imperial Guard issue, and the melta it carried was unmistakably of human manufacture. It gestured encouragement and disappeared beyond Malakai's narrow field of vision, presumably in the direction of the breach in

the wall. A moment later, his fragile refuge began to
shake, as the liberated psykers began to stampede past
him towards freedom.

Forest of Sorrows, Sepheris Secundus
088.993.M41

'WHAT'S HAPPENING?' KYRLOCK asked, beginning to
regret having given Drake the amplivisor in the first
place. The huge vessel that had wrought such spectacular destruction was continuing to circle the ruined
citadel, striking down from time to time at whatever
sporadic efforts at resistance it happened to notice, but
that wasn't what had attracted his attention. Something was happening at the breach in the wall, and he
strained his eyes through the strangely moving
snowflakes to try and make sense of the phenomenon.
It looked as though the rockcrete was liquefying, flow-
ing out across the plain surrounding the ravaged
fortification, although he couldn't imagine why that
would be.

'It's people, hundreds of them,' Drake reported, and
then, perhaps appreciating his friend's frustration, or
perhaps merely wary of being taken by surprise by
another teleporting mutant, he handed the amplivisor
to Kyrlock. 'All dressed like that... whatever she was.'

'Mostly,' Kyrlock corrected, focusing the device after
a moment of fumbling. The flood of grey-robed people, if they actually were people, which he doubted,
was apparently being directed by the soldiers they'd
seen before. Although, how so few of them managed
to control so many, he had no idea. Every now and
again, a mercenary in a distinctive high-pointed helmet would gesture, apparently at random, into the

crowd, and a grey-robed figure would scurry over to join the rapidly growing group milling around at their back. He couldn't be sure, but the mercenary seemed to be holding something, small and glowing, but the distance was far too great to make out what it might be. There was no time to puzzle over the matter any further, however. Something about the movement of the crowd, which still seemed to be pouring through the breach in the wall in a never-ending flood, suddenly struck him. 'Uh, Danuld,' he began uneasily, 'is it me, or do they seem to be heading this way?'

'WE'VE GOT A problem,' the pilot said, as a contact icon suddenly flared on an auspex screen to the left of his control station. A second later, an image appeared in the hololith, as solid and detailed as if it were an actual physical model. Text in flawless Gothic surrounded it, confirming what his eyes had already told him. 'Inbound contact. Aquila class shuttle, ETA two minutes.'

'Discourage them,' the assault leader voxed. 'We'll need a bit longer than that to finish sorting the sheep from the goats.' The cryptic phrase meant nothing to the pilot, but he nodded anyway, injecting a note of lazy confidence into his voice.

'Not a problem.' He glanced up at the gunner. 'Is it?'

'None at all,' she assured him. 'I'm running out of things to kill here anyway.'

'Then let's go hunting,' the pilot said, feeding power to the engines.

Behind him, the gunner snorted sardonically. 'You call this hunting?' she said. 'Fish in a barrel, more like.'

FOUR

Forest of Sorrows, Sepheris Secundus
088.993.M41

'KEEP RUNNING!' DRAKE yelled, crashing through the snow laden scrub. He had no idea where they were going, but he trusted Kyrlock to find whatever safety there might be in the depths of the forest. To his vague surprise, he could see more of his surroundings now, the grey light of early dawn filtering through the trees and the billowing snow clouds above them.

'I am,' Kyrlock assured him, from several metres ahead, not even bothering to turn back as he replied. There was no need to anyway, their vox channels were clear again, although neither had made any further attempt to contact the rest of the platoon. Even if someone was still around to give orders, they had no intention of following any if it meant becoming embroiled in the holocaust behind them. The forester was running easily, perfectly at home in this terrain, and Drake tried to match his fluid movements instead of floundering through the drifts in his wake. 'If we can find a thicket of needlespine we can burrow in under it until they've gone. Thought I saw one the other side of the clearing that ship landed in.'

'We'll get cut to ribbons!' Drake protested.

Up ahead, Kyrlock's shoulders moved in what might have been a shrug. 'You city boys. Worried a few scratches might spoil your good looks?' He stepped easily round a patch of ice, which sent Drake's feet slithering beneath him a moment later. 'That's nothing to what those witches behind us'll do if they catch up.'

'What the hell,' Drake said, trying to sound casual as he tripped over another hidden tree root. 'We've got body armour, right?'

'Now you're getting it,' Kyrlock said, hurdling a fallen log. The wind began to freshen, blowing more naturally again, and Drake breathed silent thanks to the Emperor. With any luck it would obscure their tracks, so once they were concealed, the mob of warp-touched abominations behind them would have no clue as to their presence. A few hundred metres further on the blizzard began again, as relentless and bone chilling as before, and he squinted through the face-scouring sleet, trying not to lose sight of Kyrlock's hurrying form, blurred almost to invisibility by the camo cape he wore.

An explosion boomed without warning somewhere above them, a new star flaring momentarily in the sky above the wind-lashed trees. Drake shuddered as the cold began to bite through his cape in earnest.

'Emperor's arse,' he swore bitterly. 'Now what?'

* * *

Lower Atmosphere, Sepheris Secundus
088.993.M41

ABOARD THE SHUTTLE, the attack had come without warning, the first indication of the aerial predator's presence being the volley of weapons fire that had slammed into its armoured hull. From his seat near the narrow door to the flight deck, Vex listened to the faltering note of the engines, the almost imperceptible whimpering of the overstressed fuselage, and the rattling roar of the slipstream through rent and ravaged metal. It was abundantly clear to him that their craft had been crippled, and was falling from the sky.

'What the hell was that?' Horst asked, gripping the arms of his seat rest with whitened knuckles.

'Three high energy impacts to the port aft quadrant,' Vex said, teasing as much information as he could from the ambient noise and the vibrations he could sense through the seat of his robe. 'Almost certainly weapons fire. Possibly lascannon, although from the sound of detonation I'd be inclined to suspect plasma bolts.'

'Pilot, report.' The inquisitor's voice was as quiet and authoritative as it always seemed to be in a crisis, and Vex could tell that his comrades were taking heart from it. Horst relaxed a little, Elyra gazed at Carolus with her usual expression of absolute trust, and Keira permitted herself to look mildly interested in what was going on. 'What hit us?'

'It's a ship... Huge! But there was nothing on the auspex, I swear!' Panic had apparently overridden the pilot's typical Secundan deference. 'They're coming round again!'

'Can we return fire?' the inquisitor enquired calmly, as though the question was only of minor importance.

'No, my lord.' Apparently reassured by someone socially superior taking command of the situation, the pilot's voice steadied. 'This vessel is unarmed.'

'Rutting great,' Horst commented sourly.

'Then I'll just have to take care of our assailants myself,' the inquisitor said. 'Can you still land us safely?'

'I'll do my best, my lord,' the man in the cockpit promised, 'but the flight systems are extensively damaged.'

'Allow me.' Vex stood, and opened the door to the flight deck. The man inside glanced up in shocked surprise for a moment. Then an expression of renewed hope crossed his face as he recognised the robes of a tech-priest. 'If I may be of assistance?'

'Please.' The pilot gestured to the vacant seat next to him. 'I can't get the nose up, and half the control surfaces aren't responding.' The edge of panic was still infusing his voice.

Ignoring his surroundings, Vex interfaced with the plummeting shuttle's machine-spirit. As he'd suspected, it had been profoundly traumatised by the damage it had sustained, and he communed with it in binary, cajoling and soothing by turns, rerouting data paths and coaxing crippled systems back on line.

'We've got lift,' the pilot told him suddenly. They were still descending rapidly, but at least it was going to be an emergency landing rather than a lethal, crater gouging impact with the ground. Then the man's voice rose again in terror. 'Here they come!'

Moved by curiosity, Vex directed his gaze through the thick armourcrys viewport, eager to see what sort of vessel the enemy was employing. Even so, he was astonished by the sight of the aerial leviathan that loomed up suddenly out of the enveloping snow clouds. Its vast size and rounded hull were utterly wrong, completely at odds with the principles of perfection striven for by Imperial technotheology. To any true acolyte of the Omnissiah, such an abomination was worse than a threat, it was blasphemy made manifest.

'Inquisitor!' Impelled by spiritual anguish, he was unable to keep the words to himself. 'It's unhallowed!' He glanced back into the passenger compartment, but the inquisitor was unheeding, lost in a psychic trance as he gathered his power.

Elyra glanced briefly in his direction, before returning her attention to their patron. 'It's all right,' she said confidently. 'He knows what to do.'

Vex had no time to doubt or dispute her words. The wounded shuttle's machine-spirit was nagging for his attention, and he soothed it as best he could, his eyes once again on the monstrous metal intruder looming ever larger in the viewport. Then, abruptly, it had gone, sheering off to starboard, flung aside by some preternaturally strong crosswind as casually as a twig.

'WHAT THE HELL happened?' the gunner demanded, looking up from her console with venom in her eyes. 'I had them cold!'

The pilot didn't answer for a moment, absorbed in the task of regaining control. The wind shear had come out of nowhere, impossibly fast, impossibly strong. Not that he'd give the frigid bitch behind him the satisfaction of admitting he'd lost control even for a moment. 'I had to evade,' he replied blandly. 'They were trying to ram us.'

'Sure they were.'

Nettled by her obvious scepticism, he shrugged, determined not to show his irritation. 'They're going down, aren't they?' he pointed out. 'What more do you want?'

'I like to make sure,' the gunner said, raising her voice over a soft beeping sound that had begun to resonate through the vox speaker.

'You'll just have to be sure enough,' the pilot said, hiding his relief at the sudden interruption. 'That's the recall signal.' Banking slowly to starboard, he began to descend towards the ruins of the fortress.

Forest of Sorrows, Sepheris Secundus
088.993.M41

'ALMOST THERE,' KYRLOCK said reassuringly, risking a glance back to see if his friend was still in sight. To his vague surprise he was, floundering through the snow as if he was trying to wade in it instead of lifting his feet properly, the flapping outline of his cape blurring his silhouette into the surrounding maelstrom of flakes. Typical city boy. Game, though, Kyrlock had to give him that. Most tenderfeet he'd met would have collapsed by now, including the rest of their platoon. He pointed ahead, through the treeline, to the open space beyond. 'Just the other side of the clearing.'

'You've been saying "almost there" for the last five minutes,' Drake grumbled, staggering closer. Kyrlock raised the amplivisor and swept the forest behind him, taking advantage of the brief pause to check for signs of pursuit, although every instinct he possessed was impelling him to keep going until they could reach the safety of the needlespine thicket; if he could find it at all in this freezing white-out, if it was even there to find. At least he could see no sign of movement behind Danuld other than the endlessly dancing snowflakes, so they still had a bit of time.

Wait. Something flickered in the trees, an eerie, unnatural light, like the faint phosphorescence around a putrefying corpse. It was moving, growing brighter, and he turned to run again. Let Danuld keep up if he could. Friendship was one thing, but this was survival, pure and simple.

Before he could take a step beyond the treeline, however, a new sound made him hesitate, a rising howl that tore through the bellowing wind like a knife through paper. Caught between two opposing fears, he vacillated, unable to decide where to run to, and Drake caught up with him a moment later, grabbing his arm.

'Come on,' he said urgently. 'What are you waiting for? They're right behind me!'

'Listen!' Kyrlock said, finally identifying the sound. Desperate panic rose within him, and he fought it down, trying to think of another plan in a hurry. The movement in the depths of the forest was more noticeable now, a few more unholy lights flickering in the darkness between the trunks, and, worse, solid blocks of shadow that moved with evident purpose. 'They're coming back!' He glanced skywards, expecting to see the baleful silhouette of the alien drop-ship descending, cursing himself for a fool for leading them both into a trap.

'I don't think so,' Drake said, glancing up too. 'The engine note's different.' He pointed suddenly. 'Look!'

'Holy Throne!' Kyrlock said. A blazing meteor was plummeting from the sky, battering through the blockading elements, a plume of smoke and flame trailing forlornly in its wake. He snapped the amplivisor to his eyes, resolving the image of a shuttle like some of the ones he'd seen landing and departing at the ravaged citadel somewhere beyond the treeline. 'It's one of ours.'

'Not for much longer,' Drake said. 'If the crash doesn't get them, the witches probably will.'

Reminded of the inexorably advancing threat behind them, Kyrlock nodded, and lowered the visor. 'Let's go, then. Maybe we can slip away in the confusion when it hits.'

'We can't do that,' Drake said, his battered military pride apparently picking one hell of a time to take one dent too many. 'Whoever they are, they're Imperial, maybe Guard. We can't just run out on them without even trying to help.'

'I didn't see you getting all noble when Kreel and the boys were having their heads handed to them back there,' Kyrlock riposted.

Drake shrugged. 'That wasn't a fight, it was a massacre. No point us getting killed too, without even a chance to hit back. This time, maybe we can. This time we might make a difference.'

'And maybe we won't.' Kyrlock hesitated, on the verge of making a run for it across the clearing, and took a final glance at the descending shuttle. It was too late anyway, he thought, with a sudden sense of fatalistic resignation. If he tried it now, he'd just get killed by the impact. He looked at Danuld again, the other Guardsman's pox-pitted face angry and tense, and sighed. If he was going to die in the next few minutes, there was no point in throwing away their friendship first. Biting back the angry words that had almost fought their way past his tongue, he nodded instead. 'But if we don't try, we'll never know.' And at least, he thought, I won't die alone.

Drake nodded too, solemnly. 'You're a good man, Vos,' he said.

'And you're a rutwitted warp magnet, but a good mate anyway,' Kyrlock conceded, venting his feelings as best he could under the veneer of masculine banter. If Drake felt moved to respond in kind, he never heard it. The howling of the doomed shuttle drowned out everything, the orange glow of its blazing engines bringing a second, brighter sunrise to the clearing. Kyrlock flung himself to the ground, burrowing as deeply as he could into the snow, behind the cover of the largest tree he could see in their immediate vicinity. A second later, Drake followed suit.

The shuttle hit the ground in a cloud of steam, the shriek of rending metal audible even over the screaming of its damaged engines and the relentless, battering wind. It bounced, and then hit again, gouging a long trench deep into the soil and loam, down into the permafrost beneath, throwing up a bow wave of frozen detritus, which descended on the two cowering Guardsmen like an avalanche, half burying them in the debris of its passing.

Part of the tail sheared off with the second impact, pinwheeling away to smash a twenty metre tree to kindling and fill the air with wooden shrapnel, while a dozen hull and wing plates ripped free of their rivets and embedded themselves in ground and tree trunk alike. Maybe a few of the approaching heretics too, Kyrlock hoped, not daring to raise his head to look. Gouts of burning fuel erupted from ruptured piping, leaving pools of blazing incontinence behind as the wreck ricocheted across the violated glade, torching stands of scrub and woodland as it went.

Fanned by the relentless wind, the fires grew quickly, and Kyrlock breathed a silent prayer of thanks to the Emperor that he hadn't tried to make a run for it before the shuttle hit after all. Even if, by some miracle, he'd managed to make it across the clearing in time, he'd almost certainly have been immolated by the forest fire within moments. He'd seen such things before, and knew with a stone cold certainty that he'd never have been able to outrun it.

'Throne on Earth,' Drake said, raising his head cautiously. 'That's something you don't see every day.'

'EVERYONE OUT! NOW!' Horst staggered to his feet, vaguely surprised to find that he still alive. Gripping his bolt pistol tightly in his right hand, he glanced around the shattered passenger compartment, and gestured towards the exit hatch with his left. They'd been lucky, there was no doubt about that. Most of the fuselage had remained in one piece, although snowflakes and smoke were drifting in through several ragged holes in the metal, and the crash webbing attached to their seats had taken the brunt of the impact, preserving everyone from serious injury. The floor was canted at an odd angle, though, and he found himself stumbling up a slope towards the door he'd indicated.

'Who died and left you in charge?' Keira asked, leaping over the intervening seats in one lithe and sinuous motion. Horst glanced at the inquisitor, worried that he might have overstepped his authority. He'd become so used to functioning as the group's leader in the months they'd been operating independently that he'd assumed the role instinctively, finding the habit of command hard to shake now that their patron was among them once again. The inquisitor, however, was looking at him with evident approval, leaning on Elyra for support as he moved out into the narrow aisle between the seats. The effort of unleashing the psychokinetic bolt, which had deflected the attacking drop-ship, had evidently been greatly debilitating, but he straightened almost at once, to the woman's ill-concealed disappointment.

'A wise suggestion,' he said mildly.

Keira tugged at the emergency release handle, and the hatch blew out, disappearing in a flurry of orange tinted snow that looked like floating embers. Her synsuit did its best to mimic the dancing flames outside, turning her into the image of a vengeful phoenix. 'No visible hostiles,' she called, sounding almost disappointed at the fact, before somersaulting through the gap and disappearing.

'After you, boss,' Horst said, standing aside to let the pair of psykers disembark. Neither bothered to draw their sidearms, no doubt preferring to rely on their innate abilities if the young assassin turned out to be wrong.

'But I can't just leave it,' a voice protested behind him, and Horst turned, to find Vex manhandling the pilot bodily from the cockpit. 'I'm responsible for this vessel, and–'

'You'll be responsible for a very large hole in the ground when the fire reaches the fuel tanks,' Vex told him briskly. 'Out while you can.'

'Damn right,' Horst said, making for the hatch. 'If anyone gives you grief for it later, tell them you were following a direct order from the Inquisition.' His sense of social order assuaged at last, the pilot scrambled out with almost indecent haste, slipping on the thin film of slush already accumulating around the rim. Horst followed, slithering to the ground down the canted stump of a wing, and glanced around, orientating himself as quickly as he could.

The shuttle would never fly again, that much was obvious, the tangled wreckage of its battered hull strewn across a wide swathe of the forest. They'd impacted in the middle of a wide clearing, and Horst suddenly found a renewed appreciation of the skill of their pilot, who was staring at the shattered corpse of his beloved machine with an expression of stunned disbelief. 'Good landing,' he said, clapping the man on the back, suddenly aware that he had no idea of his name.

The pilot turned, searching his face for any sign of sarcasm, and finding only genuine relief at their survival. His name was stencilled on the breast pocket of his flight suit, which cleared up that little mystery at any rate: Barda. He shrugged, his voice flat with delayed shock. 'I did my best, sire. Whether the guild believes that–'

'Incoming,' Keira called, from her perch on a high piece of wreckage. Horst turned, narrowing his eyes against the barrage of sleet, and tried to see movement beyond the flickering shadows cast by the spreading inferno behind them. He couldn't make out a thing, but he trusted the girl anyway, and flicked the safety of the bolt pistol off.

What can you see? the inquisitor sent to all of them, relaying the girl's reply directly into the minds of the rest of his team. Barda looked at Horst curiously as his expression changed, but there was no time to explain what was happening to him. Horst felt the words in his head echoing with the timbre of Keira's voice, blocking out almost everything else.

Two men. An image appeared in his mind's eye, vertiginously confusing for a moment, until he reconciled the spatial difference between where he was standing and the view from Keira's position. *Coming this way.* The girl's desire for bloodshed was a tangible thread in her relayed thoughts, a coppery taste in his mouth, and he felt a flicker of revulsion rising within him. *I can take them easily.*

That won't be necessary, the inquisitor admonished, to Horst's quiet relief, and broke the link.

'I should think not,' Vex said, appearing through the exit hatch at last. 'Their attire and equipment is Imperial Guard issue.' He looked at Horst with mild curiosity. 'Still here? I wasn't joking about the size of the explosion you know.'

'So what kept you?' Horst snapped, nudging Barda into motion, and following the tech-priest's rapidly retreating back. The heat of the forest fire was intense, the snow across half the glade melting into puddles and slush, beneath which his boots were beginning to churn up thick, sticky mud.

'The shuttle's machine-spirit was gravely wounded,' Vex said, 'and would be extinguished entirely by an explosion among the wreckage. I felt it only proper to administer the last rites before it merged with the Omnissiah.'

'Very commendable,' Horst said, managing to convey entirely the opposite meaning by his tone.

As they approached the inquisitor, Vex permitted himself to look smug. 'Time well spent,' he said, 'and not just in the spiritual sense.' He held up the old and battered data-slate that accompanied him everywhere, then tucked it away in some recess of his robes. 'In the process of shriving the datacore, I took copies of the sensor logs, which include some remarkably clear picts of the obscenity that attacked us.'

'Something which will no doubt aid in their identification,' the inquisitor said, nodding in approval. He directed a smile towards Barda. 'My compliments on your exceptional skills, young man. I will commend them to your masters on our return.'

'If we return,' Elyra said, with a gesture towards the running Guardsmen in the distance. 'There's something after them. I can feel it.'

'As can I,' the inquisitor agreed levelly.

'WELL AT LEAST it's warmer,' Drake said, the heat of the fires striking him like a physical blow as they approached the scattered wreckage. He flinched back from it, feeling his frozen face tingling with renewed circulation.

The blizzard scoured clearing he remembered had altered beyond all recognition, transformed into a lurid, orange tinted hell, lit by the flickering flames beyond it. The snow underfoot had become watery slush as they drew closer to the inferno, and then cloying mud, the frozen water metamorphosed by the alchemy of heat into tendrils of mist, which the fierce wind whipped away like smoke. The persistent barrage of snowflakes had changed as well, firstly into warm, driving rain, which evaporated at once from the surface of his skin, before disappearing altogether as the rising heat from the spreading forest fire sublimed them into vapour before they reached the ground.

'You were right,' Kyrlock admitted grudgingly, pointing to a group of figures trotting towards them, backlit by the flames. They were a motley collection, civilians by the look of them, and Drake began to wonder if

he'd made a mistake after all. He'd been expecting soldiers, reinforcements for the one-sided battle behind
them, allies against the swarm of renegade psykers
hard on their heels, and the disappointment was
almost physically painful.

'Drop the guns, soldier boys,' a mellifluous feminine
voice urged, and the two men turned to face it.

Drake blinked in surprise. A girl stood behind them,
although how she'd got there the Emperor alone knew.
Not a bad looker, either, if you liked skinny with all
the right curves, which Drake did, and the bodyglove
thing she was wearing left no doubt that she possessed
them. Her hair was purple, tied back with a red bandana, which made him hesitate. That alone marked
her out as an off-worlder, and he wondered for a
moment if she was somehow connected to the red uniformed soldiers he'd seen guarding the citadel.

It was the eyes in her narrow, vulpine face that really
gave him pause, though. They were green, like those of
a predatory animal, and held about as much compassion as one. Her posture, too, marked her out as
dangerous. She stood, completely relaxed, her hands
not even resting on her weapons, but poised and ready
to react to anything. It wasn't just that she clearly
didn't consider the two Guardsmen a threat; she obviously thought they couldn't possibly be, under any
circumstances.

Slowly, the hairs prickling on the back of his neck,
Drake moved to comply.

Kyrlock laughed loudly. 'Suppose we don't. You
think you can take them off us, girlie?'

'If I take them, it'll be off your corpses,' the girl said,
her hand dropping casually to the hilt of the sword
scabbarded at her waist. An almost feral eagerness

entered her expression, and Drake felt a jolt of pure terror, even stronger, if that were possible, than he'd felt when they'd confronted the mutant witch. Then he'd known he might have a chance of survival if he reacted quickly enough, but if this one decided to kill him, his life would be over, simple as that.

'Big words,' Kyrlock said, still not getting it, and Drake held his breath.

'Keira.' The grey-haired man leading the group of survivors spoke quietly, but his voice carried easily across the intervening distance. 'You might save us all a great deal of trouble simply by showing these gentlemen your rosette.'

'Well, yes,' the strange girl admitted, looking faintly petulant and disappointed for a moment, 'but where's the fun in that?' She reached into a pouch on her belt, and produced something round and edged in gold, with a crimson letter 'I' centred in it, a symbol every citizen of the Imperium knew, and which every citizen hoped never to see. She turned to Kyrlock, whose face had gone a peculiar shade of orange-flecked grey in the firelight. 'Still full of it, soldier boy? 'Cause if you are, you can argue about it with my boss over there, the inquisitor.'

'I'm Carolus Finurbi,' the grey-haired man said after a moment, inclining his head in greeting, 'of the Ordo Hereticus.' He gestured to the group surrounding him. 'And these are my associates, apart from young Barda there, who is simply assisting us.'

'Inquisitor.' Kyrlock was doing a passable imitation of a man who has just been struck by lightning, and is amazed to find himself still standing. 'I didn't mean to challenge your authority, of course, that goes without saying, but after what we've seen tonight, we wouldn't give up our weapons to anyone.'

'I can imagine,' the tall man said, 'but explanations will have to wait. Right now, I believe, we have a rather more pressing matter to deal with.'

'That's right,' Drake said, eager to regain a little of the initiative. 'We saw your shuttle coming down, and came to warn you. There's an army of witches loose, and they're heading this way.' He turned to look past the small group of Inquisition agents, and felt his mouth go dry. Behind them, the forest was ablaze from end to end, and any hope of further retreat had completely gone.

FIVE

Forest of Sorrows, Sepheris Secundus.
088.993.M41

LIKE PRACTICALLY EVERYONE on Sepheris Secundus, from the Queen right down to the lowliest mutant in the Shatters, Barda had spent his entire life surrounded by a comforting cocoon of certainty, his place in the social order as fixed and immutable as the Word of the Emperor. He was a pilot because his parents were and his grandparents had been, he still lived in the same room in the guildhouse of the Honourable Company of Cloudwalkers where his lungs had first drawn breath almost twenty-seven standard years ago, and every single decision that had ever affected him had been taken by someone else, who knew better than he did what was right and proper.

Every moment of his life since his education had ended had been spent either in the cockpit, the starport, or the guildhouse which abutted it, in the company of other guilders or, very rarely, a client who'd wanted to speak personally to the pilot they were entrusting their lives or property to.

In a handful of minutes that comfortable, settled existence had been utterly overturned, pitching him into a new and terrifying world where nothing seemed to make sense at all. His surroundings were all wrong, the environment wild and uncontrolled, the air darting randomly around him, freezing and wet.

The people with him were beyond his comprehension too, moving and talking with evident purpose, but employing words and phrases he didn't understand. They were worried, though, he'd picked up enough to grasp that. Well, fair enough, so was he. He'd have to explain to the guild masters how he'd come to lose one of their precious shuttles, a bond debt which, if they found him culpable, his descendants would still be paying off ten generations from now: if he ever had any descendents. Certainly no guilder woman would want anything to do with a man who'd lost his ship, even if the conclave of examination did eventually exonerate him.

So, bewildered and terrified, he did what any Secundan would do under stress, he gravitated to the most senior member of the party, and waited to be told what to do.

'Can you guide us to the containment facility?' the grey-haired man was asking as he edged closer, and the shorter of the two soldiers nodded.

'It's over that way.' He pointed. 'The real problem's going to be getting to it.'

'If the entire population's at large, that's something of an understatement,' the dark-haired man Barda had spoken to before put in. He seemed confident and determined, though, which the young pilot found reassuring.

'Perhaps,' the inquisitor said, 'but a lot depends on how many of them came this way. I don't suppose they'll have remained particularly cohesive, once the fact of their liberation has sunk in.'

'Good point,' the blonde woman interjected. 'Chances are they'll have scattered pretty much at random.'

'Highly probable,' the inquisitor conceded. He turned back to the Guardsmen. 'How spread out did the crowd you saw seem to be?'

'A fair amount,' the taller soldier said, after a moment's thought. 'It's hard to be sure, with the blizzard and all, but the trees seemed to be splitting them up.'

'If they're just trying to get away from the facility,' the girl with the funny coloured hair said, 'then most of them will be moving the other way by now.' She gestured towards the forest fire, with an expression curiously close to rapture. 'Can't see many being able to walk through that.'

'A few powerful pyros might try it,' the blonde woman said, 'but I wouldn't fancy their chances.'

'Then we're agreed,' the inquisitor said calmly, although Barda couldn't understand what sort of consensus the peculiar people around him might have come to. 'Our best option is simply to punch our way through, and seek refuge at the facility.'

'If there's any of it left,' the tall soldier said, not disagreeing exactly, but clearly far from happy.

His friend didn't seem too pleased about the turn events had taken either, but nodded anyway. 'It gives us a better chance than freezing or burning to death out here,' he said, his words punctuated by the muffled *crump* of the explosion the tech-priest had warned everyone about. A hot, scorching wind hit the back of Barda's neck, and he willed himself not to turn back, to see how little was left of the majestic vessel he'd once soared through the Emperor's realm with.

'Might as well get on with it then,' the dark-haired man said, swinging the gun in his hand to aim at the space in front of him as he took a step towards the shadowed bulk of the trees in the distance. Then he seemed to recollect himself, and glanced deferentially at the inquisitor. 'I assume you'd like Keira to take point?'

'She seems the obvious choice,' the inquisitor said, and to Barda's amazement the girl smiled eagerly. She wore the colour of royalty, he noted with some surprise. Perhaps she was a princess, scion of some off-world dynasty, although why someone so exalted would be part of an inquisitor's warband he had no idea.

'Thought you'd never ask,' she said, springing from her perch and bounding away, her silhouette seeming to shimmer faintly as she moved.

'Are you all right?' the older woman asked, an expression of faint concern on her face, and Barda became aware that she was addressing him.

'Yes, my lady,' he replied automatically, before honesty impelled him to add, 'just a little confused by all this.'

'I'm not surprised,' the woman said kindly. Then to Barda's horror she drew a gun from the recesses of her gown, and held it out to him. 'Here, you might need this.'

'I don't know how to use it,' Barda said, taking the thing anyway, as to refuse even an implied request from a social superior was anathema to his Secundan soul.

The woman nodded encouragingly. 'It's easy. That's why I carry one.' She pointed, as he fumbled his fingers around the pistol grip, vaguely surprised by how comfortable it felt in his hand. 'That thing next to your thumb's the safety catch. Flick it up to release the trigger, down to make it safe. Just point and squeeze, don't snatch, and pray to the Emperor to guide your bolt. It's a las weapon, so there's no recoil to worry about.'

'I see.' Barda nodded, as if he did. 'But I can't take it, my lady, not if it leaves you defenceless.' To his astonishment, the woman laughed.

'Oh, I'm far from that. Just trust in the Emperor, and you'll be fine.'

The whole group was moving, and Barda broke into a stumbling jog to keep up with them, sticking as close to the inquisitor as he dared. The tall soldier glanced at him with an expression of amused contempt as his feet slithered in the slush, and muttered something that sounded like, 'City boy.'

The group was spreading out a little, taking on something reminiscent of the formation adopted by the migrating birds Barda had so often seen from the cockpit, presumably so they could watch one another's backs more easily. He, the inquisitor and the blonde woman were in the centre of the line, the muscular dark-haired man with the big pistol a handful of metres ahead of them and to the left, the tech-priest ahead and to the right. He too was holding a handgun as if he knew how to use it, and a few fragments of prayer floated back towards them on the wind. 'Blessed be thy primer that it might spark cleanly, thy firing pin that it may strike home with the surety of thine own perfection.'

A little further back, and slightly further out, the two Guardsmen paced the main group, the tall one with the long-handled thing slung across his shoulder on the left, and the shorter one with the pockmarked face on the right, both holding their lasguns at the hip, ready to fire. Barda felt a rising tension in the pit of his stomach, although he couldn't have said why, other than the fact that all these people who seemed so used to violence were clearly expecting more.

It didn't help that the weather was worsening as they left the artificial heatwave of the forest fire behind them and began to plod grimly into the teeth of the gale. Stinging sleet began to pepper their faces, and their feet began to lose purchase in the thick, clinging snow.

The shorter soldier raised his voice a little. 'Vos, is it me, or is it easing off a bit?'

The tall one nodded. 'A bit, I think.' He shrugged. 'Either that, or we're getting used to it.'

Overhearing, Barda shuddered. He couldn't imagine ever getting used to these hellish conditions. Before he had time to brood, though, a thin, wailing scream cut through the rising howl of the wind.

'Sounds like Keira's made contact,' the dark-haired man said grimly.

The inquisitor nodded. The worst of the wind seemed to be parting around him, Barda suddenly realised, as though the hand of the Emperor was shielding him from the ravages of the elements. 'With quite a large group, too, if one of them had time to scream,' he added. As if by some unspoken consensus everyone picked up their pace, hurrying towards the source of the sound.

Then suddenly, as they burst out into a small glade no more than a score of metres across, everything changed. Without warning, the swirling snowstorm seemed to part, to reveal a vista of carnage. Bodies lay on the trampled snow, two men, a woman, and something that seemed to be neither, all dressed in the slashed remains of some dull grey material, dyed red by their own blood. Half a dozen more were still standing, pressing in towards the centre of the clearing, where Keira leapt and danced, her sword reaping lives wherever it struck.

Some of the psykers seemed to have something clasped in their hands as they attempted to strike her, strange glowing energies sparking around their closed fists, but she evaded every attack with what looked to Barda like contemptuous ease. Even as he watched, she struck down a mutant lunging for her with a chitinous claw, severing its arm and sinking her weapon into its back up to the hilt as she turned. To her evident surprise the creature rose again, almost tearing the hilt from her hand as it did so, and she withdrew the blade hastily, giving ground a little as she sought to open the distance.

There was little time to take in any more, however, as, apparently sensing the approach of the Inquisitorial party, most of the group turned to face them. A couple raised their hands, the arcane energies they manipulated seeming to hang in the air for a moment, before streaking through the intervening air.

'Get down!' the blonde woman said, pushing Barda aside, and he felt the skin of his face tingling as one of the eldritch bolts hissed past him, striking one of the trees on the fringe of the clearing. It erupted instantly into a spreading mass of stinking corruption, which gradually subsided into the snow surrounding it, stain-ing the pristine surface with bubbling filth. The other witchfire bolt slammed into a nearby bush, turning it into a pyre of blue-white flame.

Feeling as though he was on the verge of losing his sanity, Barda looked hastily away from such horrors, only to see another trio of grey-clad figures shambling into the clearing, their eyes febrile with hate. Without conscious thought, he raised the laspistol in his hand, gesturing with it like a cold metal finger.

'More of them!' he shouted. The tall soldier glanced at him and grinned.

'Oh yes. Thanks. Might have missed 'em otherwise.' He squeezed the trigger of his lasgun, spitting a hail of inaccurate fire at the newcomers. A few bolts struck home, gouging cauterised craters in flesh, blue-white from the cold, the rest whining through the air around them. Barda followed his lead without thinking, shooting wildly. He didn't hit anything that he could see, but he felt like he was doing something, and for the first time since the strange aircraft had swooped out of nowhere to strike his Aquila from the skies, he felt that he was at least partially back in control of his own destiny.

'Fire for effect!' the dark-haired man called, begin-ning to shoot at the pair who'd flung the energy bolts. His skill with the heavy handgun he held seemed astonishing to the watching pilot. The first time he pulled the trigger, the ragged torso of the man who'd set fire to the bush exploded in a geyser of blood and ruined meat, falling heavily in a cloud of steam as residual body heat met the bone-biting cold of the snowstorm. The tech-priest's gun boomed too, hardly less accurately, but with less spectacular damage to its target. One of the people pressing close to the embattled girl fell, blood spurting from a grievous wound to the head, but didn't seem to explode.

'A little help, here, Danuld,' the tall soldier called, and with a thrill of terror Barda realised the three figures they'd been shooting at were still pressing forward, too numb with the cold, or devoid of sanity, to have been incapacitated by their wounds.

'But you're doing so well,' the small soldier riposted sarcastically, snapping off a shot that took the psyker on the left in the head. It fell, twitching, and its two companions hesitated, glancing towards the larger group for a lead.

'Allow me.' The inquisitor gestured towards the tightly packed knot of heaving bodies, and it scattered suddenly, the grey-robed abominations picked up and flung aside as casually as the wind whirled the snowflakes away. Only Barda and the blonde woman were close enough to notice the way his face paled, and how close his knees came to giving way.

'I've got this one,' the dark-haired man said, his bolt pistol barking again. The man who'd flung the bolt of corruption staggered backwards, a thin crimson mist seeming to thicken the air around him. Then, to Barda's horrified surprise, he rallied, standing firm, and began to laugh. Thick, sticky fluid began to flow across his ruined chest, knitting diseased flesh together, repairing the damage almost instantly.

'Oh no you don't,' the blonde woman said, a bolt of pure orange flame winking into existence in front of her. For an instant, Barda felt its heat beating against his face, like a fainter echo of the inferno they'd left behind them at the crash site, before it streaked through the air to burst inside the partially reconstituted ribcage of the malignant witch facing them. The man screamed, high and shrill, as the cleansing flame scoured him from the inside out, and collapsed in the snow amid a cloud of steam, where he continued to flail for a moment before becoming still.

Taking advantage of the distraction, Keira ducked under the crab-thing's remaining arm, which looked a little more human, and decapitated it with a single fluid stroke. She flicked the blood from the blade in her hand with a practiced movement of the wrist, restoring the shimmering length of steel to its pristine state, but didn't resheath her weapon.

'You're one of them!' the smaller soldier shouted, an edge of hysteria entering his voice as he swung his las-gun around to aim at the blonde woman standing next to Barda. 'Get away from the inquisitor!'

'She's sanctioned, you idiot,' the dark-haired man said shortly. 'Do you think she'd be with us if she wasn't?' His bolt pistol cracked again, taking down one of the psykers that the inquisitor had felled, who was trying to clamber back to his feet, arcane energies sparking the air around him.

Looking vaguely embarrassed, the soldier switched his aim back to the pair of grey clad abominations who'd remained standing, only to find them both running for the treeline. He took the shot anyway, narrowly missing the nearer of the two, and swore colourfully.

'Better keep moving,' the dark-haired man advised, leading the way deeper into the encircling wood.

'Sound advice, as always.' The inquisitor staggered a little, and the blonde woman was at his side in an instant.

'Help me with him,' she said to Barda. The young pilot hurried forward, offering his shoulder. To his proud surprise, the inquisitor accepted it, leaning against him for support, but still managing to keep up a reasonable pace despite his evident exhaustion. 'Carolus, are you all right?'

The inquisitor smiled at her, in what looked to Barda like one of the affectionate moments of mutual understanding his parents sometimes shared. 'I'm getting too old for all this,' he said, his faintly jocular tone immediately reassuring. 'I just can't fling spacecraft around like I used to.'

'They're breaking,' Keira called from up ahead. 'Moving aside. I guess we weren't as easy to pick off as they thought.'

'Praise the Emperor,' the dark-haired man said, making the sign of the aquila.

The princess shrugged, a little ruefully. 'Would have been nice to send a few more to His judgement,' she said, 'but He'll get round to them all in the end.'

Her words meant little to Barda, but at least she seemed to be right about the rest of the grey robes avoiding them from now on. As they hurried through the forest as best they could, he kept catching glimpses of movement between the trees, but it seemed cautious and fearful rather than aggressive. As the minutes wore on, however, he had less time to look, or to think about it. The inquisitor was leaning ever more heavily on his shoulder, clearly on the verge of collapse. The blonde woman stayed close, too, keeping a concerned eye on him.

'Almost there,' the tall soldier assured her at last, after the latest of several enquiries about the matter. 'We're just reaching the treeline.' A moment later, the entire party broke out into the open again, looking down on a scene of utter devastation.

'Throne preserve us,' the dark-haired man muttered. 'What the hell happened here?'

As THE PALE light of dawn intensified to the thin grey murk that passed for sunshine across most of the surface of Sepheris Secundus, the full extent of the havoc wrought by the raiders became all too clear. From a distance, the great gash in the curtain wall of the fortress, and the charred craters where its air defence batteries had once been, were the most visible signs of damage, but the closer they got to it the more evidence they could see of the incredible amount of firepower their mysterious enemies had been able to unleash. As they trudged across the plain fronting the violated bastion, Drake felt his spirits sinking with every step, turning his head from side to side as he plodded through the snow in a futile attempt to find some trace of anyone or anything he recognised. Even Sergeant Claren would have been a welcome sight, but the reek of charred meat from what was left of the command Chimera was enough to confirm that nothing more tangible remained of him than ashes and grease.

The Imperial Guard encampment had quite simply been obliterated. Every vehicle, every hab unit, had been scoured from the permafrost as thoroughly as though they'd never existed. Even the blackened remains were disappearing from view, as the drifting snow began to shroud them, the only graves most of the casualties would ever know.

To Drake's shocked surprise there were still a few survivors, a handful of hollow eyed men in uniforms like his own, huddled warily in twos or threes, mustering under the command of one of the red-uniformed garrison troopers. A few glanced up with idle curiosity as the Inquisitorial party approached, and Drake nodded to a couple of faces that he vaguely thought he might have recognised, but no one responded, too far gone with exhaustion or trauma.

'What's going to happen to us?' Kyrlock asked, taking in the small clusters of Guardsmen with a single sweeping gesture of his arm.

The dark-haired man that Drake assumed was some kind of second in command glanced at the inquisitor for a moment, and then clearly deciding he was too exhausted to answer, shrugged. 'Reassignment, I suppose. None of you will be going back to a line regiment after what you've seen tonight.'

'Reassignment where?' Drake asked, knowing trouble when he heard it.

The man shrugged again. 'That's for the inquisitor to decide.'

Great, Drake thought. The old man looked as if the only thing he could work out was which side of the bed to collapse onto. He was leaning heavily on the skinny kid in the flight suit, and the matronly woman who'd done that scary thing with the fire was clucking around him like a mother hen.

'Halt.' Drake looked up to find that, lost in his thoughts, he'd led the group almost as far as the hole in the outer wall. A red-uniformed trooper was pointing something, which looked like a bigger and heavier version of his own lasgun, right at him, while several others kept the rest of the little group covered with hair trigger intensity. 'Who goes there?'

'Inquisitor Finurbi.' The old man was pulling himself upright, staring down the group of soldiers, his Inquisitorial sigil flashing red in the artificial light spilling from the vast gash in the wall. 'These people are with me.'

'Fine, sir. You're expected.' The NCO in charge of the detail stood aside, with a crisp salute.

The inquisitor nodded. 'Good. Let's get inside out of this infernal wind, and start trying to make some sense of this mess, shall we?'

SIX

**The Citadel of the Forsaken, Sepheris Secundus
089.993.M41**

HORST SQUINTED, NARROWING his eyes against the wan noonday sun, which was seeping through the scudding grey murk and clinging to the tops of the distant mountain peaks before bouncing feebly from the surface of the table in front of him. This side of the fortress had escaped any significant damage in the attack, and the conference room they'd convened in might have been anywhere in the Imperium: the same polished wooden table, the same uncomfortable chairs, and the same gilded aquila looming over everything, which he'd seen a hundred times before on a dozen different worlds.

Inquisitor Finurbi sat at the head of the table, only the frozen tundra beyond the large picture window behind him giving any clue as to their actual location. Fascinated by the continual motion, Horst gazed past their patron's right shoulder at the windswept snowfields, drifting and spiralling in the near-constant gales like frozen cloud, breaking like surf against the encircling forest. Suppressing a yawn, he tried to look interested in what Vex was saying.

'It was definitely sabotage,' the tech-priest concluded, having spent the last ten minutes explaining in excruciating detail how improbable it was that both primary and secondary power sources had been lost simultaneously, let alone at the same time as the citadel had come under attack.

Horst nodded, as though he'd been paying attention. 'That raises two obvious questions,' he said. 'Who and how.'

Keira snorted derisively. 'Heretics, of course,' she said, leaning back in her chair at what to anyone else would have seemed a dangerous angle. Her feet were on the table, almost opposite where Horst sat, and she looked at him sardonically down the length of her legs. Nettled by her apparent indifference, and the lack of respect it implied for their patron, Horst bit down on a sharp retort, but he was saved the bother of replying by the man at the opposite end of the table from the inquisitor.

'You won't find any of those among my command, I can assure you.' Captain Malakai scowled, his face showing clear signs of recent medicae attention, and Inquisitor Finurbi coughed diplomatically.

'I don't doubt that for a moment.' Despite food and rest, Horst suspected that their patron was still severely debilitated. An opinion Elyra clearly shared, judging by the brief expression of concern that passed across her face as the inquisitor spoke. 'But the fact remains, your security was quite clearly compromised.'

'You don't have to tell me that,' Malakai growled, manifestly in no mood for the niceties of protocol. 'I lost almost a third of my command.' His jaw tightened. 'But that doesn't mean we have a traitor in our midst.'

'I'm afraid it does,' Vex chimed in diffidently. 'If we examine the evidence dispassionately, it's the only logical conclusion. The genetorium is in the very heart of the facility, and only someone with access to it could have cut the power supply. Once we discover how it was done, of course, that should be a strong indication of who was responsible.'

'How soon will you be able to tell?' Malakai asked, with the same expression Horst had seen on the faces of arbitrators getting their first glimpse of a suspect they thought they could beat a confession out of.

The tech-priest shrugged. 'It's too early to say,' he said levelly. 'I've been consulting with Technomancer Tonis, the senior surviving acolyte of the Omnissiah, and he's of the opinion that the systems are too badly compromised to be able to tell much without a thorough examination.'

'Can you trust him?' Keira asked ingenuously. Vex looked baffled, so she went on. 'Whoever took out the power plant clearly knew what they were doing. I'd start by asking where all the cogboys were when everything went klybo.'

'A tech-priest?' Despite the studied neutrality of inflection practised by those of his calling, Horst could quite clearly detect an undertone of shock and outrage in Vex's voice. 'Absolutely unthinkable!'

'She might actually have a point for once,' Horst said, more to seize the opportunity of putting Keira back in her place by assuming a slightly patronising tone than because he actually agreed with her. To his chagrin, however, she seemed unabashed, possibly even taking the comment as a sign of his approval, and smiled at him again in that disconcerting manner. 'Why couldn't it be one of the tech-priests?'

'Because to deliberately cause a machine to malfunction would be a mockery of the perfection of the Omnissiah,' Vex explained, somehow managing to sound both condescending and outraged at the same time. 'It would be an act of blasphemy against the Machine-God. You might as well ask if an ecclesiarch was praying to the Dark Gods.'

'Well, it wouldn't be the first time one of them did,' the inquisitor conceded, 'but I don't think we should be concentrating our attention on any particular group among the staff at the moment. The raiders quite clearly had detailed knowledge of the layout of the citadel, which implies in turn that someone passed them that information.'

'A whole nest of heretics,' Keira said gleefully, no doubt picturing a wholesale purge of the unrighteous, preferably with a lot of blood and burning involved. 'Better and better.'

'That hardly seems likely here,' Horst said mildly, refusing to rise to the bait. 'This is one of the most secure facilities in the sector. Everyone connected with it has been thoroughly examined by the Inquisition.'

'Evidently not thoroughly enough,' Malakai said, looking as though he was eager to make a start on the job at once, and in person. Then, realising he had perhaps gone a little too far, he nodded to the inquisitor. 'No disrespect to your colleagues intended, of course.'

'None inferred,' Inquisitor Finurbi told him. 'Even the most faithful servant of the Emperor can be suborned or cozened into disloyalty if the right pressure is applied. Indeed, if our adversaries are as resourceful and well organised as they appear, whoever was responsible for informing them of the weaknesses in our defences may have done so entirely unwittingly.'

'You mean psykers?' Elyra asked.

The inquisitor nodded. 'We know they employ them. A sufficiently powerful telepath might have been able to lift the knowledge from an unsuspecting mind without the victim even being aware of it.'

'That wouldn't account for the sabotage,' Horst pointed out. 'Whoever did that must have had access.'

'They might have been influenced,' Elyra suggested, without sounding terribly convinced of her own argument. 'A powerful enough psyker might be able to control someone's actions from a distance.'

'Except that the psi dampers would have nullified any such power,' Malakai pointed out, 'along with those of the inmates.'

'A very good point,' Vex agreed. 'The dampers were fully active right up until the time the power failed.'

'They haven't been restored yet, though,' Elyra said.

Vex shook his head. 'They were extensively damaged, and since you and the inquisitor are the only psykers left in the facility, Tonis felt it both expedient and more courteous to divert the repair teams to more urgent matters. Of course if any of the inmates are recaptured, bringing the dampers back on line will become a far higher priority.'

Malakai snorted. 'I wouldn't worry too much about that. We're still operating under Condition Extremis. The search teams will shoot to kill.' He shrugged indifferently. 'Not that we'll find many alive in any case. Most of the fugitives will have frozen to death by now.'

'Most, but not all,' Inquisitor Finurbi pointed out. 'A few will have abilities that enable them to resist the cold, and some will simply be too bloody minded to lie down and die now that they've been given a taste of freedom. The Arbites should be warned to expect a sudden upsurge in incidents involving psykers, particularly in isolated communities.'

'Already in hand,' Malakai assured him. 'We informed the Isolarium as soon as we got communications back, in case whoever hit us tried to free the psykers they're holding too.'

'Good.' The inquisitor looked appraisingly down the table. 'Keira, you wish to say something?'

'I'm not sure,' the young assassin said, with a shrug that, from Horst's perspective, sent uncomfortably interesting ripples along the length of her body. 'It's just something Malakai said a minute ago.' She tilted her head, to regard the Guard commander quizzically. 'You said the dampers would stop a psyker from possessing anyone, but what if they were possessed by a daemon?'

The hiss of indrawn breath from everyone around the table was quite clearly audible for a moment, before being drowned out by another hacking cough and the clang of Vex's hand against his breather unit. The tech-priest shook his head doubtfully, his eyes watering a little. 'I couldn't say. The units here are powerful, most certainly, but they weren't designed with the repulsion of warp entities in mind.' He turned to the inquisitor. 'Perhaps the Ordo Malleus might have some pertinent information?'

'Perhaps.' Inquisitor Finurbi nodded thoughtfully, looking more tired and drawn than Horst could ever remember. 'I'll make the appropriate enquiries, but I don't think it's likely.' A faint air of tension, which had hung over the room ever since Keira had asked her question, seemed to dissipate as he spoke. 'I hardly think a daemon would have bothered with anything quite so subtle as sabotage, or coordinating a military strike with such obvious precision.'

'Neither do I,' Horst said firmly, trying to hide his relief, and ignore Keira's infuriating grin. 'What do we know about the forces that attacked us?'

'Well, they were human,' Malakai said, clearly relieved to have the discussion returning to a topic on which he felt at home. 'We recovered a couple of bodies, mercenaries by the look of them. Most of their kit was Imperial.'

'Most of it?' the inquisitor asked.

Malakai nodded, and produced a handful of thin metallic discs, about the size of coins, which shone brightly as the watery sun struck them through the window. He dropped them on the table with a clatter, like someone overturning a set of cutlery. One fell edge down, and embedded itself in the thick wood of the tabletop. 'We recovered these, too,' he said.

'What are they?' Keira asked eagerly, leaning forward for a better look. Her elbows met the table simultaneously with the thud of her chair legs returning to the vertical. 'They look like blades, but I don't see how you could possibly throw them without slicing your fingers open.'

'They're ammunition,' Malakai explained, 'from an eldar weapon. At least one of the raiders had some of their armour too, I saw the helmet.'

'Did you indeed.' The inquisitor cupped his chin thoughtfully in his hand, resting his elbow on the table to take the weight of his head, and Elyra glanced at him again, concern on her face. He must have reassured her telepathically, Horst thought, as she settled back in her seat almost at once, looking faintly relieved. 'I take it you're absolutely certain of this?'

'Absolutely,' Malakai confirmed. 'Before we were assigned here, my unit spent some time in the service of the Ordo Xenos. We encountered eldar face to face on two occasions, and observed them from a distance several times on reconnaissance.'

'Their spacecraft was of xenos manufacture too,' Vex put in, producing his data-slate and placing it reverently on the table in front of him. After muttering a catechism or two, he activated its projector unit, and a faintly wobbling hololithic image of the drop-ship that had downed their Aquila shimmered into existence above it. 'Does this look like an eldar vessel to you?'

Malakai shook his head. 'It's tau. Couldn't tell you its class, but the lines are unmistakable. We had a run-in with the little grey bastards a few years back, when they first started showing up on this side of the galaxy.'

'Why would the tau attack a place like this?' Elyra asked, puzzled. 'It's no threat to them.'

'I don't think they did,' the inquisitor said thoughtfully. 'It's more likely that the vessel was captured or stolen, like the eldar equipment Captain Malakai found.'

'Then how did the mercenaries manage to fly it?' Vex asked reasonably. 'Xenos tech is unhallowed, and no true servant of the Omnissiah would risk his soul meddling with it.'

'I've no idea,' Finurbi said, 'but they evidently did.' His face grew troubled for a moment, as he strove unsuccessfully to recall something. 'I've worked on occasion with a colleague from the Ordo Xenos. He mentioned something once about a heretical group that hoarded alien artefacts for reasons of their own, but the details escape me.'

'The Faxlignae,' Malakai said thoughtfully. 'It would explain the eldar stuff, and the drop-ship. They've never shown any interest in psykers before, though, as far as I'm aware.'

'Whoever they were, they were well organised,' Horst said, staring at the hololith, 'and well resourced. Wherever that thing came from, let's hope it's the only one they've got.'

Malakai nodded his agreement. 'Its firepower was phenomenal, I can tell you that. It cut through our curtain wall in a matter of moments.'

'Right where their ground troops would have the shortest route to the containment area,' Horst commented. 'Bit too much of a coincidence for me.'

'And for me,' the inquisitor agreed dryly, 'which brings us back to our hypothetical interloper.' He nodded at Vex. 'I agree with your assessment. Find out how the systems were sabotaged, and we'll be in a better position to identify the culprit. That's your job, obviously, since no one else here has the necessary expertise, but feel free to ask for whatever assistance you may require from the rest of us.'

'Of course.' Vex nodded, quoting something that had evidently struck him as apt from the *Credo Machina*. 'The purity of logic is a beacon for the truth.' He made to switch off the projection, but Horst forestalled him with a gesture.

'Just a moment,' the former arbitrator said, and stared at the image of the strangely rounded drop-ship as he mulled over the half-formed question that had insinuated itself gradually into his mind during the preceding discussion. 'Can you estimate the passenger capacity of that thing?'

'Not with any degree of certainty,' Vex said, 'but well over a hundred at the very least, possibly more than double that. May I ask why?'

'Something Drake said,' Horst replied, the reason for his disquiet becoming clearer to him as he spoke.

Malakai looked puzzled. 'Who's Drake?' he asked.

'One of the Guardsmen who helped us,' Elyra explained. She glanced down the table at Horst, evidently following his line of reasoning. 'He said he'd seen one of the raiders calling individual psykers out of the crowd.'

'Exactly,' Horst said, 'which implies they were after witches with some specific talent.'

'Or just the most powerful ones,' Elyra said. Both of them glanced at the inquisitor.

'Neither is a particularly comforting proposition,' Finurbi said, after a moment's pause.

'If they've been taken off world, they could be anywhere,' Keira offered helpfully. 'There are so many ore barges in orbit we could never search them all.'

'Assuming they're even still in the system,' the inquisitor said. 'It's far more likely their ship made the transit to the warp hours ago.' He sighed, and smiled ruefully at Elyra. 'Is it just me, or are things getting infernally complicated again?'

'How MUCH LONGER are we going to be kept hanging around here?' Kyrlock asked. At first he'd simply been relieved to be inside, out of the cold, but now the waiting was beginning to get to him. The civilians he and Drake had escorted in, an inquisitor's warband no less, had vanished almost at once, hurrying away on whatever business had brought them here in the first place, leaving him and Danuld in the company of the red-uniformed soldiers who had followed them into the building. Belatedly remembering that he was talking to a real warrior, not some quota-filling halfwit like the late and unlamented Sergeant Claren, he made an effort to moderate his tone, and added, 'Corporal. Sir.'

'No idea,' the man said indifferently, turning away, his body language eloquently proclaiming that he cared even less. Used to this sort of dismissive attitude from practically everyone he came into contact with, like any Secundan serf, it never occurred to Kyrlock to resent it. He simply shrugged, and returned to the bunk he'd been assigned.

'Told you,' Drake said idly from the next one. He glanced around the barrack room. 'He probably doesn't know any more than we do in any case.'

'So far as I'm concerned, they can leave us here till the Emperor steps down from the throne,' the man on the other side of Kyrlock agreed, referring to a widely-held superstition about the turn of the millennium, now less than a decade away. Kyrlock recognised him vaguely, although he couldn't put a name to him. 'Good food, a warm bed, beats roughing it out in the snow.'

'Enjoy it while it lasts,' Drake said cynically, more versed in the ways of the military than the average conscript. He indicated the names still stencilled on the footlockers, and the faint flecks of adhesive still clinging to the walls around the beds where picts and printsheet clippings had been hastily removed. 'These are dead men's bunks. What do you want to bet we'll be picking up where they left off?'

'Doing what?' Kyrlock asked, and Drake shrugged.

'Haven't a clue,' he said. Then he grinned. 'Cheer up, Vos. It can't be any worse than what we went through last night.'

Kyrlock was less than convinced about that, but had no opportunity to argue the point. Before he could open his mouth, the corporal in red and grey was back, two of his subordinates at his shoulders.

'Fall in!' he bellowed. Recognising the tone of an NCO who wasn't to be trifled with, Drake was out of his bunk and standing at attention faster than Kyrlock would have believed possible. Taking his lead from his friend, as he'd been doing since they'd met in basic training, Kyrlock jumped up too, stepping into line a moment later. The rest of the troopers followed as quickly as they could, scrambling into some semblance of order, though not fast enough for the corporal, who kicked the legs out from under a couple of the most tardy, dropping them heavily to the floor. 'Right, you maggots, you've been reassigned. As of this moment you are no longer soldiers of the Imperial Guard.'

A disbelieving murmur swept through the ranks, and the corporal glared. Kyrlock felt the hairs on the back of his neck stirring. The NCO paced down the line, and looked him straight in the eyes. Kyrlock tried to keep his face impassive, and not even blink. 'Did you say something?'

'No, corporal.' A flat, declarative statement.

After a moment, the man took a step back, and transferred his attention to Drake. 'How about you?'

'No, corporal.'

'No, I don't believe you did. You two fall out. The rest of you, down and twenty.' The corporal waited while Drake and Kyrlock stepped out of line, and the rest of the dozen or so survivors of their original platoon puffed their way through the press-ups. As they finished, and clambered sheepishly to their feet, the

NCO looked at them as though he'd just made an unwelcome discovery on the sole of his boot. 'As I was saying before the debating club convened, you are hereby reassigned to the service of His Imperial Majesty's most holy Inquisition. By His grace, it seems, you've survived where none of you should have done, which means you've either been blessed by His special favour, have an exceptional degree of fortitude, or are just plain lucky.' He indicated the door. 'Your training for the exalted calling of Inquisitorial storm trooper, which frankly I don't think any of you are fit for, begins now.' He indicated the two troopers with him, who turned and ran out of the door. 'With them, at the double. If you can't keep up I'll shoot you.'

After a moment of stunned silence, the assembled Guardsmen sprinted for the door, elbowing each other aside in their eagerness to get through the narrow gap. The corporal watched them struggle for a moment, and then turned back to Kyrlock and Drake, who hadn't moved. 'Think I'm joking, do you?' he asked.

Drake shook his head. 'Waiting for the door to clear, corporal. We'll catch up soon enough. Overtake most of them if it's a long run, only a few have enough sense to pace themselves.'

'I see.' The corporal nodded slowly, turning to Kyrlock. 'And you?'

Kyrlock shrugged, out of his depth but determined not to show it. 'What he said, corporal.'

'I see.' For a moment, a trace of amusement seemed to flicker across the man's face. 'The two of you might actually make the grade, but you've got other orders.'

'What orders?' Kylock asked.

The corporal smiled wryly. 'You think they tell me? All I know is you're to go with him.' He indicated the barrack-room door, through which the last of the Guardsmen had just vanished. A man was standing there, grey-robed and magisterial. 'Inquisitor.' The corporal inclined his head.

'Vos and Danuld, isn't it?' Inquisitor Finurbi smiled in an open, friendly manner which completely failed to reassure Kyrlock. 'I believe you may be in a position to help me.'

SECURE IN ITS hiding place, the intruder stirred restlessly. The attack had gone well, exactly according to plan, and it had always been prepared for the investigation that was bound to follow. Its position within the facility, unseen and unsuspected, would have allowed it to mislead and misdirect the enquiry, diverting suspicion, perhaps even evading detection altogether.

However, something had changed. The inquisitor was here, the dampers were down, and bringing them back on line would prompt too many questions. The fires of the man's talent were flickering, eroded by exhaustion, but remained a potent threat. If it could sense them, the intruder thought, then perhaps the reverse was true, and the inquisitor could sense its presence too, or might be able to when he recovered.

This was an unexpected development, and one it would have to assess very carefully before taking steps to neutralise the danger.

'WITH RESPECT, SIR, I don't really see how you expect us to help you,' Drake said. Judging by the expressions on the faces ranged around the room, it was an opinion shared by most of the inquisitor's associates. At least he could put names to them now. Belated introductions had accompanied a meal unlike anything he or Kyrlock had ever experienced before: pulses baked in a thick, rich sauce, and served on thin slices of lightly charred bread.

The room, too, was unlike any he'd previously been in. It was well appointed, there was no doubt about that, but panelled in dark, glossy wood instead of the glass he'd been surrounded by in the palaces of Icenholm. The padded seats were familiar enough, but were covered in plain fabrics, all in shades of red and grey, and a scarlet carpet covered the floor.

Clearly, the royal colour was far less exclusive off-world. Keira still wore the crimson bandana, and, to his vague disappointment, a tabard in the same shade of red now covered the body glove that had left so few of her charms to the imagination. The others were still dressed exactly as they had been the first time he'd seen them, but then he didn't suppose much of their luggage would have survived the shuttle crash. What had happened to the pilot he didn't know, there was certainly no sign of him in the strange, un-Secundan room.

'You both saw a great deal of the action,' the inquisitor explained, steepling his fingers and leaning back in his chair. His feet were propped up on a large hassock, and it looked to Drake as if he was half asleep, but the eyes behind the half-closed lids were alert enough, and he knew better than to underestimate the man. 'More than any of your comrades. You might still be harbouring information we can use, even if the nature of it isn't exactly clear yet.'

'I see.' Drake nodded, not really getting it, but damned if he'd admit the fact in front of the others.

They obviously thought he was thicker than spoil silt, good for nothing beyond toting a lasgun and dying for the Emperor on some far distant battlefield.

'I'm not sure you do,' Horst said, glancing up from a data-slate in his lap, and Drake tried not to let the flare of resentment he felt show on his face. He was evidently less successful than he'd hoped in this, because Keira suddenly grinned at him in an unexpectedly friendly fashion.

'Don't let that tone of Mordechai's get under your skin,' she advised. 'He used to be an arbitrator. They teach smug and patronising in basic training.'

'Says the self-appointed hand of the Emperor's judgement,' Horst riposted dryly. 'No inflated ego there, then.' He glanced at the tiny pict screen, and then back up at Drake. 'Your personal histories make interesting reading.'

'They do? How?' Drake asked, already wondering what else these lunatics had in mind for him and Kyrlock. If half the whispered stories about the Inquisition were true, it was probably nothing good. On the other hand, they all seemed cheerful enough, and the inquisitor was far more friendly than he would have expected. Somehow, though, that was even more disquieting, as if they were being lulled into a false sense of security.

'Danuld Drake,' Horst read aloud, before glancing up again, 'former PDF regular, good record, two commendations. Requested a transfer to the Imperial Guard tithing. That's unusual.'

'I had my reasons,' Drake said. There seemed little point in going into his dissatisfaction with the Royal Scourges, and the snobbery and hypocrisy that had hindered his progress up through the ranks.

Horst nodded appraisingly. 'Reading between the lines, you think for yourself rather too much for a military man. Do you think that's a fair assessment?'

'Speaking purely as a military man, I wouldn't be in a position to comment, sir.' Drake had only intended to stonewall, a tactic that had worked well with irate superiors before, but, to his surprise, Horst seemed pleased with the answer, nodding as he paged through the slate.

'And Vos Kyrlock.' He looked across at the red-headed man next to Drake.

'That's me,' Kyrlock confirmed, giving away no more than he had to, like any Secundan serf coming to the attention of a social superior.

Horst read a few more lines. 'You seem unusually inclined to think for yourself too: evading tithes, black marketeering. That's almost tantamount to treason on this benighted rock.'

'I'm no traitor.' A low rumble of anger accompanied the words, and Kyrlock's fists balled. Drake tensed. He'd heard this tone several times, usually just before a brawl broke out. Vos's volcanic temper, quick to erupt, and just as quick to die down, was the main reason he'd had so few friends among the regiment. He laid a restraining hand on Kyrlock's arm, pressing him back into his seat, but the forester shook him off. 'And anyone who says I am had better like sanitorium food.'

Horst didn't look worried, Drake realised, something that brought him very little comfort. The dark-haired man was simply looking at Kyrlock with curiosity, mixed with a little amusement, and the Guardsman felt a chill in the pit of his stomach. These people were Inquisitorial agents; no matter how strange he found them, they were undoubtedly dangerous.

'Horrible stuff,' Horst agreed, without moving. 'And for the record, I made no such insinuation. If anyone here believed that, we'd hardly be considering making use of you, would we?'

'Well, no, I suppose not.' Clearly confused, Kyrlock checked the movement, and, to Drake's relief, resumed his seat.

'Let's get this straight,' Drake said, turning to look at the inquisitor, 'you're asking Vos and me to work for the Inquisition?' He could hardly keep a note of incredulity from his voice, although whether that was the result of the idea itself, or his temerity in daring to address so exalted a servant of the Imperium directly, he couldn't have said. To his even greater astonishment, the man smiled.

'In a manner of speaking. Like many of my colleagues, I employ a number of operatives to help me in my work. One of those teams is with me now.' He nodded at Horst and Keira. 'It's my opinion, backed up by an exceptionally positive casting of the Emperor's Tarot, that your local knowledge may be useful in our current investigation. If you survive the experience, and manage to impress us sufficiently with your dedication and loyalty in the process, I may continue to employ you after our business here is concluded, or, if you prefer, you may return to the ranks of the storm troopers.'

'We'll help in any way we can,' Drake said, still trying to grasp the full magnitude of what he was hearing. Realistically, he knew, there was no other answer he could possibly make. Brought up to regard service as both a right and a duty, refusal simply didn't occur to him. He nudged the man next to him with his elbow. 'Right, Vos?'

'Right.' Kyrlock nodded too, his eyes unreadable.

'Good. I'm glad that's settled.' The inquisitor stood, slowly, and once again Drake found himself thinking that the man was overcoming his exhaustion by willpower alone. He glanced at Horst. 'Then I'll leave you in Mordechai's capable hands.'

'Very good, inquisitor,' Horst said, looking to Drake distinctly unenthusiastic about the prospect. He glanced at the two Guardsmen. 'First thing we'd better do is assign you some quarters.'

'Speaking of which,' the inquisitor said, starting for the door, 'if anyone needs me, you'll find me in mine. Try not to disturb me unless it's really urgent.'

'Oh, there you are.' Elyra bustled into the room, smiling in relief as she caught sight of him. 'Captain Malakai thought you should be informed at once. You've just had a message, relayed from Icenholm.'

'What sort of a message?' the inquisitor asked, and Drake thought he could detect a note of resignation in the man's voice. To his vague surprise, it was accompanied by a pang of sympathy. 'I take it this can't wait until the morning?'

'It's from the Tricorn,' Elyra said.

Drake's puzzlement must have shown on his face, because Keira condescended to explain. 'The Ordo Calixis headquarters on Scintilla,' she told him, her whispered voice suddenly coming from somewhere close to his ear. Not having noticed her move, he gave an involuntary start, which seemed to amuse her. 'They coordinate Inquisition activity throughout the sector.'

'Thanks,' he murmured back.

Elyra was still speaking. 'They've received an astropathic communication for you, from outside the sector, from an Inquisitor Grynner, of the Ordo Xenos. He won't tell anyone else what it's about.'

'That sounds like Jorge,' Inquisitor Finurbi said. 'Never trusts anyone he doesn't know.' He sighed. 'I'll have to return to Icenholm, and get hold of an astropath. If Malakai can find me a shuttle around here that still flies, young Barda can take me.' A jaw cracking yawn forced its way past his defences. 'Most intriguing. Why would Jorge need the help of a witch hunter?'

'For the same reason you could use a specialist in xenos tech?' Horst suggested. 'Maybe he's got hold of another thread of the same conspiracy.'

'Perhaps.' The inquisitor yawned again, and smiled at Elyra. 'Could I impose on you to make the arrangements?'

'Of course.' She looked at him, concern evident on her face. 'But you really should rest first.'

'I'm going to,' he assured her. 'Wake me as soon as the shuttle's ready.'

'I will.' The blonde woman smiled tolerantly. 'Now go and lie down before you fall down.'

THE INTRUDER HAD come to a decision. One way or another, the inquisitor had to die, now, while he was still vulnerable, before his strength returned. Tearing itself free of its hiding place, it prepared to strike.

SEVEN

The Citadel of the Forsaken, Sepheris Secundus
090.993.M41

NIGHT HAD LONG since fallen across the bleak tundra surrounding the citadel, only a few faint stars flaring briefly into visibility through the occasional rent in the glowering clouds before being occulted again by their insubstantial bulk, but Vex remained indifferent to the passage of time. The vital regulator built into his augmetically enhanced body allowed him to go without sleep for periods even the hardiest of men unblessed by such gifts could never have endured. Indeed, the very thought of rest, if it even occurred to him, would have been repugnant right now. Not only was it his duty as one of the Omnissiah's anointed to restore harmony to the violated systems of the fortress as quickly as possible, the intellectual challenge of working out how the damage had been inflicted was a fascinating one.

Deep in the genetorium, in the shadows of the primary power core, the untidy and ill-managed environment they'd struggled through to get here might as well have been on another planet for all the effect its presence had in this temple of order and serenity. Vex glanced up from the system schematic being projected in the air above his faithful data-slate, savouring the presence of the Machine, the purposeful, constructive world of metal and glass surrounding him. As he did so, his attention was attracted by a deferential greeting in binary, to which he courteously responded by rote.

'May I be of assistance?' one of the tech-priests on duty asked, approaching him with all the diffidence due to a colleague openly wearing the sigil of the Inquisition alongside the cogwheel emblem of his calling.

'I think you might,' Vex said, raising his voice a little over the hum of the generators. Having someone around who understood the intricacies of the system, and who could immediately answer any questions he might have, would speed up his investigation considerably. He gestured to the pieces of equipment surrounding them, many with open inspection panels, from which hastily spliced cables and a profusion of wax sealed prayer parchments spilled, mute testament to the heroic efforts made by Tonis and his repair teams over the preceding few hours. 'The damage in this section seems relatively minor.'

'Indeed it is, by the grace of the Omnissiah,' the junior tech-priest confirmed, nodding eagerly. 'The spirits of the circuit breakers confined the holy energies, preventing them from doing harm in their eagerness to be free.' He tried unsuccessfully to keep a note of pride from his voice. 'I have been made personally responsible for the appropriate rite of thanks for their timely intervention.'

'Then I have indeed been guided to your input by the gears of the Great Machine,' Vex said, seeing no harm in encouraging the young man's vanity if it helped him gather the data he needed a little more efficiently. The quick burst of binary had identified him as Brother Polk, a low-ranking tech-adept seconded here by the Adeptus Mechanicus. Like everyone else he'd exchanged handshakes with since his arrival, a secondary layer of embedded coding contained a security clearance verified by the Inquisition liaison office of the Lathe Worlds. Vex took a degree of quiet satisfaction in that, still nettled by Keira's implied slur on the probity of the order he served. 'Am I right in assuming that the secondary generators are in a similar state?'

'You are indeed,' Polk said, responding to the flattery in precisely the manner Vex's analysis had suggested was the most probable. 'The safety systems performed their functions like true servants of the Machine.'

'Excellent,' Vex said. If Polk was right, he'd just been spared a further three hours of painstaking investigation. He glanced at the schematic again, pinpointing the next most likely point of vulnerability. 'If I could impose upon you to accompany me to the primary heat exchangers, I'm sure I would find your advice equally valuable there.'

'Technomancer Tonis did say my duties here were of paramount importance,' Polk said reluctantly. 'The machine-spirits of the genetorium were gravely affronted, and must be propitiated with all due dispatch.'

'As is only right and proper,' Vex said, resigning himself to a longer, more detailed analysis without the young man's assistance. Polk nodded, his disappointment at being unable to participate further in the enquiry quite palpable, and another thought occurred to Vex. 'Although, aiding me to apprehend the person responsible for their suffering as quickly as possible might perhaps restore their equilibrium even more effectively.'

'Perhaps it might,' Polk responded eagerly, 'and you are, after all, acting in the name of the Inquisition. Perhaps I can best discharge my duty by assisting you.'

'That does seem the most rational inference,' Vex said, permitting himself a moment of amusement at the young man's enthusiasm, perhaps seeing a little of himself as he'd once been, on the day Inquisitor Finurbi had walked into a quiet Mechanicus shrine with an interesting problem to solve. He stood aside, deactivating the data-slate, and returning it to the recesses of his robe. 'Perhaps you would care to lead the way.'

THE INQUISITOR'S TALENT burned and pulsed like a psychic beacon, drawing the intruder irresistibly towards it, scorching it with its purity and power. The intruder hesitated for a moment, wondering if it had waited too long. The man's strength was increasing by the moment, his defences sharp and diamond hard, the vulnerabilities it had hoped to find scabbing over even as it watched.

Then, on the verge of turning away, it saw a minute flaw, a tiny opening that none of its kind would dare attempt under most circumstances, but it had no choice. Impelled by desperation, it lunged into the attack.

CAROLUS STIRRED, HIS dreams disturbing ones, as they so often were these days. He'd seen and done too much to ever expect to sleep soundly again, but exhaustion held him in chains of smoke, weighing him down and suffocating his soul. He was with Elyra, as he so often was in the rare, pleasant reveries, both of them younger, in the bedroom of the villa they'd shared in the mountains above Fallion, back in the days when it had just been the two of them, before they'd been joined by Roykirk the bounty hunter and Verro the ratling. Now Roykirk and Verro were dead, and he mourned them, sobbing desperately, even though they'd died half a sector away and three years after Fallion.

Carolus, what is it? Elyra asked, smiling in the way that had always made his heart sing, but that only made his grief grow stronger. Her hair was red, not yellow, and he could see beyond her, through the gap where the wall should have been, that the village in the valley below was ablaze from end to end, its inhabitants running and shrieking and dying, burning like candles or choking in their own smoke. He tried to answer, but nothing escaped him beyond racking sobs that shook his whole body, and left him howling like a child. *It's all right, I'm here.* Her arms were round him, soothing and reassuring, and he clung to her, desperate for comfort. *I'm with you now, and I'll never, ever leave you.*

Her grip tightened, impossibly, moving sinuously around him, and he began to struggle, dimly aware through the weight of the nightmare that something was wrong.

'TRY HIM AGAIN,' Horst said, tearing his eyes away from the hypnotically swirling snowscape in the darkness beyond the window of the guest quarters' lounge. Elyra looked at him for a moment, as if attempting to find a way of verbalising just how fatuous she found his advice, and then gave up and returned her attention to the vox panel.

'Carolus, the shuttle's ready. Can you hear me?'

'He must really be out of it,' Keira said, glancing up from the throwing knife she'd been playing with, balancing it on one finger by the tip, flipping it up to catch the hilt, and then moving on to the next digit. Drake had been watching her since she started, fascinated, a mug of recaf growing cold in his hand, and Kyrlock had long since gone to bed.

Horst nodded. 'Hardly surprising,' he agreed. 'I can't remember the last time I saw him that exhausted.'

'I'd better go and wake him,' Elyra said.

Keira shrugged. 'He'll be cranky,' she warned.

'He'll be a lot crankier if we let him sleep now that the shuttle's prepped,' Elyra said, making for the door.

'CAROLUS. CAROLUS, IT'S me, Elyra.' The voice echoed through the guest room, accompanied by a loud, continuous knocking. 'Carolus, are you all right?'

Deep in the coils of nightmare, the voice penetrated, clear and true.

This isn't happening! Carolus thought, tearing the *faux* Elyra from him with a single psychokinetic blast. As she flew backwards he could see that her limbs were elongated and boneless, like tentacles, dangling from a body that hung in the air before him, losing any resemblance to a human being as he focused more clearly on it. His eyes snapped open to a nightmare.

The thing that had attacked him was real, a grotesque apparition, floating a few feet above his bed, its questing tentacles already reaching down to ensnare him again. The worst thing about it, though, was that it was somehow insubstantial, flickering in and out of existence as he watched. Again, he reached out with his mind to swat the thing, but it resisted. Somehow, their moment of contact had sapped his strength again, and it rallied fast, rolling with the insubstantial blow and swooping down towards him.

'Carolus! Can you hear me?' Elyra's voice again, shrill with concern.

Hazy recollections of his nightmare began to surface, and with it a surge of anger that tore through his mind, sweeping everything else away. This warp spawned obscenity had defiled his most cherished memories, tried to turn them into a weapon against him, tried to turn his love for Elyra into the instrument of his destruction. Gathering every iota of that anger, he channelled it, forming a lance of pure hatred and loathing, which impaled the bloated body hovering over him, burning through it like a white hot blade.

'WHAT THE HELL was that?' Horst asked, drawing his bolt pistol as an eldritch keening echoed around the corridor outside the inquisitor's bedroom. Before he could use it, the door in front of them flew from its hinges, blasted aside by a ball of flame that had erupted into existence in front of Elyra.

'There's something in there,' she said, the colour draining from her face. 'I can sense it.'

'What is it?' Horst asked, pushing past the psyker, bringing his pistol up as he dived through the door, slipping easily into the room clearance drills he'd learned in the Arbites. The inquisitor was sitting up in bed, his face drained and white, staring at a point in the air about a metre in front of him.

'I don't know.' Elyra followed him in, her eyes searching. 'It's gone now.' She shuddered. 'It felt so cold.' Catching sight of the man on the bed she hurried over and embraced him. 'Carolus, what happened?'

'I killed it, I think.' He returned the gesture, holding her tightly to him for a moment, breathing deeply to restore his habitual calm. 'Drove it off, anyway.' Then, to Horst's embarrassed surprise, and Elyra's evident delight, he kissed her. 'It was your voice, the sound of it. If you hadn't called out to me I'd never have woken in time to fight back.'

'Do you know what it was?' Horst asked, taking refuge in the practical. He'd never seen the inquisitor look frightened before, or emotional, and he found the experience profoundly disturbing. He'd known intellectually that their patron had shared some kind of bond with Elyra, going back long before he or any of the others had joined the Angelae, but they'd never been particularly demonstrative with one another, at least not while anyone else was around. The idea that Carolus Finurbi could be vulnerable, despite his power and status, was a new and unwelcome one.

'Not exactly, no,' the inquisitor said, sounding a great deal more like his old self, 'but I think we owe Keira an apology.'

'You think it was a daemon?' Elyra asked, horror and incredulity contending for supremacy in her voice. Finurbi nodded slowly, leaning on her for support as he rose to his feet and reached for his robe.

'I've never encountered anything like it before,' he said slowly, 'so I can't be sure. But if it wasn't warp spawn of some kind, it'll certainly do until a real one comes along. When I get back to the Tricorn I'll talk to the Malleus, as well as seeing what Jorge is after. Maybe they'll be able to identify it for me.'

'That reminds me,' Elyra said, trying desperately to keep the conversational tone normal, 'your shuttle's ready. Barda managed to find one that didn't get too badly dented in the attack, and he's waiting to take you back to Icenholm.'

'I won't be returning to Icenholm now,' the inquisitor said decisively, a measure of his old steel beginning to reassert itself, to Horst's unspoken relief. 'Things are moving too fast. I'll need the full resources of the Tricorn if I'm going to unravel this mess.'

'I'll get Malakai on it at once,' Horst promised, reholstering his sidearm and making for the door. 'There must be a ship of some kind in orbit heading for Scintilla today, even if it's just an ore barge.'

'So long as it's capable of warp travel, nothing else matters,' Finurbi said. 'There's no time to lose.'

'I DOUBT THAT you'll find anything untoward with this system,' Polk volunteered diffidently, as Vex reached out to remove an inspection panel from the wall. 'Technomancer Tonis ministered to it himself.'

'Indeed?' Vex glanced at his faithful data-slate. 'No repairs appear to have been scheduled on it, let alone completed.'

'Before the incident, I mean,' Polk amplified. 'I met him in the corridor here just yesterday. He was correcting a minor imperfection he'd detected.'

'Was he indeed?' Vex was troubled. He knew that such routine tasks were often done without keeping a proper maintenance record, but seldom by someone of the technomancer's rank. He would have expected more devotion to Order and Correct Procedure.

Resolving to ask the man about it the next time they met, he lifted the panel clear.

An acrid cloud of dark smoke billowed out, and dissipated slowly in the current from the air vents, bringing with it the unmistakable smell of charred insulation. 'Oh my,' Polk said, shocked, and Vex's chest panel rattled with a fresh bout of coughing, 'a manifestation!'

'A grave one, too,' Vex agreed, leaning forward to inspect the damage.

'I'll inform the technomancer at once,' Polk said, reaching for a vox-panel set into the wall nearby. A moment later he glanced across at Vex. 'That's odd. He doesn't seem to be answering.'

'That's all right,' Vex replied, as evenly as he could, peering into the depths of the ducting that his removal of the panel had revealed. He'd taken a small hand luminator from a pocket in his robe, and was sweeping the beam methodically among the systems, attempting to isolate the source of the disruption. 'I suspect he already knows.' Despite the instinctive revulsion he still felt at the idea, the deduction of Tonis's guilt was all but inescapable. Tempering his horror and disgust with a strong sense of satisfaction at his own strength of mind, he began to search for any signs of evidence that would corroborate or, preferably, disprove the hypothesis.

He found it almost at once. The site of the damage was obvious: scorch marks and scattered debris the unmistakable stigmata of an explosion, a small one, but enough to disrupt the power supply, and cause the safety overrides to shut down both sets of generators. The sabotage had been carefully planned, to wreak as much havoc as possible from the smallest amount of disruption, and Vex felt a reluctant stirring of respect for its efficiency. As he moved the beam of his luminator to get a better view, it reflected off something small and metallic. Reaching into the narrow gap, and suppressing an outburst of language quite unbecoming to a man of his position as his robe snagged briefly on an obstruction of some kind, he fished it out, and regarded it closely in the light of the corridor.

'What have you found?' Polk asked eagerly, craning his neck to see.

'Evidence of treason,' Vex said heavily, still not wanting to believe that a fellow tech-priest was capable of such wanton destruction. It was a small brass cogwheel, bent and distorted, but still quite recognisable, and a thin coil of wire, once tightly wound, now a loose, yielding spiral.

'They don't belong in there,' Polk confirmed, regarding the fragments of metal curiously. 'That thing looks like a clock spring, but I don't see why anyone would leave a chronograph somewhere they couldn't look at it.'

'These are parts of a timer,' Vex explained heavily, reaching for the comm-bead in his ear. 'I need to speak to the inquisitor at once.'

'The inquisitor's shuttle just left the pad,' Horst's voice informed him crisply. 'We're working independently again. What have you got?'

'A suspect,' Vex said. 'Tonis appears to have planted a small but effective bomb in the primary heat exchangers. I'm afraid Keira's wild imaginings may not have been quite so wide of the mark after all.'

'Hey, two for two.' The young assassin's voice cut in, sounding inappropriately gleeful to Vex. 'Maybe you should start taking me a bit more seriously.'

'A couple of lucky guesses doesn't make you Chastener Domus,' Horst admonished, referring to a popular fictional detective.

'This digression, though no doubt fascinating to anyone who knows or cares what you're talking about, is hardly germane to our current situation,' Vex said, dragging everyone back to the point. He turned to Polk. 'Where's Tonis now?'

'In his quarters,' the young tech-priest said, no doubt trying and failing to infer the fragments of the voxed conversation he'd missed, 'meditating on the state of the systems. He left orders not to be disturbed.'

'Then he's in for a rude awakening,' Vex said.

IN THIS, IT turned out, the tech-priest was wrong. By the time the hastily reconvened group of operatives had forced entry to his quarters, Tonis was unequivocally and very messily dead.

'What in the warp could have done this to him?' Drake asked, looking at the scattered shreds of meat, intermixed with the fused remains of the late technomancer's augmetic enhancements, in horror. He still had his Guard issue lasgun, and clutched it with whitened knuckles, scanning the room for something to shoot, but it seemed devoid of any threat. Apart from the crimson smears marring the smooth metal surfaces, and the shreds of something that might once have been organs hanging from the teeth of the cogwheel in the small devotional alcove, everything seemed pristine, placed carefully for maximum efficiency in its use, just as one might expect in the personal quarters of a tech-priest.

'What in the warp's about right,' Horst said grimly. 'Something like the thing that attacked the inquisitor?'

Keira grinned triumphantly at him. 'Could have been a daemon,' she agreed, looking at the residue, which had once been a body, with rather less distaste than Drake was entirely comfortable with. He'd seen death often enough before, inflicted it too, whenever the simmering resentment of the serfs boiled over into rioting or an over-confident baron tried to withhold part of his tithe from the Queen, but the sheer savage butchery that had happened here was something else. The thick, metallic stench of blood was clogging his nostrils, and the unfamiliar food he'd eaten earlier seemed to be curdling in his stomach.

'Well, I'm guessing he didn't cut himself shaving,' Kyrlock said, and Drake grinned, grateful for his friend's down to earth presence.

Horst ignored the feeble witticism, and turned to Elyra. 'Can you feel anything?' he asked. 'Like you did in the inquisitor's room?'

'No.' She shook her head. 'I can only sense an active presence. If you want to lift echoes, you'll need a specialist.'

'Could it have been the same creature?' Drake asked, before wondering whether it was entirely sensible to be drawing attention to himself. He was still acutely aware that he and Kyrlock were here on sufferance, and that now Finurbi had rushed off to hitch a lift on some trading vessel due to leave orbit within the hour, Horst would be delighted to find an excuse to hand them back to the storm trooper corporal. However, the team leader was nodding thoughtfully.

'Good point,' he said, glancing across at Drake. 'Nice to know someone around here's using their head.' Keira made a derogatory gesture behind his back, and Drake kept his face straight with an effort. 'Elyra?'

'Your guess is as good as mine,' the blonde woman told him, 'but, yes, it sounds reasonable. I'd hate to think there were two of those things running loose around here.'

'You have to admit it hangs together,' Keira persisted, apparently unabashed by their leader's dismissive attitude. 'Daemon possesses the cogboy, makes him blow up the power plant, then...' Her voice trailed off. 'Makes him explode? Why would it do that, do you think?'

'To attack the inquisitor,' Vex suggested. 'It needed to be incorporeal to do that.'

'But why?' Horst clearly didn't buy it. 'Why not just walk up to him in Tonis's body and put a bullet through his head?'

'Because that would blow its cover?' Keira suggested, and then took another look at the mess in the room. 'Like this didn't. Forget I said that.'

'Gladly,' Horst said.

Kyrlock shrugged. 'If it was a daemon, who knows how it thought?' he said. 'Maybe it just didn't want this guy around to answer questions once it went back to hell, or wherever it's gone.'

'Come to that,' Elyra said, 'I've never heard of a tech-priest being possessed before. You hear all kinds of stories when you're being trained for sanction, but nothing like that. They usually go after psykers, because their minds are already open to the warp.'

'Could a tech-priest be a psyker?' Horst asked.

Vex shrugged. 'I've never heard of one,' he admitted, 'but I would have thought that a mind turned towards the perfection of the Machine would be too far removed from such matters to manifest that kind of ability.'

'He could have been a latent, I suppose,' Elyra said, 'but then something would have had to trigger his talent to attract a warp entity.' She shook her head. 'That doesn't just happen spontaneously, not in adulthood, anyway.'

'So we've hit another blind alley,' Horst said. He turned to Vex, who was still methodically searching the room. 'Have you found anything we can use?'

'Very little,' Vex admitted, 'not even a personal dataslate.' He picked something off the flat metal desk in the corner. 'He had a personal vox unit, though. Perhaps that might tell us something.'

'Maybe.' Horst nodded. 'If he was connected to the attack here, he must have been in touch to coordinate things. Maybe we can get a lead on his associates.'

'It'll probably take a while,' Vex cautioned, already relishing the challenge to come. 'Any incriminating data is bound to be heavily encrypted.'

'Then you'd better get started on what you do best,' Horst told him. He glanced around the room again, looking as eager as Drake felt to be somewhere else. 'The rest of us might as well go to bed. The inquisitor took the last airworthy shuttle, and we won't get another one in here before the morning.' He took another look at the scraps of offal littering the room, and sighed. 'Anyone got anything further to add?'

Keira grinned at him. 'Daemon,' she said. 'Cogboy. Told you so.'

EIGHT

Icenholm, Sepheris Secundus
094.993.M41

THE VILLA WAS just as they'd left it: elegant, polychromatic, and deeply boring. Keira leaned on the glass balustrade, her chin in her hand, and looked down the glittering flanks of the suspended city into the shadowed depths of the Gorgonid mine kilometres below. The dizzying drop didn't bother her. She'd grown up clinging to the belly of the walking city on Scintilla, and, if anything, she missed the constant movement, the endless need to keep adjusting her balance. Here there wasn't the remotest chance of an incautious misstep plunging her into oblivion.

'Nice view,' Drake ventured cautiously, joining her at the waist-high barrier, but remaining far enough away not to crowd her. He was the only other member of the group who felt comfortable out here, but then he'd lived most of his life in Icenholm, and was no doubt as indifferent to the chasm below as she was. The others stayed well away from the balustrade whenever they ventured outside, and Kyrlock had never even set foot on the terrace, staying firmly within the security of the semi-transparent walls.

'I suppose,' she said. Drake nodded, not speaking either, and she wondered what had brought him out here this morning. He seemed friendlier than the other Guardsman, more relaxed now he was out of uniform, and he seemed less wary of her than the others did. She'd even caught him looking at her a few times in the manner of a man harbouring lustful thoughts, quite heedless of the fact that most Redemptionist women would have killed him on the spot for such blatant sinfulness.

Not so long ago she probably would have done too, but the Collegium Assassinorum had honed her zeal. Now she was selective, reserving the Emperor's judgement for heretics and traitors, instead of squandering her talents on the pitiful wretches who barely understood how much He despised them for their weaknesses. Besides, he was one of the Angelae, at least for the moment, like her, an instrument of the Inquisition. She could hardly slaughter him on a whim, just because she didn't like his attitude.

Nevertheless, she found herself picturing how easy it would be. One kick, the skirt she wore being loose enough not to restrict her movements, an elbow to the throat, and he'd be on a one-way trip to the Gorgonid before he even realised what was happening.

'You look pensive,' Drake said easily, sipping from the mug of recaf he'd brought out of doors with him.

'Oh.' She could hardly admit she'd been thinking about killing him. 'Just mulling over some combat drills. I'm getting stale cooped up in here.'

'I know what you mean, and I've only been here a day.' Drake waved an expansive arm, taking in the houses on either side of them, and on the slope below. 'I never thought I'd even set foot in a place like this: living in luxury, anything I want just a call to a servant away, and I never realised how much I'd hate it.' He flung the recaf mug away, and watched it shatter on the roof of the house below. 'I know what the price of it all is, in the wasted lives down there.' He pointed to the deep scar of the Gorgonid. 'I've seen it all in the Scourges. The corruption starts at the bottom of the Shatters, and gets worse and more deeply ingrained the higher it climbs. Up here it's just hidden behind smart clothes and snobby manners, that's all.' Conscious that he was beginning to raise his voice, he looked a little embarrassed. 'Sorry, I didn't mean to get carried away.'

'It's all right,' Keira said, a little nonplussed. 'We all feel that way, I suppose. It's why we do what we do.' She looked at him again, surprised to find something akin to her own fervour in his eyes.

Drake nodded, still looking a little sheepish. 'I know. I feel lucky, really. I never thought I'd get a chance to make a difference, but I'd still rather be out there, doing it, than hanging around here waiting for Mordechai to come up with a master plan.'

'He's good at what he does,' Keira said, surprised by the flash of resentment she felt at the implied disparagement of Horst. Emperor alone knew, he could irritate her readily enough, the patronising... Suddenly breathless, she turned, sitting on the balustrade, heedless of the vertiginous plunge behind her.

'Are you all right?' Drake asked, moving a little closer.

'I'm fine.' A flash of movement by the sliding doors leading into the lounge caught her attention, and she focused on it gratefully. Elyra was standing there, beckoning, her violet kirtle almost the same colour as her eyes, which were looking at the two of them a little curiously.

'Oh, there you are,' the psyker said. 'Mordechai wants to see everyone in the lounge in five minutes. Sounds like a briefing.'

'Good.' Drake offered Keira an arm. Ignoring it, she jumped down from the balustrade. 'Sounds like we might be getting out of here faster than we thought.'

'So, what's changed?' Keira asked, lounging in her seat. With the inquisitor's departure, Horst had lost no time in having the floor cushions their patron preferred replaced by more conventional chairs and divans. She was wearing a blouse the colour of the overcast sky, and a loose skirt, in the patchwork blue, green and grey currently fashionable among the minor Secundan nobility. One bare calf swung below the hemline, revealing embroidered slippers, and from where he sat Horst could just make out the tell-tale bulge of a knife sheath on her thigh, supported by a crimson garter. 'Looks to me like we're right back where we started.'

'Not quite,' Horst said, quelling his irritation almost by reflex. 'Now that we've got a couple of new leads we can begin to work.' He nodded towards Drake and Kyrlock, who were sitting slightly apart from the others on the fringes of the group. 'Vos and Danuld know this city and the mines down there better than we could ever hope to. That gives us an edge.'

'I'd like to think so,' Drake said. 'What would you like us to do?' He seemed to have changed in the last day or so, Horst thought, but just how he couldn't put his finger on. He'd discarded his old Imperial Guard uniform almost as soon as they'd arrived at the villa, but his black shirt and midnight-blue trousers still had something of a military cut about them, despite the high quality of their material. He was sitting upright, his right ankle resting on his left knee, looking alert and interested.

Kyrlock, on the other hand, had disdained the luxury of fine clothing, preferring what Horst thought was probably the sort of thing he'd worn prior to his induction into the Guard: leather trousers, stout boots, and a coat of furs, apparently made up of the pelts of several small, forest-dwelling animals. Slouching in his chair, a crystal goblet of amasec in his hand despite the hour, he looked as though he'd have felt more at home in an Iocanthan warband than among these elegant surroundings.

'Vos, I'll get to in a moment,' Horst said, 'but you'll be working with me. You know this city pretty well, don't you?'

'Parts of it,' Drake said. 'I know the royal palace inside out, and I've been to several of the barons' estates for one reason or another.'

'What sort of reasons?' Keira asked, intrigued despite her pose of boredom, and Drake shrugged.

'Honour guard, additional security when one of the royal family was paying a visit, that sort of thing, and a couple of raids, of course.'

'Raids?' Elyra asked.

Drake nodded. 'Every now and again one of the barons thinks he can withhold a portion of his tithe and no one will notice. When that happens, the Scourges go in to remind them that they're wrong.'

'For His vengeance will fall on the unworthy, and scour them from His holy realm,' Keira quoted with relish, no doubt from one of her precious Redemptionist pamphlets. Horst had made the mistake of asking her about her beliefs once, in an attempt to while away the time during a tedious orbital transfer, and had found that they seemed to boil down to two basic propositions: everyone was a sinner, and the Emperor hated sin. Therefore it was the sacred duty of his most devoted followers to kill as many of their fellow citizens as possible, preferably with a great deal of collateral damage, in order to deliver them to the Golden Throne for final retribution.

When Horst had pointed out that this sounded suspiciously like doing His enemies' work for them, Keira had simply glared at him, and all but accused him of being a heretic. In the end, he'd only been able to silence her by unfastening his shirt, to reveal the aquila scar he'd cut into his chest with his combat knife during the vigil in the Cathedral of Illumination in Tarsus, which had preceded his graduation as a fully-fledged arbitrator.

He wondered if that had been the moment when she first started to challenge his authority, but he couldn't be sure; it had been so long ago, a year at least.

'Possibly true, but unhelpful,' Horst said, and she grinned at him again in that infuriating manner. Sighing under his breath, he returned his attention to Drake. 'You know how the people here think, can read their reactions, so I'd like you with me while I'm asking questions. I'm hoping you'll be able to pick up some of the subtle cues I might miss.' Keira muttered something that sounded like 'practically everything, then,' and he ignored her, provoking a self-satisfied smirk.

'Sounds reasonable to me,' Drake said. 'Where do we start?'

'The Spire of the Golden Wing,' Vex said, leaning forward to place the gutted remains of Tonis's vox unit on a glass-topped table, next to a crystal vase of flowers and a half-eaten florn cake. 'The late technomancer made several calls to an address there in the last few weeks.'

'What sort of address?' Elyra asked.

'A private social club,' the tech-priest said. 'The Icenholm lodge of the Conclave of the Enlightened.'

'That sounds like a nest of heretics if ever I heard one,' Keira said eagerly. 'Let's get in there and take them down.'

'I'm afraid they're nothing of the kind,' Horst said patiently, 'so you'll just have to restrain your enthusiasm for violence until an appropriate target presents itself.'

'They're philosophers, aren't they?' Drake asked unexpectedly. Noticing Horst's evident surprise, he shrugged. 'Prince Buchalas is an honorary member, so the Scourges keep an eye on the place, although the only studying he seems to do there is down the blouses of the female servants.'

'I'm sure they'd like to think they're genuine scholars,' Horst said, 'and it probably started out that way a few centuries ago, but these days the Conclave is basically a social club for rich dilettantes with intellectual pretensions. They have a lodge or two on most of the worlds in the sector.' He shot a warning glance at Keira. 'And before anyone points out that this is precisely the kind of gathering heretics habitually take advantage of, the Ordo Calixis monitors it closely for exactly that reason.'

'So what's the connection with our possessed tech-priest?' Drake asked.

Vex pursed his lips thoughtfully. 'He may simply have been a member. Several acolytes of the Omnissiah are, I'm told, hoping to further their understanding of the Great Machine.'

'All right,' Kyrlock said, having finished his drink, and no doubt feeling it was time he showed he was paying attention. 'Who else did he call recently?'

'Mostly colleagues within the citadel, or other members of the Adeptus Mechanicus,' Vex said. 'The former group can be left to Captain Malakai to interrogate, and the latter seem unlikely to be involved. Nevertheless, I've noted their identities for further investigation should it seem warranted.'

'You said "mostly",' Drake said, an instant before Horst could ask the question. 'What about the rest?'

Vex shrugged. 'A few random locations, which I'm attempting to identify by comparison with the planetary records, and at least one that appears to have gone nowhere at all. The unit shows signs of tampering, however, so my best guess would be that some additional components were recently inserted, and then removed, possibly to enable him to communicate with whoever attacked the citadel.'

'The conclave it is, then,' Elyra agreed. She looked at Horst appraisingly. 'So if you and Danuld are following that up, what about the rest of us?'

'Back to our original assignment,' Horst told her, eliciting a sigh of frustration from Keira.

'The one we dead-ended on, you mean?' she asked, with a touch of asperity. 'Looking for off-world people smugglers, who probably don't even exist?'

'They exist, all right,' Kyrlock said, refilling his empty goblet from a nearby decanter. 'You just need to know who to ask.'

'And you do, I suppose?' Keira enquired sarcastically.

Horst nodded, trying not to relish the petty point-scoring. 'He does, or at least who to ask about asking.'

'You hear things in the mines,' Kyrlock told her, 'if you keep your ears open, and if people know you're a bit in the shadows yourself.'

'A petty criminal, you mean,' Keira said, looking at him coldly.

'The barons might call me that,' Kyrlock admitted, 'but they've already got their hands on pretty much everything there is. Down there,' he pointed momentarily to the floor, 'trying to keep a bit back for yourself is just plain common sense.'

'And if you keep back enough, and can find the right people, you can get off-world,' Horst said.

Kyrlock nodded. 'So I've heard. Never had enough to try, nor wanted to, but there are plenty who do.'

'And now you're going to be one of them,' Horst said. Kyrlock nodded again, and he turned to the others. 'Vos and I have discussed this, and he's agreed to go undercover. Given his reputation among the serfs, it shouldn't take much to convince the right people that he wants to get off-planet, and has enough money to pay his way.'

'No offence,' Keira said, 'but have you been warp touched or something? You've known this guy barely two days, and you're already trusting him with an independent operation. What happens if he screws up?'

'I won't screw up,' Kyrlock said, his face colouring.

'I don't doubt that,' Horst said diplomatically. 'The inquisitor recruited you, and that's good enough for

me, but just in case, I'm assigning you some back-up.'
He glanced at Keira. 'Do what you're good at. Don't
show yourself unless you have to, and keep any fleas
off his back.'

The girl shrugged. 'Fine. Anything's better than hanging around here watching my fingernails grow.'

'And what's my cover?' Elyra asked mildly. Taken
aback, Horst looked at her, and she smiled gently. 'Carolus sent us here to see if there was more to this racket
than just moving disgruntled serfs to another world,
remember? If there are any psykers hidden among
them, I'm the only one of us who'd know.'

'A good point,' Horst conceded. 'But they'd know
you too.'

'They would.' Elyra nodded. 'Which might get us a
lead to whoever's harbouring the witches. If I could
pass as one–'

'No. It's too dangerous.' Horst shook his head. 'You'd
be risking far more than just your life.'

'I'm a psyker, Mordechai. I do that every day, just by
not dying. The Emperor has protected me so far, and
I've no doubt he'll continue to do so.' She smiled at the
younger woman. 'Besides, I'll have Keira watching my
back.'

'All right,' Horst conceded reluctantly. 'If you're sure.'
He glanced at Drake and Kyrlock. 'And if you can convince these two you'll be able to pass for a Secundan.'

'Shouldn't be too difficult,' Drake said, after a
moment's thought. 'Not a serf, obviously, but someone from up here, a middle-ranking servant of some
kind.'

'Hardly the sort of person I'm going to walk into a
drinkhole in the Tumble with, though,' Kyrlock
objected.

'I've got the money for our passage,' Elyra said. 'You've got the contacts. Does that sound feasible?'

'Maybe,' Kyrlock admitted, rather grudgingly, Horst thought. 'But we'll have to come up with a really good story to explain how we met.'

'We will,' Horst assured him. 'It's what we're good at.'

'Fine. While you're doing that, I'll get some exercise with the sparring servitors.' Keira stood, stretching sinuously, and glanced at Vex. 'Can you set them up again for me?'

'Of course.' The tech-priest stood too, and began to follow her out. 'If you could perhaps make some attempt to minimise the damage this time? Some of the components are difficult to come by in this system.'

As they left, Horst sighed, and shook his head. 'Is it me, or is she getting worse?'

'Worse how?' Elyra asked, as Drake and Kyrlock left the room too, commencing what sounded like an animated discussion of Secundan social mores and the most probable circumstance for a cross-caste meeting.

Happy to let them settle on a cover story for Elyra between them, Horst shrugged. 'Her attitude. She's challenging every decision I make, and she keeps staring at me.'

'Of course she is.' To his surprise, Elyra chuckled. 'What do you expect?'

'An element of professionalism,' Horst said, before the full implication of her words penetrated his shield of irritation. He looked at her curiously. 'You mean you know what's wrong with her?'

'Some detective you are,' Elyra said unhelpfully. 'Just think about it. What is she?'

'A graduate of the Collegium Assassinorum, an Inquisition operative, a Redemptionist zealot,' Horst said, 'which, from where I'm standing, adds up to a psychopathic pain in the arse.'

Elyra chuckled again. 'Not a bad list, but you're missing out the most important thing.'

'Which is?' Horst was running out of patience with guessing games.

Divining his irritation, Elyra shrugged. 'She's a teenage girl,' she said. 'Isn't it obvious?'

'Isn't what obvious?' Horst began, before, with a shock of horror, belated realisation suddenly struck. He felt his face flushing, to Elyra's evident amusement. 'Dear Emperor on Earth. You think she's got some kind of crush on me?'

'Of course she has,' Elyra said tolerantly. 'Why else do you think she keeps trying to attract your attention?' An expression of sympathy passed briefly across her face. 'Not that I suppose she realises it. Well brought up little Redemptionists tend to label that sort of feeling as sinful, and sublimate it in violence. She must be feeling really confused.'

'*She's* confused,' Horst said heavily.

NINE

Icenholm, Sepheris Secundus
095.993.M41

'THANK YOU FOR waiting so patiently, my masters,' the overdressed factotum said, bowing so low that the voluminous sleeves of his green and purple gown brushed the floor. Whatever the actual intellectual attainments of its members, Horst thought, the Icenholm lodge of the Conclave of the Enlightened certainly managed to give the impression of an institution dedicated to learning. The carpet beneath his feet was patterned in threads of blue and gold, forming a scale map of the Secundan solar system, and a softly glowing image of the galaxy had been worked into the glass wall opposite, illuminated by a hidden light source. 'A member of the governing council will see you now.'

Nodding in acknowledgement, Horst followed the man across the entrance hall, his feet sinking into the rich pile with every step. He glanced at Drake, but the former Guardsman looked appropriately impassive, the unfastened black overcoat he'd donned before leaving the villa billowing around him as he walked like a tightly contained storm cloud. Even if he'd never been here before, he had doubtless seen far greater ostentation in the royal palace, and was unlikely to be impressed. Horst had opted for sober tones too, a light grey rainslick and trousers, the coat open to reveal a hint of the shoulder rig containing his bolt pistol, which was buckled over a plain shirt in darker grey, the colour of iron.

The functionary opened a pair of double doors, bearing stained glass images of some kind of steam engine that Vex would no doubt have recognised had he been here, and cleared his throat. 'The Emissaries of the Inquisition, my lord.' Horst had never heard any-one enunciate capital letters before. Unsure whether to be amused or impressed, he walked forward, almost colliding with the factotum as the garishly dressed man halted at the threshold and bowed across it. 'The Honourable Abelard Poklinten-Grebe, Lord of the Miredank, scion of the Grimcrag dynasty, Secretary of the Minutes to the governing council of the Conclave of the Enlightened's Lodge of the Golden Wing.' Apparently exhausted by the effort of such a concen-trated spray of capitalisation without any discernible pause for inhalation, the minion backed away, leaving the doorway clear.

Horst stepped through it, finding himself in a large room full of scattered tables and data lecterns, into which the reflected radiance that illuminated the whole city was falling through a wide, yellow tinted window. Shelves of books, scrolls and data-slates filled the walls, rising to the ceiling three times a man's height above his head. Drake followed, glancing around without any apparent sign of interest.

'Please, just call me Abelard,' a thin young man said, rising from one of the tables, which was covered with books and papers. No one else appeared to be in the room. His robe was patterned in yellow, orange, and purple, and Horst found himself wondering how often it induced a migraine in its wearer. He smiled ingratiatingly, displaying an equine overbite. 'Simply can't abide all that formal nonsense.'

'It'll certainly save a bit of time,' Drake agreed, pulling a chair up to the opposite side of the table without waiting to be invited. Horst sat next to him, mildly irked that a raw recruit to the Angelae had taken the initiative, but he'd asked him along because of his understanding of the local mores, so there wasn't any point in complaining about it.

Horst glanced at the pile of books. 'Early settlement history?'

'Bit of a passion of mine,' the aristocrat admitted, looking faintly embarrassed. 'To understand where we are, we need to know where we've come from. I'm working on a short monograph, arguing that the initial settlers of Sepheris Secundus were far more socially integrated, only developing the current feudal system as the population grew too large to manage in any other way. Hierarchical systems are everywhere in nature, so it's only to be expected that human society mirrors this.' He began to rummage in the stack of books. 'If you examine Kallendine's *Benefits of Tyranny*–'

'We'll try not to keep you from your researches for too long,' Horst said, recognising a hobby horse being mounted, and hastily seizing the reins before it could canter away.

Abelard coloured slightly, and reluctantly turned his attention to the business at hand. 'Quite so.' He looked from one man to the other, as if registering their presence for the first time. 'My fellow scholars and I are eager to assist you in your enquiries, of course. May I ask what brings agents of the Inquisition to our doors?' He spoke lightly, although Horst was sure he could detect an undercurrent of apprehension in his voice. Even an aristocrat wasn't immune from the jurisdiction of the Inquisition, however much he might wish to seem unintimidated by them.

'We're investigating the death of someone we believe may have been one of your members,' Horst said smoothly, observing the young man's equine features pale slightly. 'The circumstances were sufficiently unusual to excite our interest.'

'Unusual how?' Abelard asked, with faintly studied ingenuousness.

'It got our attention,' Drake said. 'That's all you need to know.'

'Yes. Yes, of course.' A pale sheen of sweat was beginning to gather on the fop's pasty face, and he cleared his throat nervously. 'I didn't mean… How can I help?'

'You can confirm that Technomancer Tonis of the Adeptus Mechanicus was a member of this lodge,' Horst said. 'That would be a good start.'

Abelard nodded, his long face flopping on his elongated neck. 'Yes. Yes, he was.'

'You seem very sure of that,' Drake said evenly. 'Do you know all your members personally?'

'We don't have that many tech-priests.' Abelard smiled weakly. 'They tend to make an impression, as you can imagine. I can find out the last time he was on the premises, if you like.'

'Please.' Horst inclined his head courteously, and the young man rose from his seat. The former arbitrator found himself wondering, for a moment, whether he was about to make a run for it, but Abelard simply tottered over to one of the library stacks and ferreted about in it, before returning with a data-slate ostentatiously ornamented with gold filigree.

'Here we are. Our members sign in on arrival.' He paged down the pict screen, squinting a little at the miniscule font. 'He spent quite a lot of time here in the library, but then I suppose that's what you'd expect. His kind don't have much use for the dining facilities or the members' lounge.'

'I imagine not,' Horst conceded. He hesitated, just long enough to suggest that his next question was spontaneous, rather than planned in advance. 'Did he have any particular friends here?'

'I wouldn't know,' Abelard said, a little too hastily. 'We all tend to mind our own business in the Conclave, stick to our studies, that kind of thing.'

'I don't suppose you'd have any idea which records he was consulting?' Drake asked.

'Not really,' Abelard admitted. 'Tech-priest stuff, I suppose. He did have a bit of a thing about archeotech, I remember, come to think of it, kept snaffling history texts I was after, but he always put them back when he'd finished with them.'

'I see.' Horst nodded, as though this new information confirmed something he already knew, although he didn't see how it was going to get them any further along. The young aristocrat might know a little more about Tonis's cronies than he'd seemed willing to divulge, but getting it out of him looked like being a long and tedious process. Horst already had him pigeon-holed as an idiot, though a conscientious and well-meaning one. That probably accounted for his position on the governing council, someone who would get on with the dreary necessity of administration without asking awkward questions or attempting to shape policy, or, for that matter, notice anything out of the ordinary, however blatant it was. Horst had lost count of the number of complacent halfwits he'd encountered over the years who'd said something like 'but he seemed so nice!' or 'well, it's always the quiet ones, eh?' in precisely the faintly distracted tone of Abelard's voice when some damning piece of evidence against an associate was finally shoved under their noses.

'Perhaps you should try to remember some names,' Drake said quietly, 'because if you're more afraid of them than you are of us, you're making a very big mistake.' His facial muscles twitched, in something that wasn't quite a smile, and suddenly the amiable young aristocrat was leaning back in his chair, glancing dumbly at Horst like a hound hoping for a biscuit but prepared for a kick.

Surprised, but too practised not to show it, Horst nodded sympathetically. 'My associate isn't the most tactful of men, but he is quite correct.' He smiled in a rather more friendly manner. 'I'm sure you've heard a lot of wild stories about the people we work for, haven't you? Things no one with a modicum of common sense could possibly believe.'

'That's right, I have.' Abelard laughed, in a slightly forced fashion, whinnying through his nose in a manner that reinforced Horst's initial impression of equine characteristics. 'Absolutely ridiculous, some of them.'

'They're all true,' Horst assured him. 'Barely scratching the surface, in fact. So if you're protecting anyone, for any reason, it really is in your best interests to think again.'

'I'm not, really.' For a moment, Horst thought the etiolated young man was about to cry. 'I only knew Tonis by sight. He was in some kind of study group, but a lot of our members are. I couldn't tell you who else he was working with, honestly. These things are always so informal.'

'What do you mean by a study group?' Drake asked flatly.

Abelard looked confused for a moment. 'Well, a group of members with an interest in common sometimes exchange information, study a subject together. That's why we call it a–'

'I see.' Drake cut him off, nodding curtly. 'So you can't tell us who else might have been in the group with him.'

'Not as such, no,' Abelard admitted. 'They would have been on the premises at the same time, of course, but so would a considerable number of our other members. Not every member of a study group attends every meeting, and now and again someone else attends one out of curiosity, or to make a presentation.'

'But you said everyone signs in when they arrive,' Horst said, surprised to find himself playing the sympathetic role again. 'That means we could narrow down the list of people we need to speak to by looking for the names of those who happened to be here whenever Tonis was.'

'I suppose you could, in theory,' Abelard said, looking distinctly unhappy at the prospect, 'but it would take an unconscionable amount of time.'

Catching a furtive look the young man cast at the pile of papers on the table between them, Horst finally understood the reason for his reticence. He hadn't been attempting to protect anyone, just avoid a long and complicated administrative task that would take him away from his precious, and almost certainly completely pointless, research.

'I have a friend who thrives on such challenges,' Horst said, reasonably accurately. Vex would undoubtedly have found it more fun if he had to break some complicated cipher to get at the raw data first, but he should be able to produce an initial list of suspects almost at once with little difficulty. 'If you could provide us with the attendance records for, say, the last three years?'

'Of course.' Abelard positively beamed with relief. 'That would be no trouble at all.' He handed the dataslate to Drake, who looked at it as if it might suddenly explode. 'You'll find everything you could possibly need on there.'

'Thank you for your cooperation,' Horst said. 'We'll return the slate when we've finished with it.'

'Not at all,' Abelard said, with a dismissive wave of the hand. 'We've got copies of everything, and if you can't trust the Inquisition, who can you trust?'

'Right, we're done here.' Drake stowed the slate in an inside pocket of his overcoat, revealing the heavy calibre revolver he'd selected from the warband's small but comprehensive collection of weapons, now supplemented by the two Guard-issue lasguns. It was a good piece, a 9mm Scalptaker from the forges of Gunmetal City, and Horst's growing respect for the man had risen still further as he'd watched him make his choice, picking out the most solid and reliable handgun available in preference to any of the flashier alternatives.

The young dilettante flinched at the sight, as if half-expecting Drake to draw it and shoot him, now that he was no longer useful. Then, reassured as Drake turned away, he pulled his chair in closer to the table again. 'If you see one of the servants on the way out,' he said, his attention already returning to his books, 'send one in, would you?' He glanced at Horst as he spoke, but it was Drake who responded.

'Order your own damn drink,' he said brusquely, striding out without a backward glance.

Horst caught up with him in the ornate entrance lobby as the factotum trotted past in the other direction, bearing a large goblet of amasec on a silver tray and a deeply concerned expression.

'What the hell was all that about?' he asked, once the servant was out of earshot. 'I asked you along to observe, not take over the interview!'

'We got what we needed,' Drake said. 'Which is more than you would have done asking politely.' They passed through a thick glass door onto the street outside, the panels being pulled aside by a man and a woman in matching liveries, who sprang forward in perfect unison to clear the way for them. Both were missing a little finger, which Horst remembered marked them out as married serfs, but whether to one another or not he had no idea. As soon as he and Drake had reached the thoroughfare, the pair closed the door behind them, as silently and efficiently as servitors.

Horst hesitated, trying to orientate himself, and then set off after Drake, who had begun to stride away with complete confidence. The roadway was broad here, surfaced in blocks of toughened glass, which formed an intricate mosaic of an Imperial eagle wreathed in orange flames, and Horst found himself squinting a little against the glare. From this height, about midway up one of the smaller spires, most of the city lay spread out below them, scintillating in the ever-present glow, so that they seemed suspended above a glittering jewel, all but filling the gap between the mountains. The pit of the Gorgonid mine was lost to view entirely, the gaps in the superstructure through which it could be glimpsed lower down appearing merely as darker shadows, flaws in the heart of the gem, which only enhanced its beauty. Somewhere on those lower slopes was the villa they'd left a few hours ago, although he couldn't be sure where. He suspected that Drake could have pointed it out without a second's hesitation.

'What do you mean?' he asked, dodging around the crowds queuing to embark on the cable car that had brought them up here, swaying gently on what had seemed little more than a thread, one of hundreds festooning the suspended city like a bustling cobweb. He'd expected to descend the same way, but Drake had bypassed the cable car station, and was angling towards a narrow gap he'd barely even noticed between two buildings at the far end of the thoroughfare.

'You asked me along for my Secundan perspective,' Drake said, stopping at the edge of the street. A thin staircase, barely wide enough for one person to traverse at a time, descended into the shadows beside him. 'And that was it. Everyone here knows their place in the pecking order, and that waste of oxygen we've just been talking to's near the top of the heap. Politeness means deference on Secundus. The more polite you tried to be, the less important you made yourself look to him. That's so ingrained in the local culture, even an Inquisition rosette can only counterbalance so much of it.'

'I see.' Horst nodded, taking the point. He'd got so used to the fear and deference his status as an agent of the Ordo Calixis conferred that he'd almost come to rely on it, and finding that weapon blunted was both strange and disorientating. No wonder his enquiries had been so frustrating. The idea that some of the people he'd interviewed might have lied to him, might even have done so without hesitation or fear of the consequences, was new and disturbing. 'Then you did the right thing.'

'I'm glad you feel that way.' Drake smiled, hesitantly, and Horst returned it. 'I realised what was happening almost as soon as we walked in there. I couldn't say anything to you in front of history boy, so I just tried to be snotty enough for both of us.'

In spite of himself, Horst laughed. 'I think you managed that well enough,' he said. 'Where are we going now?'

'Down here,' Drake said, standing aside for a heavily pregnant young woman in some kind of servant's livery. Secundan sense of hierarchy notwithstanding, it seemed, the general hiver's convention of descending pedestrians giving way to climbers on the narrow vertical walkways apparently held sway here too. The girl smiled her thanks, with a deferential dip of her head, and disappeared into the milling crowd. As he began to descend, Drake turned to look back at Horst. 'Maybe we can narrow that list down a bit before we give it to Hybris.'

'Then lead the way,' Horst said, beginning to descend the stairs after him.

* * *

Icenholm, Sepheris Secundus
096.993.M41

THE WIND ON the terrace of the villa was rising, tugging at Vex's robes, although absorbed in the rites he was administering he hardly seemed to notice the discomfort. 'Are you sure you don't want to change your mind?' he asked, checking everyone's harnesses for the final time, and concluding the appropriate prayers with a dollop of sanctified oil on what he'd rather unnervingly referred to as the Emperor bolt. Elyra had been puzzled by that, until Keira had grinned at her and Kyrlock.

'If it breaks,' she'd said, 'you'll just have time to say "*Oh, Emperor!*" before you hit the ground.' At which point Kyrlock had turned even paler, and Vex had smiled, pointing out that in actual fact at this altitude you would have enough time to articulate an entire sentence if you had sufficient presence of mind to frame one, and then looked puzzled as both women had dissolved into tension releasing giggles.

'Absolutely positive,' Elyra said, almost firmly enough to convince herself. The harness of the glidewings felt strange, tight against her torso, and she tried to persuade herself that this was the reason her breathing felt a little rapid. She glanced over the edge of the balustrade and raised her arms, feeling the breeze fill the aerodynamic sails attached to them, and almost overbalanced.

'Careful,' Keira said, reaching out to steady her, and then hopping up to crouch on the railing with easy confidence. She unfurled her own wings, and turned them to the wind, looking like a hawk about to take to the air.

No, Elyra thought, not a hawk, an eagle, a living avatar of the Imperium, about to swoop on the enemies of all that was good and holy, talons extended to smite them with the Emperor's own wrath. Despite her trepidation at what she was about to do, the image amused her. If she kept this up, she'd turn into a Redemptionist herself. Breathing one of the prayers her father had taught her, and summoning up the image of the quiet chapel in which he'd preached the Emperor's word aboard the void station she'd called home until her fateful meeting with Carolus, she clambered up awkwardly beside her friend.

'Nothing to it,' Keira assured her. She'd donned the synsuit again, and most of it was mimicking the matt black finish of her wings and harness. Unlike the garishly coloured sets, patterned like strident butterflies, which Elyra and Kyrlock had purchased from a sporting goods emporium that afternoon, the assassin's wings had been extensively customised for speed and manoeuvrability, characteristics she'd have little chance to use this evening, escorting her colleagues down to the surface. She glanced at Kyrlock, who was still hanging back, his face pale in the dimming light of the late evening. 'Are you coming?'

'Yes,' Kyrlock snapped irritably. 'If I'm going to break my rutting neck, I might as well get on with it.' He glanced at Vex, and moved his spatchcocked orange wings experimentally. 'That way to gain lift, right?'

'Absolutely,' Vex assured him. 'Although you shouldn't have to worry too much about that. Steering will be the main thing. I'm told it's a relatively easy skill to master.'

'That's right,' Keira agreed cheerfully. 'These things take a bit of practice to get used to, but they're pretty simple really, and it's not as if you need to do any fancy flying. More of a controlled plummet.'

'If that's supposed to make me feel any better about this, it isn't,' Kyrlock snapped.

By way of an answer, Keira stepped into her steering stirrups and dived off the balustrade, opening her arms and letting the growing wind catch her wings. She swooped low over the roofs of the tier below, and then turned and ascended on the thermals rising from the mine, circling the villa lazily. There were still several score of glidewingers gyring around the high spires, where the light was better and the young aristocrats who practised the sport were closer to home, but this low down she had the sky to herself. Faint streaks of red from the westering sun were beginning to suffuse the gentle glow of ambient illumination, lowering the general light level to something close to the Secundan norm. Outside the cone of reflection, dusk would already be shading into night.

If they didn't go now, Elyra told herself, they'd never be able to see well enough to find a landing spot. Placing her trust in the Emperor, as she had done since childhood, she leapt into the void.

'No, REALLY?' DRAKE smiled easily, and sipped at the first mug of decent ale he'd enjoyed since enlisting in the Imperial Guard. They'd found a buttery catering to the myriad of servants working the middle levels of the Spire of the Golden Wing without much difficulty, blending into the rest of the clientele with an ease that had clearly surprised Horst, but which Drake, used to the subtle social game that characterised all human interaction on Sepheris Secundus, had been counting on. Their sober garb, in what was clearly high quality material, marked them of sufficiently high rank in the hierarchy of service to pass unchallenged, and he'd played the part of a naturally sociable man willing to pass the time of day with his inferiors well enough to have left a generally favourable impression on everyone he'd conversed with since they'd arrived.

The real bonus, though, had been the food and drink. As he'd surmised, most of it had come from the stores of the minor nobility who inhabited that part of the spire, rejected as being not quite up to the required standard by their chefs, or perhaps just having passed the optimum time for its consumption. Having grown used to the leavings of the palace kitchens during his time as a Royal Scourge, Drake had a far more refined palate than most Imperial citizens of his humble status, and relished the chance to indulge it again. He remained mindful of the purpose of their visit, however, and inclined his head towards the younger of the two women currently sharing their table. 'You've actually met the Prince?'

'Met him?' The girl, who was dressed in the livery of the Conclave's servants, laughed a little tipsily. 'I've still got the bruises on my arse from taking in his amasec. Hands everywhere, that one.'

'Not just his hands, if you give him half a chance,' the other woman said, brushing her mousy brown fringe from her eyes, and the two women laughed together raucously.

'Not that he isn't generous, mind,' the first one said. 'He gave Ennith that lovely whatsit, you know, with all them jewels on it. Might even be worth a go or two for something like that.'

'That's the thing, though, innit?' her friend demurred. 'It's not exactly guaranteed. Just your luck to

get him on a night when he's distracted with affairs of
state or some such malarkey, and it's just "thank you
very much, where's me breakfast?" in the morning.'

'True.' The younger woman sighed ruefully. 'But you
never know till you try, do you? And at least he's a
gent, not like those lads from the Guild of Tableware
Polishers. Think they're the Emperor's gift, they do.'
She glanced up at Drake, her glass already empty, and
he waved the hovering sommelier over to recharge it.
Like all the buttery staff, a gratuity and a few quiet
compliments about his serving skills had been sufficient to engage at least his peripheral attention for
most of their tenure at the table. The girl's eyes narrowed a little. 'What did you say you did again? If you
don't mind me asking.'

'Of course we don't.' Horst had grown a little more
accustomed to the way status was established, having
sat through several such conversations and observed
Drake's responses. Recognising an implicit challenge,
he mimicked the affable tone of a Secundan responding in a friendly manner to a social inferior. 'I'm the
household amanuensis, and my associate here is the
majordomo.' It was a variation of the answer Drake
had given in previous exchanges, and the former
Guardsman smiled a little, pleased with the progress
Horst had been making towards blending in.

'I see.' The young woman nodded, a little intoxi-
cated. 'That'll account for those nice manners of yours.'
She glanced at her friend for confirmation. 'Didn't I
say when we walked in, those two look like they've got
nice manners?' The older woman nodded. 'You talk a
bit funny, though, if you don't mind me saying.'

'My friend's from off-world,' Drake said easily, 'here
to inspect our household before her ladyship arrives.

She doesn't spend a lot of time on Sepheris Secundus, but we like to think whenever she graces us with her presence she'll find everything to her liking.'

'You work for an off-world family?' The girl looked at Drake with awestruck respect. 'We didn't know there was one of those in the spire.'

'Well if there is, it isn't ours,' Drake said, wondering if he'd gone too far. The arrival of a noble from offworld was a very juicy piece of gossip indeed, and would be all over the city within hours, at least those parts of it inhabited by servants. 'Our mistress inherited a small villa on the northern slope about a century ago, and maintains it for the odd occasion her business brings her here. Hardly fitting for the permanent residence of someone of her status,' he glanced at Horst in the manner of a Secundan aware of perhaps crossing the line in implying a degree of criticism of the behaviour of an employer in front of a superior servant, 'but she spends so little time here that it suits her well enough.'

'Indeed.' Horst nodded, apparently aware at least that some kind of response was required, and by luck or instinct choosing one that consolidated Drake's credibility in the minds of his small but rapt audience. 'The lady Keira is a woman of refined, but simple tastes. Even at home on Scintilla she prefers composing poetry to the demands of the social season.'

'That's class, all right,' the younger woman agreed, a trifle glassy-eyed. 'Sounds like she'd fit right in with our lot.'

'They certainly sound a fascinating group,' Drake agreed, dragging the conversation back to the topic he'd been hoping to raise, with a grateful glance in Horst's direction. 'Although I suppose none of them could be as interesting as a prince of the blood royal.'

'Don't you believe it,' the older servant said, apparently agreeably surprised to find her drink replenished. 'There's plenty of 'em at least as wayward as he is. In different ways, mind.'

'Oh yes.' The younger one nodded vigorously, and then appeared to regret it. 'They're all obsessed with something: Technomancy, classical drama, the Emperor's Tarot, you name it. Except Viscount Adrin, he's into a little of everything, talks to everyone.'

'Well you've got to expect that, I suppose,' the older one interjected. 'He is the Social Secretary.' She looked across at Drake. 'That means he organises things for the members, finds rooms for the study groups to meet in, sends us around with the drinks and snacks, that sort of thing.'

'A vital job,' Drake agreed, straight-faced. 'I've no doubt the Conclave would fall apart without him.'

'He'd like to think so, right enough,' the woman said, 'but if you ask me, that little weedy one does most of the work. Adrin just floats around the place taking the credit, and talking to that tech-priest friend of his.'

'Tech-priest?' Horst asked. 'I didn't think they had any friends, apart from servitors.'

The two women laughed immoderately at the feeble joke.

'Old Tonis isn't so bad, actually,' the younger one said, once she'd got her breath back. 'At least he looks at you like you're there when he wants something, which is more than most of the others do. And he keeps his hands to himself, unlike most of the rest.'

'Probably just as well,' her friend said. 'He's got so many augmetic bits he's probably got... you know, augmetic bits.'

Steeling himself against the inevitable howl of hilarity, Drake began to wonder if the information they'd just uncovered, valuable as it was, was being obtained at too high a price.

Above the Gorgonid, Sepheris Secundus
096.993.M41

AS THEY LEFT the nimbus of reflected light around the city, Keira soared, feeling the surge of air beneath her wings buoying her up like the light of the Emperor's word. She banked easily, riding the thermals rising from the vast scar in the earth below, the concentrated body heat of uncountable serfs mingling with that of cooking fires and the labouring engines of the vehicles that conveyed the day's scrabblings of ore from the tally sheds to the stockpiles. Fresh clean air rippled across her face, the chilly sting of it invigorating, and she fought down the impulse to laugh. No one would hear her, but the habits of the hunt were deeply ingrained, and stealth was of the essence.

Her companions flew steadily, maintaining a relatively straight course, and Keira soared around them, keeping an eye on their progress. There would be little she could do if either of them screwed up really badly, but they both seemed to be getting the hang of it, too scared or sensible to do anything other than use the lift the glidewings gave them to descend slowly towards the ground. Elyra smiled a little wanly as Keira swooped by, her face a mask of concentration, and the assassin dropped a few metres, catching air to slow her progress, falling back to check on Kyrlock.

For a moment, back at the villa, she'd wondered if his courage was going to fail him after all, but as she'd turned to make a rising pass over the roof he'd clambered convulsively onto the balustrade and jumped, just after Elyra. Now, to her amusement, a fierce, exultant grin was stretching the skin of his face, and he yelled a greeting as she flew past.

'Emperor's bones, what a rush!'

Keira waved, relieved, and pointed a little to the left, towards the landing site she'd picked out. Kyrlock nodded, and adjusted his course, a trifle awkwardly, but with growing confidence.

Leaving him to it, Kiera soared ahead again, intent on shepherding Elyra down safely. The Guardsman's earlier apprehension might have been forgotten in the exultation of the moment, but the potential neck-breaking part of the descent was still to come.

Icenholm, Sepheris Secundus
096.993.M41

'THE LADY KEIRA?' Drake asked, leaning on the rail of a cable car station he'd led them to shortly after leaving the buttery. The evening was well advanced, and the projecting platform was almost empty, affording an uninterrupted view of the softer splendour that Icenholm presented by night. Everywhere the two men looked, the lights of the glass city were coming on, turning the daytime jewel into something more closely resembling the galaxy that the scudding clouds permanently obscured, lit from within by a myriad of individual lanterns, which together cast a warm, serene glow across the vitreous landscape.

Horst shrugged, feeling faintly embarrassed. 'It was just the first name that came into my head,' he admitted. Hardly surprising, given how often his thoughts had returned to the girl following his dis-concerting conversation with Elyra that morning. If the psyker was right, and the young assassin really was infatuated with him, he didn't have a clue what to do about it. The obvious, and entirely dishon-ourable, course of action was out of the question. Even if, by the Emperor's grace, they did manage to make it work, it would split the team, dividing loy-alties and imperilling the operation. And if they didn't, which was far more likely, the fallout was going to be lethal.

Besides, he didn't feel that way about the irritating little brat, did he? He couldn't deny that he found her attractive, in a purely physical sense, but they had nothing in common beyond their dedication to the Inquisition. The physical side of things might be fine, for a while, but sooner or later you had to start talking as well, spending time together, caring about one another, and that simply wasn't going to happen. They were just too different.

'I can understand that,' Drake said casually, oblivious to his comrade's inner turmoil. 'She does make a bit of an impression, doesn't she?' Then he shrugged. 'Are we heading straight back?'

Horst started to nod, but thought better of it. 'Not directly,' he said. He needed guidance, and from a source far more authoritative than mere human advice. 'Do you know of any temples on our way down?'

The Gorgonid Mountains, Sepheris Secundus
096.993.M41

THE GROUND CAME up so fast, in a blur of motion, Elyra barely had time to register it. It was almost completely dark, a faint swirl of windborne snow battering into her face, and the faint air of detachment she'd felt floating above the world was abruptly gone. With shocking suddenness, the mountains below were rising above her, the smooth snowfields dappling their flanks rushing past.

Minor blemishes in their smooth white perfection resolved into potentially lethal outcrops of grim grey rock that seemed to be reaching out to snatch her from the sky. She swung her legs frantically, dipping a wingtip as Keira had shown her, and to her relief the rig she wore responded at once, turning to follow the barely visible silhouette of the assassin ahead of her. A second shadow paralleled her own, projected by the artificial star field of the city above, and she glanced up, seeing Kyrlock a few metres higher and almost a body length ahead, his great physical strength conferring a surprising degree of control over the wings he wore.

They were heading for a narrow valley, where the trees seemed thinner, and Elyra found herself reciting one of the catechisms she'd learned as a child, invoking the protection of the Emperor. Keira rose a little, soaring easily over a copse ahead of them, and Kyrlock followed, appearing to gain confidence with every passing second.

Almost caught unawares, Elyra altered the angle of her wings, felt the sudden rush of lift, and barely made it, high branches reaching up to snag her hair and clothing, leaving stinging scratches across her face and hands as she skimmed the top of the arboreal obstacle. At least her eyes hadn't been struck. For a heart stopping moment she wondered if her harness would be fouled, or the fabric of the wings ripped, but the rig held together, and then they were dropping fast towards an open expanse of snow surrounded by trees.

Keira landed first, kicking her boots free of the steering stirrups to drop lightly onto her feet, killing her forward momentum with a couple of steps. As she came to a halt, and shrugged free of her harness, she turned to watch the approach of her protégés.

Kyrlock hit hard, in a flurry of snow and profanity, losing his balance and stumbling forward before falling face down in the welcoming drifts. Elyra had no time to worry about the red-headed Guardsman, though, as the ground suddenly rose up from nowhere to smack her hard in the face. She tumbled, feeling the brace of her left wing snap under the weight of her forearm, trying instinctively to tuck into a roll, but the harness and the glass fibre skeleton of the gliding rig encumbered her, inhibiting her movements. Something slammed into the side of her head, and darkness descended.

'Sin and damnation,' Keira's voice said, from what sounded like a long way away. 'I told Mordechai this was a stupid idea, but does anyone ever listen?'

'Is she all right?' Kyrlock asked, sounding even more distant.

'She will be.' Something grabbed Elyra around the torso, rolling her over. Feeble light skewered her smarting eyes, and she blinked them clear, as Keira's face appeared above her. For a moment she thought the young assassin's head was surrounded by a halo, like the icons of the saints in her father's chapel. Then Keira moved, to reveal the shining constellation of the city, impossibly far above. 'A few cuts and scratches, and that's going to be one hell of a bruise, but I don't think anything's broken.'

'Then we might as well get started,' Elyra said, forcing herself to sit up, astonished at the number of places it was possible to hurt. She scrabbled for the release of her harness, and found it distorted into uselessness.

'Allow me,' Kyrlock said, reaching down to cut her free with what looked like a Guard-issue combat knife.

'Thank you.' Elyra accepted his proffered arm, hauling herself upright, and tried to ignore the little firecrackers of pain that erupted all along her left arm as she shrugged free of the buckled remains of the glidewings. They'd never fly again, that much was certain. Kyrlock's looked a little battered, but still serviceable, and Keira's, of course, were still in perfect condition. 'Where are we?'

'The lower slopes, above the main mine workings,' Keira said. 'I've touched down here before, on scouting trips.' She began to fold her wings, in the faint glow of light from the city above them, and gestured to Kyrlock to do the same. Elyra limped around to hers, and began to follow their lead, but the assassin forestalled her. 'No, leave that one out in the open. It'll back up your cover story if anyone thinks to check.'

'Fine.' Nursing her throbbing head, Elyra watched her companions stow their gear. 'Where are you going to hide the others?'

'Just inside the treeline.' Keira gestured towards the surrounding forest, and Kyrlock nodded approval, as a few more snowflakes flurried past in the stiffening breeze.

'Good idea. We'll be getting more snow soon, and they won't get buried too much by the drifting.'

'More snow? Good.' Keira finished stowing her kit. 'That'll cover our tracks nicely.' She tapped the commbead in her ear. 'Hybris, can you hear me?' The answer was evidently in the affirmative, because she nodded once, briskly. 'Good. We're down.' There was a short pause, during which she glanced in Elyra's direction with a faint air of amusement. 'That's right. No problems at all.'

TEN

'WELL, ADRIN WAS definitely on the premises whenever Tonis was,' Vex said, looking up from the overly ornamented data-slate lying beside his own on a convenient table in the lounge of the villa. He'd been examining the files it contained for several hours, and was beginning to draw some tentative conclusions, despite the faint irritation he still felt at the way the casing of the poor machine had been so insensitively adorned with pointless frippery, instead of the iconography properly dedicated to the Omnissiah that such a fine piece of equipment deserved. 'Of course he spends a lot of time there, but that holds true for the majority of the members.'

'But we know he had some kind of connection to Tonis,' Horst reminded him; quite unnecessarily, so far as Vex was concerned, but he refrained from remarking on the matter. Those unblessed with the clarity of thought bestowed by the Omnissiah often kept stating and restating the obvious. He'd grown so used to it since leaving the quiet of the Mechanicus shrine to begin his association with the Angelae Carolus that it barely registered with him any more. If anything, he found it either amusing or perversely reassuring, like a system with multiple redundancies, ensuring that the relevant facts kept reasserting themselves despite any distractions that might occur. Signal to noise, the vox chaplains called it, and he found the comparison apt. Unmodified humans certainly made enough of the latter.

'Quite so,' Vex said, having observed that people said that kind of thing to acknowledge the receipt of packages of redundant input. 'That means our next goal should be to gather as much information as possible on Adrin.'

'That's your job,' Horst told him, to his complete lack of surprise. 'Get into the data systems, and pull up everything you can on him. There should be plenty, given his influence and connections.'

'Isn't that rather a tall order?' Drake asked. 'It could take days to assemble a complete picture. Have we got that long?'

'Don't worry,' Vex assured him. 'I have some powerful filtration algorithms, which ought to distil anything relevant without too much difficulty.'

'Good.' Horst nodded slowly. 'And while you're doing that, there's another approach we might try.' He glanced at Drake. 'Something one of Danuld's informants said gave me an idea. We might just have given ourselves the opening we need to plant an agent inside the Conclave.'

'What was that?' Drake asked, a moment before amused comprehension dawned across his face, and for no reason Vex could see his voice suddenly became a nasal falsetto. 'Sounds like she'd fit right in with our lot.'

'Precisely,' Horst said, grinning. Since neither of them seemed inclined to share the joke, Vex ignored it, and returned to work.

The Gorgonid Mountains
096.993.M41

THEY'D WORKED THEIR way slowly down to the edge of the foothills, keeping in cover, relying on the wind and the flurrying snow to cover their tracks. Kyrlock had moved with surprising assurance, manifestly happy to be back in an environment he knew well, and Keira had been little more than a ghost in the darkness. Only Elyra had struggled, wading through the snow, sinking deep through its crust with every step. This was nowhere near as unpleasant as the blizzard they'd fought their way through after their shuttle had been downed, but it was still bad enough, made worse by the stiffness in her limbs and the jolts of pain that jarred through her with every stumbling footfall.

The cold was acute, too, sapping her strength, and she fought down a brief stab of envy at the thought of other pyrokines she'd known who were able to project a thin aura of warmth around themselves. Her talents, however, lay in a more direct and destructive direction, and, Emperor knew, she'd been grateful for that often enough. At least she'd had the foresight to don thick, weatherproof clothing. Down here, Kyrlock's furs didn't seem like such an affectation any more.

'Is it much farther?' she asked, and Kyrlock looked back at her, an unexpected expression of sympathy on his face.

'Almost there,' he reassured her, for the third or fourth time.

Keira nodded, her face pale in the all-pervading glow that surrounded them, enabling them to progress ever more quickly as it had grown in strength. The closer they'd come to it, the more brightly the city above them had illuminated the landscape, so that the small group of Angelae were able to move as confidently as they would have done in the bright moonlight of a more Emperor-favoured world. 'Just beyond that stand of trees,' she confirmed. 'I've been this way before.'

Elyra stumbled through the last patch of woodland, and stopped suddenly, awestruck. In front of her, less than a hundred metres away, a vast precipice yawned, falling away farther and deeper than the eye could see, the trees and snowfields ending as abruptly as if they'd been cut away by the stroke of a sword. Kilometres distant, the opposite face stood stark and drear, shadowed in the gentle illumination of the city above, speckled with the winking lights of the uncounted hovels and workings that clung to it. 'Golden Throne!' she breathed.

'You think that's something, wait until we're close enough to smell it,' Kyrlock said, although how much he was joking Elyra couldn't tell.

'Which way?' she asked, recalling her mind to the mission.

Kyrlock gestured to the left. 'We can get down into the Tumble that way,' he said confidently, before glancing across at Keira. 'All right with you?'

'Fine.' The young assassin shrugged, her outline blurred by the synsuit. 'This is your ground. You call it.' She stood casually, her eyes sweeping the desolate landscape. 'Go have a drink. I'll watch your back.'

'Works for me,' Kyrlock said. He glanced at Elyra. 'Coming?' Without waiting for an answer, he strode off in the direction he'd indicated.

'Of course.' After a moment's hesitation, and a final glance at Keira, Elyra limped after him, feeling almost the same as she had done before making her leap from the villa, what seemed like a lifetime ago.

Icenholm, Sepheris Secundus
096.993.M41

'Now, THAT'S INTERESTING,' Vex commented. He'd managed to download most of the pertinent information from the offensive looking data-slate to his own, which was making the most of its Inquisition level access protocols to scour the Icenholm datanet for any relevant records it could plunder. 'A distinct anomaly.'

'Something about Adrin?' Drake asked, sipping his third mug of recaf. He was looking tired, but refusing to go to bed until the surface party checked in again. Omnissiah alone knew what he expected to be able to do about it if they were in any sort of trouble, but Vex supposed his zeal was commendable. Horst, the veteran of innumerable such vigils, had turned in some time before, preferring to sleep while he could.

'No, about Tonis,' Vex said. Out of politeness he moved aside, to give Drake an uninterrupted view of the pict screen, although he doubted that anyone unschooled in the theology of data retrieval would be able to make much sense of the icons it was displaying. 'I factored him into the filters, in an attempt to prioritise any other connection there might be between the two of them, but it's thrown up something rather curious.'

'Which is?' Drake asked.

Vex shrugged, and coughed loudly, making a mental note to adjust his respirator unit again at the earliest opportunity. 'His security clearance was issued by the Inquisition office on the Lathes, like most of the Adeptus Mechanicus personnel at the Citadel, but he has a local birth record.'

'Tonis was a Secundan?' Drake asked, apparently needing confirmation of the fact before he could accept it.

Knowing this for another common trait of those unblessed by the Omnissiah, Vex merely nodded. 'That appears to have been the case. However, both his parents were minor members of the local aristocracy, with no apparent connection to the Adeptus that I can find.'

'But their son became a tech-priest.' Drake frowned thoughtfully. 'I've never heard of a Secundan noble doing that.'

'Perhaps he simply had a calling,' Vex said. 'But it might well be worth looking into.'

The Tumble, Gorgonid Mine, Sepheris Secundus 096.993.M41

KYRLOCK HADN'T BEEN joking about the smell. As she limped into the wilderness of spoil heaps fringing the mine, Elyra caught her first faint whiff of it, the unmistakable odour of too much unwashed humanity living in too close a proximity, and the sweet, sulphurous stench of raw sewage. Other, equally noxious, smells were intermingled with it, rising and falling like the melody line of a symphony of stench: the smoke and grease of uncountable cooking fires, the acrid tang of the pall of dust that hung over everything, and the sharp stink of burned promethium from the loaded trucks that still growled past in a steady stream even at this time of night. The racket of their engines was supplemented by the Waymakers who squatted on rickety platforms lashed to the front fenders or clung precariously to some makeshift perch, hallooing loudly, blowing horns, or banging drums to warn of their approach.

Suddenly the unmistakable shriek of a shuttle engine rose over the cacophony, drowning it out entirely, and snatching at her attention. Elyra glanced up, seeing the blocky silhouette of a bulk cargo lifter descending from somewhere above them, following the line of labouring transporters towards wherever they were going. Presumably there was a landing pad a kilometre or so in that direction.

'Better keep your eyes on the surface,' Kyrlock advised, not even appearing to register the spacecraft's approach, and Elyra nodded. There were people everywhere, trudging up and down the road, mostly men but there were a few women amongst them, keeping firmly to the fringes of the narrow strip illuminated by randomly scattered arc lights. The gaps in between had been plugged for the most part by flickering torches, in sconces nailed to posts driven into the ground. The mine's denizens barely seemed human, plodding along in almost complete silence, their clothes, skin and hair ingrained with the omnipresent dust. They walked, heads down, with occasional wary glances into the deeper patches of shadow fringing the highway. Occasionally one would speak, a short, mumbled sentence or two, falling silent again as their companion replied equally tersely, or merely shrugged in response.

At first, Elyra had been alarmed at the sight of so dense a crowd, expecting to attract attention, perhaps even trouble. There was no doubt that both she and Kyrlock stood out among the drab, shuffling host. Even uninjured she would have been distinctive, her stout boots, thick jacket and trousers, and rucksack as out of place as a ball gown would have been. Her limping gait, and the cuts and bruises on her face, only compounded that. Her companion simply looked like trouble, his chain axe slung across his back, and a shotgun from the Angelae's armoury held ready for use with all the assurance of his military training. He'd slipped it from his shoulder as they first entered the fringes of the Gorgonid, without comment.

Elyra had regretted stowing her laspistol in the bottom of her backpack, but she hadn't expected to need it so soon. At least her innate abilities would protect her if necessary, so she simply put her trust in the Emperor and followed her guide. To her mingled surprise and relief, none of the shuffling serfs seemed to register their presence at all, or, if they did, could not rouse themselves enough to care about the strangers in their midst.

'Down this way,' Kyrlock said, turning off the roadway at last, and slipping between two spoil heaps, which looked to Elyra no different from any of the others surrounding them. Kyrlock was looking more wary, scanning every patch of shadow, and she followed his lead, wishing the gentle light from the city suspended above them was a little brighter. Several times she caught glimpses of movement, heard hushed voices in the darkness around them, and once the distinctive aroma of lho smoke drifted across their path, the faint glow of the smouldering sticks pinpointing at least two people conversing quietly among the sheltering stacks.

'Where are we going?' Elyra asked, completely disorientated. Every mound of rubble looked the same to her, although Kyrlock continued to stride out with confidence, enviably sure-footed on the treacherous surface. Elyra stumbled several times, but remained standing by the Emperor's grace. She almost turned her ankle more than once, but the stout hiking boots she'd selected supported and cushioned the joint, preventing any serious injury. Every now and again she felt an irrational urge to glance back and see if Keira was still following them, but she fought it down. Even if she was there, which the sensible part of Elyra's mind didn't doubt for a moment, the young assassin wouldn't be visible.

'A drinkhole I know,' Kyrlock said, and then shrugged. 'Used to know, anyway. Should still be there, if Mung's made the right pay-offs.'

'And this Mung can get us off-planet?' Elyra asked, aware that other ears in the shadows might be listening, and sticking to her cover story as a precaution.

Kyrlock looked back at her as if she was simple. 'Course not,' he said, as though explaining it to a child. 'He can sell us a drink, that's all, but it's a place to start asking.' He shook his head, playing the same game as she was, laying the groundwork against later suspicion. The group they were hoping to contact would be cautious, and would ask around. A pantomime argument now would consolidate their cover, if the right people overheard it. A faint edge of derision entered his voice. 'You've got no idea at all how things work down here, have you? I should have left you where you fell.'

'And waited for the commissars to catch up with you?' Elyra scoffed. 'You need to get off this dirtball as much as I do.'

'Yeah, well, maybe I do, but I don't see you managing it on your own.'

'Funny, I was just thinking the same thing about you.' They stared at each other for a moment, and Elyra fought down the impulse to giggle at the theatricality of it all.

After a moment, Kyrlock shrugged, and turned away. 'Well, come on then, if you're coming,' he said.

MUNG'S PLACE WAS exactly where Kyrlock remembered, and didn't seem to have changed at all in the last year or so: a crude shaft, driven into the side of a millennium-old spoil heap by someone desperate or crazy enough to attempt to recover the scraps of low-grade ore discarded along with the waste by an earlier, more profligate generation. Shored up by flakboard and pit props too worn or flawed to be of any use in the mine itself, it was typical of thousands just like it scattered throughout the Tumble. Now, truncated by cave-ins, it only went back a dozen metres or so, extending about half that to the sides, creating a rectangular space with just enough room to stand upright. Large and small packing crates did their best to look like tables and chairs, and a roughly rectangular section of metal, which looked as though it had been scavenged from the chute of an ore hopper, formed a crude bar at one end.

Kyrlock reslung his shotgun and pushed aside the flap of canvas that covered the entrance, meeting the eyes of the large man with a pickaxe handle standing next to it for a moment as he did so. The fellow nodded automatically, before registering his face, and smiling a slightly strained greeting.

'It seems they haven't forgotten you,' Elyra said, stepping through the gap after him, and ignoring the frankly curious stare that followed her.

'No, they haven't,' Kyrlock agreed, scanning the faces that glanced up to assess the new arrivals. A few were familiar, glancing away again as soon as they registered his presence, the rest strangers. Well, that was to be expected, the turnover of clientele in a place like this tended to be rapid. No one seemed overly pleased to see him, but then no one seemed overtly hostile either. He tried to remember any unsettled grudges someone might still be holding from before his arrest, but none came to mind. The cuckolds who'd turned him in wouldn't dare enter the Tumble at night, and he didn't owe anyone money. Several of the customers were eyeing Elyra with barely concealed interest or suspicion, which was all according to plan. They'd intended to make an impression, and they were certainly doing that. 'Come on.' He gestured for her to follow him, and walked up to the bar.

'Vos,' Mung said, from the relative safety of the other side, a faint edge of surprise in his voice. 'I heard they hung you for tithe evasion.' He looked just the way Kyrlock remembered, thin and wiry, with lank brown hair and an insincere grin, which revealed a misshapen row of yellowing teeth. A shaggy beard covered his face, obscuring the tattoo, identical to Kyrlock's, which was still just barely visible behind a hedgerow of hair and grease.

'You heard wrong,' Kyrlock said, with a humourless smile. 'Two drinks.' He dropped a couple of coins on the counter, with a metallic rattle. 'I got tithed off myself, to the Imperial Guard. Say what you like about the nobility, they've a fine sense of humour.'

'Some of 'em you can die laughing,' Mung agreed, slopping something from a bottle into a cracked glass and a mug with a broken handle. 'Who's your friend?'

'Not really sure,' Kyrlock admitted. 'She's from up there.' He pointed skywards, and Mung nodded, taking in the quality of Elyra's clothing. 'Name's Elyra. Seems to have been the butt of another little joke.'

'Vos.' Elyra tugged at his sleeve, pretending to be nervous. 'He doesn't have to know all this, does he?'

'Course he does,' Kyrlock said. 'The right people come in here, he can tell them I'm looking to deal.' He pushed the mug towards her dismissively. 'Enjoy your drink.' He turned back to Mung. 'Kantris still show his face in these heaps?'

'Now and again,' Mung said, non-committally. 'What do you want to talk to him about?'

'That's between him and me,' Kyrlock said, and Mung nodded cordially, not having expected any other answer.

Elyra sniffed suspiciously at the pale liquid in her filthy cup, and winced. 'What is this stuff?'

'Best not to ask,' Kyrlock said, knocking his own drink back in one, with a sigh of satisfaction. 'He'll only lie about it anyway.'

'Got that right,' Mung agreed cheerfully. 'Another?'

'Why not?' Kyrlock dropped another coin on the counter. 'We've got time.'

'So,' Mung said, looking him up and down as he refilled the glass. 'You're a Guardsman now.'

'Not as such,' Kyrlock said, grinning. 'I sort of resigned.'

'I see.' Mung took in the stencilled serial number on the haft of his chain axe, next to the aquila symbol of the Guard, and the shotgun hanging casually from his shoulder. 'Do they know you're gone yet?'

'Oh yes.' Kyrlock nodded. 'I settled a couple of scores before I left.' Mung glanced at the weapons, drawing the conclusions he was meant to, and Kyrlock continued with a well-concealed sense of satisfaction. 'Since then I've been hiding out in the Breaks. Most of 'em couldn't find their arses with both hands and a map up there.' He snorted derisively. 'City boys. But then Elyra fell on me, and it turns out she's got a better idea.'

'Which is?' Mung asked, his eyes going to the woman again.

'Our business.' She took a cautious sip of the drink in her hand, and grimaced. 'Emperor's blood!'

'Knew you'd like it,' Mung said cheerfully. He turned back to Kyrlock. 'Fell on you, you said?'

'I jumped,' Elyra said, 'with a set of glidewings. I'd never used one before, so the landing was a little rough. Vos saw me come down, and dug me out.'

'I thought my luck was in,' Kyrlock said, knocking back his second drink. 'Dead aristo just dropping out of the sky like that, bound to have some good jewellery or something on 'em, you know? But she was still breathing.'

'Can't win 'em all,' Mung said, sympathetically.

'Right.' Kyrlock nodded. 'And it turns out she's in trouble too.'

'Must be, to take a risk like that.' The rodent-like barman looked at Elyra with a mixture of curiosity and respect. 'Mind if I ask what kind?' Then he smiled insincerely, in a belated attempt at tact. 'Folk'll be asking, see, when I say Vos and his friend were mentioning some business.'

'Well, if you must know,' Elyra said, managing to look both embarrassed and angry at the same time, 'my master and I fell in love with each other.' Kyrlock nodded, impressed with her acting ability. If he hadn't known she was lying, he'd never have been able to tell. She swallowed the drink in one gulp, apparently overcome with emotion for a moment, and taking advantage of the tears that the raw alcohol brought to her eyes to add extra verisimilitude. 'Which was fine, until the mistress found out. The vindictive old hag was going to have me killed, so I made a run for it.'

'Quite right too,' Mung said, sympathetically, and out of the corner of his eye Kyrlock could see that the rest of the customers were listening as avidly as they could without appearing to. Within the next few hours, the story of his desertion from the Guard and Elyra's flight from a vengeful noble would be all over the underworld that thrived in the ruins of the Tumble and the back alleys of the Commons. The barman poured more of the anonymous liquid into Elyra's cup, which, to Kyrlock's surprise, she downed too. 'Here, have another. On the house.'

'We'll need somewhere to stay,' Kyrlock said, 'until the word gets out.'

Mung nodded, pulling aside a curtain behind the bar, to reveal a shabby storeroom with a stained and grubby bedroll on the floor, and a reeking bucket in one corner. 'You can have my place,' he offered, 'for five credits, each.'

'Ten credits for that?' Elyra said. 'That's outrageous!'

Mung shrugged. 'Suit yourself,' he said, 'but you won't do better.' He glanced speculatively in her direction. 'This mistress of yours, is she hacked off enough to hire a bounty hunter by any chance?' The question was choked off as Kyrlock's fist closed around the front of his greasy and malodorous shirt, and he transferred his attention to the Guardsman, smiling in what he imagined was an ingratiating fashion. 'I'm only saying, they'll want to be sure she's dead, won't they? They'll go straight to the Commons, start asking around. If you want to stay hidden, you'll need to be with someone you trust.' He wriggled free of Kyrlock's grasp.

'Fair enough,' Kyrlock said, wiping his hand on his furs, 'but it's five for the room, flat. And any trouble walks in here looking for us, you'll be the first to die. Got it?'

'Pleasure doing business,' Mung agreed, standing aside to allow them behind the counter. Kyrlock and Elyra ducked through the curtain, letting it fall closed behind them, and the psyker lowered herself gingerly onto the bedroll, shuddering a little as her bare hands made contact with the blankets.

'Can you trust him?' Elyra asked, pillowing her head on her backpack, and relaxing with a sigh.

Kyrlock nodded slowly, seating himself on a crate of tinned food, facing the curtain, and laying the shotgun across his lap. 'I suppose so,' he said, considering it. 'He's a greedy little bastard, so he definitely won't rat us out before we pay him.' He sighed. 'And he is my brother. That still counts for something, even down here.'

ELEVEN

The Tumble, Gorgonid Mine, Sepheris Secundus
097.993.M41

DAWN CAME SLOWLY to the Gorgonid, even out on its fringes, and Keira knew from her earlier stealthy explorations that there were many parts of the vast chasm where it never arrived at all. Now the city above the mine was beginning to glow more brightly, as the rising sun reached the array of reflectors on the highest peaks surrounding it, and the shadows around her were beginning to lighten. In another hour or so the pale disc would climb above the encircling mountains, casting as much illumination as it ever did into these foetid depths, and it would become too much of a risk to move around openly. As if in anticipation of the new day's arrival, the furtive nocturnal activity that had scurried and whispered all around her during the hours of darkness had tapered off in the last hour or so, leaving the shattered landscape curiously quiet.

Aware of the need for concealment, Keira had settled into a small declivity near the crest of a spoil heap with a good view of the entrance to the drinkhole where Elyra and Kyrlock had found refuge. She lay prone, beneath a scrap of canvas as ingrained with the ever-present dust as everything else around here seemed to be, watching the entrance through an amplivisor that Vex had blessed in some fashion so that it was able to function even in pitch darkness, limning the world in muted shades of softly refulgent green.

The smell and the taste of powdered stone was every-where, scratching her eyes, clogging her nostrils, and coating the back of her throat, but she ignored the dis-comfort, considering it a fitting penance for the sin of theft; even one as petty as the robbery she'd commit-ted to protect her makeshift refuge from prying eyes.

When she'd first joined the service of the Inquisition Keira had been profoundly dismayed at the moral com-promises that doing the holy work of Him on Earth so often seemed to demand, the creed of Redemptionism having little room among its tenets for anything other than absolutes. But the more she saw of the galaxy the more she'd come to understand that sometimes the commission of a smaller sin was the unavoidable price of extirpating a much greater one. She had even come to take a quiet pride in her ability to bear the burden of such minor transgressions without giving way to the weakness and corruption they promulgated in less pious souls. Her service to the Emperor conferred some-thing akin to divine sanction on whatever she did, but she still embraced any privations He sent her way as a consequence of these petty misdemeanours.

It was as though He was looking over her shoulder on such occasions, reminding her of His forbearance, and Keira relished the idea that she might have attracted a small fragment of His attention, even for a moment.

Sometimes, however, like this morning, she found herself fretting over her actions, wondering if she'd failed Him in some way, and whether the grittiness in her throat and the hard edges of the rocks beneath her ribs were signs of His displeasure. Maybe she should have killed the truck driver after all.

She'd scavenged the scrap of canvas from an ore lorry she'd found a couple of hours earlier, pulled over next to the highway, in a patch of deep shadow where one of the flaring torches had been extinguished. Certain that Kyrlock and Elyra wouldn't be moving again so close to dawn, she'd slipped away in search of something to secure her hiding place, spotting the truck almost at once through the Omnissiah-blessed lenses. As she'd approached it, keeping to the deepest patches of darkness, slipping silently across the treacherous scree, she'd heard voices, and glanced around the tailgate to make sure the crew's attention was otherwise engaged while she rummaged through the vehicle's external tool locker in search of the material she needed.

As she'd caught sight of the speakers, only her Assassinorum training had prevented an involuntary gasp of horror from escaping her, and possibly betraying her presence. The driver had been arguing with a cloaked and hooded figure, whose body was clearly twisted in a manner far from the true perfection of humanity. Any residual doubts about its identity that Keira might have retained were dispelled almost at once, as she grasped the subject of their conversation. They were haggling over the price of some black market scrabblings from the Shatters, the lowest levels of the mine, where only mutants and renegades dared to go.

Righteous anger welled up in her at the realisation of what she was witnessing, nothing less than a traitor consorting with a mutant for mere squalid profit. Without thinking her hand went to the crossbow at her belt. Within seconds she had a quarrel nocked, the weight of the silent killer heavy in her right hand, and a throwing blade balanced in her left.

Quick and quiet, she told herself. Take the abomination with the bolt, and the man with the knife. The cavalcade of traffic continued to rumble past only a few metres away, and would drown any cries they might make.

Then she hesitated. Disposing of the bodies would be difficult in this wilderness of stone, and leaving them to be discovered was out of the question. Violent death was common enough in the Tumble, and would excite little comment, but it tended to be crude and brutal. The people Elyra and Kyrlock were hoping to infiltrate were far more sophisticated than the average mining serf, and might recognise the fact that these two had been taken out swiftly and cleanly. They might even suspect that such unusual deaths were somehow connected to the new arrivals, which would put the whole operation in jeopardy.

The mission comes first, Keira thought, one of the fundamental tenets her collegium tutors had schooled her in. Everything else is secondary. But letting such cancers in the body of the Imperium live on left a sour taste in her mouth. Resheathing the knife, and loosening the tension in the crossbow string, she prised the lid off the lorry's equipment locker and extricated what she needed.

'All right, five protein packs per tonne,' the driver said, his deal apparently concluded. 'Provided it's as pure as you say, and not mostly shale like the last lot.'

'Iss pure,' the mutant assured him. 'You think uss madmen?' It laughed mirthlessly, a phlegm laden gurgle that made Keira's skin crawl. 'We cheat the Franchisse, no one deal with uss again, everyone sstarve.'

'You cheat the Franchise, you won't live long enough to starve,' the driver said, grinding the stub of a lho stick beneath his heel.

The mutant's shoulders shifted, in what might have been a shrug of resignation. 'We deliver, night after nexsst.'

'Yeah, right,' the driver said, swinging up into the cab. 'Usual place, usual time, five packs per. Make sure you're there, 'cause the shuttle's not waiting.'

Then the engine had roared into life, and Keira had melted back into the darkness, clutching her grubby prize. As she'd anticipated, the patina of dust blended it almost imperceptibly into the pile of rubble, supplementing the more active camouflage of her synsuit, and reducing the possibility of a chance reflection from the lenses of the amplivisor giving her position away. A faint flurry of snow began to fall again, blurring the outline of her sanctuary even more, and she smiled, certain now that she had the Emperor's approval.

Relieved that she'd made the right decision after all, she mulled over the conversation she'd overheard, trying to remember the exact words. She knew that Mordechai would ask for the minutest of details, his detective's mind chewing every last shred of intelligence from the raw data. She felt the familiar warm tingling in the pit of her stomach at the thought of providing fresh information and proving her value to him. He might even drop the supercilious manner long enough to smile at her for once, or say something approving for a change, instead of being such a pompous prig all the time.

'Keira.' Preoccupied with her pleasant reverie, the sudden actuality of his voice in her comm-bead took her completely by surprise. She started guiltily, the irrational thought that he might somehow know she'd been thinking about him making her face flame scarlet, the stones beneath her rattling gently against one another as she moved. 'Are you receiving?'

'Yes,' she replied, a little of her shock and embarrassment leaking into her voice. Maybe he'd take it for simple surprise, since she wasn't supposed to check in again until dawn. 'What's happening?' They were meant to keep comms silence as much as possible, that was standard operating procedure, so something had obviously changed.

'We need you back here,' Mordechai said. 'Can you pull out?'

'Yes,' Keira replied, after a moment's thought. The Tumble was almost deserted, its nocturnal denizens gone, and the spoil tippers and heap scavengers were not due to start work until daybreak. If she moved fast, she could get clear of the mine before too many people were abroad. It would be daylight before she could make it back to her hidden set of glidewings, but they were a common enough sight around Icenholm for her not to attract any attention when she landed at the villa, and she doubted anyone else would be abroad in the foothills to notice her departure. 'What about Elyra and Vos?'

'They'll just have to take care of themselves,' Mordechai said flatly. 'We've got a possible lead, and you're the only one who can follow it.'

The warm glow in Keira's stomach intensified, leaving her breathless for a moment. He needed her, and he'd just admitted it. 'Pulling out now,' she said, trying to keep her voice level, and beginning to stow her kit.

'Are you all right?' Mordechai asked, and she flushed again, her inexplicable embarrassment metamorphosing almost at once into irritation. He thought he was so smart. 'Your voice sounds a little strange.'

'Dust in my throat,' Keira said, worming her way out from under the canvas, and beginning to pick her way cautiously down the side of the spoil heap. A few fresh snowflakes began to fall, and she breathed silent thanks to the Emperor, grateful for their help in blurring her outline. Losing herself in the disciplines of the stalk, she let the strange and unwelcome emotions leak away, until only the predator was left.

ELYRA HAD SLEPT badly, as she'd known she was going to, the discomfort of her injuries and the smell of the bedroll combining to keep her from anything other than a light doze, so when she'd woken for the third or fourth time she'd insisted on changing places with Kyrlock. She'd half expected him to argue, but the former soldier was too pragmatic for any pretence of gallantry, and had taken his turn on the rank blankets with alacrity. Now he was snoring gently, his right hand still on the stock of his shotgun, stirring at every sound beyond the curtain that shielded them from the makeshift bar.

Elyra watched him sleep, sitting on another of the ubiquitous crates, as far as she could get from both the curtain and the rancid slops bucket in the corner. Her pack was on her lap, her hand inside it, grasping the butt of her new laspistol, an identical model to the one she'd given Barda after the shuttle crash. Kyrlock might have been prepared to trust his brother to some extent, but Elyra had been an Inquisition operative for far too long to take anyone's loyalty for granted, with the single exception of Carolus. Horst, Vex and Keira she knew well enough to be reasonably certain of their reliability, although the evident tension between the former arbitrator and the young assassin was a little disquieting, not least because neither of them seemed capable of acknowledging its cause, or doing anything positive about it even if they were. Kyrlock, on the other hand, was an unknown quantity. She trusted Carolus's judgement about bringing him and Drake into the team, but neither of them had proven themselves yet, and the thought that her life might depend on a man she barely knew was hardly a comforting one.

Startled by a faint beeping from inside the rucksack, she flinched, her finger tightening involuntarily on the trigger of her laspistol, and breathed a silent prayer of thanks to the Emperor that she'd left the safety on.

'Elyra,' she said quietly, extricating the personal vox from the bottom of the pack, next to the gun. It was a standard civilian model, quite unremarkable to look at, although Vex had made some careful alterations to its inner workings, ensuring that any transmissions made to or from it would be incomprehensible to anyone else attempting to listen in. Carrying it was a risk, perhaps even more so than the gun. Her assumed identity as a fugitive would at least explain the weapon, but there was no obvious reason for her to be carrying a communications device. After some debate,

Horst had insisted she take it, and claim she'd just packed it from force of habit if anyone challenged her, but she'd only given in because Carolus had left him in charge. Now, it seemed, his insistence was justified.

'It's Mordechai,' he told her, unnecessarily. 'I thought you should know I've just had to pull Keira out.'

'I see.' Elyra kept her voice level, despite the surge of irrational panic that accompanied the words. The thought that the young assassin had been following their every move, watching their backs, prepared to intervene if they got into trouble, had been more comforting than she'd realised. 'Is she coming back?'

'I don't know,' Horst admitted. 'We need her up here, on a new line of enquiry. She's going undercover too, so she might be hard to redeploy in a hurry.'

'Well, nothing's going to happen down here for a while,' Elyra said, taking what comfort she could from that. 'Vos's contact, who turns out to be his brother by the way, doesn't seem to think this fixer he knows will show before it gets dark again. We'll be in touch as soon as we know more.'

'We'll be listening out,' Horst assured her, and broke the link.

'Who was that?' Kyrlock asked, opening his eyes, and yawning as he watched her stow the vox in the bottom of her pack.

'Mordechai,' Elyra said, wondering how he was going to react to the news of their abandonment. 'He's had to reassign Keira. We're on our own, at least for the moment.'

'No change there, then,' Kyrlock said, rolling over and going back to sleep.

* * *

Icenholm, Sepheris Secundus
097.993.M41

'THOSE WERE THEIR exact words?' Horst asked, intrigued. 'They definitely mentioned the Franchise?'

'Yes, both of them. The man, and that thing he was talking to,' Keira said, an edge of revulsion seeping into her tone. She'd arrived back at the villa a few moments before, swooping down onto the terrace like a piece of the night sky made manifest, shrugging her wings off and leaving them for Vex to stow. The conversation she'd overheard seemed to have struck her as particularly significant for some reason, and she'd insisted on recounting it verbatim as soon as she'd got inside. 'Do you know what it means?' She leaned forward eagerly on the overstuffed couch, her synsuit rippling as the kaleidoscope of colours from the stained glass walls played randomly across it.

'Yes.' Horst nodded, trying to ignore the disturbing manner in which the shifting patterns emphasised the curves of her body. 'The Shadow Franchise is a crime syndicate, which operates all over the sector. We didn't know they had an operation going on Sepheris Secundus, but it makes sense. They'd certainly have the contacts and resources to shift black market ore off-planet.'

'How about people?' Keira asked. 'Could they be the ones Elyra and Vos are going after?'

'It's possible,' Horst said, considering it. 'Probable even. We knew whoever was moving them had to have some serious backing, and the Franchise certainly fits the bill.' He nodded judiciously, and smiled at the girl, acknowledging her contribution to the investigation. 'This could turn out to be quite significant.'

'No problem.' An unexpected grin appeared on Keira's face, and Horst found himself wondering if the implied praise, mild as it was, had been a mistake. If she really was infatuated with him, the last thing he needed to do was encourage her.

'Does this change anything?' Drake asked, stifling a yawn, and taking a gulp from the mug of recaf that Horst was beginning to think was permanently grafted to his hand.

Horst shook his head, grateful for the distraction. 'No. We knew we were dealing with a dangerous and well-resourced group to begin with. Keira's given us an indication of which one it might be, which could be useful if we need to follow up off-planet, but the plan remains the same as it always was: get Elyra and Vos into the pipeline, and find out where it goes.'

'And find out if any psykers are along for the ride,' Keira reminded everyone.

'Quite,' Horst said, as diplomatically as he could, and trying to ignore a faint moue of dissatisfaction that flickered across her face at the minor rebuff.

'Shouldn't we tell the Arbites?' Drake asked, depositing the empty mug on a nearby tabletop, with a faint *clack* of glass against glass. He'd gone to bed late, and slept badly, his gamboges silk pyjamas almost as rumpled as his hair, most of his conversation since rising a litany of malediction against overly soft mattresses. 'If this Shadow Franchise is operating in the Gorgonid, they ought to know.'

'No.' Horst shook his head emphatically. 'Not yet, anyway. The last thing we need is a platoon of enforcers charging around down there, disrupting the operation before we can get our people inside. Once Elyra and Vos are in place, and we've got all the evidence we're after, we can send the local headbusters in to roll up the network.'

'Works for me,' Keira said cheerfully, before a faint shadow passed across her face. 'Still can't help wishing I'd sent those two to judgement while I had the chance, though.'

'You did the right thing,' Horst assured her, provoking a spontaneous smile that transformed the sullen mask he was used to seeing in a wholly unexpected fashion. For a brief moment the attraction he felt for her seemed entirely natural, and then the momentary glimpse of the woman she might have been without her violent upbringing faded away into the familiar neutral expression. 'We might never have uncovered the Franchise connection if you hadn't used your initiative.'

'That reminds me,' Keira said, her demeanour entirely businesslike. 'What's this new lead you want me to follow up?'

'You're going to love this,' Drake said as Vex entered the lounge, Keira's glidewings, expertly stowed, hanging from one hand.

Horst wasn't so sure about that, but he nodded anyway. 'Hybris has been constructing a new identity for you,' he said, as the tech-priest propped the wings against a convenient table leg and muttered the prayer of activation over his data-slate.

'Quite a simple task,' Vex assured him, most of his attention still on the pict screen. 'I just had to alter a few property records and some credit files, and plant a few stories in the newsprint archives. If anyone runs a background check, Lady Keira Sythree will appear to be entirely genuine.'

Until she opens her mouth, at least, Horst thought. The rudiments of imposture were standard training at the

Collegium Assassinorum, however, and Drake was familiar enough with aristocratic manners to instruct her in the
basics. They'd just have to hope that any flaws in her per-
formance were put down to her off-world origins. The
Secundan nobility tended to be an insular lot, forced by
the conventions of their feudal society to live within the
domains they administered, and few had even met an
off-worlder face to face, let alone travelled to other planets. That made Tonis's apparent emigration to the Lathes
as a young man even more intriguing.

'You want me to pretend to be a lady?' Keira asked
incredulously.

Horst nodded. 'After you've had a bath, obviously,'
he said, regretting the remark at once, both for the
mental images it provoked and for the filthy look Keira
directed at him in reply.

'I'd like to see you looking vacseal fresh after grub-
bing around in the Tumble all bloody night,' she said.

'See?' Drake interjected with a grin. 'She's talking like
an aristo already.'

'And you can go rut a mutant while you're at it,' Keira
said, completely taken aback by Drake's loud and
spontaneous laugh in response.

'Perhaps this isn't the optimum strategy after all,' Vex
ventured after the briefest of pauses, his carefully modulated tones sounding even more mannered by
contrast. He blinked at Keira in mild perplexity. 'If you
feel the task is beyond you.'

'I never said that.' Keira took a deep breath, and
looked straight at Horst. 'You're right, I do need a bath,
and some sleep.' She glanced sideways at Drake. 'I
didn't mean to jump down your throat, either.'

'That's all right,' Horst said, completely astonished
by her awkward attempt at conciliation, and hiding it

as best he could. 'My remarks were inappropriate. I should apologise to you.'

'Well, if you must.' Keira shrugged, the faint scar below her cheekbone growing more clearly visible as her face coloured. 'What do you want me to do?'

'We'd like you to become her,' Horst said, indicating the pict screen. Keira rose, and crossed the room, pulling up a chair next to Vex for a better view. 'Danuld and I have already seeded the rumour that a noble lady from Scintilla is due to arrive in Icenholm, and I'm afraid you're the closest we've got.' Realising an instant too late how this might sound if she was still determined to take offence, he winced, anticipating another glare, but Keira barely seemed to have heard him, already immersed in the details of her cover story.

'I've falsified credentials for you as a member of the Conclave of the Enlightened's lodge in Ambulon,' Vex said. 'Partly because it's the hive you're most familiar with on Scintilla, and partly because the Conclave lodge there is relatively small and obscure.'

'I see.' Keira nodded slowly. 'So as well as an aristocrat, you want me to pass for an intellectual.' A mischievous grin appeared on her face, and she glanced up at Horst. 'I'm flattered you think I can do it.'

'I wouldn't even have considered this if I didn't,' Horst said, concealing his doubts, and receiving another fleeting smile in return. He kept his own face impassive, and tried to ignore the pang of sympathy he felt at the barely perceptible expression of disappointment that replaced it. This was no time to allow emotions to get in the way of duty.

'What's my area of study?' Keira asked, pointedly addressing the question to Vex.

The tech-priest scrolled down a few lines of text. 'Theosophical poetry, with a particular interest in works produced during the Age of Apostasy. That should establish your credentials as an unconventional thinker.'

'Sounds more like you want me to play at being a heretic,' Keira said, the familiar truculent tone beginning to edge into her voice again, and Horst began to wonder if this was going to work after all. Before he could speak, though, Drake cut in.

'Not exactly,' the Guardsman said, 'but you will be looking for signs of heresy among the people you're infiltrating. If any of them are part of a subversive group, they're more likely to reveal themselves if they think they're talking to someone willing to listen to their lies.'

'Precisely,' Horst said, with a grateful glance in Drake's direction. Keira still seemed to be listening, anyway, rather than rejecting the proposal out of hand as he'd feared she was about to. 'That's why we need someone of unimpeachable faith to do this.' To his relief the girl was nodding slowly, the implied flattery doing its job the way he'd hoped.

'I see,' she said. Then a tone of doubt began to seep into her voice. 'I'm not sure I can pass for an expert in this stuff, though. What happens if some real scholar wants to discuss it with me?'

'Luckily they're pretty thin on the ground,' Vex said. 'Most of the members are dabblers and dilettantes at best, and none of them are particularly interested in that area of literature.' He paged down the screen. 'These are the most well-known titles on the subject; mention them, quote a few lines, and you should be able to bluff your way through a conversation with no real difficulty.' He brought up a fresh page of text. 'These extracts ought to serve for most purposes.'

'It should work, I suppose,' Keira conceded grudgingly. 'And if anyone realises I'm a fake, I can always just kill them.'

'Only if you have to,' Horst said, wondering if she was joking, and more than half convinced that she wasn't.

Keira yawned and stretched, and then clambered to her feet. 'Well, if that's it, I'm off to clean up and get some rest. Sounds like I'm in for a busy day.'

'Probably best,' Horst agreed, trying not to notice the way her synsuit clung to the curve of her buttocks as she left the room.

'What about us?' Drake asked, recalling him to the present. 'We can't go back there. The nobs know we're Inquisition operatives, and the servants think we're lackeys.'

'I know.' Horst nodded in agreement. 'She'll have to go in alone.' Noticing Drake's dubious expression, he smiled reassuringly. 'Don't worry, she can take care of herself.'

'I don't doubt that,' Drake said, 'but what are the rest of us going to do? Just sit on our hands waiting for Vos and Elyra to call?'

'No.' Horst shook his head. 'Hybris has managed to locate Tonis's surviving relatives on Sepheris Secundus. You and I are going to pay them a little visit.'

TWELVE

The Fathomsound Mine, Sepheris Secundus
098.993.M41

FROM THE AIR, the great gash in the earth where the Tonis family clung grimly to their holdings resembled nothing so much as a suppurating wound, the encrusted scabs of waterlogged spoil that surrounded it for kilometres reminding Horst uncomfortably of hardening pus. As Barda banked the shuttle gently to the left, descending slowly towards one of the villas clinging precariously to the lip of the vast chasm, the former arbitrator was able to get his first real view of the pit, and shook his head in bemused surprise.

'I was expecting something like the Gorgonid,' he said. 'Smaller of course, but nothing as weird as this.'

Drake, who occupied the seat next to him, leaned across for a better view. 'The Fathomsound's unique,' he said. 'No one really remembers if the lake's always been there, or if the workings broke through into an underground river one day and the pit flooded, but there's nowhere else like it on Sepheris Secundus.'

Horst could believe that. Instead of the endless turmoil of the pit under Icenholm, which he'd become almost familiar with during his stay in the suspended city, the shadowy crater below them was filled with black water, extending further back beneath the overhanging lip of the workings than it was possible to see from this altitude. Almost in the centre of it, like the misshapen pupil of a dark, malignant eye, a jumble of ramshackle buildings and other structures floated like surface scum. Only as the tiny flecks surrounding it resolved themselves into boats was he able to appreciate the full magnitude of the waterborne slum that the serfs were unfortunate enough to call home. 'How deep is it?' he asked, unable to keep a note of awe from his voice.

'No one knows,' Drake said. 'Deep enough for all kinds of wild stories though.' He shrugged. 'The usual peasant bogeymen. Some of the serfs believe there's a drowned city at the bottom, with Emperor knows what living in the ruins, but the water pressure's too great for anyone to have really got down deep enough to see. Anyone who's got back up again, at any rate.'

'You'd be surprised how many peasant bogeymen you run into in this job,' Horst told him, enjoying the brief expression of discomfiture that crossed Drake's face, before the former Guardsman nodded thoughtfully.

'A week ago I'd have thought you were jerking my chain saying that,' he said, 'but after what we saw at the Citadel…' He broke off, and tilted his head towards the narrow door leading to the shuttle's cockpit. 'Are you sure the flyboy's still keeping his mouth shut?'

'Pretty much,' Horst said, 'and the inquisitor must think he's a low security risk, or he'd never have allowed him back on-planet in the first place.' Nevertheless, he'd kept the young pilot on constant standby since their patron had departed from the system, along with the shuttle Inquisitor Finurbi had requisitioned from Captain Malakai. Barda's superiors in the Guild hadn't argued, and the pilot seemed quite happy with the arrangement, no doubt relieved to have the shield of Inquisitorial service between him and any unfortunate consequences of the loss of his Aquila for as long as possible. 'I noted his cooperation in my last report.'

There was little point in continuing to make them as conscientiously as he had been, since the trading vessel the inquisitor had departed the system aboard didn't have an astropath among its complement, but the habit was a hard one to break, and Horst had already dispatched two comprehensive summaries of their progress so far to their patron, confident that the messages would be waiting for him at the Tricorn as soon as he arrived on Scintilla. He'd also forwarded the results of Captain Malakai's investigation at the Citadel of the Foresaken, which, so far at least, had failed to identify any more traitors and heretics lurking unsuspected among the staff. That was one thing to be thankful for, at any rate.

'We're on our final approach,' Barda's voice informed them, and Horst noted the absence of an honorific with detached amusement. The young man seemed to feel more like an equal now, a part of the inquisitor's warband in his own right rather than a mere hireling, and perhaps that was just as well. If he continued to keep his head, and was willing to leave Sepheris Secundus when the time came, he might offer Barda the chance to come with them when they left. A pilot of his skill would be a valuable asset to the team, especially if Malakai could be persuaded to part with the shuttle on a more permanent basis.

'Acknowledged,' Horst responded crisply, turning his attention to the bleak landscape beyond the armourcrys. One of the villas clinging to the lip of the immense overhang was growing larger in the viewport, and he studied the peculiar structure closely as they approached it. Great chains, each link twice the height of a man, had been attached to bolts almost as large as the Rhino personnel carriers he'd ridden in so often as a newly inducted arbitrator, driven into the cliff face where it protruded out farthest over the dark and sinister waters below. From these, the house depended, built on a platform of thick, rusting metal.

As Barda circled, angling his trajectory towards the shuttle pad at one end, Horst could see that a few of the rivets holding the plates from which it was composed were missing, and a blizzard of brown flakes whirled around them, torn free of the corroding surface by the backwash of their landing thrusters. He turned to Drake. 'Do these things ever fall off?' he asked, trying to sound as if he was joking.

Drake shrugged. 'Not often,' he said, although Horst couldn't be sure quite how serious he was being in return.

'There have only been three such incidents in the past five years,' Vex put in helpfully from the seat behind, 'all in gales of exceptional force.' He craned his head for a better view. 'The structural integrity of this particular residence seems to be adequate, at least for the duration of our visit.'

'Well, that's a relief,' Horst said, and returned his attention to the layout of the villa. As he'd expected, large sections of it displayed the aristocratic fondness for coloured glass that he'd noticed in Icenholm, but other parts of the building were plain, the material used in their construction unclear from this altitude, their surfaces covered in once-garish rainstreaked paint. He pointed it out to Drake, and the Secundan nodded.

'Minor family, small holdings, small tithes. Not much income to spare on tarting the place up.' He turned to glance back at Vex. 'Pretty much what I was expecting, after what you told us about their status.' Then he leaned across Horst again, examining the architecture more closely. 'And it's all old. Nothing new's been added for years.'

'Which means?' Horst asked.

'The less a family like this actually holds, the more ostentatious they try to be,' Drake said. 'If they haven't been glassing those walls over, or adding to the building in some other way, they're either in serious financial trouble or a lot of their resources have been going somewhere else.'

'Any guesses where?' Horst asked.

Drake shrugged. 'You're the detective. If we were back on the web, I'd say casinos, obscura, or joygirls, but out here in the rubble a drawing room harp recital's about as close as you get to a wild evening. Maybe their holdings are just getting worked out, and they're running out of money. It happens.'

'That might explain why their son joined the Mechanicus,' Vex volunteered. 'If the family fortune was all but gone, he would have had very few options to look forward to.'

'Got that right,' Drake agreed. 'When a minor family goes under, it's a feeding frenzy. Their baron seizes anything left worth having, and then the creditors move in. If they're lucky, or bright enough to see it coming, they might get off-planet and disappear, but most of them hold on until it's too late.'

'What happens to them then?' Horst asked, partly from a desire to understand what might be motivating the people they'd come to talk to, and partly out of morbid curiosity.

'That depends,' Drake said. 'Sometimes a relative will take them in, but that hardly ever happens, and there are always strings if they do. Sometimes a good-looking daughter manages to get by in the way you'd expect, and the brighter ones go into service, if they've got any useful skills and they can stand saying "yes, sir," to the sort of people who used to wash their socks. Some join the night life in the Tumble, a few fall all the way to the Shatters, and a lot of them just go nuts. You see them sometimes in the temples, muttering or shouting at people who aren't there, living on handouts from the priests.' He shrugged. 'But most of them just jump.'

'Well, that's interesting,' Vex said, glancing at the screen of his data-slate, before passing it forward for Horst to take a look.

'What is?' Drake asked, most of his attention still on the suspended building. Judging by the way his eyes were flickering from window to window, Horst thought he was probably checking for hidden marksmen or other signs of ambush.

'I set up a vox-link between the slate and the datanet in Icenholm before we left,' Vex explained, 'and I've just found the Tonis family's tithe records for the last few years.'

'They seem to be meeting their obligations to their liege lord all right,' Horst agreed, after a quick glance at the screen. 'If anything, yields from their holdings are slightly up.'

'Then the money's going somewhere it shouldn't,' Drake said flatly.

Trusting his local knowledge, Horst nodded thoughtfully. 'That means we need to find out where,' he said.

'We're down,' Barda's voice informed them unnecessarily, a moment after a faint bump had reverberated through the fuselage. After a short pause, during which the whine of the engines diminished to a whisper, his eager face appeared through the door to the flight deck. 'Anything you'd like me to do while you're gone?'

'Keep the hatches sealed,' Horst told him, acutely aware that the shuttle was their only way off the pendulous mansion. 'Have you still got the laspistol Elyra gave you?'

'Yes.' The young pilot nodded, tensely. 'I've been practising with it, just in case.'

'Good. Keep your vox circuits open, and if we call, get ready for a fast take-off. Be prepared to give us covering fire if you have to, but I'm sure it won't come to that. This is only meant to be a routine questioning, so we shouldn't run into any serious difficulties.'

'Right. Got that.' Barda nodded again. 'Anything else?'

'If you're listening out on the vox anyway,' Vex suggested, 'perhaps you could run a broad frequency scan while you're about it. If anyone here really is involved in the matters we're investigating, they might try to warn a confederate, or ask someone more highly placed in their cell for instructions.'

'Good point,' Horst conceded, and then glanced at Drake and Vex. 'Let's go and meet the grieving relatives, shall we?'

Icenholm, Sepheris Secundus
098.993.M41

KEIRA WOKE INSTANTLY, her hand closing around the hilt of the blade beneath her pillow, and then checked the motion a moment before flinging it into the throat of the servant girl hovering diffidently on the threshold of her bedroom. 'Yes?' she asked, sitting up, and tucking the knife back out of sight before the maid could catch sight of it.

'Sorry to disturb you, your ladyship, but there's a message for you. An answer is required, so I was just looking in to see if you were still asleep.' The girl's gaze flickered down from Keira's face for a moment, and a well-concealed look of surprise came and went as she evidently registered the faint tracery of old scars webbing her torso.

'That's fine, Lilith,' Keira said, quietly pleased with herself for remembering the girl's name. She'd been hired that morning, before the others had left, as Horst thought a lady's maid about the place would add verisimilitude to her pose as an aristocrat. Plump, dark-haired and immaculately groomed, Lilith filled her well-cut but simple grey gown as though it was the height of *haute couture*, and walked with a poise almost as assured as Keira's own, although no doubt this was the result of a very different manner of schooling. Though she concealed it easily, Keira felt a little uncomfortable around the girl. Drake hadn't had time to instruct her in the niceties of patrician behaviour as he'd promised before leaving with the others, and if anyone was likely to see through the imposture it would be a woman used to the presence of genuine nobility. There was no point in worrying about it, though, she'd just have to do the best she could until he got back, and hope that any gaffes she might make would just be put down to her being an off-worlder. 'Could you find me some suitable clothes?'

'Of course, my lady.' Lilith started bustling through the closets, which were stuffed with items Keira didn't recognise. Drake had evidently been busy while she had bathed and rested, slipping easily into his assumed role of majordomo. 'I think something like this might be appropriate.' She extricated a kirtle patterned in violet and blue. 'Goes nicely with that unusual hair colour of yours.' She hesitated. 'If it's not too forward of me to mention it, madam.'

'I don't think so,' Keira said, trying to hide her uneasiness. She'd spent most of her life relating to people either as allies in the never-ending war for the soul of the Imperium, or as enemies of all that was good and holy to be dispatched as swiftly as possible. The girl's deference was subtly unnerving, and she didn't know how she was supposed to react to it. Then inspiration struck. 'I've spent so much time on Scintilla, I've really got no idea what's appropriate here any more.' She moved to the edge of the bed, swung her feet to the floor, and began to slip into her underwear.

'It's a very distinctive look,' Lilith said. 'Half the ladies in Icenholm will be copying it before the season's out, you mark my words.' She picked up a brush from the dressing table, and began to do something to Keira's hair. After a moment the impulse to strike out, snapping the girl's neck, faded, and the strange sensation began to feel quite pleasant. 'There, that's got it a little more tidy.' Lilith stepped back, tilting her head critically to one side. 'Although we'll have to do something about it properly later on. I don't know what your last attendant was thinking of, letting it get into that state.'

'Quite,' Keira agreed, tugging the dress on, relieved to discover that Drake had made sure it was sufficiently loose for her to fight in if she had to, despite a superfluity of lace and an excessive amount of embroidery. 'Just so long as I look respectable enough to receive a message.'

'Oh, you do that, my lady.' Lilith smoothed a few creases, and handed her a pair of slippers encrusted with garish beadwork butterflies, into which Keira slipped her feet.

The messenger was waiting for her in the villa's main reception room, an earnest young man in a livery Keira recognised at once from the briefing materials Vex had left for her to digest. There was no reason why the woman she was pretending to be would be able to distinguish it from the household colours of any other Secundan noble family, however, so she kept her face impassive as she entered the room.

'You have a message for me, I'm told,' she said, inclining her head quizzically.

The young man bowed deeply. 'From my master, the Viscount Adrin,' he declaimed, in a voice as clear and resonant as a cathedral chorister chanting the responses. 'To the right noble Lady Keira Sythree, his most humble greetings, and the welcome due a fellow scholar of the Conclave of the Enlightened. Should the noble lady find such a prospect agreeable, my master has the honour to propose a meeting at the Lodge of the Golden Wing, two hours past the setting of the sun, to confer upon her all due rights and privileges of access to their archives, and perhaps discourse a little upon matters of the intellect.' He paused, inhaled, and looked at her expectantly. After a short silence, during which Keira wondered if she was supposed to respond yet, or if he was merely catching his breath, he asked 'How say you?' in the tone of a playhouse minion giving a prompt.

Keira shrugged. 'Might as well,' she said. 'I've nothing else planned.'

The messenger raised an eyebrow. 'That is the substance of your reply, my lady?'

'It is.' Keira nodded. 'Does it sound ambiguous in any way?'

'No, my lady, both clear and succinct.' The young man cleared his throat. 'And this is the message you wish me to convey, verbatim?'

'If that's the usual procedure, I suppose so,' Keira said, beginning to feel irritated by the pointless formality. 'I'm afraid I'm rather new to all this. On Scintilla we have voxes.'

'Voxes. Quite.' The messenger made a slightly strangulated sound behind his floppy lace collar. Then he bowed deeply from the waist. 'By your leave, my lady.'

'By all means.' Keira turned towards the door, inexpressibly relieved to see her lady's maid hovering there. 'Lilith will show you out.'

Once she was sure she was alone, she vented her feelings by flicking a couple of the sofa cushions into the air with her toe, punching one across the room before it fell, and dispatching the other to the terrace with a spinning back kick. If Mordechai had known in advance what he was letting her in for with this warp

brained scheme of his, she vowed, she'd... she'd...
Well, she wasn't quite sure what she'd do to get back at
him, but she'd certainly take her time about it.

The Fathomsound Mine, Sepheris Secundus
098.993.M41

HORST STRODE BRISKLY along the main corridor of the
hanging mansion, Drake and Vex flanking him, his
Inquisition rosette clearing a path through the household servants as effectively as a flamer through a
snowdrift. Someone must have warned its owners of
their approach, though, because neither betrayed the
slightest surprise as the trio of Angelae threw open the
ornate double doors at the end of the passageway.

The room beyond was opulent, more so than Horst
had expected, given Drake's appraisal of the mansion's
exterior, boasting the usual excesses of glass sculpture
and soft furnishings, and he made a mental note to ask
his colleague at the earliest opportunity if he'd noticed
anything out of the ordinary. Not for the first time he
gave silent thanks to the Emperor for the inquisitor's
foresight in adding Drake to the team.

'I'm afraid you've come at a rather inconvenient
time,' the Lady Tonis said coldly, looking at the three
men who had dared to invade her drawing room as
though they'd just belched in the middle of a dinner
party. She looked about thirty, but Horst knew from
the records Vex had obtained that her appearance was
the result of extensive juvenat treatments, and that her
real age was well over twice that. Her husband had
apparently opted to freeze the ravages of time a decade
or so later than his wife, allowing enough grey to seep
into his hair to impart an air of maturity and wisdom,

and his face was still pallid with grief, making it look closer to his real age than his assumed one. Both were dressed in the formal oranges and yellows of mourning affected by the Secundan nobility. Drake had explained that the colours were supposed to reflect the flames of a funeral pyre, although in the case of the late Technomancer there had hardly been enough left to burn. 'We've just returned from our son's funeral, and we're expecting the ecclesiarch to arrive for the vigil of mourning at any moment.'

Determined not to repeat the mistake he'd made with the secretary of the Conclave in Icenholm, inadvertently undermining his authority by addressing him politely, Horst merely nodded briskly in response. 'Then we'll do our best not to detain you any longer than necessary, but you must realise this is an important part of our investigation.'

'Very well, then,' Lord Tonis said, in tones of resignation, 'but I don't see why you found it necessary to come all this way just to ask us a few questions.'

'Your son was a faithful servant of the Imperium,' Horst said, 'and the manner of his death is disturbing. That alone justifies the interest of the Inquisition.'

'Disturbing how?' Lady Tonis asked, exchanging an involuntary sideways glance with her husband. Horst's investigative instincts were aroused. He was sure they knew something about their son, some secret they were keeping between them.

'His mortal remains showed signs of daemonic possession,' Horst said bluntly, hoping to shock them into some further betrayal, but both aristocrats had regained their composure, merely paling at his words in the manner most pious citizens would on hearing the most feared denizens of the warp referred to so casually.

'Impossible,' Lord Tonis said flatly, making the sign of the aquila regardless. 'Our son was a faithful follower of the Omnissiah. You must have made some kind of mistake.'

'That's always possible,' Vex said, his carefully modulated tone cutting through the awkward silence that followed, 'but as yet we have found no alternative explanation.'

'The thing is,' Drake said, still leaning against the doorframe, where he was able to keep an eye both on the room and the corridor outside in case any of the household staff attempted to eavesdrop or interfere, 'that sort of thing usually happens to psykers, not cogboys.' He glanced apologetically at Vex as he used the mildly disparaging nickname for tech-priests, but his colleague, conscious of the part Drake was playing, seemed unperturbed by the insult. Horst noted the slip, but Lord and Lady Tonis appeared not to have, gaining the impression they were supposed to of an ill-mannered thug held barely in check by his superior.

'Quite true,' Vex said. 'Offhand, I can think of no other case where an acolyte of the Omnissiah was so afflicted.'

'There you are, then,' Lady Tonis said waspishly. 'You're digging out the wrong seam, and there's an end of it.'

'There's no end of it until the Ordo Calixis declares so,' Horst said. 'At the moment this matter has been delegated to my colleagues and I, but if you prefer to discuss it with an inquisitor in person, we can arrange a meeting quite easily.'

'That won't be necessary,' Lord Tonis said wearily.

His wife glared at him. 'Harald,' she said, her tone admonishing.

'What's the point?' Lord Tonis said. 'The boy's dead. There's nothing they can do to him now.'

'Why would we want to?' Drake asked bluntly.

'Because he was a psyker,' Lady Tonis snapped. 'Satisfied?'

'Not really, no,' Horst said. 'He was working in an environment where such a curse would have been immediately apparent, and he had been carefully assessed by the Inquisition before being assigned. No such taint was discovered at either stage.'

'Then it worked!' Lord Tonis said, glancing at his wife.

'Evidently not well enough,' Drake said, 'whatever it was. But you've just admitted to harbouring a psyker, which is good enough for me.' He glanced at Horst. 'Shall we take them in? The Arbites at the Isolarium can hold on to them until the boss gets back, or we can bring in an interrogator from Scintilla.'

'That might not be necessary,' Horst said, watching the last vestiges of aristocratic arrogance draining from their unwilling hosts as the full realisation of the power behind them began to sink in. He leaned forward a little in his overstuffed chair, his posture one of polite attention. 'If you could explain from the beginning?'

'Gilden was cursed,' Lord Tonis said. 'Not that we realised at first, but when he got to his early teens, things started to happen. Small objects would seem to move around on their own, stuff like that.'

'I'm surprised you noticed,' Drake said sardonically, and Horst motioned him to silence. The constant movement of the hanging house was disconcerting, like being on a boat in a slow, steady swell, and the last thing his sensitive inner ear needed was another reminder of the fact. The short suborbital hop from Icenholm had been bad enough.

'A hard secret to keep,' Horst said, hoping to prompt them to continue, and distract himself from the vague feeling of nausea in the pit of his stomach.

'You have no idea,' Lady Tonis said, her tone still brittle, but mingled with the kind of relief Horst had heard many times before in the interrogation suite of a precinct house when some petty felon eventually decided to stop lying and begin to unburden his conscience. 'Servants gossip so, and we hardly dared to see anyone in case they noticed something untoward. Our social lives were in tatters. We were at our wits' end.'

'You should have gone to the appropriate authorities,' Horst said. 'Had him tested and rated.'

'And then what?' The woman looked at him with cold contempt. 'Hand him over to be penned up somewhere with the other freaks, waiting to be taken away by the Black Ships?'

'It was your duty as citizens of the Imperium,' Horst said.

Lord Tonis sighed heavily. 'Some things are stronger than duty,' he said. 'I don't expect you to understand, but if you ever find yourself with a child, a family, perhaps you might.'

'Perhaps,' Horst said, feeling an unexpected pang of regret at the thought as he spoke, 'but that's hardly likely.'

'Then I'm sorry for you,' the old man said, sounding as though he really meant it.

'I assume that the Church of the Omnissiah offered an alternative course of action,' Vex said, his voice as level as ever, 'but I must admit to wondering how, precisely.'

'We had a visitor from the Adeptus Mechanicus,' Lord Tonis said. 'A magos from the Lathes, looking for some highly specific materials. We were able to accommodate him, although they were difficult to obtain.'

'No other holding in the Fathomsound could do it,' his wife added, with an element of pride.

'Quite so,' Lord Tonis confirmed, before continuing. 'The extraction took some time, and despite the obvious risks, we felt obliged to offer him the hospitality of our house.'

'I presume he noticed something,' Horst said, hoping to nudge him a bit closer to the point.

'He did.' The Tonis patriarch nodded. 'He was right in the room with us when Gilden's curse manifested, and a flower vase started spinning in the middle of the table.'

'We thought he'd panic,' Lady Tonis put in, 'but he didn't. He just said it was interesting.'

'If he was of sufficient standing in the light of the Omnissiah,' Vex said thoughtfully, 'he probably had an augmented cerebellum. That would have precluded an emotional reaction.' His eyes unfocused for a moment, as he recalled something. 'Technomancer Tonis was similarly blessed.'

'Yes.' Lord Tonis nodded. 'Magos Avia suggested that a similar enhancement might save Gilden, by replacing the organic parts of his brain where the taint resided with augmetic cogitators, and we were desperate enough to try it.'

'Such blessings are reserved for the Omnissiah's anointed,' Vex said, sounding either disapproving or envious, Horst wasn't sure which. Perhaps it was a mixture of both.

'Which is why he became a tech-priest,' Drake said.

'That's right.' Lady Tonis slumped in her chair, the body language of a woman her true age superimposed grotesquely on her artificially youthful frame. 'When Avia returned to the Lathes, Gilden went with him, and that was the last we ever saw of our son.'

'That's not true, though, is it?' Horst said. 'He returned to Sepheris Secundus twelve years ago. You must have had some contact with him in all that time.'

'We saw Technomancer Tonis,' the woman said, 'a half-mechanical parody of a man. But there was nothing left of Gilden, except for a few old memories that meant nothing to him. He came to the mine a few times to reopen Avia's excavations and do some work down there, but after his first visit we avoided one another. Harald and I found it too painful, and he seemed to find our emotional displays...' she groped for the right word, '...distasteful.'

'Do you know what he was doing in the mine?' Horst asked.

Lord Tonis shook his head. 'Not a clue. The seams down there were worked out years ago. We offered him all the serfs he needed, but he declined, saying he preferred to use servitors. He brought them in and out himself, in an old cargo lifter.'

'One final question, if you don't mind.' Horst glanced at his chronograph, reminding the couple that they had an appointment, and that whether or not they got to keep it was entirely up to him. 'Who's been blackmailing you?'

'Who do you think?' the woman asked, not even bothering to deny it. 'Avia, of course. He had to bend a lot of rules to get Gilden treated quickly enough. That cost a lot of credits, and a damn sight more to keep him quiet about what he'd done afterwards.' She smiled bitterly. 'At least that stops now. The Inquisition knows what we did, so he hasn't got a hold on us any more.'

'That raises the question of what you're going to do about it,' Lord Tonis said quietly.

Horst shrugged. 'Harbouring a psyker is both treason and heresy,' he said, twitching his coat aside to reveal the bolt pistol in its shoulder rig. The two aristocrats stared at him, plainly terrified, and trying not to show it. 'If it was up to me I'd shoot the pair of you right now, but my patron inquisitor may want to question you further. Consider yourselves under house arrest until you hear from us again or the Arbites arrive to take you into custody.' He turned to Drake and Vex. 'Come on. We've other matters to attend to.'

'One thing still intrigues me,' Vex said, pausing in the doorway. 'Your son's remains have already been disposed of according to the rites of the Church of the Omnissiah. Why are you having a second funeral?'

'Because we're not members of your heartless cult, and our son is dead,' Lady Tonis said bitterly.

'And because funerals aren't for the dead,' her husband added, taking her hand, 'they're for the living. But I don't suppose you'll ever understand that.'

'Probably not,' Vex agreed, following his colleagues out.

'WHY DIDN'T WE just take them in?' Drake asked, as they left the mansion and began to walk across the shuttle pad, his bootsoles ringing on the riveted metal surface. The wind was keen, making his coat flap like a banner, and threatening to nudge him off his feet.

Horst shrugged. 'People start asking questions about where they've gone and the next thing you know every lowlife on the planet's running for cover screaming that the Inquisition's coming, which klyboes Elyra and Vos's operation. They'll keep until we've dug out the traitors we're really after.'

'If you say so.' Drake shrugged too, clearly far from convinced. 'You've been doing this a lot longer than I have.'

'Some aspects of their story still strike me as anomalous,' Vex said. 'Like this Magos Avia. If he really exists, and agreed to nullify Tonis's psychic abilities, why engage in prolonged blackmail afterwards? Acolytes of the Omnissiah have no need of money, the church provides everything they require.'

'I wondered about that too,' Drake said, raising his voice a little as a second shuttle began circling the pad, waiting for theirs to make way for it. 'I think we should take a look down this hole of his.'

'My thoughts exactly,' Horst said, tapping his comm-bead. 'Barda, are you ready to lift?'

'As soon as you're aboard,' the young pilot confirmed, 'and I'm getting a transmission from Icenholm. Patching it through.'

'Mordechai?' Keira said in his ear a moment later. 'This warp-brained idea of yours has just gone klybo. Adrin's made contact already, and he wants to meet me tonight. No way I'm passing for an inbred parasite that soon without some serious coaching.'

'Fine.' Horst thought rapidly. 'Don't panic. I'm sending Danuld straight back with Barda, as soon as they've dropped Hybris and me at the mine. The two of you should be able to nail your cover story before this evening.'

'We'd better, or I'm just going to have to kill everyone in the room and let the Emperor sort them out.'

Keira paused for a second. 'And for your information, I am *not* panicking!' The channel went dead before he could muster a reply.

Horst turned to face Drake. 'Did you get that?'

'I did.' Drake nodded sombrely, a hint of amusement in his eyes. 'You want me to go back to the villa and teach Keira how to be a lady, while you and Hybris go looking for Emperor knows what at the bottom of a shaft used by a daemon-possessed tech-priest in a mine that's supposed to be haunted.'

'That's about the size of it, yes,' Horst said. 'Any other questions?'

Drake nodded again. 'Any chance you'd consider swapping?' he asked.

THIRTEEN

'THERE THEY GO,' Horst said, completely superfluously so far as Vex was concerned, as the shuttle rose from the landing pad at one end of the gently rocking raft. The tech-priest nodded nonetheless, recognising the phrase as just another example of the redundant input most of the unaugmented seemed to rely on for reassurance in times of stress.

'Almost three minutes ahead of my most probable estimate,' he agreed instead, watching the bright flare of the shuttle's afterburners ignite like a flaming star against the overarching darkness of the cavern roof a kilometre or more above their heads. 'We seem to have been most fortunate in our choice of pilot.' Few others he had met would have been sufficiently attuned to the mood of the shuttle's machine-spirit to have risked invoking the extra thrust until it had risen above the lip of the hole in the roof through which they had descended into the depths of the Fathomsound, dropping almost vertically downwards from the dangling house invisibly far above them. Barda had judged the manoeuvre to a nicety, and as they watched, the pinprick of light elongated to a streak, bouncing up and out through the ragged circle of grey sky in the stygian blackness above.

'He shows promise,' Horst agreed, the matter clearly of little interest to him at the moment. His face was pale in the light of the luminators scattered around the deck of the mining platform, the faint pallor no doubt a result of his unfortunate propensity to motion sickness. He glanced around at their surroundings with evident distaste. 'Guess this must be the way.'

Without waiting for a reply, he set off across the gently rocking surface of the landing dock towards a handful of ramshackle buildings, apparently erected from whatever materials had happened to come to hand in the course of the job. Even in the half-light, Vex was able to make out flakboard, crudely sawn planking and cretecast slabs, and that had just been in the walls of the nearest structure, a two-storey edifice illuminated by a few flickering electrosconces hanging from brackets below the roofline. It was the largest and most impressive of the buildings, and the tech-priest was hardly surprised to see a heavyset man in drab clothing hurrying down a ramshackle staircase that leaned against its patchwork wall like a drunk clinging to a pillar for support, apparently intent on greeting them.

Estimating that they still had several seconds before conversation could be initiated, Vex looked beyond the platform, absorbing as much as he could of the subterranean world they'd landed in. The scale of it was truly impressive. The vast hole in the roof through which they'd descended covered no more than two thirds of the sinister black lake, the far shore of which was lost in the gloom of the other side, so that from here the dark waters seemed to recede into infinity. Faint pinpricks of light speckled the distant walls, turning them into a miniature starscape, where the ostracised or the desperate scrabbled for specks of usable material, although the seams above the surface had been worked out generations before. The only minerals worth the effort of recovering lay far beneath the waters of the buried lake.

That was the business of the platform they were standing on. Hundreds like it bobbed all around the edges of the tarn, where the water was still shallow enough for their anchor cables to find a purchase. Further out there was nothing, except the sprawling, dilapidated floating town the locals called the Flotsam, its boundaries changing incrementally every day as another pontoon edged hopefully outwards, or was swept away by bad weather or malign currents. In really bad weather, like the winter blizzards, the entire habitat would stir with the choppy water, complete neighbourhoods sometimes vanishing overnight, to be replaced piecemeal as their waterlogged construction materials were fished out over the weeks that followed.

Vex gathered that the bodies of the drowned were so frequent a sight that the locals barely noticed them, not even bothering to recover the unfortunate victims of the lake unless their clothing or personal effects seemed obviously worth the effort, or a putrefying corpse had got entangled with the infrastructure somewhere the nearby residents found the stench of its decomposition too much to bear.

Innumerable watercraft were scudding to and fro around the gargantuan raft, propelled by sails for the most part, and he nodded thoughtfully. Whether or not the leviathans of legend that Drake had referred to really existed, something he was inclined to doubt, but couldn't dismiss entirely given some of the bizarre sights he'd seen since joining the Angelae Carolus, there were clearly sufficient fish in the murky water to keep the peasantry fed.

The few mechanically propelled vessels he could make out in the encircling gloom were considerably larger than the sailing ones, flat-bottomed mineral barges for the most part, wreathed in acrid smoke or farting the unmistakable tang of burned promethium. They chugged along with sublime disregard for anything else on the water, scattering the fishing boats ahead of them like a nobleman's bodyguard shouldering the peasantry aside in a crowded street.

'My lords.' The man he'd noticed hurrying down the staircase was standing before them now, a faint sheen of sweat turning the patina of grime across his face into greasy mud as he goggled at Horst's Inquisition sigil with undisguised fear. As the arbitrator snapped the rosette's case closed, and returned it to his pocket, the man's eyes continued to follow it as though hypnotised. 'How may I be permitted to serve you?'

'That rather depends on who you are,' Horst said, and the man nodded weakly.

'Phyron, my lord. Supervisor of Mineral Recovery for this platform.' A faint inflection of pride was still audible in the man's voice, Vex noticed, even through his understandable apprehension. In the hierarchy of serfdom, he was clearly a man of considerable stature.

'Then I'm sure you can be of assistance,' Vex said calmly, noting that Phyron's expression barely changed as his gaze moved from Horst's pocket to acknowledge his presence. That was unusual. Most of the unaugmented tended to look a trifle uneasy the first time they encountered a tech-priest, so it seemed reasonable to infer that this man had had dealings with Tonis on his periodic visits to the mine. 'We wish to inspect the workings you maintain here on behalf of the Adeptus Mechanicus.'

'Of course, my lords.' Phyron licked his lips nervously, torn between his fear of the authority the Inquisitorial agents represented and the legacy of generations of unquestioning loyalty to his feudal masters. 'But you must understand that it may not be safe down there. Technomancer Tonis was always very insistent that no one went into the shaft without him.'

'Your concern has been noted,' Horst said, in a tone that brooked no argument, and the supervisor nodded unhappily.

'Then I'll take you down myself,' he said, turning and leading the way towards a crane at the end of the platform, its boom jutting out over the turbid water. 'The shift's just finishing on number three, so the bell should be up again directly.'

'The bell?' Horst asked, dropping his voice a little, so only Vex could hear him clearly. 'What's he talking about?'

'That, I would imagine,' Vex said, indicating the point at which a tangle of cables and hoses entered the water. A large bubble rose to the surface, followed by another. A moment later the point below the derrick was a mass of churning froth. The note of the crane's engine changed, taking a greater strain as its burden lost the supporting buoyancy of the water.

'Golden throne!' Horst said, impressed in spite of himself. Uplifted by such a powerful display of the Omnissiah's bounty, Vex could only nod in agreement. A curving metal shell was beginning to break the surface, its exterior pitted with corrosion and tangled with water weeds. As the crane continued to take more of its weight, the note of its promethium-burning engine rising in pitch like a hymn of praise to the Machine-God, the enraptured tech-priest was able to take in the full glory of the construction that it was supporting. Riveted metal plates formed a rounded hull the size of a standard cargo container, the runes and sigils of protection against water and pressure applied to it still legible despite considerable weathering and wear.

Within moments the metal shell was clear of the lake, and a crew of serfs hurried to a windlass set in the decking, running around it with the unthinking precision conferred by years of repetition. With a grinding of ungreased cogwheels, which set Vex's teeth on edge, the crane began to slew, bringing its precious cargo inboard. As it did so, a thick hatch in the bell's outer hull began to open, pushed from the other side.

The crane operator slackened the cable off, and with a grinding crash that rocked the entire pontoon the diving bell met the deck almost exactly in the centre of a shallow depression hammered into the rusting metal surface by innumerable such impacts over the years. Abandoning the windlass, the deck crew ran out a ramp, which butted up against the lip of the hatch.

'Best stand back a little, my lords,' Phyron advised as the crew began to disembark, shambling down the incline like barely animate creatures, reminding Vex uncomfortably of the plague zombies they'd faced in the outer layers of Hive Tarsus a couple of years before. All were blank-eyed with exhaustion, caked with mud and dust, their shabby clothing hanging from them like sloughing skins. They lined up, wordlessly, while the deck crew trotted inside the diving bell. A moment later the men reappeared, pushing wheeled skips piled with ore down the ramp, holding them back as gravity began to overcome inertia on the gentle slope. Each truck had a name painted on the side of it, next to a crude pictogram so that the miner it belonged to could pick it out from its fellows.

Leaving his unwanted guests, with a couple of apprehensive glances in their direction as though half expecting to be called to heel, Phyron walked over to a large counterweighted slab level with the deck, onto which the first ore skip was wheeled by its attendants. A mechanical arm swung lazily against a notched wooden board as the platform sank, recording the weight of the ore it contained, and Phyron reached into a pouch on his belt, counting out a few dull metal tokens.

'Ennis,' he called, and one of the miners shambled forward, accepting the handful of tallies. From his extensive reading on the subject of the internal workings of the Secundan mines, Vex recalled that at the end of the month the workers would be able to exchange the tokens they received for food and other supplies shipped in by their liege lords, perhaps even a real coin or two. The miner slurred some routine formula of insincere gratitude, tugged his forelock, and got back in line. 'Garver.' The ritual was repeated several times, each weighed skip being wheeled away to a storage shed as soon as its contents were assayed. No

sooner had they delivered one to the stockpile, empty-
ing its contents into an echoing metal bin, than the
deckhands returned to the diving bell for another.

'Now that's interesting,' Horst murmured, pointing
to a skip that had just begun its journey down the
ramp. Unlike the others it was only half full, and its
owner lay unmoving on the heap of rubble it contained. 'Foul play, do you suppose?'

'I doubt it,' Vex replied, *sotto voce*. 'There are dozens
of fatal accidents a day in every mine on Sepheris
Secundus. I imagine this one was unexceptional.'

'Magger.' Phyron looked up from the name on the
truck, registering the corpse it contained for the first
time. 'What happened?'

'Rockfall,' Ennis said, shrugging.

That sounded plausible to Vex. From where he was
standing, the dead miner looked as though he'd sustained severe blunt trauma to the head, and his torso was
mottled with bruises. In any event, Phyron didn't seem
particularly concerned, merely motioning the nearest of
the deckhands towards the skip. Two of them heaved the
corpse out of it, and away from the weighplate. The
pointer shifted a notch as the additional burden was
removed, and the supervisor grunted approval.

'That's better. He was dumb as a rock, but a lot less
valuable.' None of the miners stirred as their erstwhile
companion disappeared over the side of the raft with a
faint splash. Phyron counted out a few tokens. 'Anyone
know his family?'

'Ent got one,' Garver volunteered after a moment of
silence. 'Swept off the Flotsam last blow but one,
weren't they?'

'Tha's right,' someone else said. 'Long of Scobie's lot,
bairns an' all.'

'Fine.' Phyron slipped two of the tokens into his pocket, and held out the rest. 'That's one more apiece then. He doesn't need it any more, and I'm sure you'd like a drink in his memory.'

'Well said, guvnor.' Ennis took the handful of copper, watched intently by the eyes of his workmates. 'We always says there's no finer gentleman on the water you could hope to work for than Mister Phyron, doesn't we lads?'

'Aye, right, happen we do.' The chorus of assent sounded distinctly insincere to Vex, but Phyron appeared to take it at face value, nodding judicially, with a sideways glance towards the Inquisition agents to make sure his fairness and probity were being properly noted.

After the task of weighing the day's delvings had been completed, and the surviving miners had shuffled off towards the boat waiting to return them to the dubious comforts of the Flotsam, the supervisor gestured towards the diving bell. 'Ready when you are, my lords,' he said.

The Tumble, Gorgonid Mine, Sepheris Secundus 098.993.M41

'WHAT DO YOU want?' Kyrlock asked, as Mung twitched the grubby curtain aside and stuck his head into the room behind the drinkhole. The bartender shrugged.

'Just wondered if you were getting hungry, that's all.' He grinned insincerely, with a nod at Elyra. 'Not interrupting anything, am I?'

'No,' Kyrlock said shortly, irritated at the insinuation. His mood had been growing ever more sullen as the day had worn on, the tedium of their enforced confinement growing on him with every passing hour. If something didn't happen soon, he thought, he'd have to go back into the taproom and pick a fight just to relieve the monotony. Only the reflection that doing so would be really stupid, possibly compromising their mission, had restrained him so far; that, and the fact that until night fell and the customers started to arrive there would be no one to pick on but Mung. He had no objection in principle to beating up his brother, but the scrawny little bartender was hardly a challenge, and they needed his help in any case. So, deprived of the solace of cathartic violence he fell back on brooding instead.

Elyra hadn't been much of a companion either. Reluctant to talk about herself, or any of the other Angelae, in case Mung overheard something that cast doubt on their cover story, she'd spent most of the day meditating, or whatever the psyker equivalent of press-ups was, staring into space with a vacant expression that made Kyrlock feel as though something small with too many legs was running up and down his spine.

The trouble was, he felt trapped. He hadn't asked to join the Inquisition, any more than he'd wanted to join the Imperial Guard. All his life, other people had been telling him what to do, and now he'd seen for himself that there were alternatives he was beginning to grow sick of it. At least as a forester he'd been left alone for most of the time, able to slip through a few of the cracks in the feudal system, albeit not quite as successfully as his brother had done, reliant on no one else, and with no responsibilities beyond turning in enough raw timber to at least look as though he was meeting his obligations to the baron. Now Horst and the others expected things of him, and momentous consequences he barely understood apparently hinged on the decisions he'd have to make over the coming days and weeks.

Maybe he should get out while he could, just walk away and leave them to it, go and hide out in the Breaks like he'd been pretending to when he repeated his cover story to Mung. But that would leave Danuld with no one to watch his back if it all went klybo, which he was morbidly certain would only be a matter of time, and how could anyone hope to outrun the Inquisition anyway?

'I could do with something to eat,' Elyra said. Her injuries were healing a little, her movements slightly less stiff than they had been, but half her face was still covered by a livid purple bruise.

'Then you're in luck.' Mung came fully into the room, a sack across one shoulder, the familiar ingratiating grin still plastered to his face. 'I managed to bag a couple of rockrats, enough for stew.' Apparently misinterpreting the expression that crossed the psyker's countenance, he added, 'No extra charge.'

'Very generous,' Kyrlock said flatly. There was no denying he was hungry too, and the food they'd brought with them would last a lot longer if they accepted Mung's hospitality, but he was in no hurry to taste the rank meat of the rockrats again. One thing about being in the Guard that he'd quickly learned to appreciate was food that was actually palatable.

'No problem.' Mung rummaged on a shelf in the corner, finding a large knife with a stained and rusting blade, and sat on a nearby crate, producing a rodent the length of his forearm from the sack that he'd dumped on the floor between his feet. Still chatting happily he slit its belly open, flung a handful of guts in the general direction of the slops bucket, and began to skin it. 'More than enough of 'em to go around.'

'How did you manage to catch it?' Elyra asked, trying not to look, and Kyrlock felt a flash of surprise that a hardened Inquisition agent could be so squeamish about something so minor. 'We would have heard shooting, even buried away down here.'

'So would the overseers,' Mung said, looking up just long enough to grin at her, before decapitating the rat and beginning to joint it. 'Besides, guns need ammo, which costs, even if you can get hold of one in the first place.' An expression of sly knowingness slithered across his features. 'Not saying I couldn't lay hands on one myself if I needed it, mind, or for anyone else who asked, if the price was right.'

'I've got a gun,' Kyrlock said shortly, his hand still on the stock.

Mung nodded appraisingly. 'So I see, nice piece. I won't ask who lost it, 'cos I know you won't tell me.' He shrugged. 'If you need any shells for it, I can ask around.'

'I've got enough,' Kyrlock said. He'd forgotten just how much his brother could run off at the mouth given the opportunity, and began to wonder if coming here had been such a smart move after all. But the man he wanted to see used to be a regular in Mung's place, and apparently still was. Finding him anywhere else in the Tumble would have taken far longer, and left them dangerously exposed while they searched.

Mung shrugged, and began to work on the second rat. 'Suit yourself, Vos. Offer's there, that's all.'

'If you didn't shoot them, what did you use?' Elyra asked. 'Snares?'

By way of an answer, Mung put down the knife and the half-dissected rodent, and pulled something from his belt. 'This.' He handed the Y-shaped piece of laminate to her with a hint of diffident pride. 'Made it myself.'

'A slingshot?' Elyra asked in surprise, taking the crude stonethrower, and checking the tension of the elastic cord by pulling on the neatly sewn leather cup in the centre of the line. 'I haven't seen one of these in a long time.' Then to Kyrlock's surprise, a nostalgic smile appeared on her face. 'I used to have one when I was a girl. Not as good as this, though, and I was never very accurate with it.'

'You have to have the knack,' Mung agreed. 'But once you've got it, you don't lose it.' Remembering the number of long-range snowballs that had hit him in the face while they were growing up together, Kyrlock didn't doubt that. 'And there's always enough ammunition in a place like the Tumble, just lying around at your feet.' He stood, scooping up the jointed meat, and leaving the skins where they'd fallen. 'I'll let you know when it's cooked.'

'Your brother has hidden depths,' Elyra said, once the curtain had swung closed behind him.

Kyrlock shrugged, obscurely irritated by her apparent approval. 'Oh, definitely,' he said. 'And most of them better left buried, if you ask me.'

Icenholm, Sepheris Secundus
098.993.M41

'You LOOK AMAZING,' Drake said, unable to stop himself, as Keira entered the drawing room of the villa. To his surprise she smiled back, acknowledging the compliment, and turned slowly on the spot for his inspection.

'Well, I look the part at any rate,' she conceded.

Drake nodded his agreement. 'You'd turn heads in any salon in the hive,' he said, quite truthfully. Lilith had evidently been working some alchemy peculiar to ladies' maids in his absence, changing the young assassin's appearance in some subtle fashion he couldn't quite put his finger on, but wholeheartedly approved of. Her hair seemed fuller, framing her face in an artfully flattering manner, and carefully applied make-up smoothed her complexion, hiding the faint scars on her face. Her gown was low-cut, revealing just enough to hint at a great deal more, pale green threads worked through the white satin to create an effect like the first shoots of spring through an undisturbed snowfield, subtly echoing the colour of her eyes.

'Yes. Well.' Keira coughed, looking mildly embarrassed. 'When you've quite finished staring at my body, maybe we ought to get on. Adrin's expecting me in a couple of hours, don't forget.'

'I wasn't...' Drake began, before realising that he had been, and shrugging apologetically. 'Sorry. It's just been a long time since I've seen a woman quite so worth staring at.'

'You shouldn't say things like that,' Keira said, her face and intonation hardening abruptly, and Drake belatedly remembered that she belonged to some puritanical cult that probably thought flirting with someone was the fast road to hell. Now he came to think about it, that was a real shame, not to mention a waste.

'I'm sorry if I offended you,' he said, as diplomatically as he could. 'I just meant that you look exactly the way you should do to make this work.'

'Oh.' The girl was clearly struggling to believe him. 'Then I suppose it's all right.'

'I'm glad you think so,' Drake said, relieved. He smiled tentatively. 'So, if we can just agree, in a purely objective way, that you look beautiful enough to pass for a genuine aristocrat, we can start on the protocol stuff.'

'Do you really mean that?' Keira asked, her tone softening, and Drake nodded briskly.

'The sooner the better. I can't tell you everything about noble etiquette in a couple of hours, obviously, but I can give you enough of the basics, and the fact that you're an off-worlder ought to explain any minor *faux pas*. If anyone looks at you strangely, just make some off-hand remark about how they do things at the Lucid Palace on Scintilla, and watch them fall over themselves trying to imitate you for the rest of the evening.'

'I meant what you said about how I look,' Keira said, shifting her weight awkwardly from foot to foot, and Drake found it curiously difficult to look her in the eye. Every time he tried, she moved her head, although he felt certain that she was still observing every nuance of his expression.

'Well, yes,' Drake said uncertainly. 'Adrin would have to be blind not to notice how attractive you are, any man would.' For a moment, he wondered if he'd inadvertently insulted or angered her again, but to his surprise a faint flush of red was colouring her cheeks.

'I don't think of myself in that way,' she said.

'Well, you're not a man,' Drake replied reasonably, wondering how to move the conversation back towards the business of the evening. 'But trust me, you're something special. I thought so the moment I saw you.'

'It's nice of you to say so,' Keira said slowly, as if needing time to translate his words from some arcane xenos tongue into plain Gothic, 'but if you've got any ideas about, you know, sinning with me, forget it.' She met his gaze at last, and Drake saw the cold eye of the assassin looking straight into his own. There was something else there too, though, a hint of confusion, and he nodded again.

'I understand. For what it's worth, I've never had the slightest intention of making a pass at you. I know it's against your beliefs, and I respect your convictions, even if I don't share them.' He shrugged. 'Besides, I can see how things are between you and Mordechai, and I'm not nearly stupid enough to put myself in the middle of that.'

'What are you talking about?' Keira asked, the tightness of her voice growing again, along with the confusion on her face.

'This isn't really the time,' Drake said, hoping to head off whatever was coming before it was too late. 'We've got a lot of ground to cover before you go off to meet Adrin.'

'Rut Adrin. What did you mean about Mordechai and me?' Keira asked angrily.

Drake sighed. 'I just meant it's pretty obvious how you feel about him, that's all. I know I wouldn't have a chance of competing, so I'm not going to try.' To his astonishment, the girl sat heavily on a nearby sofa, and laughed so hard he began to worry that she was in imminent danger of choking.

'You think I'm… that I feel… about *Mordechai*?' She doubled over again, gasping for air, and Drake tried not to stare down her cleavage. 'Danuld, that's priceless!'

'Well, I'm glad you find it so amusing.' Drake sat too, on a convenient chair, and waited for the storm of hilarity to blow itself out. 'Now, precedence. Normally a viscount would be further up the pecking order than a mere lady, but because you're from off-world the obligations of hospitality supersede local distinctions of rank, unless you're in the presence of a member of the royal family.'

'So I'm top canid. Good.' Keira wiped her streaming eyes, smearing Lilith's artfully applied makeup, and tried to adopt a posture of polite attention.

Feeling as though he'd just been doing handsprings in the middle of a minefield, Drake nodded decisively. 'Almost certainly, although one of the Queen's relatives is a member of the Conclave. If he's there, you'd better try to avoid him, although given his reputation he'll certainly do his best to spend some time with you. Under no circumstances should you agree to be alone with him.' That would be all they needed, Keira killing a member of the royal family in outraged defence of her virtue.

'Right, got that.' Keira nodded too, brisk and businesslike. 'Now, what about all these different kinds of fork they use? What's the point?'

Sighing heavily, Drake began to explain the complexities of place settings, wondering, with a trace of envy, how Horst and Vex were getting on in the depths of the Fathomsound.

The Fathomsound Mine, Sepheris Secundus
098.993.M41

DESPITE ITS SIZE, the diving bell felt distinctly claustrophobic, and Horst found himself hoping that the descent wouldn't take too long. The air inside it was rank, thick with the smell of old sweat and desperation, mud, decay and damp. It was cold, too, which he hadn't been expecting, his breath puffing visibly in the wan light of the luminators set into the domed metal ceiling, while chill droplets of condensation fell on him wherever he stood, like fitful raindrops.

As the crane had lifted the vast metal construction from the dock it had oscillated wildly, both he and Vex keeping their feet only with difficulty, although Phyron had managed well enough. The motion had steadied somewhat after they'd entered the water, though, diminishing to a slow oscillation, which troubled his sensitive inner ear just enough to be mildly annoying. Occasionally a more violent movement shook the metal bubble, provoking an audible groan from the hull plates, although what caused them Horst could only guess at: cross-currents, perhaps, or maybe one of Drake's leviathans chewing on the jumble of cables and air hoses that formed their only fragile connection to the surface. With a sigh of irritation, he forced such childish imaginings away. This was no time to be psyching himself into a claustrophobic panic attack.

'Truly remarkable,' Vex said, gazing at the featureless slabs of riveted metal enclosing them on all sides as though they were icons of the saints, and Horst shrugged, trying to look unimpressed. In his opinion, it wasn't seemly for agents of the Inquisition to express enthusiasm, or anything else apart from grim purposefulness, in front of outsiders.

Not that Phyron seemed to notice the remark, fully absorbed as he was in the business of piloting the bell. He stood at one end of the echoing metal space, on a small dais protected by a railing to which devotional scrolls, icons of the Emperor and sacred cogwheels had been fixed by wax seals, along with less identifiable items, which Horst assumed were intended to propitiate the more capricious spirits of the Fathomsound. Singularly unsuccessfully, it seemed, in the case of the late and unlamented Magger.

'Three more fathoms,' Phyron said into the speaking tube next to where he stood, one of the tangle of umbilicals linking them precariously to the surface world, 'and left one.' His eyes were fixed on a flickering auspex screen, marked in concentric circles, a single bright dot wavering two rings from the centre. As Horst watched, it shifted its relative position, the crane above moving to follow Phyron's instructions, and drifted across to kiss the outer edge of the bull's-eye. 'Left again, one half, and lock off.' Phyron breathed an audible sigh of relief as the glowing pinprick centred, and glanced up in the direction of the Inquisition agents. 'Almost there, my lords.'

'Good,' Horst said, trying not to let the relief he felt at hearing those words become too evident in his tone. He must have succeeded, because the supervisor's attention returned immediately to the task at hand, without so much as a glance in his direction.

'Keep paying out,' Phyron said to the speaking tube, studying the runes flickering at the bottom of the auspex screen intently. 'Another six fathoms should do it.' A few moments later a metallic clang echoed through the confined space, as though the thick hull surrounding them had just been struck by a gigantic hammer, and the supervisor smiled thinly. 'Contact,' he reported to the surface. Two runes on the auspex screen turned green. 'And we have a hard seal.'

'Which means what, exactly?' Horst asked, his ears still ringing.

'That it's safe to disembark, my lord,' Phyron said. Horst took a step towards the hatch in the wall they'd boarded the bell by, and Vex laid a restraining hand on his arm.

'I believe that exit is only for use on the surface,' he said, pointing to a section of the floor from which chains rose to a hoist on the ceiling.

Phyron nodded diffidently. 'Quite correct, my lord Magos.'

Vex, Horst noted with wry amusement, didn't bother to correct his sudden elevation several degrees up the Mechanicus hierarchy.

'Access to the mine is through the ventral hatch.' He pulled a lever, and a thud like a handful of bolts being withdrawn reverberated through the confined space. A moment later he activated the hoist, and a slab of metal as thick as the length of Horst's forearm rose into the gloom above their heads, admitting a slow trickle of water, which seeped towards the arbitrator's boots like blood from a clotting wound.

'How do we get inside then, swim?' Horst asked irritably, staring at the rectangular pool of water thus revealed.

'That won't be necessary, my lord,' Phyron assured him hastily, lowering the slab of hull metal to one side. Abandoning the hoist controls, he splashed into the pit, which proved to be no more than knee deep, and groped around below the surface. A moment later he straightened, tugging at something, and the water abruptly vanished, disappearing down a square hatch no more than a metre wide, which the supervisor had lifted bodily out of the way. 'Will this do, or would you prefer to use the cargo lift?'

'That will be fine,' Horst said, calculating the time it would take to unship the slab of hull plating, reattach the chains to the retaining bolts at each corner of the thick metal plate, which he could now see almost filled the space below the rectangular hole in the floor of the submersible, and lower the whole arrangement into the mine below. No doubt that was how the trucks full of ore were lifted into the belly of the diving bell at the end of every shift. He pointed to a number painted on the wet metal surface. 'What does that mean?'

'Shaft number five, my lord.' If Phyron thought the question strange, or idiotic, he gave no sign of the fact. 'The one you were interested in.'

'I see,' Horst said. He'd assumed that the whole mine was interconnected in some way, but evidently it wasn't, the bathysphere they'd descended by the only form of access to any of the individual workings. That would make this the perfect place to hide something illicit, as well as the perfect trap. Judging by Vex's expression, he'd just come to the same sobering conclusion.

'Do you wish me to accompany you, my lords?' Phyron asked, his evident trepidation or recent immersion in the freezing water making his voice tremble as he spoke, it was hard to be sure which. Possibly it was a combination of the two.

Horst shook his head. If anything happened to the diving bell they were all as good as dead, and he was rutted if he was going to take the risk of leaving it unattended. 'No,' he said. 'Stay here. Make sure everything's ready in case we have to leave in a hurry.'

Phyron nodded eagerly, unable to hide his relief. 'By your command, my lord,' he said, bowing.

Horst turned to Vex, but the tech-priest was already moving, dropping through the hatch with barely restrained eagerness to see whatever it was that Tonis and the mysterious Magos Avia had concealed in the depths. The square of darkness in the hatch plate suddenly glowed orange, and the tech-priest's voice echoed up from below.

'There's a luminator down here.'

'Good,' Horst said. If the worst came to the worst, at least they'd be able to see what was trying to kill them. With a last glance round at the interior of the bathysphere, which suddenly seemed a lot more inviting than it had done, he jumped after his friend.

FOURTEEN

The Tumble, Gorgonid Mine, Sepheris Secundus
099.993.M41

'HE'S HERE,' MUNG said, poking his head briefly round the curtain screening the storeroom from the bar, through which the sound of voices and the smell of lho smoke had been drifting for some time. Elyra stood slowly, shouldering her pack, and trying to ignore the firecrackers of crepitation that the movement seemed to detonate in her bruised and aching muscles.

Kyrlock had been sitting at a crate in the corner of the taproom for some time already, and glanced up briefly to nod a greeting as she emerged from the storeroom. He was talking to a man dressed in the same rough garments as most of the mine workers she'd seen, although they seemed both cleaner and better cut, and his hands weren't so ingrained with the ubiquitous dust as those of everyone else within sight. His hair was red, and thinning slightly, and as he looked up to follow Kyrlock's gaze and nod affably at her she could see a scar on the side of his face where his liege lord's tattoo had been crudely removed.

'You must be Vos's friend,' the man said as Elyra sat between them, easing her pack into her lap, where she could grab the laspistol at the first sign of treachery. Her gifts would protect her just as effectively as the gun if necessary, of course, but revealing them would effectively end the mission, and she would only use them as a last resort. He held out a hand. 'Emyl Kantris, at your service.'

'Elyra Yivor,' she replied, shaking it firmly, and Kantris smiled, evidently forming a favourable opinion of her.

'Vos tells me you jumped from the city,' he said casually. 'Not something you do every day.' His expression was open and genial, but his eyes remained guarded, scrutinising her visible injuries carefully.

'Once was enough,' Elyra said flatly, and Kantris smiled, turning back to face Kyrlock.

'You're right, she doesn't give much away. But I'm a busy man.' He emptied a cracked glass of whatever Mung served his customers, and signalled for another. The bartender scurried across to refill it, and then retreated hastily, his shoulders hunched a little, as though trying to fend off the dangerous knowledge of what might be going on around the makeshift table. 'What do you want?'

'To get off-world,' Elyra said. 'Vos says you can fix it. If you can, let's talk terms. If you can't, just say so, and we can stop wasting each other's time.' She reached out and took the drink from in front of him, draining the glass in one, preventing herself from choking by a considerable effort of will. One thing she'd learned long ago in her career as an Inquisition agent was that self-assurance, or the appearance of it, was the key to dealing with lowlifes like Kantris. Any sign of weakness on her part would be ruthlessly exploited.

'I might be able to fix it,' Kantris said, all pretence of affability gone. 'But it'll cost, and the people I need to talk to are going to ask questions.'

'Good for them,' Elyra said. 'Vos told you why I'm running?'

Kantris nodded. 'You were rutting some lordling and his wife found out. She's not the forgiving type. That about cover it?'

'More or less.' Elyra made her voice hard, as though suppressing anger at his bluntness. 'She's vindictive enough to have me killed, if that's what you mean, and who's going to make a fuss about an assistant clothier? She's probably hired a replacement already.'

'I'll need more than that,' Kantris said. 'Names, for a start. If one of the highborn's really gunning for you, the risk goes up, and so does the price.'

'The marquise de Granbie,' Elyra said at once, confident that the profile of the non-existent noble house Vex had seeded in the Icenholm infonet would be proof against any scrutiny Kantris's associates could subject it to.

'I'll check it out,' Kantris said, a little too casually. He turned back to Kyrlock. 'And you want to get your feet on the star road too, I take it.'

'Probably best,' Kyrlock agreed. 'I can go to ground in the Breaks again easily enough, but the Guard'll shoot me for sure if they ever catch up.' He took another swig of his drink. 'Dunno what's out there, but it can't be any worse than this.'

'If I had a credit for every time I've heard that,' Kantris agreed, the mask of affability back in place, and he signalled for more drinks. After they'd arrived, and Elyra had gulped the foul concoction down, reflecting that at least it was numbing her tongue enough to kill the lingering flavour of the rockrat stew, he nodded in a businesslike fashion. 'Which brings me to the crux of our little meeting. How are you proposing to pay your way?'

'I picked up a few things before I left,' Elyra said, delving into her backpack, and adopting a suitably vengeful grin. 'If the bitch wants them back, she can come down here and ask nicely.' She laid a couple of items of jewellery on the shabby planking between them, and Kantris showed the first genuine expression she'd seen on his face since sitting down: astonishment, followed almost at once by naked avarice. The pieces had been carefully chosen to fit in with her cover story, opulent without being garish, finely crafted, and with sufficient signs of wear to have obviously passed through several generations of previous owners. Precisely the kind of things a noble-woman would cherish, and exert all the influence she could to recover, along with the body of the thief who'd dared to take them, the kind of things that could only be safely fenced off-world. 'Would these be enough for a couple of tickets?'

'They might,' Kantris said, reaching out towards them, all pretence of reluctance to deal swept away by sheer greed. 'What else did you get?' Before his hand could close on the precious trinklets, Kyrlock lifted the barrel of his shotgun, his finger looped casually round the trigger, and the fixer checked the motion, gazing at him with thinly disguised apprehension. It seemed Kyrlock hadn't been exaggerating about his reputation down here after all.

'That's her business,' Kyrlock said levelly.

After a moment Kantris nodded. 'I'll pass on the offer, and see what they say.' His eyes followed the glittering prizes as Elyra scooped them back into her pack, and he stood, with a final effort at appearing casual, which he didn't quite manage to pull off. 'If they think it's enough, and your story checks out, I'll be back later. Enjoy your drinks.' With a perfunctory wave of farewell, he hurried to the doorway and vanished into the night.

'Are you mad?' Kyrlock asked, as soon as he was sure Kantris was out of earshot. 'Just showing him the stuff like that?'

'It was a calculated risk,' Elyra told him shortly. 'I've met his kind before. We'd have been going round in circles half the night before he even agreed to talk to his contacts, and Emperor knows how long it would be before we got anywhere after that. This way we get moving straight away.'

'Unless he decides to stab us in the back and just take the shinies,' Kyrlock said, knocking back his latest drink.

Elyra shrugged. 'He'll probably try,' she agreed. 'I know I would.'

'Oh, right.' Kyrlock shrugged too, evidently determined not to seem any less casual about the possibility than she did. 'So long as you know what you're doing.'

'Of course I do,' Elyra assured him, with as straight a face as she could manage. 'I'm making this up as I go along.'

'Terrific,' Kyrlock said, waving to his brother again. As Mung approached the makeshift table, he held out his hand. 'Just leave the bottle.'

* * *

The Fathomsound Mine, Sepheris Secundus
099.993.M41

AT FIRST IT hadn't seemed so bad down here, Horst thought, Vex's discovery of the luminator system a welcome surprise. He'd expected they'd have to make their way through pitch darkness, with only the thin beams of their hand-held flambeaux to guide them. Instead, he'd found himself in a cavern roughly twice his height, fitfully lit by a string of electrosconces, which clung precariously to the cracked and irregular rock walls. A few broken tools and the rotting corpse of a wheelbarrow lay scattered about the chamber floor, their metal parts corroded with rust, presumably not worth the effort of recovering when the shaft was abandoned, and the broken ground underfoot was littered with chunks of rock and other detritus. Horst had no idea whether they were the result of human activity or natural erosion, although Vex could probably have told him if he'd seen any reason to ask.

With a final glance overhead, to the square hatch leading back to the sanctuary of the diving bell, and the rope ladder giving access to it, Horst drew his bolt pistol. There was nothing to shoot at that he could see, but the weight of the weapon in his hand, and the power sword at his waist under the concealing folds of his overcoat, were obscurely comforting.

'I'd be careful with that down here if I were you,' Vex told him conversationally, reaching inside his robe to loosen his autopistol in its holster nonetheless. As his hand emerged, he gestured to the moisture slick walls surrounding them, down which water was trickling from a thousand cracks too small for the eye to see.

'Blow a hole in the wrong place and we'll be swimming back to the bell.'

'I'll bear that in mind,' Horst said uneasily, keeping the gun in his hand regardless. He glanced round the dank and freezing chamber, trying to orientate himself. 'Which direction do you think we should go?' There were several tunnel mouths scattered around the cavern, all equally uninviting so far as he could see, the faint glow of widely spaced lux globes forming a flickering path into the depths of each one.

After a moment's thought, Vex gestured towards a tunnel mouth, which looked no different from any of the others to Horst's untutored eye. 'Down here,' he said decisively, setting off along it without further ado.

'How can you tell?' Horst asked, catching up with him a moment later. The tunnel was cramped, the air moist and cold enough to catch in his throat, and he found he was stooping a little as he hurried along, even though the headroom was more or less adequate, almost as if he could feel the weight of the rock and the immense depth of water bearing down above him.

'The cabling for the luminators is newer,' Vex said, 'which implies that this shaft has been used more recently than any of the others.'

They walked on in silence for a while, save for the scuffling of their bootsoles and the endless dripping of water, the sounds of which echoed and re-echoed in the confined space, folding in so tightly that Horst found himself straining his ears for any other noise that might indicate that they were no longer alone. Apart from Vex's persistent cough, which the cold, moist air seemed to be triggering more frequently than usual, he heard nothing, which, far from reassuring him, merely intensified his sense of unease. The chill and the all-pervading dampness were subtly debilitating, his clothes clinging wetly to his skin, and his hair plastered to his scalp, dripping water into his eyes with annoying regularity. The lux globes were getting further and further apart, so that, although not exactly dark, the narrow passageway was growing steadily more gloomy, the patches of shadow more profound, the deeper they descended into the mine.

On several occasions the two Angelae found their way blocked by thick metal doors, orange with rust and slick with mould, which had to be shouldered aside with protesting squeals before they could proceed. Mindful of Vex's words of caution about using the bolt pistol, Horst was able to divine their purpose without too much difficulty, and tried not to picture the torrent of water sluicing through the constricted workings these heavy barriers had been placed there to stop.

From time to time they passed similar portals sealing side passages, and in a number of places the tunnel widened to a fair-sized cavern, where, evidently, a lode of some useful ore had been discovered and scraped out. By contrast, in other spots, the excavation narrowed alarmingly, the walls constricting so much that there was barely room to proceed in single file, or the roof descending so far that Horst had to bend almost double to make his way past the obstruction. A couple of times he might have given up entirely, believing that they'd come to a dead end, and determined to try their luck with one of the side galleries instead, if it hadn't been for the faint glimmer of another lux globe in the distance beyond the latest obstacle.

'We must be getting close,' he said at last, not for the first time, and Vex nodded.

'I believe so,' he agreed. 'The degree of illumination is beginning to grow.'

Now that he came to mention it, Horst realised that his colleague was right, but chilled and exhausted as he had been, the fact hadn't registered with him before. Just as his eyes had adjusted slowly to the gathering darkness as they'd descended, they were adjusting again to the growing brightness ahead of them, where a more intense light shone around an outcropping of rock. 'What is it?' he whispered, wiping the sheen of moisture from his bolt pistol as best he could.

'Judging by the refraction patterns and the echoes,' Vex said, 'I would conclude that it's a cavern of some kind.' He drew his autopistol, and blessed it quietly under his breath. 'Whatever we've been looking for, I suspect we've just found it.'

Icenholm, Sepheris Secundus
099.993.M41

'MY LADY KEIRA. You do us much honour,' Viscount Adrin said, bowing formally as she entered the library of the Conclave of the Enlightened. Keira dipped a curtsey, as Drake had instructed her, the instinctive balance of the practiced assassin bestowing as much elegance on the unfamiliar movement as if she'd been practising it all her life.

'Thank you for your kind invitation,' she responded, assessing him carefully, amused to note that he was taking in every detail of her personal appearance just as avidly as Drake had done back at the villa. That thought reminded her uncomfortably of their conversation, and she forced the memory aside with a flare of irritation. The idea that she could be harbouring some kind of affection for Mordechai was absurd, she would surely have known if she was, but the Guardsman's words had embedded themselves like thorns in her mind, refusing to be dislodged however much she scratched at them.

This was no time to be distracted, she told herself firmly, smiling at her host, and taking refuge in the dispassionate analysis of what could be a potential target.

Adrin was younger than she'd expected, at least physically, although since someone of his status would have access to juvenat treatments that didn't mean much. She knew he was in his early sixties chronologically, but he looked around half that age. *As if he's about Mordechai's age*, a treacherous thought whispered in her mind, before being slapped aside by the disciplines of duty. His hair was dark, like the arbitrator's, but elaborately coiffured, falling in oiled ringlets around his shoulders, and his eyes were brown instead of blue. His features were regular, to the point where anyone more susceptible to such things than Keira might have thought of him as handsome, and he comported himself with an easy charm that the Redemptionist in her instinctively distrusted, but which was hard not to respond to nevertheless.

Since the lady she was supposed to be would have taken him at face value, at least to begin with, Keira smiled and nodded at his quips, and tried to avert her eyes as unobtrusively as possible from the indecent tightness of his dark green hose. His shirt was mercifully loose fitting, but open at the neck to reveal a well-muscled torso, the paler green silk of the chemise shot through with streaks of white.

'We evidently have a taste for certain colours in common,' Adrin said, holding out a hand into which a servant placed a glass of some local wine. Keira accepted one too, and, remembering Drake's instructions, overrode the impulse to thank the girl. The drink was pleasant enough, though a trifle sweet for her palate, and she nodded.

'Or my maid and your valet do,' she said.

'Quite.' Adrin laughed, a little more spontaneously than mere politeness demanded. 'I wouldn't have a clue what to wear if Noblet didn't lay it all out for me.' An expression of exaggerated confusion crossed his face, and Keira found herself smiling without quite knowing why. 'Come to think of it, I wouldn't even know where to find a fresh cravat if I needed one. I think he keeps them in a drawer somewhere.'

'That's the usual procedure, I believe,' Keira agreed, wandering over to the bookshelves. Night had fallen completely, and the great room was lit by chandeliers hanging from the ceiling, their level of illumination precisely calculated to give enough light to read comfortably by without being glaring or harsh. Beyond the glass wall the city glittered, light bouncing from a million facets, bathing everything in an aurora of shimmering radiance.

Spotting one of the titles Vex had briefed her about, she extracted it from the shelf. 'Oh, you have Philemon's *Comedia Theologica*.' She opened the heavy volume, and flipped a couple of pages. 'With the Grobius illuminations.' She snapped the book shut, and replaced it on the shelf. 'And the Haldenbruk excisions, unfortunately.'

'I'm afraid that's the only edition we've got,' Adrin said, looking at her with a vague air of bafflement. 'The unexpurgated text is almost impossible to come by.'

'It doesn't matter.' Keira drank a little more of the sickly wine, finding it increasingly cloying with every sip. 'The missing passages aren't really crucial to his argument, and some of them are didactic in the extreme. I just prefer to work from a complete text whenever I can.'

'You've read the full version?' Adrin seemed more surprised than ever. 'Wherever did you manage to find one?'

'In the Lucid Palace, of all places.' Keira adopted a slightly affected air of self-satisfaction. 'I was doing some cataloguing there, just as a small favour to Marius, you understand, and stumbled across an original copy. Judging by the amount of dust on the spine, no one had even looked at it since it was published.' For a moment she wondered if dropping the Sector Governor's name, and implying that they were acquainted, had been overplaying her hand, but Adrin seemed hardly to have noticed.

'I thought the missing passages were a bit... you know.' He lowered his voice, like a prudish gossip about to discuss some intimate illness. 'Heretical.'

'Not really,' Keira said blandly. 'Not quite in tune with the current orthodoxy, I'll grant you, but then the Ecclesiarchy never quite seems to make up its mind what that is anyway. There seem to be as many One True Paths to the Emperor as there are priests.'

'You're not afraid to speak your mind, are you?' Adrin asked, sounding a little awestruck.

Keira shrugged. 'When you get to my age,' she said, remembering that she was supposed to be over a century old, 'you find that it saves a lot of time.' The irony of trying to seem older and more experienced than a man three times her age, who undoubtedly believed

that her genuine youth was as artificially maintained
as his own, suddenly struck her. Her face must have
remained straight, though, because Adrin was nodding, a smile on his face.

'I rather gathered that from your response to my
message,' he said. 'The poor fellow was quite put out.
His family has been in the Guild of Heralds since the
Gorgonid was just a couple of serfs with a spade,
apparently, and no one's ever been quite so cavalier
about the correct forms of address before.'

'I'm sorry if my reply struck you as overly blunt,'
Keira said, managing to sound more irritated than con-
trite, 'but I'm not used to all this formality. We're a bit
more straightforward about things on Scintilla.'

'I know. You have voxes, I hear.' Adrin smiled, inter-
cepting a tray of canapés as a servant orbited past with
it. Keira took one too, biting into a small salty cracker
covered in something the consistency of lube gel,
which smelled faintly of fish guts. Under the pretext of
examining the bookshelves again she turned away,
slipping the remains of the snack between two vol-
umes on the history of a local noble house she'd never
heard of, and selected another title she recognised
from the list Vex had given her. 'What else has caught
your fancy?'

'Typhius. The *Lamentations*.' She flicked through the
pages in a desultory fashion. 'Rather a favourite of
mine, I must confess. All the exuberance of Philemon,
but with none of the concomitant vulgarity.'

'But rather less controversial,' Adrin said easily.

'Perhaps that's why so few commentators seem to
take him seriously any more,' Keira said, returning
the book to its place, and handing her empty wine
glass to another passing servant. 'He's seen as more

orthodox, less challenging to the accepted order of things.'

'You sound as if you disagree,' Adrin said.

'I do. His more popular works fall quite clearly into the mainstream, that's beyond dispute, but some of his monographs push the boundaries of what was considered acceptable even during the age of apostasy.' She shrugged. 'Needless to say those are not particularly easy to find, but they are well worth the effort of seeking out.'

'Perhaps to someone in your field of endeavour,' Adrin said blandly. 'I doubt that I'd find much I could understand in any of them.' He gestured towards the main door of the library. 'If you would care to continue our discussion over supper, I've taken the liberty of informing the dining room that I'm expecting a guest this evening.'

'How very thoughtful,' Keira said, taking his proffered arm in the manner Drake had tried to show her earlier. 'But enough about me. I'm sure a man like you must have some fascinating lines of research under way.'

'You flatter me, lady,' Adrin said, leading her across the opulent entrance hall towards the dining room, from which both appetising aromas and the murmur of conversation could be heard, 'but I spend so much time on administrative trivia that I have little time for any enquiries of my own.'

'Nevertheless, you must have some particular areas of interest,' Keira persisted, as another of the ubiquitous servants pulled a chair away from a table containing two place settings to allow her to sit. As she did so she glanced around at the other occupied tables, where half a dozen or so small groups of men and women were chatting idly over their meals. Most were richly dressed, flaunting their aristocratic status as gaudily as possible, although she was faintly surprised to note the plainer robes of Administratum adepts on a couple of the diners, and an elderly ecclesiarch talking earnestly with a couple of young fops in the corner. By and large, though, the simplicity of her own dress, which Lilith had offset with a single violet pendant on a gold chain, echoing the shade of her hair, and Adrin's restrained ensemble, set them apart from the others with their air of understated refinement.

Adrin ate a mouthful of his starter, something pink and gelatinous, before replying. 'I try to keep abreast of whatever the main study groups are doing,' he said, 'in case they need anything to assist them, so I sit in on a few of their sessions from time to time. Some are more interesting than others, of course.'

'I imagine so,' Keira agreed, taking a cautious spoonful of her own portion. It tasted better than it looked, to her well-concealed relief, and she suddenly realised how hungry she was getting. 'Do you have any particular favourites?'

Adrin nodded, and swallowed hastily. 'A couple. A friend of mine runs... used to run an archeotech group. He died recently, though, so it's probably going to fold. No one else in the Conclave has the necessary expertise.' He licked his spoon thoughtfully. 'We do have a couple of other tech-priests among the membership, but they never made any secret of the fact that they thought Tonis was being frivolous, so I don't suppose any of them will be willing to take it over. And there's the philosophy group, of course. If I'm honest, most of the discussion there goes over my head, but the debates are never less than stimulating.'

'I can imagine,' Keira said, and waited for a hovering servant to remove her empty plate. The wine accompanying the meal was rich and dark, far more to her taste than the one she'd been drinking in the library, and she sipped at it thoughtfully. 'Perhaps I'll sit in on a session while I'm here.' If there were any hidden heretics among the conclave's membership, that seemed the most likely place for them to show their hands openly, hoping to entice additional moral weaklings into their web of deceit.

'You'd be very welcome,' Adrin assured her, with a hint of eagerness. It seemed Drake wasn't the only one to find her alluring that evening. Feeling unexpectedly flattered, despite her disapproval of Lustful Thoughts on principle, Keira nodded, and turned her attention to the main course, which proved to be braised grox in a rich mushroom sauce. 'I'm sure you'd find it interesting.'

'I'm sure I would,' Keira agreed.

The Fathomsound Mine, Sepheris Secundus 099.993.M41

THEY ENTERED THE cavern cautiously, guns at the ready, keeping to the deepest patches of shadow they could find. There was no sign of movement in the brightly-lit space beyond, but Horst was too seasoned a field operative to let that count for much, the habit of caution too deeply ingrained to ignore. Crouching behind a boulder next to the entrance of the cavern, he steadied the bolt pistol in his hand and swept the area in front of him, searching for a target.

At first sight it seemed little different from any of the other worked-out faces they'd travelled through to get here, the broken walls still showing signs of the tools that had gouged them from the stone beneath the ever-present film of moisture. None of the other caverns they'd seen had been as brightly illuminated as this one, however, the arc globes on scaffolding posts ranged around the centre of it seeming almost dazzling by comparison. And none had had a small prefabricated habdome erected in the middle of them.

'That must be it,' Horst said, and Vex nodded tightly, his autopistol levelled at the entrance to the dome. It was a standard model, perhaps half a dozen metres in diameter, and generally, ones of that size only had a single doorway. Neither man would take that for granted, though, and by common consent they began to circle the structure, keeping a close watch on it, but remaining equally wary of the shadows beyond the circle of arclight.

'No visible security systems,' Vex said, as they returned to their starting point.

Horst nodded. 'But it's the ones you don't see that kill you.'

'True,' Vex agreed, before coughing loudly again, and slapping his respirator unit irritably with the heel of his empty hand. Cautiously, the two Inquisition operatives began to move towards the incongruous edifice, their weapons held ready for use. 'I assume you wish to enter first?'

'Of course,' Horst said evenly. He'd carried out this kind of manoeuvre innumerable times as an arbitrator, both in training and in earnest, and as the team leader it was his place to take point. Nevertheless, he glanced briefly at Vex as they advanced. 'Unless you'd rather, in case there's some special system rigged you think you might recognise.'

'An unlikely possibility,' Vex said.

Horst sighed. 'I knew you'd say that,' he said, flattening himself against the gently curving wall.

Vex followed suit on the other side of the door, reaching out slowly to grasp the handle. It turned as he twisted it, and he braced himself, nodding at Horst. Silently he mouthed the words, 'On three.'

Horst returned the nod, and the tech-priest counted off the seconds as noiselessly as before. Just as his lips finished shaping the third and final number, he jerked the door open. It slid awkwardly on corroded runners, squealing loudly, and Horst dived through the widening gap, rolling to cover as much distance as possible, his weapon seeking a target as he rose to a crouch. An instant later, Vex appeared in the doorway behind him, his autopistol levelled.

'Clear,' Horst said, and the tech-priest nodded.

'I deduced as much from the fact of you not getting shot,' he agreed cheerfully.

Letting the remark go, Horst walked a little further into the dome. It was completely open, uncluttered by any partitions, and he was able to see across to the other side with little difficulty. The habitation module was warm and dry inside, in stark contrast to the mine in which it stood, and the sudden change of environment was making him feel even more uncomfortable than he had been outside, his steaming clothes clinging uncomfortably to his skin, leaching any residual warmth from it.

'Someone's been staying here,' he said, stepping around a bedroll. Several of them had been laid out around the perimeter of the dome, and he bent down to examine the nearest one, hoping to find some clue as to who'd occupied it, but the blankets were empty.

An idea struck him, and he glanced up at Vex. 'The Franchise, do you think? It's the ideal place to hide the people they're smuggling.'

'Possible, but unlikely,' Vex replied, his attention almost fully engaged with the tangle of equipment he'd discovered in the centre of the dome. 'That would imply some connection between them and either Tonis or Avia, which we have no cause to suspect at this time.'

'True,' Horst conceded. 'What do you make of it, then?'

'I lack sufficient data to draw any firm conclusions,' Vex said, a trifle primly, 'but I would venture to suggest that Tonis was engaged in some highly unorthodox research; research that may have involved the cooperation of psykers.'

'Psykers?' Horst echoed, surprised. 'Why would you think that?'

By way of reply, the tech-priest indicated the jumble of devices filling the centre of the dome. Cogitator banks and data lecterns formed an outer ring, pierced by gaps in which tangles of cabling snaked in all directions, connecting them in some manner beyond Horst's comprehension. Stepping cautiously over the nearest potential trip hazard, he found his colleague staring intently at something laid out on a metal table in the middle of the torus.

'This looks like one of the psy dampers they use at the Citadel,' Vex said, an unfamiliar tone of confusion seeping into his voice. 'But it's been heavily modified.'

'Modified how, exactly?' Horst asked, and then corrected himself hastily. Carried away with enthusiasm for some unfamiliar device, Vex was quite likely to answer the question in minute and incomprehensible detail. 'I mean, what's it meant to do?'

'I really have no idea,' Vex said, intrigued, poking a damp and grubby finger into the guts of the machine as he spoke. 'It certainly wouldn't dampen a psy field in this state.' He glanced at the nearest cogitator bank with the sort of expression Horst was more used to seeing on the face of a hungry hound spotting a bowl of food, or Keira catching sight of a heretic she'd been given permission to terminate. 'I'll have to download as much of his data as I can access, and analyse it properly when we get back. I just hope there's enough storage space left on my slate.' His expression changed to one of profound surprise, as he removed a sub-assembly of brass cogs and vacuum tubes, and peered into the cavity. 'Omnissiah's cogs, what's that?'

Horst craned his neck to look, as the tech-priest lifted something from the bowels of the device. It looked like a small piece of polished ivory, so smooth that the light seemed to hang around it in a faint nimbus rather than being merely reflected. Its surface was scratched, in a manner that suggested careful carving rather than accidental wear, although Horst couldn't discern any recognisable pattern in the marks.

'I haven't the faintest idea,' he said. 'But you'd better hang on to it.'

Vex nodded in agreement, slipping the strange object into a pocket inside his robe, and bent his head again to take another look at the housing he'd opened. Then he looked up, an uncharacteristic expression of alarm on his face. 'I think we'd better run,' he said, before hurdling the nearest tangle of cable and pelting towards the door.

Horst followed hard on his heels, slipping on the wet rock underfoot as he left the sanctuary of the dome. As he recovered his balance he could see Vex's

white robe flapping in the distance, like a child's drawing of a ghost, already halfway to the tunnel they'd
come in by. 'What is it?' he called, hitting his stride and
catching up fast.

'Timer,' Vex said breathlessly, vanishing into the tunnel mouth. 'Counting down. And a genecode scanner.'

'That's insane,' Horst said, glancing back, but disinclined to slacken his pace. The cavern was out of sight
already, the brighter glow of its arcglobes attenuated
by distance and the intervening twists of the narrow
passage.

'No,' Vex panted. 'Clever. It must start whenever
someone handles the device. Only an authorised user
can abort the countdown. If I hadn't taken that trinket
out to examine it, I'd never even have known the trap
was there.'

'How long have we got?' Horst asked, not bothering
to inquire why they were still running. Even a moderate explosion would be magnified and channelled by
the confined space, endangering them far beyond what
would normally seem like a safe distance. There was
no telling how large a charge Tonis had left behind to
ensure the security of his heretical endeavours either.

'We haven't,' Vex gasped, an instant before the moisture slick rock beneath Horst's boots seemed to
shudder. A moment later both Angelae lost their footing entirely, as a massive hand seemed to strike them
between the shoulderblades, sending them sprawling.

'Up! Quickly!' Horst yelled, scrambling to his feet,
heedless of the slick of mud plastering the front of his
clothes. He seized a handful of Vex's robe, yanking him
upright, and forcing the tech-priest into a stumbling
run. A faint rumbling sound could be heard in the
depths of the mine, and a cold, wet wind began to

blow from somewhere behind them, the stale air of the cavern being displaced by a rush of incoming water. 'The shaft's been breached!'

It was like running in a nightmare, the arbitrator thought, unconsciously anticipating the dreams that would wake him on occasion for the rest of his life. The faster he tried to move, the more his bootsoles seemed to slip on the wet stone of the passage floor, and Vex was stumbling, still winded from the effects of the explosion, yanking him off balance with almost every step. The rumbling behind them and the unnatural wind were constantly increasing, and he fought down the impulse to turn and look behind, knowing that giving way to it would cost a vital second or two, and that if the roaring death was close enough to see it was already too late in any case.

'There!' Vex cried, pointing, as they rounded an outcrop of dull grey rock, and with a sudden flare of hope Horst caught sight of the last of the bulkhead doors they'd passed through on their descent. It was no more than a score of metres away, the rising passage beyond it still lit by the flickering lux globes, and he breathed a silent prayer of thanks to the Emperor that they'd left the portals open as they'd made their way down the shaft.

Horst nodded, feeling a sudden burst of renewed energy at the prospect of their imminent deliverance, and picked up the pace a little in spite of his fatigue. The cold wind of death was almost a gale against his back, and as he half helped, half threw the dazed techpriest across the rust pitted threshold, he felt his boots splashing in a deepening film of water. Leaping through the gap after Vex, he turned, seizing the handle, and almost froze in terror as he began to pull the door closed.

The passageway behind them was gone, replaced by a moving wall of water, which filled it completely, bearing down on them as rapidly and unstoppably as a rut-frenzied bull grox. Horst strained against the corroded hinges, the muscles of his back cracking with the effort, and with a reluctant shriek the door began to move. Too slow, he thought, too late.

'Let me help.' Vex leaned across him, grabbing a reinforcing bar, and pulled too. Howling like a damned soul, the portal began to swing shut. Then the wall of water reached it, and with a bang which reverberated painfully in the confined space, reminding Horst uncomfortably of the moment Barda's Aquila had hit the permafrost, the door slammed, propelled by the force of Emperor alone knew how many tonnes of water crashing into it from the other side.

Both men were thrown through the air by the shock of impact, and Horst fell bruisingly against the hilt of his power sword, which jammed painfully into his hip. Fortunately, the force of the blow didn't activate the weapon, or he might have lost a limb, instead of just his dignity and a layer or two of skin. A thin storm of rust particles whirled in the air around them, forming an itchy slurry with the film of water on their clothes and bodies, making them look uncannily as though they were both caked in drying blood.

'Are you all right?' Horst asked, staggering to his feet.

'I believe so,' Vex confirmed, catching his breath. He kicked a nearby chunk of rubble, the first time Horst had ever seen him give way to visible anger. 'No thanks to my own stupidity. If I hadn't tried to meddle with that device, we'd have all Tonis's records to examine.'

'I doubt it,' Horst consoled him. 'If the cogitators weren't rigged as well, you can call me a heretic. From the moment we set foot in there, it was only a question of which trap we set off first.'

'Then it seems you were right,' Vex said ruefully. 'It is the ones you don't see that kill you.'

'But you did see it,' Horst said, clapping the disconsolate tech-priest on the back, and trying to sound encouraging. 'And it's only thanks to you that we're both still alive.' He turned resolutely towards the passageway leading up to the entrance chamber. 'We may not know exactly what Tonis was up to down here, but we do know it had something to do with psykers. Inquisitor Finurbi was right.'

'That may be so,' Vex said, turning to trudge wearily after him, 'but we still don't know nearly as much as we might have done.'

The Tumble, Gorgonid Mine, Sepheris Secundus 100.993.M41

THE BOTTLE WAS almost empty before Kantris returned, but Kyrlock felt as sober as ever, his unease at the situation he found himself in too acute to allow the alcohol to dull the edge of it. Elyra had remained where she was, occasionally sipping at her drink, but the conversation between the two of them had been stilted, and largely fictional, intended to be overheard by the other patrons, many of whom would undoubtedly repeat the carefully seeded nuggets of verisimilitudinous detail to Kantris or his associates before the night was over. The psyker might know her business when it came to hunting heretics, but he knew the teeming underworld of the Tumble, and he knew she'd made a mistake in her handling of the expeditor. Kantris was a weasel, everyone knew that.

The only reason he was still walking around was because he was a useful one, to all sorts of people, for all sorts of reasons.

'It's all set,' Kantris said, lowering his voice as he approached their corner of the barroom. 'There's a group leaving on an ore barge the night after next, and they've got room for two more.'

'Good,' Kyrlock said, reflecting that for a prize like the one Elyra had dangled in front of them, the smugglers probably wouldn't have thought twice about freeing up some additional space with a couple of bullets if necessary. 'When and where?'

'Not here,' Kantris said, with a suspicious glance round at the other patrons, who pretended a sudden deep interest in the contents of their glasses. 'There's a safe house I can take you to.'

'We're safe here,' Elyra said, and Kantris shook his head pityingly.

'Of course you're not.' He glanced at Kyrlock for confirmation. 'If the de Granbie bitch really has got a bounty hunter on your tail, he'll be working the drinkholes for sure.'

'He will,' Kyrlock agreed. That much was obvious, and insisting on staying here would only tip Kantris off that they didn't really fear pursuit, which would beg the obvious question of why. He grinned mirthlessly at the red-haired expeditor, and shrugged. 'City girl.'

'Fine.' Elyra stood, and hefted her pack, letting it hang casually from one shoulder. 'Let's go.'

'Might as well,' Kyrlock agreed, hiding his disquiet as best he could. He rose slowly, collecting his gear, and unobtrusively ensured that the chain axe was loose enough in its sling to draw one-handed. 'Back in a moment.'

'Where are you going?' Elyra asked, although whether the note of unease in her voice was genuine, or being assumed for Kantris's benefit, he couldn't be sure.

'We still owe Mung,' Kyrlock reminded her, making for the bar. So far, it seemed, the people Kantris worked for hadn't been able to poke any holes in their story, but he didn't think they'd stop trying.

'You're off, then?' Mung said, glancing up from rearranging the dirt on the countertop with a damp and filthy rag as his brother approached.

Kyrlock nodded. 'Five creds for the room,' he said, dropping a handful of clattering change on the metal surface, 'and something for the drinks.'

'More than fair,' Mung agreed, scooping up the coins, and flashing a brief grin as he registered the two extra credits his brother had added in. Far more than the raw distillate had been worth, but Kyrlock reckoned the Inquisition could afford it, and they were unlikely ever to meet again. 'So you're off, then?'

'Looks like it,' Kyrlock agreed.

'One for the road,' Mung said, reaching under the counter and handing over a bottle of the colourless liquid. 'For the old times.'

'They weren't all bad, were they?' Kyrlock said, taking it, and stowing it in his pack. Neither of them could think of anything more to say, but he suddenly felt reluctant to leave.

His brother shrugged. 'Yes they were,' he said, 'but we got by.' A faint air of wistfulness passed across his face. 'Look after yourself out there, Vos,' he said, ''cause I guarantee you, no other bugger will.'

'No change there then, is it?' Kyrlock said, turning away. Elyra and Kantris were already waiting beside the curtain leading to the open air, and pushed through it without a word as he moved up to join them. Kyrlock hesitated on the threshold, raising a final hand in farewell, which his brother returned, and then the filthy scrap of fabric sundered them forever.

'Which way?' Elyra asked impatiently, and, recalled to more immediate matters, Kyrlock nodded. The night was well advanced, closer to dawn than dusk, and the furtive night life of the Tumble was winding down, its nocturnal denizens scurrying away to hide from the authorities in whatever bolt-holes luck or the right bribes kept secure, or to resume their daytime lives unnoticed among the teeming mass of serfs swarming towards the face. It was still dark enough for the soft light of the suspended city to be the only reliable source of illumination, though, and he looked around, scrutinising the shadows. A faint scrape of dislodged stone echoed in the stillness of the night, and he tensed, wondering if they were being watched by anything more inimical than rockrats.

'Down here,' Kantris said. 'It's not far.' He gestured towards a narrow defile between two spoil heaps, and Kyrlock raised his shotgun.

'After you,' he said.

'Well of course,' Kantris said easily. 'How else am I going to show you the way?' He set off at a confident pace, his footing on the treacherous shale instinctively sure, and after a moment Elyra began to follow. His senses straining, Kyrlock took up the rear, silently cursing the woman for her impatience. She was blocking his shot at Kantris, and if the expeditor tried anything, he couldn't fire without hitting her.

At first, it seemed, he was being overly cautious. Despite his expectations, Kantris showed no sign of turning and drawing a gun. However, as they made their way between another pair of spoil heaps, some way from Mung's place in a part of the Tumble Kyrlock didn't recognise, the treachery he'd been anticipating materialised.

His first and only warning had been the familiar rattle of stone against stone, which he'd heard several times since leaving the drinkhole, and generally dismissed as more rockrats going about their business, or equally furtive night folk, as eager to avoid detection as he was, kicking an unregarded pebble as they'd hurried away. This was louder, however, and more sustained, and he turned, bringing up the shotgun just in time to see a man rising up from the spoil heap behind him, throwing aside the tattered blanket with its thin coating of shale that had so effectively concealed him. City light gleamed on a long, serrated blade as the ambusher rushed at him, sweeping the end of the filthy piece of cloth out and around in an attempt to entangle his arms.

Kyrlock pulled the trigger, and the fellow fell, half his chest transmogrified in an instant to bloody scraps, the boom of the shotgun echoing flatly through the canyons between the artificial hills. Even before the brigand's knife clattered against the stone the Guardsman had turned, and cursed under his breath.

There was a whole gang of bandits erupting from the dirt around them, two closing on Elyra, and a big fellow charging towards him swinging a length of rusty chain. Unable to fire for the fear of hitting the psyker instead of his intended target, Kyrlock ducked under the improvised flail, reaching round for his chain axe, and thumbing it to full power as he tore it free of its retaining straps. The whining metal teeth met the man's chest as he swung it in a short, flat arc, grating on some steel plates sewn into the fellow's coat as Kyrlock stepped in behind him. The makeshift armour held for a moment, raising a shower of bright golden sparks, before the blade penetrated, extinguishing them in a sudden shower of dark blood. Kyrlock kicked his assailant in the back of the knee, knocking him down, and sliced through his neck as he fell.

As the brigand with the chain gurgled and went silent, Kyrlock whirled, aiming the shotgun one-handed, but still couldn't find a target without endangering Elyra. Slinging the weapon, he switched to a two-handed grip on the chain axe and charged towards the nearest of her attackers, a short fellow in a hooded cloak, holding a long metal pipe roughly his own height, which he thrust at the woman's midriff like a spear.

Before Kyrlock could get within striking range, though, Elyra had pivoted easily, stepping in close to the man with the pipe, increasing the distance the other outlander attacking her had to travel, and seized the weapon halfway down its length. She twisted again, using her hand as a fulcrum, and brought the end up rapidly, flicking its erstwhile owner off the tip like a clod of earth from a stick. He fell heavily, entangling the legs of the last bandit, who went down hard, dropping the knife he was carrying. Before either man could rise, Elyra spun the thin tube of metal, bringing it down hard, twice in rapid succession. They both went limp, and she hurdled their prostrate bodies, flinging herself at Kantris, who staggered backwards, raising both hands.

'Hey,' he protested frantically, 'hold on! I'm on your side, remember?' A faint, sickly echo of his bar-room grin tried to gain a foothold on his face as he retreated.

'Since when?' Kyrlock asked, moving up to stand shoulder to shoulder with Elyra, holding the whining teeth of his chain axe where the sweating expeditor could get a good look at them. He shot a glance at the grim faced Inquisition agent. 'I told you he'd try something like this.'

'I didn't try anything, swear to the Emperor,' Kantris said. He glanced from one operative to the other, the grin coagulating. 'Lucky you were so quick off the mark, or they'd have had us for sure.' He heaved an exaggerated sigh of relief. 'Better get on, then, eh?' He looked at Elyra speculatively. 'Those were pretty sharp moves for a lady's maid.'

'She's got enemies,' Elyra said. 'Apart from me.' She threw the pole away, where it clattered among the stones, and glared defiantly at Kantris. 'All right, I lied. I was the bitch's bodyguard. The rest of it's true, though, and I thought you'd be more trusting if I played the helpless little girlie. How else did you think I got out of the house in one piece?' She glanced sharply at Kyrlock. 'Do you have a problem with that?'

'If you can get me off planet before the commissars catch up, I don't care if you're Abaddon the Despoiler,' Kyrlock assured her, slipping easily into the fallback story they'd agreed on in case her more lethal skills became obvious to an outsider. They hadn't expected something like this to happen so early in the mission, but, paradoxically, it might even work to their advantage. Kantris would be congratulating himself on his cleverness for having exposed Elyra's apparent deceit, and with any luck he and his shadowy associates would take everything else they were told at face value, believing that the real lie had been successfully found out.

'How about you?' Elyra asked, turning back to Kantris. 'Do we still have a deal? Or am I going to have to make alternative arrangements?'

'That won't be necessary,' the fixer assured her, with a quick glance at the inert bandits, and a covetous glance at the backpack he'd almost certainly intended to ransack. 'The deal stands. Vos here'll tell you, I'm a man of my word. Well known for it.'

'Is that true?' Elyra asked, and Kyrlock nodded slowly.

'I've never heard of him reneging on anyone he's afraid of,' he agreed slowly. 'And if he's not afraid of you by now, he ought to be.' He shrugged, and glared at the expeditor. 'And even if he isn't, he knows damn well I'll snap his miserable neck if we have any more problems, don't you Emyl?' He switched off the chain blade, and stowed it.

'There's no call for that sort of language,' Kantris said, making an unconvincing attempt to sound affronted. 'We're all friends here. On my mother's life, I never laid eyes on any of these scoundrels before.' He shot a nervous glance at the two Elyra had struck down. One of them was beginning to stir, and making a low groaning sound, which Kyrlock knew was the prelude to regaining consciousness. 'Best get moving, eh? It'll be light soon, and we need to get you under cover.'

That much, at least, was true, and waiting until one of their unfortunate assailants was in a fit state to answer questions would be far too great a risk.

With a last regretful look at the feebly twitching bodies, Kyrlock nodded. 'Right behind you,' he said, unslinging the shotgun again.

FIFTEEN

Icenholm, Sepheris Secundus
101.993.M41

EVERYONE ELSE HAD slept late, leaving Drake with little to do except enjoy a leisurely breakfast and listen out for an emergency signal from Kyrlock and Elyra, which he didn't really expect to hear. They were both in deep cover, somewhere in the sprawling pit of the Gorgonid, working their way into the pipeline. Their chances of being able to call without being observed by someone around them would be minute. Vex's shrine in the corner was still murmuring to itself, though, the runes he'd pointed out before leaving for the Fathomsound flashing reassuringly to show that the vox-unit in Elyra's pack was still functioning, so Drake had been able to enjoy his mid-morning recaf and a stroll around the terrace with a relatively easy mind.

'Good morning.' Keira joined him in the open air, apparently unconcerned by the chill, clad in a yellow silk robe, which clung closely enough for Drake to be reasonably certain that she wore nothing beneath it, held closed by a knotted cord. Her slippers matched the fabric, and her hair swung loose around her face, which still held the faint flush of a long, leisurely bath. Her eyebrows shifted a little closer together as she registered his scrutiny. 'You're doing it again.'

Drake smiled, and tore his attention away from the shapely and well-muscled calves below the folds of cloth.

'Hard not to,' he admitted cheerfully. 'But we covered that last night.' He suppressed a moment of unease. 'At least I thought we did.'

'That's what I wanted to talk to you about,' Keira said, moving distractingly close, and lowering her voice. 'I've been thinking about what you said.'

'Oh.' Drake had hoped that she would have forgotten the awkward exchange by now, but she clearly hadn't. He kept his gaze on her face, despite the temptation to let it wander appreciatively downwards, seeing once again a flicker of uncertainty in the depths of her emerald eyes. 'If I embarrassed you, I apologise. I can't pretend I don't find you attractive, but I understand you don't feel the same way about me, and I won't let that get in the way of our working together.'

'I believe you,' Keira said, to his heartfelt relief. 'But I meant the other thing you mentioned.' To his surprise, Drake saw a flush of crimson, too deep to be the legacy of her bath, spreading across her face and neck. 'About Mordechai.'

'I'm sorry about that too,' Drake said, feeling as though the solid balustrade behind him was suddenly as insubstantial as smoke, and that he was teetering on the brink of the abyss. 'That's entirely your business. I should never have brought it up.'

'It's just that… I was wondering…' Keira hesitated again, and then ploughed on with her usual directness. 'What made you think that I felt… something like that for him?'

'Well…' Caught by surprise, Drake floundered a little. 'The way you act around him, I suppose.'

'And what way's that?' Keira asked, an edge of irritation beginning to enter her voice.

Remembering how dangerous she could be if she lashed out in angry frustration, Drake tried to collect his thoughts.

'Edgy,' he said at last. 'And you challenge him all the time. It's as if you're trying to antagonise him, because it's the only way you can attract his attention and still feel in control.'

'That's ridiculous,' Keira said, although the note of belligerence Drake had expected was absent from her voice.

'If you say so,' he replied, as neutrally as he could, 'but if a girl started acting like that around me, I know what I'd think.'

'Which is what?' Keira asked, a little breathlessly.

Drake shrugged. 'That she was either the biggest bitch in the sector, or my luck was in.'

'I see,' Keira said coldly, 'but maybe Mordechai doesn't have quite such a high opinion of himself as you seem to do.'

'I'm sure he doesn't,' Drake said easily, 'but I thought it was your opinion of him you wanted to discuss.'

'What's the point?' You're as bad as he is,' Keira said, turning sharply away. 'Thanks for your help.'

'Any time,' Drake assured her, quietly appreciating the spectacle of her retreating rear as she returned to the house.

By the time he'd finished his recaf and wandered back inside, the others were up as well. Horst greeted him affably enough, but still seemed exhausted after his ordeal in the mines, lying on an overstuffed chaise with his head on a cushion embroidered with the coat of arms of the family from whom the villa was rented. He was dressed in a simple grey shirt and trousers, his brocade jacket hanging from the back of a nearby chair. Vex, in a freshly laundered robe, was already hard at work on his data-slate, muttering prayers and tapping the keyboard with single-minded diligence, barely looking up to acknowledge the Guardsman's arrival.

Spotting Keira on a sofa at the end of the room, Drake braced himself for some sign of overt hostility, but from her demeanour their conversation on the terrace might never have happened. The young assassin merely glanced up, smiled, and nodded at him with every impression of ease. She'd got dressed in the interim, in a simple ochre kirtle that suited her well, and Lilith was fussing over her hair, coiling it neatly at the nape of her neck. 'If you're hungry, we were about to have an early lunch,' she said brightly.

'Works for me,' Drake agreed, settling himself comfortably in a nearby armchair. 'I trust you had a pleasant evening at the Conclave?' The servant knew where Keira had gone the previous night, and would no doubt think it odd if no one asked her mistress whether she'd enjoyed herself.

'Most enlightening,' Keira said, in exactly the right tone of bored condescension, examining her reflection in the mirror her maid held up for her as she spoke. 'Thank you, Lilith, that's a tremendous improvement.'

'Very becoming, if you don't mind me saying so, my lady. It wouldn't suit everyone, of course, but you've got the bone structure for it. Breeding always tells, in my experience.'

'I'm sure you're right,' Keira said, completely straight-faced, and turning to face the servant. 'That will be all for the moment.'

'Very good, my lady,' Lilith said, and bustled out, followed a moment or two later by a pair of domestics, who had been busily laying a side table with a small but comprehensive buffet.

Horst approached the table as soon as the servants were out of earshot, and ladled out a generous plateful of kedgeree, which he began to devour the moment he'd sat down again. 'Better grab something to eat while you can,' he said. 'We've got a lot to discuss.'

Having breakfasted well before the others rose, Drake contented himself with a small portion of pancakes, which he soused in ackenberry syrup. Glancing round for a fork, he became suddenly aware of Keira's presence at his elbow, noting her quiet amusement as he suppressed a reflexive start. 'Can I help you to anything?' he asked, determined to seem affable. If she was as willing as she seemed to gloss over any lingering awkwardness between them, he was certainly ready to reciprocate.

Keira considered the range of dishes on offer. 'Some of those kidneys,' she said thoughtfully, 'some mushrooms, a bit of whatever that is…' she pointed at a nearby platter.

'Kenil omelette,' Drake said, spooning up a generous portion, and transferring it to her plate. He sniffed at the fragrant steam. 'Kenil seems fresh, too.'

'Never heard of it,' Keira said. 'Guess it must be a Secundan thing.'

'It's a kind of lichen,' Drake told her, 'which grows wild in the mine workings. The Fratery of Comestibles cultivate it in the worked-out seams, to improve the yield and flavour.'

'Oh.' Keira took a cautious nibble at the omelette, and nodded approvingly. 'Tastes pretty good. I suppose they grow the mushrooms down there too?'

'That's right.' Drake smiled easily. 'Not a lot else you can do with a hole in the ground.'

'I wondered why fungi were so popular with the cooks here,' Keira said, taking her plate to a nearby chair.

'Hybris?' Drake asked. Vex looked up, with a faintly distracted expression. 'Want anything?'

'Whatever you deem most nutritious,' the tech-priest said, returning to work. Not having a clue what that might be, Drake filled a plate with a random selection of foodstuffs, which he placed within easy reach of the data-slate.

'We're definitely making some progress,' Horst said, setting his plate aside with a sigh of satisfaction. 'My latest report to the inquisitor contains some significant new information.'

'Which he won't be able to respond to for another month at least,' Vex reminded them, glancing up from the keyboard for a moment. 'Assuming the warp currents remain favourable.'

'That makes it all the more important to ensure that everything we know is available to him the moment he arrives at the Tricorn,' Keira said, a trifle indistinctly.

'Exactly,' Horst said, looking momentarily taken aback at this sudden unexpected support. 'If the worst comes to the worst, he'll be able to pick up where we left off.'

Drake nodded soberly. It was becoming increasingly evident that they were facing a powerful and well-concealed conspiracy, which meant that it was entirely possible they could all be killed before they had a chance to meet Inquisitor Finurbi in person again. If that happened, Horst's periodic progress reports would enable him, or another group of Angelae, to follow the same trail, preferably to a happier conclusion. 'Then let's try to save him the trouble,' he said dryly.

'What's our next move?' Keira asked. 'Adrin seems convinced I'm a genuine scholar from Scintilla, and that I'm at least open to heretical ideas, even if I don't actually harbour them.'

'That's excellent,' Horst said, nodding in approval. Keira smiled at the implied praise, and Drake felt an unexpected pang of jealousy. If the man really couldn't see that, despite her protestations to the contrary, she was besotted with him, he was an idiot. 'Do you have any idea how to build on that?'

'Maybe,' Keira said. 'He belongs to a study group, where I could drop a few more hints about holding heretical views without committing myself too openly. If there really are cultists among the Conclave, it might tempt them to approach me.'

'Good.' Horst nodded again. 'How soon can you move on that?'

'Tonight,' Keira said, swallowing a mouthful of omelette. 'They're holding a meeting, and I've already expressed an interest in attending.'

'Excellent.' Horst rose, and returned to the sideboard, helping himself to a fragrant plate of gently steaming offal. 'Keep your eyes and ears open, but don't take any unnecessary risks.' He glanced at her, a trifle warily, evidently expecting some scornful or sarcastic rejoinder, but Keira simply nodded in response.

'Don't worry,' she said, 'I'll stay focused.' Then she smiled at him. 'Could you get me some recaf while you're up?'

'Sure.' Horst poured the drink, stirring in the mix of spice and sweeteners he knew she favoured from the array of bowls standing next to the pot, and handed her the delicate glass cup on his way back to his chair. 'That about right?'

Kiera sipped, and nodded, and then smiled at him again. 'Just right, thanks.'

'You're welcome,' Horst said, with a trace of unease. He glanced at Drake. 'Anything from Elyra and Vos yet?'

'They've moved out of the drinkhole,' Drake said, determined to keep his mind on the business at hand, despite the unexpected entertainment. 'She hasn't checked in since last night, but according to Hybris's auspex her vox has shifted about a kilometre. That probably means they're in the pipeline by now.'

'Can we get a more precise location?' Horst asked. 'If they call for extraction or back-up, it would help to know exactly where they are.'

'Already done,' Vex assured him. 'According to the overlay, they're in an old airshaft, leading down to one of the subterranean galleries on the fringe of the Tumble.'

'In the mine itself?' Horst asked. 'That sounds a bit risky.'

'Maybe not,' Drake said. 'None of the miners would stray into an air shaft, there's nothing to extract there. Is the gallery still in use?'

'One moment,' Vex said, communing with the data-slate. He glanced up, his eyes focusing again. 'Worked out seven years ago, currently leased to the Fratery of Comestibles for the cultivation of edible fungi.'

'You mean we're facing a conspiracy of mushroom farmers?' Keira asked incredulously.

'I doubt it,' Horst replied, taking a mouthful of his recaf. 'They probably have no idea what's going on down there.'

'Good. I'm starting to get a taste for the stuff,' Keira said brightly, and Horst glanced in her direction again before returning his attention to the tech-priest.

'Who's renting it to them?' he asked.

'A good question,' Vex replied. 'Technically, that part of the mine belongs to one of the barons, but it may have been conferred on one of the lesser houses that owes him fealty.' His eyes lost focus for a moment as he communed with the datanet in binary. 'The records will take some time to disentangle.'

Drake nodded his agreement. 'I imagine they will,' he said. 'Holdings like that tend to change hands regularly among the minor nobility, for all kinds of reasons.'

'I'll do the best I can,' Vex said, chewing absently on a mushroom, his attention already absorbed by the data-slate display.

'I'm sure you will,' Horst said, and then turned to Drake. 'Do you feel up to running recon tonight? That should be Keira's job, but she's going to be busy.'

'Reckon so,' Drake agreed, before an alarming thought struck him. 'I won't have to glide down, will I?' To his relief Horst was shaking his head, while Keira grinned at him sympathetically.

'The cable will do,' Horst said. 'We've got a ready-made cover story for you, which means you'll be able to walk in pretty openly.'

'At least to begin with,' Keira agreed. 'If our targets bought Elyra's story, they're bound to be looking out for a bounty hunter on her trail. If they think they've spotted one it'll keep her cover solid.'

'Exactly,' Horst said. 'The trick will be to fade out of view before you approach the air shaft. If the Shadow Franchise really is running the operation, they'll have lookouts posted all around the place.'

'I can take care of myself,' Drake said.

'I don't doubt it,' Horst said, 'but try to avoid contact. All you have to do is confirm that our people are there. Keep your head down, and report back as soon as you can.'

'Maybe I should go instead,' Keira said. 'If I use the wings, I can get in and out before the meeting tonight. I'm sure Danuld can manage, but I'm a lot better at sneaking around than anyone else here, and it means he won't have to shake any tails after playing bounty killer.'

'I've thought of that,' Horst replied, shaking his head doubtfully, 'but it's cutting things too fine. You can't risk being delayed and missing the meeting.' He looked sharply at the girl, clearly anticipating an argument, but she simply nodded her head.

'Good point,' she conceded, and grinned at Drake. 'I'll be thinking about you crawling around in the mud while I'm sipping wine and eating sweetmeats.'

'I'll try to think kindly of you too,' Drake riposted, returning the smile, although he wasn't entirely sure if it had really been meant for him. He turned to Horst. 'What about you?'

'I'll be trailing Keira,' Horst said. 'If she really makes contact with a heretic group, she might need back-up in a hurry.'

'I'm flattered,' Keira said, turning the smile briefly on him. Then she shrugged. 'If there's nothing else to discuss, I'd better hit the books. If I'm going to bluff my way through a philosophy seminar tonight, I'll have to at least look as though I know what the conversation's about.'

'I think we're about done here,' Horst agreed, and Keira withdrew, dropping a final mischievous curtsey in the doorway. As soon as she was out of sight, he turned a perplexed expression on Drake. 'Do you think she's all right?'

'She looks fine to me,' Drake said. 'Why do you ask?'

Horst's air of puzzlement grew more pronounced. 'She seems different, somehow. Not quite herself.' He began to look worried. 'Hell of a time for her to be sickening for something.'

Despite himself, Drake couldn't quite suppress a smile. It seemed that his talk with the girl on the terrace that morning was having unexpected repercussions.

'Maybe she's getting used to playing the lady,' he suggested, 'staying in character for the servants' benefit.' It was hardly the time to mention his suspicions about her feelings for the man, even if he'd been willing to take the chance. None of his business, simple as that.

'You're probably right,' Horst said slowly, and then smiled. 'In any case, it's a distinct improvement.'

* * *

The Gorgonid Mine, Sepheris Secundus
101.993.M41

THE REFUGE KANTRIS had led them to was a long, echo-ing tunnel, the perpetual chill in the air raising goosebumps on Elyra's arms even through the thick padding of her jacket. A constant wind seemed to be blowing past them, into the depths, and she'd won-dered about that until Kyrlock had told her they were in a ventilation shaft of some kind. Hazy about the lay-out of the mine, she'd simply shrugged and taken his word for it.

'I've seen worse,' she said, ignoring his expression of scepticism. If he felt inclined to argue about it, or press her for details, he kept the impulse under control, con-scious of the other ears that might be listening.

There were at least a couple of dozen other people sharing the chilly refuge with them, but she had no idea of their exact number, the fringes of the crowd lost in the enveloping gloom. Most were clearly serfs, hud-dled together in mute, mistrustful groups. There were a few families among them, whose children ran about the place with the directionless energy of the young and unconcerned, or grizzled in their mothers' arms, depending on age or temperament. Elyra marvelled at the desperation their parents must have felt to subject their infants to such an ordeal, but Kyrlock had simply shrugged when she verbalised the thought.

'What else have they got to look forward to?' he countered. 'They'll spend their whole lives down here otherwise, or somewhere just like it.' He looked at the gaunt and haggard faces of the adults suspiciously. 'You'd do better wondering what they did to raise the price of their passage.'

Elyra nodded soberly. She'd often seen what desperation could drive people to, in her years of service to the Inquisition, and had no doubt that many were here as the result of some reckless criminal act.

Apart from the families, there were many men, and a few women, who sat alone, or in huddled groups of two or three. Like the parents and their children, they all carried small bundles of possessions, perhaps everything they owned, which they clung to as much for reassurance as the fear of theft. A handful were better dressed than the serfs that surrounded them, their faces etched with even greater misery if that were possible, and Elyra wondered if they were former servants who'd fallen foul of their employers, as she was pretending to have done, or luckless aristocrats whose fortunes had declined too far and too fast for them to have found any other way of escaping their debts.

None of their fellow refugees seemed inclined to engage in conversation, however, Kyrlock's visible weapons creating an intangible cordon around them, which no one dared to breech, apart from the occasional curious child, who would turn and run as soon as Elyra smiled in their direction. The pair of them looked like trouble, that much was obvious, and everyone else already had more than enough of that.

'This looks like a well-established route,' Elyra said quietly, rejoining Kyrlock after a short and necessary trip to the makeshift midden that her nose had led her to with little difficulty.

Kyrlock glanced up. 'How can you tell?' he asked.

Elyra made a grimace of disgust, the stench still hammering at her sinuses. 'An awful lot of people have been through here,' she said, 'just trust me on that.'

'OK.' Kyrlock nodded. Then he took a tighter grip on the shotgun. 'Company's coming.'

Elyra turned her head, feeling the faint crackle of tension against her skin, like the first presentiment of a distant thunderstorm, which meant the presence of another of the warp-touched in close proximity. 'I know,' she said.

Shadows were moving in the depths of the tunnel, further into the mine, and she strained her eyes, trying to make them out. A small group of people stumbled out of the darkness, and she shuddered in spite of herself, recognising the taint they carried. They were a motley group, a trio of youngsters, two boys and a girl, all in their teens, and an older man, who seemed to be in his mid-thirties. The juvies were all dressed soberly, in clothes not too dissimilar to her own, while the adult wore a long coat against the chill, its fabric of noticeably higher quality than the garments of his protégés.

As they reached the straggle of refugees, the ragged crowd seemed to part, making way for the new arrivals, as though they could feel the corruption of the warp seeping from the bodies approaching them. A second or so later, Elyra realised that the innate deference of the serfs was responsible for their actions, not the miasma of psychic energy she alone could feel. Their leader glanced up, meeting her eyes, and she knew he'd recognised her at once for what she was.

'You're gifted,' he said, approaching to within easy conversational distance, where his voice wouldn't carry as far as the other refugees. His little group of acolytes hung back, staring at her mistrustfully.

Elyra nodded, affecting an air of nonchalance. 'Takes one to know one,' she said easily.

The man nodded, dark oiled ringlets brushing against the shoulders of his expensive coat. 'Can you do anything useful?' he asked casually.

Recognising the implicit challenge, and responding in the way most rogue psykers would, Elyra smiled ferally in response. 'Want to find out?' she asked, her voice low and dangerous. Most of the wyrds she'd encountered before had been marginally sane at best, and wouldn't think twice about using their talent aggressively if they felt threatened.

The man smiled. 'I don't think you need to demonstrate,' he said quietly. He gestured around them, taking in the crowd of refugees. 'Not in front of the sheep.' He glanced briefly, and without interest, at Kyrlock. 'I take it this one already knows what you are.'

'He does,' Kyrlock agreed, raising the shotgun, 'and he doesn't give a flying rut about it if she can get him off-planet. Think about that, if you want to give us any grief.'

'Far from it,' the man said, with a hint of amusement. 'Please put the gun down.' Kyrlock's knuckles whitened with the effort of trying to hold the weapon on aim, but its barrel dipped anyway, to point harmlessly at the cavern floor.

'So that's what you do,' Elyra said, contriving to sound unimpressed.

'She's a pyro,' one of the teenage boys said suddenly, spasming. A trickle of drool ran out of the corner of his mouth. 'I can see the flames in her aura.' His voice was cracked and reedy, and Elyra fought down a moment of panic. If he was a telepath, he might be able to read a lot more than that. Then reason reasserted itself. Her blocks would be secure against an untrained talent, even if he was able to read minds, and there was no guarantee that this lad could, since all he'd demonstrated so far was a knack for divination.

'Thank you, Ven,' the man said, glancing around briefly, and then returning his attention to Elyra. 'He's a sensitive. Limited at the moment, but with the right training, who knows?'

'If he doesn't burn out, or the Black Ships don't get him,' Elyra said.

The man nodded thoughtfully. 'Neither of which has happened to you. You must have been in hiding for a long time, and mastered your gift on your own.'

'It happens,' Elyra said neutrally.

'I know. I'm another case in point.' The man smiled, in a self-deprecating fashion. 'But not all our kind are as lucky, which is why I try to help them whenever I get the chance.' He looked across at the trio of teenagers. 'I send the most promising off-world, where they can find a safe refuge.'

'How very generous,' Elyra said. 'What's in it for you?'

'Nothing, beyond the satisfaction of knowing I've saved a life that would otherwise be blighted, and cut short.' The smile became a failed attempt to convey sincerity. 'My friends and I think of ourselves as a charity, working to make the galaxy a happier place.'

'How nice,' Elyra said, her mind racing. Carolus's instincts had obviously been correct, the people-smugglers providing a conduit between worlds for rogue psykers, but there was clearly more to it than that. This man, whoever he was, had all but told her in plain Gothic that he was part of a wider conspiracy, but how far across the sector it spread was still a mystery. What she said in the next few seconds would determine whether she would still be able to follow the chain to its next link, or perhaps be unmasked as an Inquisitorial agent, with fatal consequences. 'I hope you enjoy your trip.' She turned to Kyrlock. 'Pack up your stuff, we're leaving.'

'What?' Kyrlock had given up trying to regain control of the shotgun, leaving it hanging limply from his hand, but he was still quick enough on the uptake to cling doggedly to their cover story. He picked up his rucksack in his other hand, glaring at her angrily. 'You said you were going to get us off-planet!'

'I am. Just not this trip.' Elyra shrugged her backpack into place. 'Kantris can make other arrangements for us.' She glanced contemptuously at the trio of teen psykers, a few paces behind their enigmatic mentor. 'I've spent years learning how to hide what I am, and I'm not going to risk getting caught by the Inquisition because there's a wyrd crèche along for the ride.'

'Good point,' Kyrlock said, following her lead.

The man smiled. 'I don't think you need worry too much about that,' he said. 'They're all housebroken, and one of my associates will pick them up on arrival.' He paused, waiting for her to ask who his associates were. When she remained silent, he went on. 'Don't feel you have to change your plans on our account.'

'It's too big a chance,' Elyra said. 'I've survived this long by keeping my head down, and I'm not about to start taking stupid risks now.' For a moment, as she began to turn away, she wondered if she'd overplayed her hand. Then the man spoke again.

'Suppose you didn't have to keep your head down any more,' he said quietly.

'What's that supposed to mean?' Elyra asked, checking the movement.

The man looked her in the eyes, his sincerity as palpable as if he'd just sworn on the aquila. 'My associates would be prepared to offer you refuge too,' he said. 'You'd be protected, your gifts made full use of, and you'd never have to fear the Black Ships again.'

'Yeah, right.' Elyra laughed in his face. 'Like I'm about to trust someone I've only just met. For all I know you're an Inquisition skag paid to deliver suckers like me to the interrogators. I'll take my chances, thanks. I've done all right so far.'

'Then why are you running?' the man asked reasonably. 'You must be desperate to get away, or you wouldn't be here. My guess is, you're not doing as well as you'd like to think.'

'I've got somebody after me,' Elyra said, 'but it's nothing to do with my gift. I slept with her husband and stole her shinies, and she's got a bounty killer on my arse. Satisfied?'

The well-dressed man broke into peals of laughter, which sounded perfectly genuine to Elyra. They echoed from the broken walls around them, eliciting startled glances from the surrounding refugees, who averted their eyes again almost at once. The unforced merriment sounded entirely out of place in this despairing oubliette, making the milling serfs restive and nervous. 'Oh my,' he said at last. 'And that's your idea of keeping your head down, is it?'

'I never said it was easy,' Elyra said, allowing a reciprocal smile to soften the truculent expression she'd adopted. Her strategy had worked, after all. The mysterious psyker had swallowed her story, all the more readily for her apparent reluctance to trust him, and the next stage was to build on the rapport she'd established. 'A girl's got to have some fun, after all.'

'I suppose so,' the man said. He'd check up on who she was supposed to be, that much was certain, but she'd been careful to lead him in the direction of her cover story, so whatever he discovered would probably check out. If it didn't... Well, she'd just have to worry about that when the time came. 'Think about my offer. If you decide to trust us, we'd be pleased to help you. If not, go your own way when you reach Scintilla, and may the Powers protect you.'

'I'll think about it,' she said grudgingly.

'Good.' He turned back to his trio of protégés, and conversed with them for a short while in an undertone. Then, leaving them to settle as best they could on the hard stone floor, he turned, and disappeared back down the passage from which he'd emerged.

'Holy Throne,' Kyrlock murmured as the man disappeared. 'Some piece of work.' He made the sign of the aquila, and spat, glaring at the trio of disconsolate teenagers. 'Pus-rotted wyrds.' Then he cleared his throat, and glanced sidelong at Elyra. 'Sorry. No offence.'

'None taken,' Elyra reassured him, swallowing the old bile, which still tasted as bitter as ever. 'I've been called a lot worse.'

'That was really clever,' Kyrlock ventured a moment later, and Elyra smiled, appreciating the clumsy attempt to make amends, 'getting him to trust you like that.'

'I just turned his suspicions against him,' Elyra said. 'The more hostile and distrusting I seemed, the more he ended up trying to win me over. Now he thinks it was his idea to pass me on to the next link in the chain.'

'I get it.' Kyrlock nodded. 'Like the thing you did with that piece of pipe, taking it off the guy who was trying to hit you with it.'

'Pretty much,' Elyra said, surprised that he was capable of such insight. 'It's all a matter of using their strength to your own advantage.'

'Then let's hope we're facing a lot of strength,' Kyrlock said soberly, "cause I think we're going to need all the advantage we can get.'

SIXTEEN

The Gorgonid Mine, Sepheris Secundus
102.993.M41

THE SUN WAS setting behind the western peaks, throwing them into silhouette in a manner that reminded Drake uncomfortably of fangs in a closing jaw, as he began his descent into the Gorgonid. It was a trip he'd only made a handful of times before, despite having spent most of his life in the glittering glass city suspended above it, and he stepped onto the platform of the elevator with a tingle of exhilaration. This was the first time he'd been entrusted with an assignment entirely on his own since joining the Angelae, and he was determined to vindicate Horst's apparent confidence in him.

Keeping his expression impassive, he'd walked past the red-uniformed Scourges manning the security point with barely a glance in their direction, a wide-brimmed hat pulled down low to shade his eyes. This had been a small, but calculated risk. The chances of one of his former comrades being on duty at the cable head, part of the perpetually bored detail assigned there in case a serf rebellion should unexpectedly erupt in the mine below and attempt to send a suicidal raiding party up the wire to annoy their betters, was minimal, but still a remote possibility. None of the faces seemed familiar, though, and he strode briskly past them, conscious of the part he was supposed to be playing, exuding an arrogant self-confidence that plainly warned anyone in the vicinity that he wasn't to be trifled with.

The apprentice from the Guild of Elevation and Descent manning the creaking metal gates had scanned the papers Vex had spent most of the afternoon preparing, identifying him as a servant of the non-existent Marquise de Granbie on personal business for his patroness. Without meeting his eyes, he waved him through with a deferential tilt of the head appropriate to a functionary of the highest status, clearly wary of provoking him. If the lad found those credentials intimidating, Drake thought, he could barely imagine his reaction if he'd produced the Inquisitorial rosette that Horst had entrusted him with shortly before he'd left the villa. Where it had come from, he had no idea. Perhaps Inquisitor Finurbi had left badges of office in the team leader's charge, to be given to the new recruits whenever he felt they'd proven themselves. Either that, or it had belonged to a former member of the group who'd fallen in the service of the Emperor.

Dismissing the irrational impulse to take it out and examine it for bloodstains, he leaned against the grille enclosing the platform, looking down towards the vast pit in the ground, attempting to orientate himself. The spoil heaps of the Tumble were clearly visible in the distance, and he narrowed his eyes, trying to locate the shaft where Vos and Elyra were hidden. There was no obvious sign of it, though, just as he'd expected, and he shrugged indifferently. He'd find them, he had no doubt of that. Vex had given him a portable auspex unit, no larger than a data-slate, which was communing in some fashion with Elyra's vox. All he had to do was perform the rituals the tech-priest had shown him, and the little machine-spirit would guide his footsteps unerringly to their hiding place.

The platform shuddered as the Guild journeyman in charge of the motivators threw another shovelful of coal into the furnace, kicked the steampipes, recited the prayer of descent, and pulled the lever in front of him. With a grinding shriek of abused metal the whole structure jerked into motion, and began to slide stiffly down the guide tracks, the steel hawsers at each corner of the platform humming gently as the great drums in the winding house above it began to pay out.

There were few other passengers at this time of the evening, as Drake had expected, increasing his chances of being spotted by the people he wanted to notice him. By law, the barons had to reside in the mine holdings they owned, although most maintained apartments in the city above as well. Later, the elevators would be relatively full of the highborn and their retinues fleeing the squalor of the Gorgonid for the more pleasant environment above them, or returning to their groundside homes for as short a time as possible to maintain their property rights before decamping for Icenholm again.

Now, however, the platform was almost empty, apart from a couple of sullen looking noblemen discussing the

laziness and cupidity of the average serf in loud and braying voices, and a lady whose exquisitely cut gown and
preternatural beauty marked her out as a high-class cour-
tesan paying a house call. Clearly noticing Drake's
scrutiny she yawned delicately, and fluttered flirtatious
eyelashes in his direction, but mindful of the part he was
supposed to be playing he simply scowled and turned
away. Amused, the woman made a vulgar hand gesture
implying that he preferred the company of his own gen-
der, which Drake also ignored.

After about twenty minutes of uncomfortable
tedium the platform clanked and wheezed to a stop,
and the apprentice scurried forward to open the gates.
Waiting until the braying fops had disembarked, and
the lady of negotiable virtue had undulated her way to
a waiting litter, Drake stepped out of the elevator and
onto the cracked stone surface of the Gorgonid.

'I'm down,' he voxed briefly, tapping the comm-bead
in his ear just enough to draw attention to it if anyone
was watching.

'Acknowledged,' Vex replied at once. 'Listening out.'
The faint hiss of static in his ear died away again, and
Drake looked around, orientating himself. A couple of
loitering mine workers glanced away with elaborate
casualness, and he nodded quietly with satisfaction. So
far so good; his arrival had been noticed, and word of
the expected bounty hunter's arrival would soon be
spreading through the underworld of the Gorgonid,
consolidating Vos and Elyra's cover. Spotting the artificial hills of the Tumble in the distance he set out
towards them, the weight of the Scalptaker in its shoulder rig a quietly reassuring presence beneath his coat.

* * *

Icenholm, Sepheris Secundus
102.993.M41

'MY DEAR, YOU look even more ravishing than you did last night,' Adrin said, welcoming Keira into the opulent foyer of the Conclave lodge. From Horst's position across the street, the viscount looked genuinely pleased to see the girl as he ushered her inside. His voice, attenuated by the tiny speaker in Horst's ear, came through clearly enough, along with a persistent and vaguely irritating thudding sound, which he'd eventually identified as Keira's heartbeat.

Sending the young assassin in with a hidden transmitter had been a risk, but one Horst had decided was acceptable under the circumstances. If the Conclave did turn out to be a nest of heretics, even her redoubtable combat abilities might not be enough to get Keira out in one piece, and he wanted to be aware of the first sign of trouble.

Part of him wondered about this. He'd ordered her into far greater danger before, without a qualm, but this time he felt an unusual degree of concern for her safety. Perhaps it was the way she'd been acting at the briefing, he thought, so unlike her usual self. He'd never even considered the possibility that she could be vulnerable before, her habitual self-confidence only serving to underscore her innate lethality, but her uncharacteristically quiet demeanour was disturbing. If she was preoccupied with something it might distract her at a crucial moment, with fatal consequences.

For some reason, his conversation with Elyra came to mind, and with it some worrying new reflections. Supposing the psyker had been right, and Keira was just beginning to realise the true nature of her feelings for him. What would that do to her judgement and objectivity, not to mention her screwed-up Redemptionist world view? And if he was suddenly feeling irrationally protective of her, what did that say about his own judgement, and his fitness to lead the group? Perhaps he should mention his doubts in his next progress report, and ask Inquisitor Finurbi's advice.

If he did that, what then? The inquisitor might simply assign one of them to another team, and solve the problem that way. The thought of that happening, perhaps never seeing the girl again, brought an unexpectedly sharp pang with it. Irritating as she was, she was still his responsibility, and if she was attempting to wrestle with some inner daemons his presence in her orbit had somehow unwittingly raised, he felt obliged to help her deal with them. Besides, if she was undergoing some kind of personal transformation, the new Keira might be worth getting to know: perhaps a lot more intimately than he'd ever thought of getting to know the old one.

Vex's voice suddenly sounded in his comm-bead, and he seized on the distraction gratefully. 'Danuld's down,' the tech-priest reported.

'Good.' Horst continued to watch the foyer across the street, thankful for the Secundan predilection for glass, and the concealing bulk of a solid iron stanchion supporting the causeway a level above where he stood. 'Let me know when he makes contact.' That wouldn't be for some hours yet, he suspected. The former Guardsman would have to go through the motions of trying to find Elyra and Vos first, and then fade quietly into the shadows. It would have been much easier if the two undercover agents could have carried hidden microphones too, like Keira, but Vex had insisted that nothing that small had sufficient range, and even if it had, the risk of discovery would be far too great. An ordinary vox could be explained away if it was discovered in Elyra's pack, but obvious espionage gear could have only one purpose.

'Of course,' Vex said, and cut the link, leaving only the sound of Keira's heartbeat pulsing gently in Horst's ear.

'Leaving so soon?' Adrin's voice enquired, still idly conversational, and Horst returned his attention to the Conclave lodge across the street. The viscount and Keira had been joined by two other figures who seemed vaguely familiar, a man and a woman in sober garb, who had paused for a moment as they crossed the lobby.

'There's nothing else to detain us,' the man said levelly, his face coming into profile as he turned to reply, provoking a sudden shock of recognition in the hidden watcher across the street. Shorn of their garish mourning clothes, away from their own domain, Lord and Lady Tonis seemed shrunken and diminished. 'Our business is concluded, and our attorney has already left. Thank you for providing a discreet place to discuss our affairs away from prying eyes.'

'It was most appreciated,' Lady Tonis added, taking her husband's arm.

'It was no trouble,' Adrin assured them. 'The Lodge of the Golden Wing has always prided itself on being more than a mere academic institution. Your son was a valued and popular member, and we're only too happy to offer whatever assistance we can at this most difficult of times. Please don't hesitate to call on us again, if you feel the need.'

'Thank you,' Lord Tonis said, his air of politeness
sounding slightly strained even through the attenuat-
ing vox link, 'but we won't need to bother you any
further. Everything is quite in order.' He nodded formally, and turned away, his wife still attached to his
arm. Their dull grey clothes blended easily into the
bustling crowd as they stepped out onto the street, and
Horst had to exert all his old arbitrator's instincts to
keep them in sight .

'Hybris,' he voxed, moving out of the shadow of the
stanchion. 'Tonis's parents were here. They must be
preparing to run.' He hesitated for a moment, wondering if he should stay to back up Keira after all, but
dismissed the thought. She wouldn't have entertained
a moment's doubt in the same position, and neither
should he. 'Get Barda on standby, we might need the
shuttle.'

'Acknowledged,' the tech-priest said coolly.

Triggering a brief series of coded vox clicks to warn
Keira of his withdrawal, Horst slipped easily into the
flow of foot traffic, praying silently to Him on Earth
that he was making the right decision, and that he
wouldn't lose the fugitive aristocrats in the hurrying
throng. Within a few score metres the rhythmic thudding of Keira's heartbeat in his ear had faded away, to
be replaced entirely by the pounding of his own, and
after that he had no time to consider anything beyond
the necessity of keeping his quarry in sight.

As THE CODED pulse rattled briefly in her hidden
receiver Keira felt a brief moment of surprise, but
masked it easily, continuing to chat to Adrin as though
she had nothing on her mind beyond another pleasant
meal and a little intellectual jousting to look forward

to. *Forced withdrawal: new target.* What in the warp was that supposed to mean? There was no point verbalising the question, though, even if she'd been able to. Her jade earrings, chosen to offset the green of her eyes, weren't large enough to conceal a full vox receiver, and the matching pendant nestling comfortably just above the low-cut neckline of the rich purple gown Lilith had selected to complement her hair only had room for a minute, short-ranged transmitter.

Not that it mattered; she was used to working alone, preferred it even. That said, the knowledge that Mordechai had been listening in, hovering just out of sight in case things went wrong, had been reassuring in a peculiar kind of way.

She didn't know why he'd departed so radically from their usual operating procedure, which had been mildly unsettling, but what the hell, he was in charge, he could make whatever arrangements he liked. Maybe he'd noticed she was trying to be more cooperative this morning, and offering to watch her back had been his way of reassuring her that he appreciated the effort she was making. Danuld had been talking complete nonsense, of course, but he was right about one thing: she'd fallen into the habit of challenging Mordechai needlessly over trivial matters, and that was bad for the mission. Or maybe she'd pushed him too far, before the talk on the terrace this morning had brought her back to her senses, and he simply didn't trust her to operate independently any more. Well, if that was the case, she'd just have to show him she still deserved his confidence.

There was another possibility, a small, insinuating voice suggested, despite her best efforts to ignore it. Perhaps he'd drawn the same ridiculous conclusion about her behaviour that Danuld had, and felt some-how responsible for her apparent loss of focus. That would explain why he wanted to keep an eye on her. Or perhaps he felt some well-hidden affection, recip-rocating the feelings he thought he'd detected in her, which would at least explain why he was such a pompous prig most of the time. Just what Danuld had said, in fact, but about the wrong person.

This startling thought struck her with the force of a shock maul, driving the breath from her lungs. Recov-ering as best she could, she forced herself to concentrate on Adrin's casual conversation, hoping he hadn't noticed anything unusual in her demeanour. To her relief, he was still looking the other way, watching the couple he'd greeted a moment before as they passed out of sight along the street.

'They seemed pleasant enough,' she remarked, as though the matter was of very little interest.

Adrin nodded. 'Lord and Lady Tonis. Their son was a tech-priest, who used to run one of our study groups before he had an unfortunate accident.' He frowned, as if trying to recall something trivial. 'Did I mention that?'

'Last night,' Keira said, nodding. No wonder Mordechai had taken off so fast. The sudden appear-ance of two proven heretics, right where they expected to find a cell of them, was too strong a lead to ignore, and following them was bound to take priority over a routine back-up assignment. 'Archeotech, wasn't it?'

'That's right.' Adrin nodded casually. 'He was con-vinced there were still a few artefacts from the first colonisation lying around somewhere on Sepheris Secundus. The problem was finding them, if they ever even existed.'

'Do you think he was right?' Keira asked, taking his arm and strolling towards the dining room.

Adrin shrugged. 'Possibly. The whole planet's either wilderness, or holes in the ground. If you wanted to lose something, I can't think of anywhere in the sector more suited to the purpose.' Then he grinned. 'If he was right, though, he never found anything. Not to my knowledge, anyway.'

'How very disappointing for him,' Keira said, catching the enticing aroma of sautéed mushrooms, and trying to ignore the quickening of her appetite.

The Gorgonid Mine, Sepheris Secundus
102.993.M41

THE DAY HAD passed slowly, with little to mark the passage of time in the dank, chilly darkness. Kyrlock had busied himself as best he could in checking his weapons, which had done little to ease the visible apprehension of the refugees surrounding them, but that could only engage his attention for so long. Unable to take refuge in the traditional soldier's time killer of sleep, he simply kept watch as best he could, exchanging the occasional desultory remark with Elyra, lapsing ever deeper into the sullen silence that Drake would have recognised at once as a precursor to trouble.

The more he thought about the situation they were in, the less he found to like. Kantris had already attempted to kill them and steal the jewellery Elyra was carrying, and now they were stuck at the bottom of some Emperor forsaken hole guarded by the man's confederates. True, having seen how badly he'd under-estimated them, he was unlikely to try anything quite so direct again, but there was still plenty of scope for treachery before they found their way aboard a starship.

And that was another thing: despite his display of eagerness to get off-planet, so essential for the mission, Kyrlock was scared witless at the prospect. All his life he'd heard dark stories about the malign nature of the warp, and the prospect of entering that shadowy realm was not one he relished. Even that, though, was less disturbing than the presence, no more than a few metres away, of the trio of young psykers that the mysterious man from the depths of the mine had left with them.

It hadn't been so bad at first, they'd kept themselves to themselves, which he could more or less live with, but after a while the girl had approached Elyra and attempted to strike up a conversation. Now, the psyker was chatting with all of them, albeit with the same surliness she'd affected in front of their patron, and Kyrlock didn't like that at all. Something about their eyes, their quick, febrile movements, reminded him all too vividly of the inmates of the Citadel he and Danuld had encountered after the breakout.

'How did you manage to survive for so long?' the girl asked, her pale blue eyes fixed on Elyra with disturbing intensity. Her face was narrow, and framed with shoulder length hair, so blonde it seemed almost white. A faint sheen of radiance appeared to cling to it, although that could just have been the reflections cast by the intermittent light sources scattered around the cavern. At least Kyrlock hoped that was what it was. Her name, he gathered, was Zusen. The pale, twitchy lad with curly brown hair who'd somehow known what Elyra could do was Ven, and the other one, with the shaved head and the acne, answered to Trosk, when he could be bothered to say anything at all.

Elyra shrugged. 'I've been lucky.'

'I don't think so.' The girl looked at Elyra with feral intensity. 'You're strong enough to make your own luck, we can all feel that. We want to be strong too.'

'Good for you,' Elyra said. She pantomimed thinking deeply about the girl's question. 'Don't use your talents where anyone can see, that's a good start.'

'I told you,' Trosk said. 'You're wasting your breath. Bitch like that's only ever going to be out for herself.' He stretched out on the hard rocky floor, pillowing his head on his folded jacket, with elaborate casualness.

'Damn right she is,' Elyra said. She glanced at Kyrlock for confirmation. He shrugged and nodded, and she went on. 'I take what I want, and I do what I want, but I'm careful.'

'Careful enough to be running for your life,' Trosk said. He'd obviously had the sense to listen while Elyra had been talking to their mysterious guardian.

'I was getting bored on this mudball anyway,' Elyra said. 'Bodyguarding parasites was a meal ticket for a while, but it's not much of a challenge.' She grinned, apparently struck by a new and amusing thought. 'Maybe I'll turn bounty once we get to Scintilla, try chasing instead of running for a change.' She glanced across at Kyrlock. 'Like the sound of that, Vos? You get to beat people up and get paid for it.'

'Sweet,' Kyrlock said shortly. 'But we're not there yet.'

'You'd really do that?' Zusen was looking at Elyra with something approaching contempt. 'Waste your time chasing bounties with a deadmind?' She glanced at her compatriots. 'You talk pretty big, but we're the ones who are really going to shake the galaxy.'

'Zu,' Ven said in a warning tone, 'remember what they said.'

'Yeah, Zu,' Elyra said mockingly, 'do as you're told, like a good little wyrd. That's one way to stay out of trouble.'

'You don't know anything about it!' the girl said, her face colouring as she rose to the bait. 'The people we're with are powerful. They can protect us. If you want to keep looking over your shoulder for the Inquisition every day for the rest of your life, that's your choice, and it's a stupid one.'

'They haven't caught up with me yet,' Elyra said, 'and I don't have anyone telling me what to do either.' She grinned, and patted the girl condescendingly on the shoulder. 'I tell you what, I'll wipe your noses till we get to where we're going, and your babysitter shows up. If I like what the grown-ups tell me, I might decide to tag along after all. Sound fair?'

'Lucky us,' Trosk said. 'And if you don't?'

'Bust heads with Vos for a while,' Elyra said, shrugging indifferently. Then she grinned again. 'At least if there's a price on yours, I'll have a good start on the opposition.'

'I'd like to see you try,' Zusen said, with a flash of vindictiveness that had Kyrlock reaching surreptitiously for the grip of his shotgun. There was no telling what abilities she had, and if she was about to lash out in some way he'd drop her where she stood and to hell with the consequences. 'You've really got no idea what you're dealing with.'

'Like I haven't heard that before,' Elyra said, a smile quirking at the corner of her mouth. She ruffled Zusen's hair affectionately, apparently oblivious to the clenching of the girl's jaw in response. 'Don't sweat it, kiddies. If your little gang's as good as you say, I'll make sure you get through to your nursemaid. Think of it as an audition.' Leaving them muttering resentfully among themselves, she ambled back to Kyrlock and sat on her pack.

'Was that really sensible?' Kyrlock asked, looking up. 'Riding them like that?'

Elyra nodded. 'Rogue psykers are generally paranoid sociopaths. If I was trying to be their new best friend they'd smell a rat in a heartbeat.'

'I see.' Kyrlock echoed the gesture thoughtfully. 'The same technique you used on the other guy.'

'Exactly,' Elyra said. 'Now they're desperate to impress me. We'll have weeks on the ship together to let them think they're winning me round, and when we tag along with their escort once we get to Scintilla they'll think it was all their idea.'

'Hm.' Kyrlock considered this for a moment. 'They might take you, you're a psyker, but there's no way they'll just let me come along for the ride.'

'Maybe not,' Elyra agreed, 'but in my experience heretic groups can always do with more muscle. We'll have time to work out a strategy before we reach orbit, anyhow. If the worst comes to the worst, I'll just have to follow the underground while you make a run for the Tricorn and contact Carolus. He'll know what to do.'

'I guess,' Kyrlock said, surprised at how uncomfortable that thought made him feel. If he really wanted to go his own way once they made planetfall, that would be the perfect excuse. On the other hand, it would leave Elyra's life hanging by a thread, and he wasn't sure he could do that. It wasn't as if they were friends or anything, but she trusted him, and so had the inquisitor. That was a novel sensation, and one he rather liked.

Ah well, as she'd just pointed out, the journey would give him plenty of time to consider his options.

Icenholm, Sepheris Secundus
102.993.M41

THE FOOD WAS as pleasant as Keira had been expecting, and the dining room a little more crowded than it had been the previous night. She remarked on the fact, round a mouthful of fungi *en croute*, and her host nodded.

'The philosophy group's a popular one,' he said. 'Most of them are here for the debate.' He nodded affably to the ecclesiarch she'd noticed the evening before, who appeared to be holding forth to a tableful of interested listeners, and who broke off briefly to acknowledge the greeting with a discreet tilt of his head. 'Quarren there's proposing the motion that in order to truly preserve itself, Humanity must make greater use of the psykers among us, turning the taint of Chaos against itself.'

'Hm.' Keira nodded, pausing thoughtfully in the act of spearing some local vegetable she didn't recognise. 'Hardly a new idea, but quite radical coming from a member of the Ecclesiarchy.' She smiled at Adrin. 'Does he really believe that?'

'Who knows?' Adrin replied, sipping at the crystal goblet of wine beside his plate. 'The debate's the important thing. Do you have an opinion on the matter?'

For a moment, Keira was at a loss. Her Redemptionist upbringing had left her in no doubt that anyone touched by the warp was a walking embodiment of Chaos, deserving of nothing less than utter annihilation, but then she'd met Inquisitor Finurbi, who'd turned his formidable psychic powers against the enemies of the Emperor, and Elyra, who'd become one of her closest friends, and that old certainty had crumbled. The woman she was pretending to be would have no emotional response to the question, though, so she merely nodded, as if they were playing an intellectual game.

'I think he has a point,' she agreed, allowing a mischievous glint to enter her eyes. 'If it's good enough for the Emperor, it ought to be good enough for anyone.' The taste of blasphemy was bitter on her tongue, but she forced herself to smile nevertheless. If she was going to establish herself as someone with heretical tendencies, she might never get a better opportunity. She watched Adrin carefully, for signs of shock or outrage, but to her surprise he simply leaned back in his chair and bellowed with laughter, heedless of the startled glances he was attracting from all corners of the room.

'Oh, my dear, that's absolutely priceless. You must repeat that in the debate tonight, it'll completely knock the props out from under him.' He dabbed his eyes delicately with a napkin, and leaned across the table, his expression suddenly earnest. 'But perhaps that's a view you'd better not express too openly in less cosmopolitan company.'

'Absolutely,' Keira agreed, responding in kind to this unexpected shift of mood. 'A lot can be said in a hypothetical debate that wouldn't go down at all well if there was an inquisitor in the room.' She smiled playfully at him. 'You don't have one of those among the members too, do you? You seem to have everything else.'

'No, we don't,' Adrin said, 'but we have attracted their attention recently.' He nodded in the direction of a pale young man sipping soup in the corner, a litter of data-slates around his place setting. 'Abelard had rather an unsettling interview with a pair of their thugs the other day.'

'Did he?' Keira asked, peering curiously in his direction, and making a careful mental note to repeat the remark verbatim to Mordechai the next time she saw him. Just because she was trying to be a bit more cooperative didn't mean she had to give up teasing him entirely. 'He doesn't look like a heretic to me.'

'I don't think they generally go around carrying a placard saying, "I'm a heretic,"' Adrin said mildly, 'but you're right, of course he isn't. They were asking questions about Tonis.'

'Your tech-priest friend? Really?' Keira feigned rapt attention. 'What for?'

'Emperor knows,' Adrin said. 'Something to do with his work, probably. He never talked about it, but it was pretty obvious it was sensitive.' He shrugged. 'I just thought I should mention it. They might still be keeping an eye on the place. Or an ear.'

'Don't worry,' Keira said, 'I'm used to being discreet.'

'I'm sure you are,' Adrin said thoughtfully, and took another sip of his wine.

HORST MANAGED TO keep Lord and Lady Tonis in sight more easily than he'd been expecting. They seemed completely unaware of his presence, and if they were anticipating interference or surveillance they gave no

sign of the fact. They strolled easily along wide boule-
vards of glittering glass, talking little, but sharing the
kind of quiet companionship years of close affection
alone can confer. Watching them, Horst was barely
able to contain a stab of envy, knowing that he was
unlikely ever to know such a state. For a moment, he
allowed himself to imagine what it would be like to
walk like that with Keira, but he knew that the path of
duty they'd both chosen would lead them in an
entirely different direction.

Even though he still had only the sketchiest idea of
the layout of the city, his years of experience in shadowing fugitives allowed him to read a great deal into
the couple's unhurried progress. They seemed to be
moving almost at random, as the mood took them,
spiralling outwards towards the edge of the spire, stopping now and again to admire a particular statue or
fresco. Taking advantage of the milling crowds, Horst
edged as close as he dared, hoping to overhear a snatch
of conversation, but the constant cacophony of other
voices drowned out whatever his quarry might be discussing, and their heads remained too close together
for him to try reading their lips on the odd occasion
they turned enough to allow him a glimpse of their
faces.

'Barda's airborne,' Vex reported, distracting him just
long enough for the fugitives to vanish into the crowd.
After a moment of panic-stricken head turning, Horst
caught sight of them again, and closed the distance a
little, determined not to lose them.

'Good,' he responded, keeping his voice level. 'Patch
him through.'

'Receiving you,' Barda said after a moment. 'I can be
with you in three minutes.'

'No,' Horst instructed after a moment's thought. 'Keep clear. If they see the shuttle they'll know we're on to them.'

'No problem,' the young pilot agreed. 'I can establish a holding pattern around the spire.'

'Good,' Horst said, sprinting up a narrow flight of stairs. The steep alleyway was a perfect place for an ambush, and he reached instinctively for his bolt pistol, but found himself in another broad, well-illuminated thoroughfare before he could draw it. The passers-by here were fewer in number, more elaborately and expensively dressed for the most part, and he allowed the distance between him and the Tonises to increase a little. 'Keep scanning for any other aircraft in the vicinity. They might be heading for a pick-up point.'

That would make sense. There were plenty of landing platforms up here, both commercial and private, not to mention innumerable plazas, terraces and gardens where an aircar could set down with little difficulty. His money would be on a shuttle, though, ready to take the fugitives to a waiting starship, which would narrow the number of possible extraction points significantly. He allowed himself to feel a degree of quiet satisfaction for a moment. His judgement had been vindicated; allowing them to remain free would lead the Angelae to more members of the shadowy conspiracy of which Lord and Lady Tonis were undoubtedly a part.

'Will do,' Barda acknowledged. 'What happens if I spot one?'

'Let it go,' Horst said. 'Keep it on auspex, and follow it. If it docks with a starship, record its ident beacon, and if they go somewhere else planetside I'll want the coordinates.'

'You'll have them,' Barda promised, and Horst cut the link. The fugitive couple was entering an empty plaza, dotted with statues of the saints in exquisitely formed glass, and sweet-scented shrubs in neat, formal beds. Acutely aware that there was no crowd left to hide in, and few shadows in the gently glowing vitruvian architecture surrounding them, Horst determined on boldness. Drawing his bolt pistol, he strode confidently into the garden after them.

It was Lady Tonis who noticed him first, glancing up from a hushed conversation with her husband. The two of them had been leaning on the balustrade fringing the far end of the square, their arms around one another's waists, looking down towards the gently glowing pit of the Gorgonid. 'Mr Horst,' she said coldly. 'Come to see us off?'

'I'm afraid not,' Horst said, walking unhurriedly towards them. He tapped the comm-bead. 'Any incoming yet?'

'Not yet,' Barda confirmed.

'You can't stop us, you know,' Lord Tonis said, looking at the bolt pistol with aristocratic disdain.

'I can and I will,' Horst said. 'I'm arresting you both in the name of the Inquisition, on charges of heresy, conspiracy and abetting the enemies of the Emperor. Arbites officers will be here shortly to take you into custody.' At least they should be, if Vex had alerted them as he'd requested.

'If trying to protect our son was an act of heresy, then I'm proud to plead guilty,' Lady Tonis said vehemently.

Her husband nodded. 'As am I.'

'I'm sorry for you both,' Horst said, stepping around a low bench, and surprised to find that he meant it, at least in part. To his even greater surprise, Lady Tonis smiled sadly back at him.

'You know, I believe you are,' she said, 'but Harald and I have had a good life, on the whole.'

Her husband nodded, and kissed her. 'The Emperor's seen fit to bless us in many ways,' he said, 'but with each other most of all.'

'Still nothing incoming,' Barda reported in his ear, and with a sudden surge of horrified understanding, Horst realised the truth.

'There isn't going to be!' he replied, and began to run, still unsure of exactly what he intended to do, but already certain that he'd be too late to find out. With a few final words to one another, which were spoken too low to reach his ears, Lord and Lady Tonis leaned over the balustrade together, kicked up their heels like divers leaving the side of a swimming pool, and vanished over the edge, still locked in one another's arms.

Horst stared downwards, trying to discern some sign of disturbance in the dust wreathed moonscape of the Gorgonid so many kilometres below, or of the couple still falling towards it, but the distance and the darkness robbed him of any sight of either. After a moment, he sighed. 'We've lost them,' he reported simply. 'Resuming surveillance at the Conclave.'

As he turned away, he found the image of the last look the couple had given one another floating in front of his eyes, and he sighed again. He wasn't quite sure what the predominant emotion it stirred within him was, but he strongly suspected that it might be envy.

SEVENTEEN

Icenholm, Sepheris Secundus
103.993.M41

ANYONE ELSE MIGHT have been bored by the long overnight vigil, but Vex rather appreciated the air of tranquillity that permeated the villa now that the servants had retired. Since joining the Angelae, he'd grown used to the almost constant presence of the other members of the team, even finding their relentless undisciplined prattling quite pleasant in a companionable kind of way, but there was no denying that it could be a distraction, especially when Keira and Mordechai started bickering with one another. Why Horst let her get away with such blatant insubordination was a mystery to the tech-priest, but then so was a lot of the interaction between people untouched by the Omnissiah's gift of logical thought, and if their leader was content to let the matter go then he supposed it couldn't have mattered very much.

The villa was almost silent this deep into the night, save for the muted sounds of the city drifting in through the open windows.

He'd dimmed the illumination to a level that allowed the flickering runes on the pict screen to absorb most of his attention, enjoying the soothing familiarity of the rituals of data retrieval. He would have preferred to commune with the mechanism directly, but his responsibilities to the rest of the team precluded that. Merging his consciousness with the pure stream of information would have left him unable to monitor the vox channels as Horst had requested.

So far this evening he'd relayed several messages on the team leader's behalf, all routine, apart from the unexpected scrambling of the shuttle and its tragic aftermath. Deducing that Horst had been shaken more badly than he was willing to admit by the unforeseen suicide of his suspects, Vex had taken it upon himself to liaise with the local Arbites units dealing with the matter, politely deflecting most of their questions with the unassailable authority of his crimson rosette.

A few moments ago he'd passed on another progress report from Drake, who had apparently got bored with shaking down drinkholes and had begun making his way towards Elyra and Kyrlock's hiding place, confident that he'd managed to shake any surveillance.

Vex hoped he was right, or things could get very inconvenient. In any case, there was nothing he could do to influence events in the Gorgonid, so he put the matter out of his mind, and returned to the more satisfying challenge of teasing the shreds of data he wanted out of the great tapestry of records piece by piece, file by file, following innumerable trails with the tireless patience of his calling.

The task had been long and painstaking, but he was finally beginning to get the first nebulous sense of a pattern forming, which, he was quietly confident, would yield some significant information. The ownership records of the mine shaft in which the *faux* fugitives had taken refuge were as labyrinthine as Drake had intimated, but some of the connections they were throwing up were very interesting indeed.

The Tumble, Gorgonid Mine, Sepheris Secundus 103.993.M41

DRAKE WAS GETTING close to the air shaft. The icon on the tiny auspex screen that Vex had given him, which marked his current location, was almost on top of the gently glowing rune indicating the position of Elyra's vox. He'd shaken the shadows he'd picked up at the cable foot some time ago, by the simple expedient of making himself highly visible from the moment he'd first set foot on the mine floor.

Once he was sure he'd attracted the right kind of attention he began blustering and threatening his way around the drinkholes, ostentatiously talking on his comm-bead as he did so, apparently reporting a complete lack of progress to his patron in the city above.

Certain that so egregious a target would be easy to keep in sight, the watchers on his trail had quickly become complacent, and then sloppy. By the time he'd pretended to believe Mung's lies about his brother finding a woman's body up in the Breaks, and ordered a non-existent aircar to meet him on the perimeter road, they'd got so careless they hadn't even followed him out straight away, staying to finish their drinks first.

With a faint smile of satisfaction, Drake had watched
them emerge a moment or two later, glancing around
with an air of faint befuddlement, before heading off
in the direction of the roadway. Once he was sure they
were out of both sight and earshot, he'd moved away
from the shadows that had concealed him, and begun
picking his way carefully through the rubble towards
his colleagues' hiding place.

His progress had been slow and cautious after that,
in marked contrast to the grox charge he'd been displaying before, mindful that even if he'd shaken the
men set to follow him there were still plenty of other
denizens of the nightworld at large in the Tumble,
many of them willing to kill to protect the secrets of
their clandestine business if they were unexpectedly
disturbed. Moving silently at night was almost second
nature to a veteran soldier, though, and he'd managed
to evade any other rovers easily enough. The black
overcoat he wore allowed him to blend easily into the
shadows cast by the spoil heaps, as well as keeping the
night time chill at bay. The cool, even glow of the city
overhead was more than adequate to see by, and he
was able to pick his way through the rubble with confidence, placing each foot carefully before allowing it
to bear his full weight, in order not to disturb the
treacherous surface and betray his position with a care-
lessly dislodged stone.

'I'm almost there,' he voxed, his voice low, and Vex
acknowledged him perfunctorily. Warned by the clatter
of sliding shale ahead, Drake froze, letting the shadows conceal him, as a couple of men walked past a few
metres away, the unmistakable silhouettes of stubbers
slung over their shoulders, a comet tail of lho smoke
drifting in their wake. Drake smiled, thanking the

Emperor for the favour, and slipped through the sentry line around his objective on the heels of the careless guards.

'SOMEONE'S COMING,' KYRLOCK said, nudging Elyra's arm. Startled out of a light doze, she looked up sharply, to see Kantris and another man she didn't know walking towards them down the tunnel with an air of evident purpose. Assuming the air of arrogant self-confidence she'd adopted before, she rose to her feet, slinging the pack she'd been sitting on across one shoulder, angling it so she could grab the laspistol inside instantly if she had to.

'Who's this?' she asked Kantris, seizing the initiative before either he or his companion had a chance to speak. The newcomer was better dressed than anyone she'd encountered since leaving Icenholm, with the possible exception of the man who'd accompanied the fugitive psykers, a cloak of some dark material thrown around a jacket and leggings of unmistakably off-world cut. The colour of his clothes was indeterminate in the gloom, as was the colour of his eyes and hair, all three appearing to Elyra as shades of grey. There was no tingle of recognition to mark him out as warp-touched, but all the same she was disinclined to trust him.

'Felcher Greel,' the man said, his voice showing no sign of warmth, which Elyra found strangely reassuring. Either by accident or design, Greel projected an air of businesslike efficiency completely at odds with Kantris's edgy opportunism. 'I'm the one you pay your fares to.' Out of the corner of her eye, Elyra saw Kyrlock give a faint shake of his head, which merely confirmed the opinion she'd already formed.

'I'm not paying anyone until I see a shuttle or talk to a voider,' she said evenly.

Greel shook his head. 'Doesn't work like that. You pay me, and I pass on their cut to the ship folk, clean and simple.'

'If you want what I've got,' Elyra said, 'you show me you can deliver a foot on the star road. Otherwise my friend and I might start to think we're being set up, and that would be a very big mistake.'

'I told you,' Kantris said, with a resigned sigh, 'this one wouldn't trust her own mother.'

'Neither would you if you had a mother like mine,' Elyra said, feeling a faint twinge of guilt at posthumously slandering the quietly pious woman who'd nurtured her. 'You want the shinies, you convince me there's a ship up there ready to take us.'

'Fine,' Greel said, with a trace of impatience. 'You can talk to the loadmaster if it makes you feel any better. He's down tonight to look over some other business anyway.'

'Works for us,' Kyrlock said, with another mistrustful look at Kantris. However, the fixer's attention had already moved on to the trio of psykers, staring at them with undisguised hostility.

'Who the hell are they?' he demanded.

Greel shrugged. 'More passengers. That's all you need to know.'

'Rut that,' Kantris said. 'I'm supposed to get a cut of everyone who comes through here. Why wasn't I told?'

The grey man's expression turned hard. 'Because you're just the errand boy, Emyl. You scout prospects, and bring them to us. You're not the only one, and you can easily be replaced. You'll get a good commission on these two. If I were you, I'd be content with that.'

He turned and walked away, leaving Kantris's jaw to clench in anger.

'You think that's funny, do you?' Too afraid of Elyra and Kyrlock to risk provoking them, he elected to vent his frustration on the trio of teenagers instead, glaring from one to the other, daring them to make eye contact.

It was Ven who made the mistake of doing so. 'We don't want any trouble,' he began, before Kantris grabbed the front of his jacket, jerked him forwards, and kneed him sharply in the groin. Ven folded, with a squeal of anguish that echoed around the tunnel, drawing startled glances from the surrounding refugees, who then began edging away from the fracas as though the violence might somehow be contagious.

'Well you've got some anyway,' the fixer snarled, kicking him in the ribs for good measure, and rounding on Trosk. 'You want some too?'

'I'll pass,' Trosk said, taking a step backwards, and raising his hands defensively, although Elyra felt sure he was putting on an act rather than being genuinely frightened. He glanced in her direction with what looked suspiciously like sardonic amusement, clearly not expecting her to make good on her earlier promise.

'Smart boy.' Kantris turned to stare at Zusen, his expression growing even uglier. He took a step towards her. 'How about you, girlie? You like it rough?'

'Leave me alone!' To Elyra's surprise the girl was backing away, a shrill note of panic in her voice, every trace of the overweening self-confidence she'd displayed before evaporating like dew in the morning. 'Don't touch me!' Elyra reached into her pack, her fingers closing around the butt of the weapon inside it.

'I'll touch you all right,' Kantris gloated, grabbing her by the arm and yanking her towards him. Zusen screamed, and tried to pull away. 'If you behave yourself, you might even enjoy it.' A spiteful leer spread across his face as the girl squirmed desperately in his grasp.

'Fun's over, pusbag,' Elyra said, drawing her laspistol and levelling it, her voice a disdainful drawl. 'Put her down, right now, or I'll blow your nads off.'

'Don't think so,' Kantris said, pulling Zusen into a smothering embrace, and grabbing a handful of yielding flesh as he kept her body between himself and Elyra. 'Not without dropping her too.' He grinned lubriciously. 'But if you want her that badly you can have a turn after I've finished.'

'Nice offer, but she won't play,' Kyrlock said, taking a pace towards the pair. 'She's strictly orthodox.' He smiled, aping Kantris's malicious expression. 'Me, now, I'd be tempted.'

Elyra hesitated. She hadn't known Kyrlock for long, but this seemed wholly out of character. If she was wrong though, and he was genuinely about to turn his coat, things were going to get ugly really fast. There would be no second chance if she didn't get it right. Making up her mind instantaneously, she swung the pistol around to cover him instead.

'I'm warning you, Vos, you lay a finger on that girl and I'll be shipping for Scintilla alone.'

'It wasn't my finger I was planning to use,' Kyrlock said, grinning, and taking another step towards the struggling girl. Then he shrugged, regretfully, beginning to turn away. 'You win. I need to get off-world a damn sight more than I need a quick...'

'Just you and me, then, girlie,' Kantris said, eliciting another wordless wail of protest from Zusen, and dragging her back a pace to keep Kyrlock between them and the muzzle of Elyra's pistol.

'Wrong,' Kyrlock said, turning suddenly, the chain axe coming free of its retaining straps in one fluid movement, and the clumsy weapon spinning effortlessly in his hands. With a *crack* that resonated around the cavern, the butt of the shaft slammed into Kantris's temple. As the stunned expeditor fell, he released his hold on the terrified girl, who ran, howling, towards her friends. Even before he hit the ground Elyra fired once, making good on her earlier promise.

'Nice move,' Elyra said quietly, stowing the laspistol, and stepping over the whimpering fixer.

Kyrlock shrugged. 'I wasn't sure he'd buy it,' he said, 'but I knew you'd realise what I was doing.'

Elyra nodded, unwilling to admit just how marginal her decision to play along had been, and thanking the Emperor for His guidance as always. 'Are you all right, kid?' she asked, as though she didn't much care one way or the other.

'Yes,' Zusen said, sniffling. She looked at Elyra and Kyrlock with something like awe. 'Thank you. I could feel what he wanted to do to me.' Her shoulders shook.

'So you're a 'path,' Elyra said, reflexively strengthening her mental blocks. She was sure that none of them could read minds. She would have recognised the faint insistent pressure against her thoughts if they could, but you couldn't be too careful.

'I can pick up on people's emotions,' Zusen said, to her carefully concealed relief. 'Usually just flashes.' The girl's face crumpled. 'But the images in his mind were so strong... Oh, Emperor...' Tears began to run down her cheeks.

'It's all right now.' To Elyra's surprise, Kyrlock smiled awkwardly at the girl, attempting to calm her, and spat at the whining residue of her would-be violator. 'He won't be trying that again.' He stowed the axe, with rapid expertise. 'I'm sorry if I scared you, but I had to get close enough to take him.'

'You were wonderful,' Zusen said, to his manifest astonishment, flinging her arms around him and burying her face in the Guardsman's grubby furs. 'A real hero.'

After a moment, Kyrlock returned the embrace with a single hesitant arm, his expression that of a man who has suddenly found himself holding a ticking parcel. 'How are the others?' he asked awkwardly.

'I'm fine,' Trosk said, shrugging as he helped his friend to his feet, 'and I imagine Ven'll live.' He looked at Elyra appraisingly. 'I must admit, I'm surprised you bothered to get involved, let alone him.' He nodded at Kyrlock.

'Not half as surprised as he was,' Kyrlock said, glancing at the feebly twitching Kantris with vindictive satisfaction. Despite his evident unease at being so close to an unsanctioned psyker, he looked a lot happier and more relaxed than he had done at any time since they'd left Mung's drinkhole the night before, the brief burst of cathartic violence finally presenting him with a situation he knew how to deal with.

Elyra shrugged. 'I promised I'd get you to where you're going in one piece,' she said. She glanced sardonically at Zusen, who seemed in no hurry to leave the shelter of Kyrlock's arm. 'Still think the deadmind's a waste of space?' Zusen's face flamed scarlet, although she seemed unable to think of a suitably pithy rejoinder.

Hurrying footsteps echoed along the tunnel, and Kyrlock tensed, reaching for the shotgun at his back, before Elyra forestalled him with a gesture. Greel was approaching, a laspistol in his hand. A couple of men in the rough costume of the local peasantry walked at his shoulders, both carrying shotguns. Going for a weapon now could result in a bloodbath. The men slowed as they approached, and Greel glanced down at the feebly twitching Kantris.

'What happened?' he asked, holding the laspistol casually, but clearly ready to use it if he had to.

Elyra breathed a faint sigh of relief, keeping her expression neutral and both her hands in view. At least he seemed willing to ask questions before he started shooting. She shrugged, affecting an air of wry amusement, and chose her next words very carefully. 'I think we've just saved you some commission,' she began.

Icenholm, Sepheris Secundus
103.993.M41

'A MOST STIMULATING evening,' Keira said, and yawned elaborately. The lights were dim in the member's lounge of the Conclave, the comfortable chairs clustered in companionable groups around low glass tables unoccupied for the most part, the vast majority of the self-styled philosophers having long since departed. 'Time I was in bed, I think.'

'I was just thinking the same thing,' Adrin said, tilting his glass of well-matured amasec with every sign of satisfaction, and peering at her speculatively over the rim.

Suppressing the urge to snap his neck for his presumption, Keira smiled easily in return, and reached for her drink. What was it about men, she thought irritably. Suddenly, it seemed, every single one of them she came into contact with wanted to sin with her. At least Danuld had been honest about it, and had apologised for his weakness. And if Mordechai really had been harbouring lustful thoughts, if not the purer form of affection her imagination kept returning to in spite of her rational mind insisting on the ridiculousness of the whole idea, he'd had the decency to keep them to himself.

Contemplating that remote possibility ignited the curious fluttering sensation in the pit of her stomach again, and her skin tingled, as though in anticipation of a caress. Her mouth felt suddenly dry, and she sipped the smooth alcohol gratefully. Although she knew that sinning involved touching one another, she was vague about the details, and, secure behind her redoubt of Redemptionist rectitude, had never thought to ask.

Perhaps when Elyra returned she could seek her advice. The psyker had been intimate with men, with the inquisitor even, and everyone knew that inquisitors were the hands of the Emperor and therefore incapable of sinning. So maybe that meant that if His truly pious servants indulged in that sort of thing it wasn't a sin at all. It wasn't if you were married, she knew that, at least according to the Ecclesiarchy, although, since most of them were lamentably lax on the doctrine of Divine Wrath, she wasn't sure how far they could be trusted on other moral issues.

'Then I really shouldn't detain you any longer,' she replied airily, noting a flicker of disappointment cross his features with a certain amount of vindictive satisfaction.

'Most considerate, as always, my lady,' Adrin said, taking another sip of his amasec. He glanced at the elaborate gold chronograph on a chain around his neck, and nodded thoughtfully. 'Especially as I'm afraid I've rather a late night to look forward to tomorrow.'

'My dear Adrin,' Keira said, deciding she might as well pretend to take the lure, 'I'm beginning to think that you simply live for pleasure.'

'I would that were so,' Adrin said, allowing the foppish mask to slip a little, 'but in some matters, I can assure you, I'm very much in earnest.'

'You certainly seemed so in the discussion this evening,' Keira said. To her surprise he'd vigorously opposed the motion, arguing eloquently that psykers in general, and unsanctioned ones in particular, were the greatest single threat facing the stability of the Imperium. Partly from devilment, and partly to further establish her credentials as a heretic *manqué*, she'd taken the liberal view, arguing for greater tolerance of the warp touched, despite the ashen taste such blasphemous words had left on her tongue.

'It went quite well, didn't it?' Adrin said blandly. 'Though I must admit I was a little surprised by the fervour of your argument: rather more passion than logic there, I fancy.'

'Perhaps there was,' Keira agreed, sipping her drink thoughtfully, 'but it's easy to daemonise people if you don't understand them.' In this, at least, she was speaking from experience, having had far too many of her old Redemptionist certainties battered beyond recognition by her exposure to a wider, more varied galaxy than she'd ever dreamed existed while clinging to the underside of Ambulon. Despite that, she told herself that the power of her faith was still undiminished and her core beliefs were still intact, even though experience had eroded a few of the peripheral tenets.

'I've heard it argued that psykers aren't really people at all,' Adrin said blandly, 'just lumps of the warp walking around among us.'

'That rather proves my point,' Keira said easily. 'None of them asked to be touched by the empyrean.' She used the archaic term deliberately, conscious of her pose as a student of metaphysical poetry, and aware that heretics often affected it as a way of distancing themselves from the truth about what they were actually discussing: the realm of Chaos itself. 'There must be something more positive we could do than just rounding them up and treating them like daemonspawn.'

'An easy stance to take in a debate,' Adrin said, his intention of leaving apparently forgotten, 'but I'll wager you'd feel differently if you were faced with a genuine wyrd.'

'Then you'd lose,' Kiera snapped, allowing the appearance of tiredness and overindulgence in alcohol to make it seem as though she was letting her guard down inadvertently. 'I did see one once. There was a servant on one of my aunt's estates who had a gift for training animals. Everyone knew he was a bit simple, but he was a good-hearted lad, and whatever creature you were having trouble with you just took to see him. He'd pat it, and talk to it, and you'd never have a moment's trouble with it again.'

'That's a familiar enough story,' Adrin said, 'and one that seldom ends well.'

'It didn't,' Keira said. 'They came for him one morning when I was twelve, a whole squad of arbitrators, and some Inquisition lackey. They beat him to a pulp, threw what was left into a shuttle, and took him off to Emperor knows where. He never stopped screaming the whole time, just begging them to leave him alone. Then they burned down his cottage, and shot every animal he'd ever touched.' She allowed her voice to catch, as though fighting back tears. 'They even killed my pony. I never forgave them for what they did to Mordechai.' A small corner of her mind wondered why she'd picked on that particular name, and then dismissed it. She'd needed one in a hurry, and just said the first thing that came to mind. Aware that he was probably listening, she felt another faint stirring in the pit of her stomach, and forced her mind back to business.

'I see.' Adrin was gazing levelly at her, his expression evaluating. Keira knew that look. She was sure she had him. He'd taken the bait. Then he rose, and offered her his arm. 'Perhaps I owe you an apology, for doubting your word, and for making you relive some unpleasant memories.'

'It was a long time ago,' Keira said, as though attempting to recover her composure.

Adrin nodded. 'Nevertheless, perhaps you'll allow me to make amends. If I could prevail upon you to accompany me tomorrow evening, I'm sure you'd find it most rewarding.'

'Another discussion group?' Keira asked, allowing herself to be steered towards the lobby.

Adrin shook his head. 'A rather more exclusive gathering, at my downside residence.' He gestured towards the floor. 'Rather tiresome, I know, but I have to spend a little time among the grubbers if I'm going to retain my holdings.'

'Really?' Keira smiled, as though the idea was appealing. 'I've never visited the Gorgonid. I'm sure I'll find it very interesting.'

'I'm sure you will,' Adrin said, the mask of vacuity settling once more across his face.

The Tumble, Gorgonid Mine, Sepheris Secundus 103.993.M41

THE HEAD OF the airshaft was surrounded by ramshackle structures, around which a surprising number of people came and went. Used to the diffuse citylight, Drake found the pole-mounted luminators marking the periphery of the site glaring and harsh, but he was grateful for them all the same. They meant he had a clear view of everything going on inside it, while the sentries peering out past them in his general direction would see nothing but darkness and the silhouettes of the surrounding slag heaps. He'd found one with a clear view of the site, and had inched his way to the top on the far side. He lay just behind the crest, only his head protruding, its outline blurred nicely by the brim of his hat.

'I'm in position,' he reported, speaking quietly. The prevailing wind was towards him, but there was no telling who else might be listening out there in the darkness. The chill in the air foretold snow by morning, but not much, and he hoped his greatcoat would keep most of the cold out. He'd brought a flask of recaf with him, but he was reluctant to reach for it. A wisp of steam from the warm liquid would give away his position at once to anyone sufficiently alert to notice. Resigning himself to a long, uncomfortable vigil, he slipped the amplivisor out of its case and raised the lenses to his eyes.

'Acknowledged,' Vex said. 'Can you tell much about their disposition from where you are?'

'Surly,' Drake said, unable to resist the feeble joke, before his military training took over and he began to assess the site below with professional detachment. 'It's a fortified compound. Berms on all sides, three to four metres high, look like they've been made from the waste cleared to level the ground on the inside. One gate, pretty solid, probably made from old pit props and scrap metal. Open at the moment, two guards, one with a lasgun, one with a stubber, probably more inside. There's a hut near the gate, could be a guard post. Sentries walking the walls, teams of two, various small arms, but I'll need to see a complete circuit before I can tell you how many there are.'

'From which we can infer that they're quite determined to keep intruders out,' Vex commented dryly.

'I'd say so,' Drake confirmed. 'Frontal assault's out of the question, unless we can borrow a platoon or two of Scourges.' He'd spoken in jest, but the tech-priest seemed to take the remark quite seriously.

'It might be quicker to mobilise Captain Malakai's storm troopers if that becomes necessary,' he replied.

'It might at that,' Drake said, trying to keep his voice level. That option hadn't even occurred to him, and for the first time since joining the Angelae he began to understand quite how much power the badge in his pocket enabled him to wield. No wonder Mordechai was so serious so much of the time. He swept the amplivisor across the compound. 'Five large huts, and what looks like a tunnel mouth. I'm guessing that's the air shaft.'

'A reasonable deduction,' Vex agreed. 'Anything else?'

'No sign of Vos or Elyra,' Drake said, unable to recognise any of the people milling around below. A small group was leaving one of the buildings, and he trained the device on it, sharpening the focus. 'There's one face that doesn't fit: Void-born by the look of him.' He'd encountered starship crew on occasion, usually while providing a guard of honour at official functions for members of the royal family, and the loose-limbed gait of those subconsciously poised to compensate for minute fluctuations in the gravity surrounding them was unmistakable.

'Interesting,' the tech-priest commented. 'Can you get a pict?'

'No problem.' Drake eased the imagifer out of his pocket, centring the man in the little pict screen, and zooming the image as much as he could. 'He's got some kind of insignia on his jacket.' The image froze momentarily as he captured it. 'I can't magnify it enough to make it out from here, though.'

'Not a problem,' Vex assured him. 'I can enhance the image when you get it back to me.'

'Good.' His attention attracted by a growing noise, Drake went back to the amplivisor, training the device on the gates. The guards had been joined by a handful of others, their weapons levelled, but looking too relaxed to be expecting any real trouble. 'Something's happening. Looks like a large group approaching the compound.'

A moment later, his deduction was confirmed, an inchoate mass of human sized figures resolving themselves in the amplivisor. As they came fully into focus, Drake's breath froze in his throat. 'Muties,' he breathed, unable to suppress his instinctive revulsion at the sight.

There could be no doubt about the true nature of the shambling figures approaching the compound. Most were swathed in hooded cloaks, which concealed face and form alike, but the fall of the cloth made it abundantly clear that the limbs and bodies beneath them were grotesquely misshapen. The few exceptions were dressed like most of the other denizens of the pit, their deformities apparently subtle enough to allow them to pass unremarked among the pure, at least with the aid of the darkness.

Drake tried to estimate their numbers, but the lumbering cavalcade stretched back into the void beyond the lights, most of its members pushing crude handcarts piled high with ore. By the time the tail end of it had reached the gate, the first arrivals had long since tipped out their piles of clattering stone on the periphery of the wide open area that filled the centre of the compound, and returned to the darkness whence they'd come.

There must have been three or four dozen at the very least, unless some of them were making a round trip, returning with another load or two before leaving for good. Drake couldn't be sure, so few of the shrouded obscenities below displaying enough individuality to pick out again even if he did see them twice. At any event, there was no mistaking their leader, who had hobbled over to the void-born as soon as the head of the column had passed through the gate, and begun a conversation, which seemed to involve a lot of arm waving and head shaking on both sides.

'Looks like a business deal of some kind,' Drake concluded, having filled Vex in on as many of the details as he could in a few terse words. He'd abandoned the amplivisor, and resumed taking picts, assuming that

Horst would want as much evidence as possible to
help identify the guilty. He took a couple of images of
the guards on the walls, their weapons pointed
inwards to cover the steady stream of mutants passing
by below, and a close-up or two of the crude crossbows
and carefully fashioned slingshots that most of the
new arrivals seemed to be carrying, ready for use if necessary. 'I don't think either side really trusts the other.'

'Hardly surprising, given its clandestine nature,' Vex
concurred.

'Well, they seem to have reached an agreement,'
Drake reported a short while later.

The pile of ore had grown to a surprising volume,
spreading out from its original dumping point as it
had grown too high for the carts and barrows to be
tipped out easily, and the voider had inspected it carefully, picking out lumps at random and running some
kind of hand-held auspex over them. After a while he
nodded in satisfaction, and gestured to a couple of the
men accompanying him, who led a party of the
mutants over to a nearby shed. Before long the remaining barrows had been piled with sacks, and the
misshapen band had departed with their booty.

'That's about it,' the Guardsman added, as the last of
the mutants shuffled away into the darkness. 'Excite-
ment's over.' The guards on the walls were relaxing,
lighting lho sticks and resuming their leisurely circuit,
while a couple of the others heaved the heavy gate into
place. Settling as comfortably as he could on the pile
of stones beneath him, Drake swept the amplivisor
across the compound, resigning himself to a long and
tedious vigil. As he did so, a flicker of movement in the
mouth of the tunnel caught his attention, and he stiffened. 'Wait, there's movement in the airshaft.'

'Interesting,' Vex commented, a faint thread of tension becoming evident beneath his habitually level tone. 'Elyra seems to be on the move. Is it her?'

'I can't tell yet,' Drake said, his attention wholly absorbed by the tunnel mouth. The figures emerging from it were becoming more clearly visible as they moved closer to the pool of light cast by the luminators, but they were still little more than shadows in the gloom. 'There's a whole group of them. Five are walking, and the two in front seem to be carrying a body.' He paused for a moment. 'No, scratch that, it's still twitching. Don't give him long without seeing a chirurgeon though.' He craned his neck, as if he could somehow see past the obstructing silhouettes, and catch a glimpse of the trio walking behind them a few paces further down the tunnel.

'Do you recognise the casualty?' Vex asked, the more specific question he didn't want to ask hanging in the air unspoken.

'Never seen him before,' Drake reassured the techpriest. As the injured man and his bearers moved aside, he was able to see into the shaft without hindrance at last, and sighed with relief as he recognised the distinctive silhouette of his friend, the familiar chain axe jutting unmistakably over a fur-clad shoulder. 'Vos is behind them, still armed.'

'Then I think we can safely infer that their cover story has been accepted,' Vex said, not quite managing to keep a faint note of relief from his voice.

Down below, Kyrlock and his companions stepped into the full glare of the luminators at last, and Drake fumbled for the imagifer, hoping to get a pict of the man accompanying him. 'Elyra's there too,' he reported, 'talking to someone: a man, early middle age, civilian garb. Looks like an off-worlder.' Another flash of movement caught his eye, and he turned his head. 'The voider's going to meet them. They're talking.'

'Can you read their lips?' Vex asked.

'Not from here,' Drake said. 'I can use the amplivisor.'

'I would advise you to continue taking picts,' Vex said. 'They might give us more to go on.'

'That's what I thought,' Drake agreed. 'They're still talking, making introductions by the look of it. Elyra's saying something to the voider, and Vos is nodding. Looks like we're in business.' He tensed a little as the psyker reached into her knapsack, acutely aware of the laspistol secreted in there, and wishing for a moment that he still had his lasgun with him instead of the Scalptaker. He was good with the longarm, and could have provided covering fire easily if things looked like turning bad. However, Elyra was smiling, something shining in her hand for a moment as she held it out for inspection. The man with her nodded and said something, and everyone laughed.

The discussion went on for a few minutes longer, between Elyra and the voider at first, and then she switched her attention to the man at her shoulder. They conferred earnestly, with the air of two people both used to striking the bargain they wanted and unwilling to give any more ground than they had to. On a couple of occasions, she turned to Vos for support or to confirm something, which he did in a few terse words or with a brusque nod of the head. Then she handed over the jewellery with a smile that looked almost genuine, and the anonymous fellow in the grey cloak nodded in satisfaction. Their business concluded, Elyra and Kyrlock turned away, heading back to the airshaft, and the middle-aged man began to confer with the voider.

'That's it,' Drake reported, beginning to pack up his equipment with an odd sense of anticlimax. 'The deal's done. They're on their way.'

'Excellent,' Vex said. 'I'll inform Barda. He should be waiting for you at the extraction point by the time you reach it.'

'Thanks.' On the verge of pulling out, Drake raised the amplivisor for one final time, following the distant figures of Vos and Elyra until they were both swallowed by the gloom of the airshaft, and tried not to wonder if he'd ever see either of them again.

EIGHTEEN

Icenholm, Sepheris Secundus
105.993.M41

THE ALMOST PERPETUAL cloud cover had broken a little while Horst slept, allowing a haze of unfamiliar blue to appear in irregular patches above the suspended city, and shafts of sunlight to illuminate it sporadically in sudden effusions of dazzling polychromatic light where they struck the stained glass frontages of buildings and spires. As he entered the villa's living room he found his colleagues making the most of the glittering spectacle, enjoying a midday breakfast facing the terrace, the wide glass doors thrown open to admit a chill but invigorating current of air.

'Did you sleep all right?' Keira asked, glancing towards the door as he entered, and Horst nodded brusquely.

'Fine,' he said, before his sleep-addled mind fully registered the fact that her tone was free of the sarcasm his expectation had loaded the question with. Noting the flicker of disappointment that crossed her features at his curt response, he smiled wearily, and added, 'thank you for asking.' If she was still trying to rein in her habitual truculence, he might as well encourage her.

'You're welcome,' she replied, smiling. The effect was astonishing, and as unexpected as the sunlight slicing through the murky skies of Sepheris Secundus, softening her features in a manner he'd never seen before. For the first time he could remember, her brittle mask slipped, revealing a glimpse of the woman the girl might one day become if she allowed herself to, and he found himself wondering if playing the role of a lady was beginning to have a more profound effect on her than either of them could possibly have anticipated. 'We've saved you some food, and I don't think Danuld's quite managed to drink all the recaf yet.'

'I can always chime for some more,' Drake offered, glancing at the crystal mug in his hand with a faint air of guilt.

Horst shook his head, finding enough remaining in the pot for his own needs, and ladled a thick layer of ackenberry syrup over a plateful of waffles from one of the chafing dishes cluttering the sideboard. 'I've got enough,' he assured him, picking up some cutlery, and turning to skirt the sofa on which Keira was sitting, still swathed in her yellow dressing gown, while Lilith braided her damp hair into an elaborate *coiffure*. As he brushed past her, he caught a faint, lingering scent of warm water and bath oil. Comfortably seated at last, and settling his composure behind the shield of plying his fork, he risked a glance in the girl's direction. 'You seem to have had an interesting time with your tame philosophers last night.'

'Most enlightening,' Keira agreed, taking the hint, and glancing up at Lilith. Talking openly about their business with a servant in the room would be out of the question. 'Will this take much longer, do you think?'

'Almost done, my lady,' the plump maid assured her, fussing a few final strands into place, and holding up a mirror to allow her to inspect the final result.

'It looks very striking,' Keira said. 'This is the latest Secundan fashion, you say?'

'The queen herself wore her hair like that to the mass last St. Angevin's Day,' Lilith assured her. 'Since then it's been all the rage. Of course, with your unusual colouring, the effect will be very different. Heads will turn, I can promise you that.'

'Well, I am hoping to make a good impression,' Keira said, smiling at Horst in a fashion that, in anyone else, he would have thought of as flirtatious. Once again, the memory of his conversation with Elyra rose up to tease him with doubts and unwelcome distractions, not unmixed with some guiltily pleasurable fantasies, and he wished she was here to turn to for advice. Women had always been something of a mystery to him, Keira more than most, and he felt considerably out of his depth.

'I've no doubt you'll do that,' he agreed, bracing himself for whatever her response might be, but she'd already turned back to her servant.

'Do you think you can find something for me to wear that would set it off properly?' she asked.

'Of course, my lady.' Visibly swelling with pride at being entrusted with so momentous a decision, Lilith trotted from the room. As soon as she'd vanished, Keira picked up the looking-glass again, and grimaced at her reflection.

'You look great,' Drake assured her, a little awkwardly, Horst thought. Clearly the job of tutoring her in Secundan etiquette had been a taxing one.

'I look like a caba nut pastry,' Keira said, with a flash of her old belligerence. Then she smiled thoughtfully. 'But at least I should be able to hide a couple of surprises in there.'

'Good.' Horst nodded, not bothering to disguise his relief. 'I want you as tooled up as possible. The rest of us will be ready to intervene if we have to, but if it all goes ploin-shaped it may take us a while to get in.'

'Quite true,' Vex agreed, projecting a schematic of the Adrin estate on the hololith built into his data-slate. The mansion seemed relatively modest by the standards of most of the noble houses Horst had visited across the sector, but down in the Gorgonid the only space to build on would be the unproductive worked-out areas of the family holding. 'Like most of the highborn dwellings in the pit, the majority of the house has been constructed underground.' He rotated the image, allowing everyone to appreciate the scale of the problem they faced. 'The outer wall encloses a roughly semi-circular depression in the main face, with a relatively small surface structure abutting on to the centre of the cliff. Details of the interior layout are sparse, although I have been able to infer a speculative configuration from the old mining records, given that the main dwelling areas will have been enlarged from the worked-out shafts.'

'Meaning there are bound to be back ways into the mine,' Drake put in.

Horst nodded thoughtfully. 'Can you pinpoint those?' he asked.

Drake shook his head. 'They'll be secret. Only the family would know them all, and their most dependable retainers. Not even the household guards would be trusted with that kind of information.'

'Does Adrin have guards?' Keira asked.

'Not officially,' Vex said. 'Household troops are a prerogative restricted to those of baronial rank, and the royal family. In practice, however, I'd be very surprised if he doesn't have some kind of security in place.'

'He does,' Drake confirmed. 'They all do. It's a status thing. They just don't wear uniforms, or carry visible weapons.'

'How many men are we likely to be facing?' Horst asked. This was the former Scourge's area of expertise, and, not for the first time, he found himself grateful for Inquisitor Finurbi's foresight in recruiting the man.

'No more than a dozen, I would think,' Drake said. 'A lot of the minor nobility have one or two personal bodyguards, who follow them around at a discreet distance, but Adrin doesn't seem to.' He glanced across at Keira, who shook her head.

'Not that I've noticed,' she confirmed.

'Then he doesn't,' Horst said, a trifle indistinctly around a mouthful of waffle. 'You'd have spotted a tagger within seconds of making contact.' Again, the smile flickered across her face as she registered the compliment, and he returned it awkwardly, feeling as though he was suddenly edging across a minefield. Infuriating as their old antagonistic relationship had been, it had at least felt settled. Now, new doubts and uncertainties were muddying the waters just when he needed to remain focused.

'That probably means he fancies himself as a fighter,' Drake counselled. 'A lot of the highborn go in for duelling or melee sports.' He looked at Keira with a little more concern than Horst would have expected, but then he hadn't known her for long enough to realise just how deadly she could be. 'Don't underestimate him if things turn bad.'

'I won't,' Keira said, her usual breezy confidence reasserting itself, 'but I don't suppose he'll have any tricks up his sleeve that I haven't seen before.'

'Leaving aside any resistance from the target,' Drake went on, warming to his theme, 'his household security shouldn't prove much of a problem. If it follows the usual pattern, he'll only have two or three competent fighters among them, and maybe twice that in meat-head muscle. They'll be carrying hand weapons mostly, blades or pistols for the leaders, and basic melee kit for the rest.'

Vex coughed, and slapped his respirator panel reflexively. 'That may not be an entirely safe assumption,' he said. 'If Adrin really is involved with a heretical group, which seems extremely likely, then he almost certainly has access to far more resources than most men in his position. I think it only prudent to assume a greater number of guards than normal, and with significantly greater firepower.'

'Based on what?' Horst asked, pushing his empty plate aside.

'On Danuld's observations last night,' Vex said, displaying the picts that Drake had taken of the fortified compound at the head of the airshaft. 'Note the number of armed men, and the variety of firearms apparently at their disposal.'

'That doesn't mean they're guarding his house too,' Drake pointed out, 'and you still haven't tied the people smugglers directly to Adrin in any case.'

'On the contrary,' Vex said, managing to inject a distinctly smug timbre into his usual monotone. 'I followed your suggestion of tracing the ownership records of the mineshaft, and found them most illuminating.'

'Illuminating how, exactly?' Horst asked, returning to the sideboard for more recaf.

Vex shrugged. 'To summarise the conclusions of a most interesting rummage through the archives, the holding formed part of the dowry settlement on the occasion of the marriage of Lord Harald Tonis and Lady Sibella Adrin, some forty-seven standard years ago. I can give you the exact date in a moment, if you like.'

'Wait just a minute,' Keira said, in tones of outraged astonishment. 'You're telling us Adrin and Tonis were related?'

The tech-priest nodded. 'First cousins, to be precise.'

'And you only just got around to telling us?' The familiar sarcastic tone was back in her voice, and Horst wasn't quite sure if his predominant feeling was one of regret or relief. 'Anything else you're sitting on that we might need to know?'

'I completed my cogitations this morning,' Vex replied levelly, unperturbed as always, 'and am currently presenting my conclusions at the earliest opportunity. It's hardly my fault that those unblessed by the Omnissiah require regular periods of sleep to remain functional.'

'Then carry on, by all means,' Horst said, anxious to prevent the discussion from getting bogged down in pointless recrimination. He took a mouthful of recaf, considering the implications of this fresh revelation. 'I suppose that would give Adrin a motive for aiding fugitive psykers, knowing his cousin had been one.'

'It would,' Vex agreed. 'In any event, his family's ownership of their base of operations clearly implicates him in the Shadow Franchise smuggling racket.'

'You seem very sure of the Franchise's involvement,' Horst said. 'Do you have any further evidence of that?'

'It's a matter of probabilities,' Vex said. 'Keira overheard one of their operatives conferring with a mutant about a consignment of contraband ore, to be delivered last night, and just such a transaction took place while Danuld was watching the compound.' He gestured towards the data-slate's pict screen, and the recording the Guardsman had made flickered across it. 'It is, of course, entirely possible that another such exchange was taking place elsewhere in the Tumble at the same time, but given the amount of ore involved, I consider it far more likely that this was the arrangement Keira heard being discussed.'

'So do I,' Horst agreed, considering the implications uneasily. A pattern of some sort was beginning to form, that was undeniable, but too much of it still didn't make sense. Taking refuge in the methods of assessing evidence he'd learned as an arbitrator, he began trying to make connections between the facts. 'So, we can assume that Adrin is involved in the smuggling ring, possibly at his cousin's behest, and that the Shadow Franchise is moving fugitive psykers off-planet. That raises the question of whether or not they realise that.'

'Would they care if they did?' Drake asked.

'Probably not,' Horst conceded. 'Not if they were making money. In either case, they're only providing the means of transport. Someone has to be offering the wyrds refuge at the other end. Our primary goal is to find out who.'

'We'll know more about that when Elyra reports back,' Keira said. A faintly troubled expression crossed her face. 'Assuming we'll be able to track her through the warp.'

'Fortunately, I've been able to identify the ship she'll be on,' Vex put in, stilling another coughing fit with a resonant blow to the chest. Picking up a nearby screwdriver, he began poking about beneath his robe. After a moment, he put the tool down again, inhaled cautiously, and called up a fresh image on the pict screen. 'Danuld was able to get this pict of a voider, who subsequently spent some time consulting with Elyra and Vos. I think it's safe to assume that he's part of the crew of the ship they'll be travelling on.'

'That doesn't narrow it down all that much,' Horst pointed out. 'There must be hundreds of ore barges in orbit at the moment.'

'Quite so.' Vex coughed again, and slapped his chest plate, looking vaguely disappointed. 'But I was able to enhance the pict. Under the right degree of magnification, the crew patch on his jacket became clearly visible.' He did something to the slate, and the display changed, zooming in on a small portion of the man's upper sleeve, until the picture of a bear astride something small and cylindrical, surrounded by water, appeared centred in the screen. 'He's from the *Ursus Innare*, a Diurnus Line bulk transport, registered out of Scintilla. Traffic control has a flight plan logged back to the home system, departing tonight.'

'Good,' Horst said, nodding in satisfaction. 'Then find us a ship. If we can't get there ahead of them, we can at least be hard on their heels.'

'Should we inform the Tricorn?' Keira suggested, with uncharacteristic diffidence. 'They could intercept the barge as soon as it drops out of the warp.'

Horst shook his head. 'Too great a risk. We need Elyra and Vos to move further up the chain and see where it goes. If the Ordos tip their hand before our people have a chance to make contact, we lose the lead.' He considered for a moment. 'I'll forward a report to the inquisitor before we leave. He'll be in the Scintilla system before the *Ursus Innare* arrives, and I'm sure he'll know what to do.'

'Works for me,' Keira said.

'Glad to hear it,' Horst said, his words sounding a little strange as he spoke them, the simple pleasantry shorn of the sarcasm he'd normally have loaded it with. He turned back to Vex. 'Have you any idea what Tonis was up to in the Fathomsound yet?'

'None whatsoever,' Vex admitted. 'The presence of psy dampers would imply that he was dealing with extremely powerful psykers, but the modifications he'd made to them would have rendered them completely inoperative. Quite honestly, I'm baffled.'

'Fair enough.' Horst gave that line of enquiry up as a bad job for the moment. 'We'll just have to wait for some more evidence to turn up. Any luck yet identifying that other thing you found?'

'No.' Vex picked up the strange piece of ivory, and shook his head. 'I've no idea what this substance is. It's certainly not listed among the *Materia Codicie*.'

'What about the carving on it?' Drake asked. 'That must mean something, surely?'

'It might if I could read it,' the tech-priest admitted, 'but I've never seen anything like these marks before. In some ways they resemble circuit diagrams, but I haven't found anything comparable in the annals of my order.'

'Perhaps it's archeotech,' Keira suggested. 'We know Tonis was using the Conclave archives to look for stuff like that. Maybe he found some.'

'It's possible,' Vex conceded, doubt colouring his voice, 'but if this were of human origin, some record of a similar system ought to have survived.'

'The raiders who attacked the Citadel were using xenos tech,' Drake reminded him, 'and Tonis was probably in league with them. Perhaps that thing was the price of his treachery.' He stared at the milky white object with undisguised loathing.

'Perhaps it was,' Horst agreed. He held out his hand for the tiny object. It was heavier than he'd expected, and felt uncomfortably warm against his palm. After a moment, he returned it to the tech-priest, resisting the urge to wipe his hand against the leg of his trousers. 'Perhaps it's a talisman of some kind. If he was a psyker before this Magos Avia replaced that part of his brain with augments, he might still have needed some protection against the warp.' If Elyra was here, of course, she might be able to answer that question, but their only expert on such matters was kilometres away, as effectively cut off from them as if she was already transiting the realm of Chaos.

'He might,' Vex agreed, looking far from happy. 'That might explain why the daemon attacked him as soon as the dampers went down.'

Horst shook his head, and sighed in frustration. It was all connected somehow, he could feel it, but the specifics just wouldn't come into focus. They needed more pieces of the mosaic, and right now he didn't have a clue how to get them. Perhaps they'd know more after tonight.

'Right.' He took a deep breath, and poured himself another recaf. If he kept this up, he thought wryly, he was going to become as addicted to the stuff as Danuld seemed to be. 'Let's focus on specifics. As soon as the *Ursus Innare* transits into the warp, we hit the Franchise compound, and close down the pipeline from this end. Malakai can handle that, he's itching for some payback, and it'll do his men good to have something to shoot. Any objections?'

'Don't the Franchise come under Arbites jurisdiction?' Drake asked. 'They're only common criminals.'

'If they've been consorting with psykers and heretics, they're ours,' Keira said, a predatory gleam beginning to kindle in the depths of her eyes.

'Think of it as damage limitation,' Horst explained. 'There's no telling what kind of taint they've been exposed to, even if they don't realise it themselves. Far safer to cut out the cancer before it spreads.'

'You'll get no argument from me,' Drake agreed, 'after some of the things I've seen in the last few days. What are we going to be doing while Malakai's having fun?'

'Keira's going to a party,' Horst said, 'and the rest of us are going to crash it the moment we get the evidence we need.'

'Sounds good.' Drake slipped the Scalptaker from his shoulder rig, and spun the chamber thoughtfully, checking the load. Then he looked up, grinning. 'Do you think they'll have those little cheesy things on sticks?'

NINETEEN

The Gorgonid Mine, Sepheris Secundus
107.993.M41

'My DEAR, YOU look positively stunning,' Adrin said, as a quietly spoken servant ushered Keira into the drawing room of the underground mansion. The house was more opulent than she'd expected, and airier too, the corridors broad, and the ceilings high. Finely woven carpets and tapestries covered most of the walls and floors, the few uncovered surfaces polished so smooth that it was easy to forget they were actually tunnels hacked into the surface of the planet, and everywhere was illuminated by crystal chandeliers of elegant and intricate design. If it hadn't been for the complete absence of windows, Keira thought, there would have been no visible clue that they were underground at all.

'I thought I should make an effort,' Keira replied, smiling. Lilith had selected a loose tabard in violet silk, slashed at the sides, from her bulging wardrobe. Ignoring her maid's barely concealed air of disapproval, she'd passed over the formal gown that the conscientious servant had laid out beside it, slipping it on over her synsuit instead.

The skintight garment was now mimicking the precise shade of the material, blurring the outline of her body where the loose fabric fell, concealing the weapons beneath it, while revealing enough of her lithe, athletic build to distract the attention of almost anyone looking at her. After a show of careful consideration, Lilith had nodded thoughtfully, conceding that the makeshift ensemble did indeed set off the result of her hairdressing to perfection, and that a breath of off-world exoticism would set tongues wagging in the salons of Icenholm for days to come. 'It's all a bit last season, to be honest, but it's comfortable, and fads come and go so fast in the Lucid Palace it's impossible to keep up with them anyway.'

'It may be a little *passé* on Scintilla,' Adrin assured her, 'but here you'll have set the trend.'

Noting the expressions of the other women present, a mere half dozen or so scattered around the overstuffed divans or circulating slowly through the small groups of quietly chatting guests, Keira somehow doubted that. All were wearing the kind of gowns the Secundan nobility seemed to favour, loose and voluminous, and few if any looked as though skintight garments would do them any favours.

Most had elaborately sculpted hair, which made Lilith's efforts seem positively restrained by comparison, and many were glancing in her direction with barely concealed hostility. Ignoring their reactions, and the murmur of conversation through which the phrase 'ten credit joygirl' seemed to be forming the leitmotif, she inclined her head towards the assembled company with every appearance of indolent ease. 'These must be your friends,' she said, just loud enough to be overheard. 'I can see that everything I heard about Secundan hospitality is true.'

'You'll have to forgive a certain amount of reserve,' Adrin said. 'This is a very exclusive gathering, and we've found over the years that it pays to be cautious with new arrivals.'

'How thrilling,' Keira said, appearing not to notice the way two of the men had moved to unobtrusively block the door. They both wore ceremonial duelling swords, with ornately gilded hilts, apparently no more than part of their typically elaborate outfits, although the stances they'd fallen into left her in no doubt that the blades were perfectly functional, and their owners were skilled in their use. She suppressed a smile. No matter how good they might be against other fops, she was certain that neither of them would prove anything but a minor irritation to a graduate of the Collegium Assassinorum. 'You sound as though you're about to tell me the Inquisition might be listening to us again.'

She sincerely hoped they were. Wearing the pendant, with its concealed vox circuit, would have attracted too much attention, the colourful jade at odds with her severely functional attire, but Vex had secreted a similar unit among the mass of braids on her head, which obscured it nicely. So long as the layers of rock above the mansion weren't too deep to block the signal, her friends would be able to track her position to within a handful of metres, and hear most of what was going on around her.

'That's not something we like to joke about,' Adrin said, the bantering tone slipping from his voice. Heads around them nodded in agreement, and Keira found herself assessing the odds if she really had to fight her way out of here. The women she discounted immediately as any kind of threat, but there must have been almost a score of men present too, and at least half of them looked as though they could put up a reasonable amount of resistance before she cut them down. 'They're dangerous, like all misguided fanatics.' As he spoke, he studied her face carefully, attempting to read her reaction to the casually uttered treason.

'Misguided?' Keira asked, shading her voice with just the right amount of caution, as though hesitant to agree too quickly in case she was mistaking his meaning. 'They're certainly fanatical, I grant you that, but most people seem to think they're a necessary evil.' She placed just enough stress on the phrase 'most people' to hint that it meant 'most *other* people.'

'Do you?' Adrin asked, picking up on the implication, and apparently tiring of the game. Sensing that it was time to commit herself, Keira looked at the faces surrounding her, as though appraising them carefully.

'Do I what?' she asked, as a palpable air of tension began to rise in the elegantly furnished room. Overdressed aristocrats were enclosing her on all sides, their expressions intent, and for a moment she found herself wondering how many loyal servants of the Emperor had answered the question incorrectly, never to leave the secluded chamber alive. 'Think it's right for them to go charging around the galaxy like a bunch of ignorant greenskins, slapping down anyone who dares to think for themselves? Of course I do.' She judged the fractional pause just long enough to note which of the fops, and, surprisingly, a couple of the ladies, began to move towards her with obviously murderous intent, before laughing as though the whole thing was a tremendous joke. 'At least if there's a chance that their thugs might still be listening.'

'There's no fear of that here,' Adrin said, joining in her feigned merriment with every sign of sincerity, while the thunderstorm crackle of incipient violence dissipated as suddenly as it had erupted. 'You're among friends here.'

'I'd like to think so,' Keira said, noting the guarded welcome beginning to appear on some of the faces. 'Do any of them have names?'

'None that we share,' Adrin said. 'They all know me, of course, and I know them, but in general we prefer to preserve our incognito.'

'How very wise,' Keira said, concealing her vexation beneath another display of relaxed good humour. A prolonged round of introductions, assuming the vox hidden in her hair was getting through, would have identified the key players in this shabby little cabal of heretics, and allowed the Arbites to round them up in a single coordinated strike the following morning. She glanced around the room, as if searching for refreshment. 'I take it this evening's discussion will be rather less inhibited than it was in the Conclave.' An air of polite amusement rippled around the assembled conspirators.

'I think you'll find we do something more constructive here than mere debate,' Adrin said.

'Really.' Keira raised an eyebrow. 'You do intrigue me.'

'Then it would be impolite to keep you waiting any longer,' Adrin said, turning towards the door. 'If you'd care to accompany me?'

* * *

Above the Gorgonid, Sepheris Secundus
107.993.M41

'SHE'S MOVING AGAIN,' Vex reported, his attention on
the pict screen of his data-slate, where the schematic of
Adrin's house was being displayed. A red rune marked
Keira's position within it, and was wandering steadily
through the maze of conjectural corridors he'd extrap-
olated. With a sense of quiet pride, he noted that it
hadn't deviated through any of the areas he'd marked
as solid rock, at least so far.

'What about Elyra?' Horst asked, from his seat near
the narrow door leading to the shuttle's flight deck.
He'd visited the cockpit a couple of times since they'd
taken off, ostensibly to consult the auspex for any sign
of the lander from the *Ursus Innare*, but mainly, Vex
suspected, to relieve the tension of waiting.

Barda was keeping them in a wide holding pattern
over the vast pit of the Gorgonid, where they could
intervene at either site if they were needed, but so far
events seemed to be proceeding precisely as planned.
Vex was pleased about that. It was a matter of faith
with him that every eventuality could be predicted,
given enough information, and enough time to
process it.

'Still holding position,' Vex assured him, switching
his attention to the screen of the gaudy data-slate
Horst had obtained from the Secretary of the Conclave.

Despite its offensive casing, the mechanisms within
it were sound enough, and he'd set it up to display
both women's positions on a smaller scale map of the
Gorgonid. Drake glanced across from his own seat,
where he was checking over his old Guard issue lasgun

with practised precision, and grinned sympathetically. Vex had answered the same question several times already, and, he suspected, would continue to do so at regular intervals until the group of fugitives the psyker had managed to infiltrate had left the ground.

'Good.' Horst nodded. 'What about Malakai's men?'

'Still inbound from the Citadel,' Vex reported, privately wondering just how much progress their leader had expected them to make in the five minutes since the last time he'd asked. 'ETA seventeen minutes, assuming the headwinds remain constant.'

'Then I guess we've got nothing else to do but wait,' Horst said grimly.

'I've got a contact on the auspex,' Barda chipped in, his voice attenuated slightly by the comm-bead in Vex's ear. 'Traffic control just tagged it as a lander from the *Ursus Innare.* Looks like you're in business.'

'I'll be right there,' Horst said, rising and disappearing through the door of the cockpit.

Vex returned his attention to the pict screens in front of him, trying to extrapolate the most likely course of events, and monitoring the sporadic chatter from Keira's hidden vox. It appeared that the heavy lifter from the ore barge would be down and away before the shuttleful of storm troopers arrived, which would simplify matters. The *Ursus Innare* would undoubtedly break orbit before the raid began, and enter the warp in blissful ignorance of the fate of their planet-bound confederates. That would leave the Angelae free to extract Keira, should the situation demand it.

Suddenly aware that Drake had left his seat, and was hovering, somewhat diffidently, at his elbow, Vex glanced up. 'Can I be of any assistance?' he asked politely.

'If it's no trouble,' Drake said, holding out the las-gun, 'I was just wondering if you'd mind blessing this for me.'

'A wise precaution,' Vex assured him, taking the weapon. Beginning the simple ceremony, he was surprised to find how much the familiar litany settled his own mind. As he chanted the hallowed words he glanced out of the viewport, and wondered which of the descending lights in the distance was the lander on which Elyra and Kyrlock were about to embark.

The Gorgonid Mine, Sepheris Secundus
107.993.M41

'THEY CAN'T BE much longer,' Kyrlock said, as Elyra glanced at her chronograph for what felt like the thousandth time. 'Greel said 107, and it must be almost 108 by now.' His voice was casual, but his posture betrayed a tension almost equal to her own. The payment had been made. If the Franchise was going to betray them, now would be the time.

'There's still almost an hour until then,' Elyra replied, striving to sound relaxed. The person she was pretending to be wouldn't want to betray any sign of weakness in front of her partner, let alone the trio of juvies they'd unexpectedly found themselves saddled with. She glanced in their direction, adopting what she thought would be an appropriately patronising expression. 'Don't worry, we won't leave without you.'

'How very reassuring,' Trosk replied dryly. Out of the three of them, he was the one who worried her the most. She still had no idea what his abilities were, and couldn't ask directly without undermining her pose of indifference. He was the sharpest of the group, though, of that she had no doubt, and she was quite resolved not to underestimate him. Ven just looked dazed and confused most of the time, periodically muttering in an undertone, which was normal enough for a diviner, even one as weak and untrained as he appeared to be. Zusen was still quiet and withdrawn, apparently traumatised by Kantris's assault on her the day before, hardly bothering to speak unless she was addressed directly, and even then responding in little more than monosyllables. The contrast with her earlier overconfidence was striking, and Elyra had to remind herself not to be too sympathetic. Any overt sign of compassion would be incompatible with her cover story, but even more importantly, the girl was a rogue psyker, a living embodiment of the Great Enemy, an abomination that could unleash the power of the warp at any time, and she couldn't allow herself to forget that for a moment.

As I was once, a faint voice whispered in the back of her mind. *There but for the grace of the Emperor...*

She knew that she'd been lucky, the strength of the faith her parents had imbued her with protecting her against the perils of the outer darkness until the blessed day she'd met Carolus. He'd spotted her potential, had arranged for her screening and her training as a sanctioned psyker, and had brought her into the service of the Inquisition. Perhaps she could do the same for Zusen when all this was over, but she was realistic enough to doubt that. The chances were strong that the girl was already tainted by the warp, and a zeta grade would hardly be worth the effort of trying to salvage anyway.

'All right there, Zu?' she asked, hoping to break the dismal chain of thought.

'Fine.' The girl lapsed back into silence, sitting on the rough stone floor with her chin on her knees, as she had done for hours. She was still sticking close to Kyrlock, as though the solid bulk of the man lent her confidence, and if he found her presence as uncomfortable as Elyra suspected, he at least had enough tact or common sense to conceal the fact.

'Good.' Elyra's casual tone suddenly became businesslike, as a flurry of activity began to manifest itself further up the tunnel. 'Look alive, I reckon we're moving out.' The shuffling of feet and the low murmuring of voices was all around them in the darkness, growing louder and more purposeful as the word rippled down from group to group, and the nearest clusters of refugees were already gathering their meagre possessions together with an air of hopeful expectation.

'About time,' Kyrlock said, rising easily to his feet, and slinging the pack he'd been sitting on across his shoulder. After a moment of irresolution, which only Elyra could see, he steeled himself and held out a hand towards Zusen. 'Come on if you're coming, kid.'

'I'm not a kid,' Zusen said, a tentative smile appearing on her face for the first time in hours, in spite of her petulant tone, and she took the proffered hand, rising easily as Kyrlock hoisted her to her feet. Once upright, she relinquished it slowly, with palpable reluctance. 'I'm a grown woman.'

'Yeah, right.' Kyrlock cleared his throat awkwardly, and glanced at Elyra, clearly seeking some kind of distraction. 'You got everything?'

'Right here,' Elyra assured him. 'Is Ven still with us, or away with the cherubs again?'

'I've got him,' Trosk said, prodding his friend into motion.

After a moment, the young seer's expression cleared. 'I can manage perfectly well on my own,' he said pettishly.

'Great.' Elyra shouldered her pack, still keeping it where she could draw the laspistol if she had to. 'Let's get this crèche on the shuttle, shall we?'

KEIRA HAD THOUGHT she was prepared for any eventuality, but when she stepped into the room Adrin had conducted her to, it took all of her training to keep an expression of shock from her face. They'd been walking for several minutes, the rest of the gathering trailing in their wake like a comet tail of rustling silks, conversing in low voices, and she'd been surprised at how sprawling the underground mansion had turned out to be.

The luxurious corridors down which they'd passed at first had narrowed as they moved deeper into the labyrinth of tunnels, their rich hangings giving way to bare rock. The surface on which they trod was now the naked stone of the Gorgonid, the multitudinous footfalls of the assembly pattering from the solid surface like distant rain. It was evident that few people came this way, although the carpeting of dust along the corridors was a little thicker close to the walls, indicating that the passageways they were treading still saw a little traffic from time to time.

The illumination was dimmer too, the electrosconces, which had replaced the chandeliers, set at wider intervals than in the habitable part of the sprawling house, although they still gave enough light to see clearly by. Mindful of Horst's description of the conditions he and Vex had found in the depths of the Fathomsound, Keira could only be grateful for that. At length, Adrin had paused in front of a plain wooden door, no different to Keira's eyes than a dozen they'd already passed.

'Go on ahead,' he said to the rest of the group, who nodded their acquiescence, and disappeared further up the corridor, still conversing quietly among themselves. Once they were alone, he smiled at Keira. 'I think you should prepare yourself for something of a shock.'

'And I think you should stop watching those melodramas,' Keira replied, still acting as if she regarded the whole situation as something of a joke. The weight of her throwing knives, and the sword she'd slung across her back, were comforting beneath the concealing fall of her tabard nonetheless.

'What would life be without a little melodrama?' Adrin threw open the door with a theatrical flourish, and ushered her through with a faintly self-mocking bow.

Whatever Keira might have been expecting, this wasn't it. The room was large, and comfortably furnished, and a man sat within, reading a book. His age was indeterminate, and as he glanced up and met her eyes, the young assassin felt the force of the madness blazing in his own like a physical blow. Before she could fully comprehend what was happening, the book closed, and floated to a nearby shelf, where it nuzzled gently into place between two others.

Adrin looked at her closely, a faintly mocking smile on his face. 'Remember, I asked you last night how you'd feel face to face with a real wyrd?' he asked. 'Is it at all like you expected?'

'I haven't forgotten my manners, even if you have,' Keira replied coolly, taking refuge in her aristocratic persona. She inclined her head in formal greeting. 'Since our host hasn't seen fit to introduce us, I'm Keira Sythree, visiting from Scintilla.'

'Is it time?' the man asked, ignoring her completely. He rose awkwardly from the chair, leaning heavily on an ornately carved walking stick, and Keira could see that his feet were little more than frostbitten stumps. One of the escapees from the Citadel, then, left behind by the raiders, either by accident or because he was unsuitable for their mysterious purposes.

'It is,' Adrin answered him. 'Are you fully prepared?'

'Of course.' The man stared at him, as though the viscount was an insect he'd just discovered in a forkful of salad. 'The husks are waiting?'

'They are.' Adrin hesitated. 'You do understand the risks involved? My cousin's technique was far from perfected, and now that he's gone we're simply following the ritual he designed and hoping for the best.'

'I understand you can increase my power,' the psyker said, with an intensity that sent chills running down Keira's spine. Subvocalising one of the litanies the Collegium had taught her, she kept her face impassive, and fought down the impulse to draw steel and put an end to the abomination in front of her at once. He was clearly a delta grade at the very least, and wouldn't die easily. Even if she succeeded, she'd reveal herself as an agent of the Inquisition prematurely, and all too many of the cabal would escape before back-up arrived.

'Can you really do that?' she asked instead, letting her horror at being so close to incarnate blasphemy appear no more than incredulous surprise.

'I really have no idea,' Adrin said. 'Gilden developed the technique. He found something on one of his archeotech forays that put him on the right track, I think.' He shrugged. 'Or it might have been his mentor from the Lathes. I gather they were conducting experiments together.'

'This is irrelevant,' the psyker said, flinging the door open with a passing thought, before hobbling past them without so much as a glance in their direction. 'When I've fed on the souls of the husks, and added their power to mine, I will lead you all against the Isolarium. Its walls will crumble before me, and our brothers there will be liberated!'

Shocked beyond measure, Keira glanced at Adrin, surprised to see something of her own feelings mirrored on his face. Evidently the wyrd's new agenda, and manifest insanity, had come as something of an unwelcome surprise to his host. 'Hadn't we better go with him?' she asked.

'Yes.' Jolted back to the present, Adrin nodded, his face ashen. 'Yes, I rather think we should.'

'WHAT DO YOU mean there's going to be a delay?' Elyra asked, her hand hovering close to the hilt of her laspistol. Out of the corner of her eye, she was relieved to see that Kyrlock was reaching unobtrusively for the haft of his chain axe, using the interposing bodies of the three juves to hide the fact from Greel.

Clearly aware of what the pack concealed, after witnessing Kantris's fate the day before, Greel tried to force a placatory expression onto his face. 'Nothing to worry about, I can assure you,' he said, glancing around for the nearest guards, and manifestly taking heart from the close proximity of a couple of shotgun toting Franchisemen. 'The muties brought in a bit more ore than we expected, that's all. Got to get it loaded before we can lift.'

'*We* lift?' Kyrlock asked. 'Does that mean you're coming too?'

'Damn right it does,' Greel said, with a dismissive glance around the compound. Over a dozen men, sweating profusely despite the freezing night temperatures, were shovelling the pile of broken rocks onto a rattling conveyer belt, powered by a loudly snorting steam engine, the far end of which disappeared somewhere among the ore bins of the lander. The shuttle was huge, its angular metallic bulk almost filling the clear space in the middle of the enclosure, looming over the cluster of storage sheds like an ogryn in a crèche. 'I belong on a civilised world, not a cesspit like this.'

Kyrlock spat derisively. 'Thought you were a pansy city boy the moment I saw you.'

'That's right,' Greel said, with a faint trace of malice. 'I like my creature comforts. Which is why I'm travelling as a passenger, instead of cargo.' He glanced around scornfully at the milling refugees, who were being kept in some kind of order by the Franchise guards.

'How much longer?' Elyra asked, before Kyrlock could respond to the insult.

Greel shrugged. 'Fifteen, twenty minutes. We'll be long gone by dawn, if that's what's worrying you.'

'Glad to hear it,' Elyra said, trying to ignore the knot of tension drawing itself tighter in the pit of her stomach with every passing moment.

Above the Gorgonid, Sepheris Secundus
107.993.M41

'MORDECHAI. WE'VE GOT a problem.' Vex's voice crackled in Horst's comm-bead. 'It sounds like Keira's walked right into the middle of some kind of Chaotic ceremony. I'd recommend immediate intervention.'

'Noted,' Horst responded crisply, glancing up from the auspex screen in the cockpit, and trying to ignore the sharp stab of alarm the tech-priest's words had sent through him. It was hardly the first time Keira had been in mortal danger, and he was vaguely surprised at how concerned he felt. Forcing the unwelcome distraction away, he assessed their options. The lander from the *Ursus Innare* had already been on the ground longer than he'd expected, but the shuttle with Malakai's storm troopers aboard was still several minutes away. After a second or so of agonised internal debate, he reached for the vox. 'Talon one, this is Raptor. Bypass the primary target, and hit the house.'

'Confirm that, Raptor.' If Malakai was surprised, he was too consummate a professional to betray the fact, or question the change in his orders. 'Diverting now.'

'Good. Be advised that we could be facing psykers, or worse.' Horst broke the link, certain that he'd made the right call, and that his confused feelings for Keira hadn't been a factor in the decision. If Adrin and his confederates really were attempting to call on the power of the warp, they had to be stopped at all costs. The Franchisemen could wait. The Angelae had already seen how dangerous rogue psykers could be, and if their suspicions about the cause of Tonis's death were true, the consequences of allowing the heretics to complete their ritual could be nothing short of catastrophic. He turned to Barda. 'Get us down there, fast.'

'I'm on it,' the young pilot assured him, and a moment later Horst felt the shuttle bank sharply, already falling towards the pit beneath the city like an iron meteor.

'Forcing an entrance might prove problematic,' Vex said, his dry, pedantic tones forcing their way past the buzzing in Horst's inner ear. 'Judging by some of the remarks Keira made on the way in, the walls of the above-ground part of the structure are strongly fortified against the possibility of a peasant revolt. I doubt that our personal weapons would be able to breach them.'

'Leave it to me,' Barda said, glancing across at Horst with every sign of confidence. 'I'll get you inside.'

'The outer wall, maybe,' Horst said. 'We can just fly over it, but Hybris is talking about the structure of the house itself.'

'I know,' Barda said. 'Don't worry about it. I know what I'm doing.' He flung the agile little craft around a slower moving heavy lifter, bouncing a little in the backwash of the larger ship's afterburners.

'I don't doubt that for a second,' Horst assured him, unobtrusively making the sign of the aquila, and hoping it was true.

The Gorgonid Mine, Sepheris Secundus
107.993.M41

KEIRA WASN'T SURE where she expected the ceremony to take place: a gloomy cave, perhaps, lit by flickering torches, its walls defaced with blasphemous sigils, like the shrines to the Ruinous Powers she'd discovered among the Shatters in her earlier scouting trips.

To her surprise though, she followed Adrin and the hobbling psyker through another anonymous door into what could have been a small but well-regulated medicae facility anywhere in the Imperium. Subdued lighting reflected from clinical white walls, and banks of instruments that she recognised from previous post-mission convalescence in the sanitorium of the Tricorn hummed and chattered, monitoring the vital signs of the occupants of three hospital beds ranged around the room. No sanitorium she'd ever been in before had had a warp-touched lunatic in the middle of it, though, or about a dozen overdressed aristocrats forming a loose circle around each of the invalids. As the rogue psyker entered they all bowed, a respectful murmur of 'Magister' rippling among them.

'What's going on here?' Keira asked, partly because it would be the natural thing to do under the circumstances if she was really who she was pretending to be, but mainly because she hoped her colleagues were still listening, and the more information she could pass on to them the better the chance they'd have of surviving whatever they were about to get into. 'Who are those people?'

'They're the husks,' Adrin said. 'Psykers we rescued too late to save their sanity.'

'Unlike him,' Keira said sarcastically, gesturing towards the hobbling wyrd.

Adrin scowled. 'The magister sees deeper into the warp than any of us. I hardly think we're qualified to comment on what that does to his state of mind.'

'If you say so,' Keira said, 'but you don't seem to have had much trouble making the same judgement with these poor souls.' Mindful of the part she was playing, she corrected 'damned' to 'poor' just as the words left her tongue, and walked across to the nearest bed as she spoke. Its occupant was still wearing the grey robe of a Citadel inmate, which tended to confirm her guess at the origin of the wyrd apparently leading this coven. The shrunken figure in the cot appeared to be a man, although the degree of emaciation made it hard to be sure, the eyes in the pale face closed in sleep.

'They were raving,' Adrin said shortly. 'We help the lucid ones as best we can. The rest, we sedate for their own safety, and everyone else's.' Picturing the havoc that might be wrought by a group of psykers lashing out at random with their powers, Keira could only nod. 'We have another twenty like these in adjacent rooms, but we only need three for the ritual.'

'Which does what, exactly?' Kiera asked, an unpleasant crawling sensation prickling her scalp. The preparations for it were clearly well advanced, the aristocrats taking up positions around the beds, while a few of their number connected the cabling of a jumble of unfamiliar equipment in the centre of the room. No doubt Vex could have divined its purpose were he here to see it, but anything to do with the rites of technology was a complete mystery to the young assassin.

'As the magister said,' Adrin replied, 'we hope to augment his power with that of the husks. Gilden thought we should use the technique to make the lucid wyrds stronger, so they have a better chance of survival, but that was before the Inquisition started poking their noses in.'

'I see.' Keira nodded briskly. 'You think if you can make him strong enough he'll be able to defend you against the wrath of the Emperor.' She spoke without thinking, and, seeing a flicker of doubt in Adrin's eyes, shrugged dismissively. 'Or his errand boys, at any rate.'

'Something like that,' Adrin said, regarding her narrowly. Before he could pursue the matter, however, his attention was seized by the psyker.

'Come!' the madman's voice was resonant, commanding obedience and respect. Even Keira felt a little of it, although the strength of her devotion to Him on Earth protected her from the worst effects. 'It's time!'

Adrin turned away at once, hurrying to the control lectern in the middle of the room, and beginning to check the settings of the levers and dials. Left alone for a moment, Keira risked speaking aloud, her voice low.

'Mordechai,' she said quietly, hoping the hidden vox was still working, 'they've started. If you're going to do something about this, you'd better do it fast.'

TWENTY

The Gorgonid Mine, Sepheris Secundus
107.993.M41

'DOWN THERE,' HORST said, pointing to one of the gently glowing lights, which stood out clearly among the sharp-edged shadows littering the darkened expanse of the Gorgonid. The houses of the nobility were muted beacons in the broken landscape, easily distinguishable from the harsher lights of the industrial areas, which continued to hum with activity throughout the night, and the dimmer ones of the Commons, where the serfs snatched whatever meagre respite they could from their unremitting toil. Keira's warning, relayed by Vex, still rang in his ears, and he prayed to the Emperor that they'd be in time.

'I see it,' Barda assured him, bringing the shuttle's nose round, and skimming over the outer wall of the estate. Horst just had time to catch a glimpse of a formal garden flashing past beneath them, planted with whatever vaguely aesthetic plants might flourish in the

perpetual gloom at the bottom of the vast pit, before
the surface structure of the house loomed up ahead of
them, external luminators striking polychromatic
aurorae from the garish glass mosaic encrusting its
exterior. The young pilot hit the forward mounted retros, killing their momentum with an abruptness that
slammed Horst against his seat restraints, to leave
them hovering motionless a couple of metres above
the ground, and what seemed like little more than a
stride or two from the elaborately ornamented front
porch. 'Still think you'll need help getting in?'

'Looks like it,' Horst said, as a group of armed men
appeared by the wide front door, a slab of bronze
embossed with the Adrin family crest, and began pep-
pering the hull with ineffectual pistol fire. He glanced
round the narrow cockpit. 'Does this thing have an
amplivox?'

'Right there.' Barda gestured towards the vox unit.
'You use the same handset as the transmitter, you just
need to switch over to the external speakers.'

'Right.' After a moment's fumbling, Horst found the
right controls, and cleared his throat. 'Desist and sur-
render, in the name of the Inquisition,' he declaimed,
feeling a little self-conscious at the dramatic gesture.
'The owner of this house is charged with treason and
heresy, and any attempt to aid him will be treated as
active complicity in his sacrilege.'

Barda glanced out of the armourcrys viewport, and
shrugged. 'They're still wasting bullets,' he reported.
The shuttle had been built to military specifications,
capable of withstanding even heavy weapons fire, and
the light calibre small arms available to Adrin's retainers would barely be able to scratch the paintwork.
Unfortunately, from Horst's point of view, it had also

been built simply to haul troops and cargo, relying on the protection of specialist gunships in a war zone, and was as devoid of armament as Barda's old Aquila had been. Belatedly realising that they couldn't hope to down the shuttle, the liveried retainers scuttled inside and slammed the heavy metal portal behind them.

'Just what I'd have expected,' Drake put in, his head and shoulders appearing around the frame of the narrow door to the passenger compartment. 'Their loyalties will be to the family they serve. Even the name of the Inquisition won't outweigh ten generations of fealty.'

'Great,' Horst said. He turned back to Barda. 'Whatever you had in mind, you'd better try fast.'

'Right.' The young pilot hesitated, looking troubled, and Drake scowled at his back.

'Any time before we become daemon bait would be good,' he suggested.

'I'm on it,' Barda assured him, his hands hovering over the controls. 'It's just that I never thought there'd be people in the way. They'll all be killed.'

'If their master summons a daemon they'll be a lot worse than that,' Horst told him. 'They'll be damned, along with Emperor knows how many other innocent souls.' He patted Barda sympathetically on the shoulder. 'Doing His work isn't often easy, but the alternatives are unthinkable.' For a moment he wondered if perhaps he was overdoing it, but the young pilot merely nodded tightly by way of a response.

'You're right, of course. In His holy name...' The shuttle lurched as he worked the flight controls with expert precision, spinning the hovering craft in place on its landing thrusters. The house rotated out of view, the armourcrys in front of them being filled instead with the dressed stone of the six metre high outer wall of the estate, and the scrubby planting that filled the intervening space.

'What are you…' Drake began, just as the retros in the nose fired without warning. Despite the flare of retarding energy the shuttle jerked forwards, sending the Guardsman sprawling in the aisle of the passenger compartment, and pinning Horst back in his seat with a wave of vertiginous motion. Though he couldn't see what had happened to Vex the arbitrator distinctly heard the tech-priest utter an uncharacteristic curse, in a tone that betrayed rather more emotion than an acolyte of the Omnissiah was supposed to acknowledge. An instant later the vessel shuddered to a halt, what looked to Horst like a mere handful of metres from the looming wall.

'Oops,' Barda said. 'Cut that a bit fine.' It seemed that he had. They were close enough for Horst to be able to identify the individual stones making up the huge rampart in front of them.

'What the rut was all that about?' Drake demanded, reappearing in the doorway rubbing his head.

'Getting us in,' Barda replied, rotating the shuttle again. As the house came back into view, Horst felt the breath catch in his throat.

'Emperor on Earth,' he breathed. 'What did you do?' The front of the building around the metal door had completely disappeared, leaving a wide tunnel spattered with molten bronze and liquefied glass blasted deep into the structure. The orange glow of flames flickered around the periphery of the hole, which Horst could have driven a Rhino through, secondary fires started by the intense blast of heat from the shuttle's engines.

'Cut in the afterburners, just for a second,' Barda said, his face paling as he took in the full extent of the destruction he'd wrought. 'Like taking a blowtorch to a dolls' house.'

'Great idea,' Drake grumbled. 'I particularly liked the bit where you nearly rammed us into the wall.'

Barda shrugged. 'We're doing the Emperor's work, right? I knew He'd protect us.' He cut the power, and the shuttle settled on the seared ground beneath it as gently as a snowflake.

'Good thinking.' Horst patted the young man on the back, with rather more sincerity this time. 'Keep the engines running. If the heretics really do summon another daemon, we might want to leave here in a hurry.' If that actually happened, he rather doubted that they'd get the opportunity to flee, but even a slim chance was better than none, and it would avoid wasting precious moments arguing Barda out of accompanying them.

'Will do.' The pilot nodded grimly, and made the sign of the aquila. 'Good luck, and may the Emperor protect.'

KEIRA FELT THE faint trembling of what she guessed was her comrades' arrival through the soles of her feet, and glanced around the chamber, but engrossed in the preliminary stages of their ritual, none of the cultists surrounding her seemed to have noticed. The fops and ladies had all joined hands, forming circles around each of the comatose psykers in their hospital beds, and were chanting quietly, fragments of the ancient language of the tech-priests she'd sometimes heard Vex use among his colleagues, interspersed with the liquid cadences of a tongue she'd never encountered before.

Unlike the harsh gutturals of the Khornate cult she'd helped Inquisitor Finurbi eliminate in the bowels of Ambulon, it seemed eerily beautiful, raising a storm of strange and unwelcome emotions in her chest. Successive waves of melancholy swept over her as she listened, receding a little each time the congregation lapsed into the occasional phrases of *tech*, and she felt her eyes stinging with unshed tears for the first time she could remember since childhood.

Moving as far as she could from the nearest group, she began to subvocalise a calming litany, but that didn't seem to help. At least they hadn't expected her to join one of the circles, familiarity with the ritual apparently being an essential precondition of taking part in it, so there was little chance of her prayers to the Emperor being overheard and challenged. She exhaled, hard, fighting for calm, seeing her breath puff into visibility as a thin film of frost began to crackle across the floor.

'Magister, we have a problem,' Adrin said. He glanced up from a book of handwritten notes, his expression apprehensive, and gestured towards the patchwork of apparatus his acolytes had assembled. 'There appears to be a component missing.'

'Then find a replacement,' the wyrd demanded, a localised wind ruffling his robes and hair as his anger manifested itself physically. 'I refuse to be thwarted, with our hour of victory at hand!'

'At once, magister.' Adrin began to rummage through the haphazard assemblage of equipment, his agitation growing as he searched the leftover pieces. 'The problem is, I don't know what I'm looking for. Gilden would have, but–'

'Just find one that fits!' the wyrd shouted, the eldritch gale intensifying. Keira felt his rage brushing against the fringes of her mind, and seized on it eagerly, allowing it to counteract the debilitating effect of the chanting. Giving up on the litany she'd learned at the Collegium Assassinorum, she sought refuge in the creed of the Redemptionists instead, allowing the holy wrath of the Emperor to fill her with righteous fury. He was blood, and He was fire, and He was vengeance incarnate. As she allowed the familiar words to roll through her mind, the lassitude induced by the chanting receded. The Emperor was all, the Emperor was pure, and every last trace of the sin that stained His galaxy would be swept away so that the righteous could bask in His radiance forever.

Moving slowly, careful not to attract any attention, Keira reached beneath the tabard and drew a knife from its sheath. The Emperor was clearly incensed by the cultists' blasphemy, His holy rage pounding in her temples, just as it used to do in the lurching bowels of Ambulon every time her family's congregation prepared to purge another nest of Sinners, and she was His judgement made flesh.

'I've found it,' Adrin said, grabbing something more or less at random, and jamming it into the mechanism. A shower of sparks erupted, and the dials on his lectern flickered for a moment before steadying.

The wyrd nodded, a cold smile playing across his face. 'Then we begin!' he howled.

THE HEAT WAS intense as the small group of Angelae hurried into the depths of the house, skirting gently glowing puddles of solidifying metal, and dodging the occasional burst of flame, which erupted as the spreading fires in the rest of the house reached something else combustible. At least the blaze gave enough light to see by, although the flickering illumination was accompanied by thick, choking smoke, and Drake had paused almost at once to tie a scarf across his face. Horst had done the same, and both men coughed repeatedly as they ran, their eyes stinging and their lungs raw from the acrid fumes, despite their makeshift masks. Only Vex seemed comfortable, trotting between them, his autopistol drawn, the breath hissing easily through his respirator unit. Under more propitious circumstances Drake might have savoured the irony of that, but now was hardly the time for idle reflection.

'Ten o'clock!' Horst warned, swinging his bolt pistol up, but Drake was faster, spraying a burst from his lasgun that made the pair of looming figures up ahead duck for cover behind the smouldering remains of an overturned banqueting table. Both were carrying pistols of some kind, so it seemed that, despite his untimely attack of conscience, Barda hadn't quite managed to eliminate all the security staff after all.

'I see them,' Drake said, wishing he'd had the foresight to bring a grenade or two with him as well as his guns, but Horst had no need of anything so crude, the first bolt from his pistol blowing a hole through the thick slab of wood, and the second finding a softer target beyond in a spray of blood and viscera. 'Second one's mine.' He snapped off a single shot, taking the other man in the head as he tried to flee.

'The air seems to be clearing,' Vex said, and to his relief Drake found that the tech-priest appeared to be right. The pall of smoke was thinning, and the yellow gleam of artificial light was beginning to overwhelm the redder glow of combustion. 'We must be into the bedrock.' He hesitated, coughed loudly, and looked faintly surprised. 'I really must adjust that properly.'

'Time and place, Hybris,' Horst said, and, his mind recalled to the mission, the tech-priest nodded, consulting the screen of his data-slate. Horst tapped his comm-bead. 'Malakai, where are you?'

'Three minutes out,' the storm trooper captain assured them, his voice buzzing slightly in Drake's ear like an irritable wasp, although whether that was due to some defect in the tiny transceiver or the effects of smoke inhalation making him light-headed he couldn't be sure. 'If you've torched the place already, we've got you on visual.'

'That's us,' Horst confirmed. 'We're inside, moving on the objective. As soon as you're down, seal the perimeter, and take out everything that tries to leave and isn't carrying a rosette. If we need back-up we'll call for it.'

'You'll get it,' Malakai promised.

'This way,' Vex said, beginning to move off down a corridor still illuminated by strongly glowing electrosconces. 'She's about two hundred metres ahead.'

'Her vox is, anyway,' Drake said, trying not to think about the possibility that the girl was no longer attached to it.

Horst glanced at him, his expression grim. 'She's fine,' he said, in the tone of a man not prepared to accept any other alternative. To Drake's relief, the tech-priest was nodding in confirmation.

'She's praying,' he said. 'Some Redemptionist credo, by the sound of it.'

'She's doing what?' Horst asked, his face a mask of astonishment. 'Can't the heretics hear her?'

'I don't think so,' Vex said, in the manner of a man evaluating the possibilities carefully. 'I imagine the screaming is enough to drown it out.'

WHATEVER THE HERETICS thought they were doing, Keira thought, this was certainly not it. As Adrin had pushed home the final switch, the bodies of the comatose psykers had spasmed, keening in unison, a raw, ugly sound, which ripped through the air, disrupting the gentle cadences of the chant. The levitating wyrd had howled too, even louder, the crackle of arcane energies surrounding him intensifying, shrouding him in what seemed to be a miniature lightning storm a mere couple of metres across. Confused, their concentration broken, the cultists fell silent, staring in horrified bafflement at the ghastly apparition.

'Cut the power!' Keira yelled, flinging the knife in her hand at the shrieking, flailing madman at the centre of the maelstrom. She couldn't be certain that killing him would avert whatever catastrophe was about to befall them all, but it was what she was good at, and she couldn't think of any other options. The knife spun through the air, straight at the magister's heart. Then, to her dismay, it reached the penumbra of mystical energy surrounding him and stopped, fingers of lightning reaching out towards it. Crackling electrical discharges earthed themselves through the razor-edged steel, for what felt like several seconds, but in all probability had been the merest of instants, and then the twisted lump of metal spun away to impact somewhere in the corner of the room.

'I can't, it'll kill them all!' Adrin snapped back. Still engrossed in his flickering and barely understood instrumentation, he glanced up in shock, just in time to see her rip off her tabard and draw the sword from across her shoulder. The crimson sigil of her Inquisition rosette, on a chain around her neck, flamed brightly as she bounded towards him, cutting down a stray heretic who'd had the misfortune to be standing in her way in a welter of blood and viscera.

'Good!' Kiera replied, slashing at the nearest cable. The monomolecular edge of the master-crafted weapon sheered through it easily, sending a jolt of energy up her arm even through the insulating glove of her synsuit, and she staggered momentarily before recovering. The three husks fell silent, and the wyrd plunged headlong to the rock floor behind her with a faintly liquescent smack, as the storm around him was abruptly curtailed, his body burned and twisted beyond all recognition as something that might once have been human. 'This abomination ends now, in the name of the Emperor!'

'She's Inquisition!' one of the fops shouted, catching sight of her badge of office, and the cultists began bleating in panic, some running for the door, while others, mainly the faces she'd picked out by her stratagem in the salon, began to close in on her with obviously murderous intent. The fops with swords drew their blades, dropping into formal fencing stances better suited to affairs of honour than a genuine fight for survival, and several of the others produced hidden weapons from places of concealment. Keira noted with some amusement that the two women in the group seemed to favour long metal hair combs, which turned their hands into razor-edged claws, no doubt with venomed tips. Fine, if they expected to get within an arms' length of her, but the extra metre of reach the sword gave the young assassin made that possibility distinctly remote. So far, no problem.

'Get a grip,' Adrin said, with studied disdain. 'She's just one woman.' He drew a compact autogun from the depths of his sky blue blouson, and aimed it at her, his finger tightening on the trigger.

'That's true,' Horst's familiar voice put in from the door, and Keira felt her heart begin to race with something more than the usual fierce rush of exhilaration she normally felt in combat, 'but I think you'll find she's quite an exceptional one.'

Adrin turned to confront the unexpected intruder, bringing his gun around to seek a fresh target, and the overdressed mob around Keira rushed her as one.

'Why, Mordechai, you say the nicest things.' Keira pivoted gracefully, evading a clumsy sword thrust and disembowelling her first would-be murderer with casual ease, before turning to reap a rich harvest of heretic souls for the Emperor's judgement in a flurry of blade strokes. One of the men managed to nick her arm before she ran him through. Furious with herself for leaving him an easy opening, she resolved not to make the same mistake twice, and pivoted, taking one of the women in the stomach with a spinning kick as she attempted to take advantage of Keira's momentary distraction and strike her down from behind with her venomed claws. As the woman fell, Keira leapt across her, kicking down to snap her neck, and engage the third and final swordsman face to face.

'Drop the gun,' Drake advised, raising his Guard-issue weapon to cover Adrin, while Horst and Vex casually shot a brace of heretics who'd attempted to charge them with hastily drawn swords.

'Why don't you drop yours?' Adrin suggested. Drake looked as if he was about to reply with some equally sarcastic comment, when his expression changed abruptly to one of surprise and alarm.

'What the hell...?' he expostulated, before the weapon twitched easily out of his hands and spun away, to fall noisily to the floor several metres from him. Heartened by this sudden reversal, the cowed cultists began to look more belligerent, and one of them stooped to pick up the fallen lasgun.

'You're a wyrd too,' Horst said, as though it should have been obvious, his knuckles whitening with the effort of trying to bring the bolt pistol round to aim it at Adrin. Despite his best efforts, it was moving off-target. A second later, it tore free of his grasp, to be sent skittering into a corner with a casual flick of Adrin's mind. 'Malakai, get in here!'

'Calling for help?' Adrin asked, ripping the comm-beads from everyone's ears with another thought, and sending them spinning across the room. 'Hardly the die-hard heroism you expect from the Inquisition's lackeys, given their reputation.' Another psychokinetic shove sent Vex and Keira sprawling, their weapons flying from their hands as they hit the floor. He shrugged, glancing regretfully at the young assassin. 'Any more surprises for us before we kill you?'

'How about this one?' Drake asked, drawing the Scalptaker and pulling the trigger in one fluid movement, while the psyker's attention was momentarily distracted. The rugged revolver cracked loudly in the confined space, its heavy dum-dum bullet ripping a hole through Adrin's torso that Keira could have put her fist through. She rolled lightly to her feet, drawing another knife from the sheaths around her waist.

'Pretty good,' Adrin admitted, staggering, an expression of bemusement beginning to flicker across his face, 'but not quite good enough.' He must have been drawing on the power of the warp to stay on his feet. Drake's aim began to waver again, an instant before Keira buried her knife in his eye socket up to the hilt. Horst straightened, his bolt pistol back in his hand, and the back of the psyker's head exploded in crimson mist. He fell heavily to the floor, and the light in his remaining eye clouded at last.

'Anyone else fancy their chances?' Keira asked, picking the sword up in one lithe motion. The cultists around her paled, and fell back, and she grinned ferally. 'Didn't think so.' The impulse to slaughter them all anyway was almost irresistible, her blood singing with the old Redemptionist fervour, and she fought it down with a hint of regret. Once she wouldn't have hesitated to bring them all to the Emperor's judgement, but her duty to the Inquisition overrode her desires. The survivors would have to be interrogated, the intelligence they provided assessed, and the knowledge used to make sure that this particular cancer in the soul of the Imperium had been excised forever.

'I'll take that.' Drake strode forward to reclaim his lasgun, snatching it from the hands of the youth who'd picked it up, and striking him in the face with the butt. The fop folded, blood spurting from his nose, any ideas of attempting to use it clearly long gone.

'Fascinating.' Vex had retrieved his weapon as well, and was stowing it absently, his attention almost entirely taken up with the equipment in the middle of the room. 'This is almost exactly the same as the mechanism we found in the Fathomsound.' He poked around in the bowels of the machine for a moment, and looked relieved. 'Apart from the booby trap, of course.'

'I'm glad to hear it,' Horst replied grimly, glancing up as a squad of crimson and grey clad storm troopers appeared in the doorway, respirators still concealing most of their faces. He smiled. 'Captain Malakai, thank you for responding so promptly.'

'You seem to have managed well enough on your own,' the veteran replied, a hint of disappointment in his voice. He gestured to the nearest troopers. 'You, you and you, secure the prisoners. Shoot any that resist.' A whinny of dismay rose from the surviving cultists as the men he'd detailed began to round them up and herd them, none too gently, from the room. He looked around, as much of his face as Keira could see behind the breathing mask displaying clear signs of puzzlement. 'What were they doing down here anyway? This isn't like any Chaos shrine I've ever seen.'

'Trying to siphon off psychic energy,' Keira said, more for Horst and Vex's benefit than to satisfy Malakai's curiosity, 'from those people in the beds to him.' She gestured towards the broken body of the magister. 'But it all went klybo on them.'

'I'm not surprised,' Vex said, lifting the fused remains of the component that Adrin had added at the magister's urging from the bowels of the machine, an expression of amused disdain on his face. 'This would have reversed the polarity of the neutron flow.' He glanced scornfully at Adrin's corpse. 'None of the Omnissiah's anointed could possibly have made so elementary a mistake.'

'There was a piece missing,' Keira explained. 'That one was about the right size, so he thought it might be it.'

'Oh no.' Vex shook his head. 'This was where I found the artefact, in the installation at the Fathomsound.' His voice took on a speculative tone. 'The question is, was it made to fit into a system like this, or was the system built around it, to take advantage of some innate property it has?'

'Maybe Tonis's notes will tell you,' Keira suggested, pointing to the bundle of papers on the control lectern. 'Adrin seemed to be using some kind of instruction manual his cousin left.'

'Did he indeed?' Vex said, grabbing the notebook with what under most circumstances he would undoubtedly have regarded as unseemly haste. 'I'll have to examine this carefully.'

'Somewhere else,' Horst said sharply, before the tech-priest could become engrossed in the slapdash calligraphy. 'That fire's still spreading.' He glanced around the room, as the few remaining cultists left it at gunpoint, clinging to what shreds of dignity they could for as long as possible. 'Is that the last of them?'

'The last of the live ones,' Malakai reported, giving Adrin's corpse a contemptuous kick. 'The ones in the beds are all dead too.' He glanced across at the remains of the magister. 'And he's very dead indeed.'

Looking at the corpse of the wyrd, Keira found herself inclined to agree with the veteran storm trooper. She'd seen lives end more times than she could count, frequently at her own hands, and could generally tell at a glance whether a body was damaged beyond all hope of retaining the *igniculus vitalis*. This one, however, had belonged to a potent psyker, and there was no harm in making absolutely sure. She raised her sword, preparing to cut off his head, and froze momentarily in shock as the charred flesh at her feet began to stir.

'He's alive!' She swept the blade down, feeling the familiar faint resistance as the keen edge parted flesh and bone, and grinned in vindictive satisfaction. 'Now he's not.'

'Get back!' Horst yelled, an unfamiliar edge of alarm in his voice, and, startled, she leapt away instinctively. 'Something's not right!'

'No cak,' Drake said sarcastically, opening up with his lasgun at the spasming corpse. 'What was your first clue?' The seared flesh was distorting even as they watched, stretching and splitting, with a faint cracking of dislocating joints and tearing tendons. Something pale and bulbous, which seemed far too large to have been contained by the bag of flesh it was birthing from, reached out a tendril, which Kiera leapt over as it tried to snare her ankle, slashing down with her sword to sever it as she did so.

'It's a daemon!' she shouted, trying desperately to recall anything her Collegium tutors might have had to say about their vulnerabilities. Precious few came to mind, apart from holy water and weapons blessed by priests, neither of which seemed particularly likely to be lying around in a den of heretics.

'Fire!' Malakai roared, and his storm troopers began pouring hellgun rounds into the bloated monstrosity, while Horst and Vex added what firepower they could with their hand weapons. The tentacled horror rose clear of the mangled corpse, shrugging it off like a soiled cape, and swooped across the room, shimmering insubstantially as each shot slammed into it. Tentacles lashed out, striking down a couple of the storm troopers, and flinging another into the wall.

'So that's what killed Tonis,' Vex said, a note of wonderment entering his voice for the first time since Keira had met him. Ducking a flailing tentacle, he snapped off another shot at it, pulled his data-slate out of his robe with the other hand, and began recording whatever he could of the encounter.

'Hybris, look out!' Horst called, as another tentacle snared the tech-priest.

Keira heard something crack as it constricted, and slashed at it with her sword. For a moment, it seemed, there was nothing there to strike. Then she felt some resistance, and the strange flesh parted. Vex fell heavily, his face ashen, but there was no time to check on him. Keira braced herself, commended her soul to the Emperor, and began moving the sword in a defensive pattern, resolving to sell her life as dearly as she could as the mass of writhing tendrils fringing the thing's body stretched out towards her.

An instant before it could strike, however, Drake emptied his power pack into the thing on full auto, somehow managing to remain on aim despite the rapid movement of his target, and the entity shuddered, losing momentum. A moment later it vanished entirely, disappearing back into the warp with a howl of frustration and a crackle of arcane energies, and she let out a long, slow breath. 'Thanks,' she said simply.

'You're welcome.' Drake grinned at her, and turned to Vex. 'Lucky I asked you for that benediction on the way in.'

'The Omnissiah certainly seems to have guided your hand,' the tech-priest agreed gravely, rising to his feet with some difficulty. He turned to Keira. 'Thank you for your timely intervention.'

'You're welcome,' she told him. 'Are you sure you're all right?' None of the storm troopers the thing had attacked seemed to be moving.

'Nothing that can't be repaired,' Vex assured her. 'Fortunately my augmetic systems are considerably more robust than the organic ones.'

'So they were summoning daemons after all,' Horst said, an expression of wonderment in his eyes. He shook his head. 'I've never seen anything like it.'

'They may not have intended to,' Vex said cautiously. 'If they were experimenting with psychic energy, they might have opened a portal to the warp by accident. I'll need to read Tonis's notes before we can reach any definite conclusions.'

'Then let's get out of here while we still can,' Horst said, 'before the paper combusts.' He looked at Keira with an expression she couldn't quite make out. 'Are you all right?'

'I'm fine,' she said, feeling that oddly pleasurable tingling in the pit of her stomach again. Unsettled by it, she resheathed her sword, and followed the others into the purifying flames that were slowly consuming the works of those who'd sought to challenge the word of the Emperor.

The Gorgonid Mine, Sepheris Secundus
108.993.M41

'ABOUT RUTTING TIME,' Kyrlock grumbled, as the last of the ore rumbled off the end of the conveyor belt and into the bowels of the waiting shuttle. The skinny little wyrd was still hanging around him, and he forced himself to smile at her, ignoring the way her presence made his skin crawl. Elyra had made it abundantly clear that keeping the girl and her friends sweet was the key to the next stage of the operation, so he'd better do his best to seem friendly. She smiled back, tentatively, the first real expression she'd shown since Kantris had jumped her the previous day, and for a moment he felt an unexpected flicker of sympathy.

'Will it be much longer, do you think?' she asked.

Kyrlock shrugged. 'Better ask them,' he suggested, inclining his head towards where Elyra and Greel were huddled together in muted conversation. Becoming aware of his scrutiny, Elyra glanced up.

'We're boarding now,' she said flatly, as Greel turned away, and began ambling towards the ramp leading up to the cargo hold. 'Better step it up.' She turned to indicate the milling mass of refugees, who were beginning to drift hopefully towards the grounded shuttle. 'It's going to be a grox pen in there, so we need to stick close.'

'We will,' Zusen assured her, moving up to Kyrlock, and seizing his arm. The Guardsman fought down the urge to flinch.

'If you say so.' Trosk prodded Ven into motion again, and the little group walked purposefully towards the boarding ramp.

'Is it dawn already?' Zusen asked, and Elyra shook her head.

'Another couple of hours yet. Why?'

The young wyrd looked confused, and pointed off into the distance. 'The sky's red over there.'

'Blood and burning,' Ven mumbled. 'Pain and death.'

Kyrlock and Elyra looked at one another, the same unspoken thought occurring to them both simultaneously, and Kyrlock shrugged. If their colleagues were responsible, they had no way of knowing. 'That's night life in the Tumble for you,' he said. He smiled at Zusen, trying to sound reassuring. 'I'm going to miss this place.'

'Are you really?' she asked, her voice disbelieving.

Kyrlock paused at the bottom of the boarding ramp, took one last look at the world of his birth, and shook his head. 'No, not much,' he admitted.

EPILOGUE

The Tricorn, Scintilla: Calixis Sector
231.993.M41

'YOU'RE ABSOLUTELY CERTAIN of this?' Inquisitor Grynner asked, looking at Pieter Quillem with his habitual expression of mild curiosity.

'Absolutely,' Quillem confirmed, sitting down on the opposite bench. The cloister his mentor had suggested they meet in was a quiet and secluded one. Nowhere in the headquarters of the Ordo Calixis was truly far from the ceaseless activity of the thousands of inquisitors, interrogators and acolytes charged with preserving this far-flung province of the Emperor's realm from the perils that constantly assailed it. There were, however, a number of nooks and half-forgotten crannies where a little peace could be found to discuss sensitive matters in as much privacy as anyone could hope to find here, and Inquisitor Grynner seemed to know them all. The bench the two men occupied ran around all three sides of an alcove between two of the buttresses supporting the high vaulted ceiling, and would be almost invisible to any casual strollers retreating here for a little peace and relaxation. 'Your friend Finurbi seems to have vanished without trace.'

'How very like the man,' Grynner commented, with a quiet sigh of resignation. He removed his spectacles, breathed on the lenses, and polished them thoughtfully with the end of his neck cloth. 'Are there any indications of foul play?'

'Nothing overt,' Quillem said cautiously. 'He seems to have gone blue entirely of his own accord.'

'Hm.' Grynner replaced the spectacles, after examining them minutely for any lingering traces of dust. 'Did he see fit to inform the Ordo of why he's decided to invoke Special Circumstances?'

Quillem shrugged. 'Well, he wouldn't, would he?' An inquisitor only invoked the right of Special Circumstances, effectively removing himself from the oversight, support and resources of his sector's Ordo, if he felt that his own colleagues couldn't be trusted, or that his activities might expose them to some unacceptable level of danger. The young interrogator found neither possibility particularly reassuring.

'No, I suppose not.' Grynner sighed again. 'It seems we must proceed without his aid after all.'

'Unless we can find him ourselves,' Quillem suggested.

Grynner cocked his head slightly to the left, and looked searchingly at his assistant. 'Pieter,' he said carefully, 'have you been up to something I'd rather not be appraised of?'

'Of course not,' Quillem assured him, reaching inside his robe for a data-slate. 'I simply pointed out to the senior custodian that, prior to his departure from

Sepheris Secundus, Inquisitor Finurbi sent us an astropathic message agreeing to meet us here. That must have meant that he was willing to share whatever information he had with us.'

'A reasonable inference,' Grynner agreed, with a slight tilt of the head. 'Unfortunately, whatever information he may have had disappeared along with him.'

'Not all of it,' Quillem demurred. He activated the screen of his data-slate. 'He left a cell of his Angelae network following up some leads on Sepheris Secundus, and their leader has been quite punctilious about filing reports on their progress.' He handed the slate to Grynner. 'I think you'll find they make interesting reading.'

Grynner glanced at the screen, deactivated it, and stowed the slate in the pocket of his jacket. 'I'll peruse them at the first opportunity.' He nodded approvingly at his apprentice. 'Well done, Pieter, commendably resourceful. Was there anything else?'

Quillem nodded. 'According to their last report, they were about to take ship for Scintilla. If the warp currents were favourable, they might even have arrived in system by now.'

'I see.' Grynner looked thoughtful for a moment, allowing the young interrogator to see beyond his habitual veneer of vagueness to the razor-sharp mind it so effectively concealed. 'Then it's possible that Carolus might break cover to contact them.' He stood. 'Perhaps it would be prudent to keep an eye on these Angelae, Pieter. I take it I can trust you to make the arrangements?'

Quillem rose too. 'They're already in hand,' he assured the inquisitor.

ABOUT THE AUTHOR

Sandy Mitchell is a pseudonym of Alex Stewart, who has been working as a freelance writer for the last couple of decades. He has written science fiction and fantasy in both personae, as well as television scripts, magazine articles, comics, and gaming material. Apart from both miniatures and roleplaying gaming his hobbies include the martial arts of Aikido and Iaido, and pottering around on the family allotment.

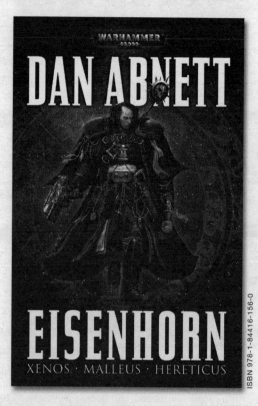